THE
FARM

THE FARM

JESSICA MANSOUR-NAHRA

hachette
AUSTRALIA

Published in Australia and New Zealand in 2025
by Hachette Australia
(an imprint of Hachette Australia Pty Limited)
Gadigal Country, Level 17, 207 Kent Street, Sydney, NSW 2000
www.hachette.com.au

Hachette Australia acknowledges and pays our respects to the past and present
Traditional Owners and Custodians of Country throughout Australia
and recognises the continuation of cultural, spiritual and educational practices
of Aboriginal and Torres Strait Islander peoples. Our head office is located on
the lands of the Gadigal people of the Eora Nation.

 A catalogue record for this
book is available from the
National Library of Australia

ISBN: 978 0 7336 5288 2 (paperback)

Cover design by Alex Ross
Cover photographs courtesy of Getty Images
Author photograph courtesy of Johnny Rocks
Internal images courtesy of Shutterstock and Dreamstime
Typeset in 13/18 pt Granjon LT Std by Bookhouse, Sydney
Printed and bound in Australia by McPherson's Printing Group

MIX
Paper | Supporting
responsible forestry
FSC
www.fsc.org
FSC® C001695

The paper this book is printed on is certified against the
Forest Stewardship Council® Standards. McPherson's Printing
Group holds FSC® chain of custody certification SA-COC-005379.
FSC® promotes environmentally responsible, socially beneficial
and economically viable management of the world's forests.

Dedicated to Charlie and Buddy

Thank you for changing my life

MENSTRUATION

(men·stru·a·tion) *noun*
a cyclical discharging of blood and tissue debris from
the uterus that recurs in non-pregnant breeding-age
females at approximately monthly intervals.

The sickness reminds me of my mother's before she died. I vomit three times a day. As I scrub the toilet bowl or the bathroom basin, I recall her yellowing face. I can't keep down the essentials – food, water, not even painkillers. Simple words like *milk* or *keys* are struggled for and not found. I'm bloated, constipated, exhausted.

I look down at the plastic stick and feel relief: I'm pregnant. Pregnancy isn't death, it's celebration, but I receive the news in a quiet way, just as I did when my mother told me she was ill. I wrap the test in layers of toilet paper then bury it in the bottom of the bathroom bin, piling empty toilet rolls, dirty tissues and hair pulled from my brush over the top of it. I won't tell James yet; not until it's definite.

I walk into the bedroom and pick up my phone. The medical clinic finds me an appointment for tomorrow, a small miracle.

—

The general practitioner is a woman I've now met a handful of times. She scans my blood test results.

'You're pregnant, Leila. Congratulations.'

I laugh a little; the diagnosis doesn't feel real. It seems like a dream, one James and I thought might take much longer to come true. The doctor gathers pamphlets, glossy and colourful, and hands them to me. The one on top has an image of a heavily pregnant woman and a list of safe foods to eat, each approved with a garish tick – *safe,* because there is danger in my condition. I swallow a burning sensation in the back of my throat and check the room for any kind of receptacle, just in case.

Our appointment is only ten minutes, and the doctor is swift; she issues instructions about blood tests, scans, timeframes, and asks whether I will go public or private. I set the pamphlets aside and confirm that yes, I have private health insurance. She asks if I have a preferred obstetrician. I don't know the names of any obstetricians. Am I supposed to? A week ago, I didn't know I was pregnant, I just thought I was dying.

'Is this good news?' the doctor asks, finally.

I nod and nod and nod. 'Why wouldn't it be?' Then I add, to make sure: 'I'm thrilled.'

This is what I want. It's not cancer, a thing that shadows you and then scrapes you out from the inside. I am not my mother. And yet, anxieties of a different kind tumble forth: what kind of mother will I be? Will I be any good? My career could suffer. Don't women with children lose half their superannuation? I read that somewhere. James will want to move – somewhere bigger, more appropriate for a growing family. More expensive. My chest is tight. I thumb the buckle of my already-snug jeans; soon they won't fit at all. I know I'll resent feeling frumpy in pants with a rubbery, elastic waistband.

'Folate and iron every day, and a dating scan at nine weeks. Dr Nikolaou is an excellent obstetrician; I highly recommend him.'

I take the referral letter and smile, rising to leave. Darker questions gnaw at me: what if something goes wrong?

What if I am the thing that goes wrong?

—

I wait for James in my small Coogee apartment, checking my phone more than I should. His last client finished at five and it's now after six. At my office, the pre-Christmas and New Year cheer has evaporated; post-holiday blues have left us with an unspoken malaise, and we all trooped out of the building a little early, as if that would help snatch back the frittering away, on our commutes, of precious free time. The sun is still high, bright light streaming in through the balcony's sliding door, so I lower the blinds and crank the air-conditioner. The apartment heats like an oven during summer, January being the worst month for it, and I resolve not to let the stuffy air and James's lateness dissipate the excitement I conjured as I prepared this little announcement. On the kitchen counter, I have a glass of whiskey poured for him and a wine glass filled with sparkling water and a slice of lemon for myself. A fresh pregnancy test, taken and fastidiously cleaned, sits between the glasses. I googled *cute ways to tell your partner you're pregnant* and this seemed the easiest; I didn't have time to screen-print a t-shirt or organise a cake that said, *Congratulations, Daddy!*

James and I talked about trying for a baby not long after we first met, amped up on pheromones and captured by limerence. Falling in love was a sudden and intense experience. James is kind, generous, sexy. We met online a year ago. He pursued me vigorously: no *u up?* messages in the app, no communication by abbreviations. He steered our chat to work and social activities; he set up an in-person date before the end of our first online interaction. No-one had ever done that before: most men on the app disappeared after realising there would be no sexting or sharing of naked pictures. Our date went well, and so did subsequent dates; during that time, James said he was attracted to not only my looks, my body – all the external, physical things – but also my intelligence, my successful career and my independence, that these things quickly set me apart. I liked how he seemed to always understand me, that he's a planner and – despite him admiring my success as a single woman – the promise of being part of a real family.

Before we met, I'd not thought of child-rearing much, being too busy working and travelling, drinking and spending and carousing, but the more we discussed it, the idea grew roots, holding me in place. James was certain he wanted children, and with him it seemed a genuine possibility for the first time. Our entanglement became something more than romance: it included the beguiling notion of creating a home.

The sex in our early months of dating was athletic, sweaty and frequent; since we agreed to try and get pregnant, it had become scheduled. Not a chore, we would tell ourselves after finishing.

Impatient, I tap the phone screen again to see the time. Six twenty-two. The front door lock clicks and jiggles, and I feel a surge of adrenaline as James's footsteps travel up the short hallway. I stand, holding the drinks, grinning, unsure what else to do. When James enters the kitchen, he smiles broadly at me.

'Hey, baby.'

He takes both glasses from me and sets them down on the counter, and we hug. He kisses me, wetly, on the lips. 'Traffic was a nightmare. Bloody Friday afternoons.'

James's office is in central Sydney. He insists on driving to and from work rather than taking public transport; he's a psychologist, and he doesn't want to run into a client in an environment where he can't quietly slip away. He also drives between Sydney and his family's rural property each week: helping his parents with farm jobs on Mondays and Tuesdays, and then rising at dawn on Wednesday mornings for the three-hour drive back to Sydney for his client work. And to spend time with me. Then he leaves again late on Sunday afternoon, and the routine repeats like clockwork.

He takes off his suit jacket as he leaves the kitchen, calling, 'Was that a whiskey for me?'

Answering is pointless; the door to the ensuite slams. I look at the glasses and the blue and white plastic oracle. It's so ordinary, but nothing will be the same once James sees it.

I wait to hear the flush of the toilet, listen to him washing his hands. My apartment is a tiny cocoon, a two-bedroom 1970s brick with a small concrete balcony. It's located several hilly streets away from the beach, which makes for a hot, uneven walk to the ocean. Even so, being that close to the sea still seems amazing to me, compared to where I grew up in stifling, suburban Brisbane.

I bought the unit when I turned thirty, to prove my independence to myself, but since James moved in, on the days he's here, it's become a cosy bubble that shelters us from the outside world. We do everything within these rendered walls: eat, sleep, shower, talk, plan, shop, watch television, search for properties we can't afford, play board games, scroll our phones, debate, curl up together, fuck. Occasionally, we make it outside, dressed for brunch or dinner, or half-clothed, carrying bulky towels for a swim.

James reappears. 'Should we order food?'

'Have this first.' I pass him the whiskey and hold up my glass to clink against his.

'Cheers,' he says. 'What are you having?'

'Sydney's finest water spritzer,' I say. 'Delicious. I think I'll drink it for the next nine months.'

He's mid-sip when my words register, his body tensing slightly. I put my glass down with a firm clink, next to the pregnancy test.

'Oh my god!' He grabs the test and peers closely at it. 'Leila!'

'I know.'

We pause for a beat and then his eyes fill and he makes a noise I've not heard before – a sort of gasping sob – and I suddenly burst into tears.

His face turns red and splotchy, and he pulls me to him and holds me tightly; he whispers, 'I am going to worship this baby, and you.'

Pressed against his body, I take in shallow breaths, tears and snot staining his shirt. The joy feels overwhelming; the same way falling in love with James did. I never thought this would happen to me. Now I have something so desired, I'm acutely aware of the inverse emotion: fear. I have a lot to lose.

I push that aside and focus on the present: James's sturdy chest; James's arms; James's face. It's like every television show I watched growing up: *We're having a baby!* Something my mother certainly didn't experience; those scenes were far from the reality of my childhood.

James pulls back. 'How far along are you?'

'Six or seven weeks? It's not exact. I have a scan in a couple of weeks, to check everything is okay.'

'Everything will be perfect,' he says, and I nod, but the twinge of worry returns; a familiar sensation when my mother comes to mind, however briefly.

'Of course it will,' I say. *Of course it will.*

'I bet it's a boy,' he says, swallowing the rest of the whiskey in one gulp.

'I bet it's a girl,' I counter, and he laughs.

'The Crawley line is all boys, I have to warn you.' He goes to the cupboard and pulls out the whiskey, pours another glass.

'How should we celebrate? Let's go out. Wherever you want. Steak? Seafood?'

'I don't know if I can eat seafo—' I stop, nauseated. I swallow hard but the queasiness builds, quickly. I wave a hand at him: *Move. Move out of the way.*

'Leila, you're pale.' James's voice echoes behind me uselessly while I lean over the kitchen sink and vomit; the contents of my stomach – half-digested oats from breakfast, nothing from lunch and too many glasses of fizzing water – stream into the stainless-steel basin. My stomach seizes and I'm helpless against the force of matter hurled from my body. Once it stops, I try to straighten up; woozy, I lean forwards to grab the paper towel. Wipe it over my mouth. Breathe slowly. James sidles up next to me, lays a hand on my back and looks in the sink.

'Full boot,' he says, and laughs, which stings unexpectedly. 'How about you go to bed? I'll bring you a hot water bottle and clean this up.'

'No, I can do it,' I say, throwing the paper towel in the bin. 'It's my mess.'

'Don't be silly,' he says. He leans in and kisses my clammy forehead. 'It's our mess. We're a family.'

There's something about the easy way he says it – *our* – the shared nature of it; it's somehow the most alluring, most comforting thing he has ever said to me. *Our. Us. We.* Finally, the word 'family' means something utterly different: it's not just Mum and me.

It's not just me.

The air-conditioning at the imaging clinic is on full blast, and the antiseptic smell of medical-grade cleaner permeates the room. The counters at the front desk are grey and the women behind them efficient. One types my name into a computer and directs me to the waiting area, calling for the next person before I've even turned away. The carpet wouldn't be out of place in a casino: dark grey with swirls of yellow and red. Effective at disguising anything that might fall upon it.

It's a few minutes past my appointment time. I took the earliest, seven-thirty am, but my phone is already vibrating with texts and emails. I'm a business consultant, and the work is ramping up: clients have returned from holidays, wanting to maximise the last of their paid-for time before the end of the financial year looms and contracts need renewal.

Even this early in the morning, the waiting room is full. Directly opposite me, a white-haired woman of indeterminate age, dressed in navy slacks, Homypeds and a neat floral blouse, sits with her husband. She has one hand on his knee while the other flips through an old *Women's Weekly*. I stare at her for longer than is polite. There's a faint waft of the soapy scent of her perfume, or perhaps it's talcum powder, blending with the acidic air. A dark silhouette appears in the corner of my eye, and I startle.

'Sorry I'm late,' James says.

'It's fine.' I'm relieved he made it. 'The sonographer is running behind.'

James spent his usual days at the farm; he smells like cut grass, and his forearms are a patchwork of small nicks and sticky conifer resin. Dressed in jeans, a flannel shirt and workboots caked in dried mud, he's an earthy, grounding presence in the sterile room. Based on the resin, I'm guessing he was cutting back overgrown pine trees yesterday. To make it here in time, he had to get up at four-thirty this morning. I said he didn't have to come – an insincere offer, one I was nervous he'd take me up on – but he wouldn't hear of it. He takes the seat next to me, his shoulder nudging mine, and kisses me. I taste coffee on his lips.

To pass the time, I read the pregnancy-related posters attached to a large corkboard on the wall. *Breast is best!* one declares, featuring a chubby baby with a gummy pink smile. Another shows a young mother holding her baby, looking highly competent. The text reads: *Ask your doctor about vaccination.*

There are no photographs of men in the posters; it's as though parenting is a burden that falls to women alone.

James squeezes my hand. He cannot wait to see the baby, to share ultrasound pictures with his family and friends. Holding back the news has been difficult for him. He's distracted himself by creating a list of the things we need to buy and it's growing steadily. He researches everything, reading product reviews to discern which crib is best and which pram is safest and has the highest-rated turning circle. I've reminded him I'm only nine weeks along, and we may not see much during the ultrasound at all, but he is thrumming with anticipation.

I pull my hand away from his and rub it on my suit pants. The waistband presses into my stomach, and I feel the twinge of my bladder. I had to drink two litres of water before the appointment and can't urinate until after the scan.

'You look tired,' James says. 'Are you sleeping?'

I shake my head.

'You need me there with you,' he says, and leans in to kiss my temple. The soothing muskiness of his skin obscures the other smells in the room; momentarily, my eyelids droop. Then he leans back, and I face forwards again.

I have my own list, too. A list of names, secreted away in my phone. They are all for girls: Ruby, Maeve, Gracie. Like James with his shopping list, I keep adding more to it: Elizabeth, Olivia, Lauren. I picture a perfect little girl in a neat school uniform, hair in plaits, playing with her similarly named peers: the Emmas, the Isabellas, the Evies. Hannah or Hilary for a sporty, fun type of girl. Helena, Julia or Sophia for a studious one. Then, some outliers: India, Luna, Frieda; names for girls who can draw or perform or sing. James and I agreed not to discuss names until we get the vital first trimester all-clear, but I can't help indulging these private inventions of who my child might be.

Truthfully, I don't mind if the baby is a boy or a girl or ends up choosing to be neither. The recurrent part – the most important part – of my fantasy is that my child is happy in every scenario I imagine them in. It keeps away the apprehension, the worry that I've committed to something I have no idea how to do. On the nights that James is away, I lie awake, worrying about my total lack of skill and experience. I don't know how to be a mother. I don't have siblings and have had no practice nieces or nephews. I don't want my child to feel like I did growing up.

Reading and googling and researching hasn't helped; it's only highlighted all the physical concerns I've been trying to ignore. I'm older. Doctors consider my pregnancy geriatric, high-risk. I wonder how I will ever give birth to this child because either method – vaginal or caesarean – will damage my body. The kind of damage that might not be undone. Medicine, and all its associated instruments and procedures, is unnerving. It pretends to be rational, stainless, until the first incision: the need for doctors to look inside you, past skin, muscle, nerves and veins, strikes me as messy and unnatural, driven by a desire to see more than they should.

These were things I didn't think about before the positive test result. Back then, when I imagined being pregnant,

I thought of family: nuclear, shiny, *normal*. I thought of love; the unconditional kind, the kind I've never known and thought I'd never experience.

A woman appears in the corridor, paperwork in hand.

'Leila Haddad?'

We stand, and I hold my breath.

'Come along, Dad,' the woman says to James, and he beams.

—

After an ultrasound of the outside of my lower abdomen, the cold gel raising goosebumps on my skin, the sonographer asks for permission to complete an internal scan. I consent. She opens a condom from its wrapper, pulls it over the wand and smothers it in clear lubricant. When I first had sex, my boyfriend bought pink cherry lubricant to use, and the smell was so intense and overly sweet, it nearly stopped us before we started. With James, we never needed lube, and I took this to mean our bodies instinctively chose each other.

The medical jelly is scent-free. As directed, I put the provided piece of foam under my bottom and draw my legs up, feet pressed together on the table, knees dropping to each side, inner thigh muscles pulled tight. The sonographer taps my right knee and tells me to relax. I smile at her and try to let everything go loose, a big ask when you're splayed out in front of a stranger and desperate to pee. She inserts the wand inside me, pressing it high and hard against my cervix. James's hand rests on my shoulder. After some internal pressure, I hear the keyboard clicking and look at the screen.

The inside of my uterus appears grey and blurry. The sonographer points out a round, fluid shape – the yolk sac. James told me about it over eggs one morning. It means there's no attachment to my bloodstream yet because the placenta hasn't formed; I can still have a glass of wine, though I probably shouldn't.

The wand pokes around inside me for what seems like a long time. The sonographer peers closely at the screen. There is a pause in the wand's movements. Then she says: 'I'm afraid I can't detect a heartbeat.'

James withdraws his hand, moves to my side to be closer to me, but he stands rigid and abject.

'Can you do a different scan?' I ask. My gaze flickers between his face and the screen. I take in the sonographer's upturned chin as she squints at the black and white images.

'You'll need to see your doctor to discuss that,' she says. 'It does look like you're measuring around seven weeks. How far along are you?'

'Nine.'

'Okay. I'll check your ovaries and other parts of your uterus now.'

There is more manoeuvring. The wand between my legs makes me feel plugged like a sink. I drop my head back on the bed and stare at the ceiling. Before this, my body worked exactly how I liked it: without limitations or malfunctions. It had never let me down – no broken bones, no health conditions, not even asthma.

We'd not have been able to afford any illnesses for me, anyway.

No-one speaks. The sonographer moves quickly, tapping the keyboard with a series of purposeful clicks to take images at every nudge of the wand.

'What are you seeing now?' I ask.

'Not sure,' she says. 'Fibroids. Perhaps cysts. I'll take the wand out now.'

It slides out and I close my legs, striving for dignity. The sonographer leaves me to tidy myself up. Before James can say anything, I tell him to meet me in the waiting room. When he's gone, I clean the sticky gel off as best I can. The paper towel is cheap and thin; I try to get the gunk off the bottom of my shirt, pubic bone, belly button. My labia. It leaves a slick sheen no matter how much I dab and rub. I shove the gluggy paper in the bin and squirt sanitiser on my hands, pull on my underwear and pants and find the bathroom. At last, I sit on the toilet, head in my hands.

When I reach the reception, James is waiting inside the glass entrance doors. We step out onto the hot sidewalk and the morning sun slaps us with glare. James points. His ute is parked down the street, and we make our way in silence. Halfway there, I stop. James reaches out as if he expects this, as if he wants to hold me, but I push my hand against his chest. 'I knew I'd fail at this.'

'There's still hope. Maybe she just couldn't see the heartbeat. We might have miscalculated the weeks.'

'She should have been able to see it.'

He rubs my shoulder awkwardly, the keys in his hand poking against my blouse. 'We'll try again,' he says.

Try again. I'm thirty-seven years old.

We reach the truck and get inside. Cars glint in front of us as we pull onto the road. It's the same peak-hour traffic Sydney is always stuck in. I wonder about the people in the cars and buses around us. People heading to work after dropping off children, people driving babies to day care. People with families.

—

I wake to a deep, sharp tug low in my gut and know it's beginning.

The GP sent me quickly for blood tests to confirm that, indeed, there was no heartbeat. The foetus wasn't viable – the words *died* and *miscarriage* weren't used, but they floated into my brain anyway as the doctor spoke in a low, flat tone, and I stared at the floor. The doctor's preference was that I wait to pass the foetus naturally. So, each day since, I've worked from home, unwilling to risk miscarrying in an office toilet cubicle.

I don't say anything to James. He leaves for work, and for a couple of hours, I answer emails and take calls. By mid-morning, the cramps intensify, and I sit on the toilet and wait. The spasms are mysterious but familiar; briefly, I'm impressed that my body performs the function so instinctively. Then crashing pain rolls over me like an avalanche, it seems like my uterus has awoken, angry and pulsing and struggling against the stiff membrane of my abdomen, and I grip the wall while everything is expelled.

A wet mass slips from my vagina. My body does the work, all I must do is keep breathing. Everything worsens:

my shuddering, the stabbing pains, the feeling that hands are inside me, squeezing and twisting. More matter splashes into the toilet bowl. I think I leave my body. It doesn't need me; it knows exactly what to do. I hover somewhere above myself and wait for it to finish.

I clean myself up, flush the blood and clots away and cry for a while. Splash my face with water. Line my underwear with a pad to catch any last remnants. I'm sure nothing of substance is left behind to infect me, that I will not need a curette. All of it – *it*, I can no longer bring myself to call it anything else, it didn't even have a *heartbeat* – is gone. I lie down on my bed and pick up my phone, open the Notes app and stare at my list of names until they blur into unfamiliar shapes and it's time to delete them: letter by letter, one by one, until they do not exist, not even in my imagination.

—

I don't recover from the miscarriage the way other women seem to. I don't go back to the doctor to discuss the internal scan results; I don't want to know about my damaged, faulty uterus. Grief pelts me in all sorts of ways, and it's almost as bad as when my mother died. It's not seeing other pregnant women or babies that hits the hardest; I don't look at them. It's panic attacks on the bus to work, brutal headaches. It worsens into recurring dreams of dying in childbirth, then all-night long insomnia, and, finally, periods of lying in bed, mute. I request extended leave from work. My boss squeezes my hand and agrees. James does everything: showers me, brings me food and feeds it to me in bed. He doesn't go back to the farm for the rest of January and all of February.

By March, he insists on taking me back to the GP for a check-up, for help. To begin recovery. She has the decency not to show disappointment or sympathy, instead prescribing medication for sleep and anxiety. She refers me to a gynaecologist to assess the fibroids and cysts.

The gynaecologist tells me, based on the scan, that I am riddled with every kind of fibroid, inside my uterus and out. There are three large cysts – two on my right ovary and one on my left. She recommends surgery to remove them – swiftly, if we hope to conceive again. James agrees, and she fits me in within the week. 'Lucky,' James says.

When I wake up from the surgery to remove everything, these wild growths, the gynaecologist stands by my bed. She says, 'There's good news and bad news.'

I keep my uterus, but the recovery from the surgery will be painful: they had to cut through my abdomen and uterine muscle. And the number of fibroids the gynaecologist had to remove means there is scarring that will still develop, on my organs and in my uterus, and adhesions that will thicken, tighten and bind inside my abdomen, causing painful cramps. The adhesions carry a high risk of blocking my fallopian tubes, reducing my chance of conceiving naturally. And there is no guarantee that this is over – new fibroids can grow, lurking like weeds ready to emerge and strangle a plant.

James says it's okay, that it shows I can still get pregnant, even with all my uterine problems. He says there's no reason to think the fibroids will return or that the scar tissue will be as bad as I fear. 'Doctors are obligated to give you the worst-case scenario,' he repeats. He is relentlessly positive. He talks about diet, insemination, in vitro, egg freezing: 'There's lots of things we can do.'

I take painkillers and sleeping pills, then lie awake, eyes on the ceiling, until the benzos force me to sleep. James doesn't approve, he thinks I'm wallowing, but I'm not. It's just that there's no way to explain to him what it's like to lose something so fundamental, especially when you were frightened you couldn't do it, that maybe you shouldn't do it, or you didn't deserve it; and it turns out your body agrees with you. I can't do it. Perhaps I never could. *Fibroids are hereditary,* the gynaecologist told me. *Your mother would have had them, too.*

Another consequence of my mother; another thing she has forced me to endure. And here I am again, trying to survive it.

We're on the Great Western Highway, on a stretch of road with guardrails and speed signage, but few exits. A train weaves alongside us for a bit, then disappears. It's freight, not passenger, pulling rusty brown carriages filled with materials essential for rural life. Between the little towns dotted along the route, the view outside changes from houses and shops to clusters of eucalypts and scrubby bush. It's mostly green, thanks to La Nina and a couple of years of drought-breaking rain, and I'm relieved to see it. Drought can be ignored in Sydney, but not out here.

I've never lived inland, or outside a major city. I left Brisbane years ago to travel: Europe, Hong Kong and New York with friends, and a couple of years working in London. Settling in Sydney, I worked my way up to consulting on corporate projects – my specialty is leading people through transformation. Change. A huge part of successful change is understanding people's fears and desires: managing their emotional responses, without them realising, and it's something I've always been good at. Professional, paid people-pleasing. On weekends, I shook off the expectations of work with exercise: running the Coogee to Bondi track, walking along the coast to Maroubra, swimming in the saltwater pools. Then I'd brunch or wine with women I met through work or the gym; people I didn't know well, but well enough to drink with.

'Are we any closer?' I ask. James says we're about halfway, and that the view of the mountains coming up is spectacular. He looks at me often while we drive, assessing me, the way a mechanic might approach a repair job. Just fix the broken part and click everything back together, good as new. I shift in the car seat, rearranging the cushions I brought to ease the bumps on my stomach. The dressing and stitches were removed a few days ago, two weeks after the procedure; the skin has knit together in a swollen scar, no infection. The gynaecologist was pleased.

'You okay?' James rests his hand on my knee and I nod. Emboldened, he adds, 'This year will be good for us. You'll get to rest and recover. Do some writing. And I'll finally be able to stop driving to Sydney.'

'Sure,' I say. 'But living at the farm isn't suddenly going to make me fertile.'

He takes his hand from my knee. I face the window.

'I'm sorry,' I say after a while. 'I know this is a good idea. I'm excited. I'll finally be able to write. I've wanted a year off for ages.'

He smiles and says, 'It's okay, I know.'

As we pass by the towns in the Blue Mountains, the foliage changes; the dry scrub peters out. The air here is colder than I'm used to in Sydney in April. The trees lining the road have transformed from green to deep red. We drive through a little town with bright shopfronts: a bakery, deli and book-store. The sign says 'Blackheath' and the streets are awash with autumn leaves, gold and auburn. It won't look like this at O'Connell, where James's family home is. By his description, it's a beautiful hamlet, filled with acreage and farms, but barely any conveniences. The local pub is patronised mostly by retired farmers and locals, and only open for half the week. The farm itself is just a house, sheds and acres of sloping plains.

We pause at the lights, beside a coffee shop. The chairs are dark wood, French bistro style; the espresso machine is gleaming silver, and the barista wears all black with a shaved head, save for a blonde quiff. If not for the lack of traffic and the crisp bite in the air, I could almost pretend I'm still in the city.

James notices me looking and suggests we stop for coffee or a snack; I shake my head. I'm not hungry. Eating breakfast this morning felt like a chore, but James insisted.

We push on, and the notion of a city, with city amenities, leaves me for good. The shops thin out and then disappear entirely; here, only small brick houses line the road. Soon they are gone too; there is only bitumen ahead, and a thicket of trees around us. I glance at the side mirror. Civilisation is out of sight.

Then, the road itself changes. It becomes steep, and James slows the ute as we weave our way down. Without warning, we emerge into a new world: on both sides of the road, everything suddenly drops away. I can't see ground. There is only bitumen, guardrail, and then – abyss. Mountains rise from the chasm – so many mountains, in stilled waves. Turning in every direction, I see green, tree-covered peaks that I feel I can almost touch. My ears pop and ring as we descend.

'Amazing, isn't it?' James says, and I nod in agreement, struck by the view. I've never seen anything like it, and I've been to plenty of places. But it is overwhelming too: one wrong turn, a slip, and you might lose it all.

—

We come through a place called Tarana, which is covered in tall poplar trees turning from khaki to gold. The road is pitted and narrow and winding, and I worry whether two cars driving in opposite directions can fit, but James says it's fine, and we don't see anyone else anyway. He suggests the landscape looks like Italy – like Tuscany – and I try not to disagree. In Italy, the poplars are a rich green and even the ruins are like art, sculptures made from stone, but here, the old corrugated iron sheds are full of holes and dark red from corrosion.

The road dips and we drive alongside a river. The bank widens and there are tents in blue and grey. Men in rugby shorts and jumpers guard the barbecues, and women in tracksuits watch the kids: families on holiday. I remember Mum's few attempts at camping holidays – eating nearly expired snags on sale from Coles and shivering in a thin sleeping bag. Friends went to hotels and resorts; one even went to Europe for a month, an adventure that left the rest of us speechless.

Once, Mum and I took a drive up to Bundaberg with one of her boyfriends. Ian was his name. I was eleven; she was thirty-five. He paid, so we stayed in a basic family resort, one of those places with a cheap restaurant, a greenish pool and multiple A-frame cabins that stank of bleach. Early one morning, Mum woke me up and made me get dressed. It was dark, but the silver-blue sky was creeping forth. She led me down a path to a gate where Ian was waiting, and we pushed it open and found ourselves on the beach. I took my thongs off and carried them, my feet sinking into the cold sand, damp grit sticking between my toes. A group of people were gathered there, some squatting low, some sitting on the sand. There was a man standing at the front, talking. We joined the group at the edges and squatted, too. There was a dark round shape in front that everyone was looking at: a turtle.

'She's laid her eggs,' said the man, and the group murmured in wonder. 'She'll swim away now. In a couple of months, they'll hatch and make their way to the sea.' The turtle shuffled down the sand to the shore. We watched, silent, as she entered the water, her flippers reaching out wide, paddling into the waves. The man said only half the baby turtles would make it to the ocean. The rest would be eaten by snakes or birds.

People stood up, brushing the sand from their bums. Mum nudged me, told me how lucky we were to be staying here, to have such a lovely holiday and that I should tell Ian how grateful I was. He walked ahead and she hurried to catch him, clutching at his hand, fingers curling into his. I tried to spot the mother turtle in the water, but she had gone. I did thank Ian later, but it was pointless. He left us soon enough.

I reach over and take James's left hand, place it on my thigh while his right hand turns the wheel, guiding us expertly along the curving road. I lace my fingers through his; he squeezes them and does not let go.

—

We drive up a hill, into O'Connell. On the left is a tiny field of headstones chipped by wind and rain; the smallest cemetery I've ever seen. 'The old boneyard,' James says. There are no posies, just weeds. We continue past cleared paddocks with metal fencing and signs that read: *Danger, electric fence, keep off.* James points ahead and says, 'If we keep going straight, it'd take us to Bathurst,' and I murmur a response. Instead, we turn onto a single-lane bitumen road. It takes us into a thicket of pale gum trees; the tallest ones twist and stretch over the road, the tops of their branches like arthritic fingers reaching for something, but the only thing to grasp is the air. Sections of them are bent forwards in what looks like design but must simply be the effect of strong winds. There are no houses along here, just rocks and bush, and white, otherworldly trees.

A few minutes later, we turn off the lane and pull in towards a driveway. It's rocky and blocked off by a double wooden gate. There's a weathered animal skull hanging off it, the eye sockets gaping. James opens the console between us and pulls out a key. He gets out and unlocks the gate, pushing both halves back. We drive through and he stops again, gets out and closes them. I watch in the rear-view as the two sides meet; they stand together, nose to nose, and he slings the padlock chain around them. We continue slowly. Small rocks fly up, making sharp, tinny sounds on the underside of the car. The driveway is graded but not paved or cemented. More bumps. I nestle my hands under the cushion, holding my abdomen, trying to gird my stomach. I can't see a house yet, just sprouted tussock on all sides. The sun is mild, and the air has a slight chill. I can smell shit.

'How far up is the house?' I ask.

'Not too far,' James says. 'About seven kilometres.'

'What was the dead skull on the gate?'

'A bull. It's good luck.'

'I'm not in Kansas anymore, am I?'

He grins. 'Don't worry, you'll be country before you know it.'

A rusted wire fence encloses the paddocks on either side of the driveway. Spiderwebs are strung between the fence wires, iridescent with late-morning dew. I spot an enormous brown and yellow spider, suspended in gossamer, its legs spread so wide they are almost a circle, like the spokes in a wheel. A herd of cows in different tints – black, camel, and one the colour of tawny port – crowd the fence up ahead. As we approach, one lets out a bellow; soon the others join in. The noise is harsh and prolonged. They press against each other, vibrating like a single organism.

'I didn't know you ran cows,' I say.

'We haven't for a long time. They're Matt's.'

'Who's Matt?'

'Local bloke. We won't see him.'

The radio sputters out and the cows disappear as we drive on. It is suddenly deeply quiet, with the crunch of rolling tyres and bird calls the only sounds. I twist slowly to look out the back window; the gate can no longer be seen. Ahead of us, there are mountains in the distance, endless land and grassy hills. There's enormous airspace. Gums and eucalypts are scattered around. Some are just stumps – lightning strike, James tells me. The next time we pass one, I look closer at the bark: it's burnt black.

'It's isolated out here,' I say.

We round another bend and fly up a small rise, accelerating; we hit some grassy bumps at speed and then we're on the flat.

'We made it,' James says, braking hard, and I'm jerked forwards. I shriek involuntarily and he looks confused, then stricken. 'Sorry – sorry.'

I press both hands on my stomach and my head drops. Black dots swarm my vision, and I shut my eyes. There had been no chance of a laparoscopy, the gynaecologist said. The incision was a large one.

'Shit,' James says. 'I didn't think. I'm so sorry.' His hand finds its way to my knee, his thumb rubbing back and forth in a smoothing motion, asking for forgiveness. I nod. He pats my leg and says he'll get the bags.

He gets out of the car and flings the door shut, and I flinch. James is coarse sometimes: pitching cutlery into drawers, scraping chairs back with force. I grew up making as little sound as possible. After some deep breathing, the adrenaline subsides and the pain settles into a throbbing discomfort. I pick up my phone, I don't know why, other than to feel connected to something beyond the car, this farm. There's no mobile reception. It's not a surprise, James had warned me it was intermittent, that there's better coverage from the road. I hear the clap of a door and look up to see that James has entered the home: the farmhouse in which we are to live.

After travelling along the rocky driveway amid the hills, a house seems incongruous in this place, like a fish trying to survive on land. The building is a long rectangle, one storey, with a small dormer window in the middle of the roof. It's beige sandstone with white French windows and a silver corrugated iron roof that conjures the clang of rain on tin, a comforting memory of summer storms in rickety old Queenslanders. Stone steps lead up to a covered verandah and a wooden front door. Terracotta pots displaying tiny purple flowers stand along the verandah pavers; down in front, overgrown rose bushes run along the length of the house. They're still in bloom.

I get out of the car and close the door. Standing before me on the grass is a black bird, not a cockatoo, but almost as healthy a size. It regards me with curious eyes but doesn't move as I walk past it, each step careful, gentle. The grass is long and springy underfoot. When I reach the front steps, I turn and look at the bird. It's still watching me. James comes outside and kisses my cheek.

'I'm going to Bathurst,' he says. 'We need groceries, and you need a rest. Will you be right on your own? I'll be an hour or two.'

'I'll be fine.'

'I'll call Mum and Dad from the road, let them know we made it. Be back in a bit.'

'Tell them thanks again for the house.'

He gives me a thumbs up and I watch him drive away. The white truck's undercarriage is stained by gritty dust, the way the yellow of cigarette smoke clings to walls. James's parents vacated the farmhouse in favour of their beach home at James's request. I don't want to imagine what he said, most likely in serious, hushed tones, to convince them I needed this. I wish we could have taken over the beach house instead, but the area is too under-developed: located between the beachside towns of Eden and Pambula, there'd have been nowhere practical for James to resume his practice, no decent-sized town nearby; and Sydney about seven hours away.

I walk up the steps and enter a large foyer. I try closing the screen door, but it's slightly off its hinges and won't stay fastened. After it swings open a few times, I pull the wooden door shut instead, locking out any fresh air, and breathe in the musty scent of soft furnishings and varnish.

I take off my shoes and place them by the front door, stepping onto a colourful Persian rug. Underneath, the floor is a buttery, polished oak. The walls are beige, the ceilings high and painted white with intricate decorative moulding. A pendant light hangs from a slightly chipped ceiling rose, the glass of the shade turned dull with age, but all of it, taken together, is quite classically beautiful.

In the foyer stand two antique mahogany sideboards crowded with framed family photos, including several black and white portraits of previous generations: I take in the unsmiling faces and dated clothes, then move on to a picture of James's parents' wedding. Patricia is in a soft pink dress that falls to mid-calf, a small bouquet of white baby's breath in one hand. Her hair is permed, and she's smiling and bashful. Her other hand grips her new husband's arm. John stands tall and appears emotionless in a dark suit, his lips a thin line, Patricia pressed up against him.

I first met John and Patricia over coffee in the city; they were visiting friends and seeing a show. James was excited for us all to meet, and they seemed genuinely delighted that James had met a woman he was serious about. The opportunity to be part of their family excited me, and Patricia made me feel welcome, inviting me to the farm any time and asking for my number. It felt official: I was a partner, not just a girlfriend.

Patricia began texting me on occasion, and I always responded quickly. A career midwife, the topics of her messages soon grew limited: hints of marriage and babies, articles on *not leaving it too late!* I pulled back, unable to contain my reaction to what felt controlling, interfering of her, somehow, and she noticed. At first, I tried to repair it as I would with any tricky stakeholder: appeasement. Make her happy. Give her what she desires, and she'll respond in kind. I was extra bubbly on the phone when

James would call her. I 'hearted' every article on midwifery and *tips for conception* that she shared on Facebook. But the damage, unspoken and lingering, was done. Our communication became less frequent; other than James, we had little in common. I stopped promising to spend weekends at the farm, using work as an excuse for never finding the time. At Christmas, she and John went overseas, and I wondered if it was some sort of retaliation for my perceived lack of interest. James and I spent Christmas Day at Coogee, swimming in the ocean, eating fresh, sweet prawns, and daydreaming about when it might be three of us instead of two.

I follow the line of photo frames. James as a baby. James in primary school, an imp in maroon tartan, squinting into the camera. James at his senior formal in a shiny, too-big blue suit, standing stiffly next to a blonde girl, the posture echoing his parents' wedding portrait.

I linger on the photos of James as a young man, wondering if I've ever known *this* James: what made him laugh, how he spent his time, who he had a crush on. What his school friends were like. He's in a green flannel, with a group of pimply teenagers, holding up a fish with a slack mouth. He's with friends at an outdoor party, esky at their feet, all of them sitting in camp chairs and raising beer cans to the camera. Then he's older, with long hair curling around his face and a bloodied, dead pig at his feet, his hands holding a rifle.

I lean on the sideboard and close my eyes briefly. Sudden fatigue comes over me as cramps corkscrew my insides. It's as though standing after sitting in the car for so long has forced my organs and membranes to jostle each other as they return to their rightful positions. After a minute, I wander down the hall to the main bedroom, skirt around the suitcases James left in the doorway and pull out a packet of Endone from my handbag. I take two pills out. From the ensuite, I run the tap and scoop water into my mouth and swallow. Then lie down on the bed, close my eyes, and wait for sleep.

—

Frogs are snapping and croaking outside the bedroom window. Behind my head, I hear squeaking and scratching in the walls. Country mice. James told me the cooling weather sends rodents scurrying indoors; they slip in through the slimmest of cracks, like they have no spines. How they survive in the cold walls, I have no idea. I check the time on my phone. It's after five. A cracking noise echoes in the distance and I wonder if James is fiddling with tools or machinery somewhere. I take a box of medication from my bag and slip it in my pocket, find a blanket in a chest of drawers and then go to the kitchen for a bottle of wine.

James has left a case of pinot noir on the kitchen table. I yank at the cardboard, tearing it in my haste. Once I've made a decent sized hole, I grasp a bottle and pull it out. Find a large glass. Snaffle a packet of crackers from the pantry. I'm not hungry, but wine sits better with my pills if I eat something.

I carry everything out to the front verandah, letting the screen door swing behind me; it bangs a few times against the door-frame. There's a little wrought iron table with two chairs.

Sitting down, I dump the pills on the table, pop one in my mouth, unscrew the top of the wine bottle and give myself a generous pour, right to the rim. I take a long sip; then swallow and shiver in relief.

'You're having a drink without me?'

James approaches from the far end of the verandah, pulling off gloves. He reaches in through the front door, flicks a switch and the light above me comes on. Flying insects rush to crowd the naked bulb. He walks over and sits on the other chair, frowning at the set-up: wine, pills, crackers. No proper food.

'The car ride really hurt my stomach,' I say, pulling the blanket over my lap.

'Have you taken Valium with the wine? You know you're not supposed to.'

I shake my head.

He points to the packet, open on the table.

I glance at it. I've left the foil poking out of the cardboard box. I jerk my head in the direction of the door. 'That screen door needs fixing.'

I swig another mouthful of wine. James gets up and drags a pot plant to the screen door, propping it open, then enters the house, closing the wooden door behind him. He's annoyed, but still leaves the outdoor light on for me. I lean over the Valium box; the sticker on it bears my name and the pharmaceutical instructions: *Do not take while under the influence of alcohol. Do not drive or operate machinery. May cause drowsiness. Do not take with other medications.* The tablets line up, ready to be plucked. I pop a second one from the foil and swallow it.

It's not the only medication I take. Slow-release Targin in the mornings and afternoons; Valium or temazepam when I feel anxious or can't sleep. Endone for emergencies, when the stomach cramps are too painful to bear. The gynaecologist was liberal with the painkiller prescriptions – *Just talk to your GP when you want to wean off them,* she said when I questioned the multiple repeats – and the GP agreed, issuing sleeping and anxiety prescriptions too, though she did ask if I'd tried meditation. I keep the meds stored in different handbags and jackets, some still in packets, some wrapped in tissue and zipped tightly in the pockets. I can't face the thought of not having easy access to them.

Mixing wine, pain relief and sleeping pills isn't allowed, medically, but it should be. When they combust, the aftermath mutes not only your body, but your mind too. It had this effect on my mother, well before the end. She took morphine and drank – vodka mainly. I didn't police it; I bought the alcohol for her. When she was lucid and in pain, she tended to talk, to try and share memories; a history she rewrote even as she told it. It was easier when she was quiet. Her tight expression would slacken, and sometimes there'd even be a loose, ghoulish smile. The moans stopped, and her constant fidgeting and squirming to try to get comfortable ceased. She was so thin that her hipbones jutted into her mattress, and it rubbed the skin, causing sores. The bed was cheap. It didn't seem worth buying a new one to alleviate her pain when it wouldn't be used for long.

Besides, pain is something we had always lived with. When I was young, I observed it daily, treated it with deference and tiptoed around it. My mother, caught in the midst of it, careened through the days looking for forgiving places to ease her suffering. Often the soft landings came in the form of men: men with shifting eyes and sharp tongues, especially after a few drinks. Welders, carpenters, doctors, lawyers, advertisers, businessmen – their profession was irrelevant. They said all the right things until my mother asked a little too much, leaned a little too heavily. Then they appeared less frequently, and only late at night, usually gone before I was awake.

The pain returned when they no longer did: my mother would rage and sob for hours, demanding comfort. It was stifling, but it was a demand I couldn't deny. On other days, I'd enter the house and she'd look past me, not as if I wasn't there, but as though she was picturing what that might be like. If it might be better.

My mother taught me that pain – physical or otherwise – is a state of loss. And I came to learn that it's avoidable if you never obtain anything you can't part with.

Through the kitchen window behind me, I listen to James chopping, hear the tap running. He's preparing dinner, but as soon as I feel nothing, I'll go straight to bed.

Melting over the chair, I watch the colours of the farm change: dusk softens the sky, throwing purple and pink light across streaky clouds. The Great Dividing Range, humming blue in the distance, guards the mix of irrigated crops and gum-strewn bushland. Bright and verdant, the crops appear cartoonish: not natural or honest, but, rather, how we wish they would.

I wake to see James plucking his wallet and watch from the dresser. He's getting ready for work in Bathurst, thirty minutes away. James has shifted to working full time out here for the year. One of his father's friends owns a large psychology practice and found room for him. The morning light is dim with the curtains closed, and I watch him through lazy lids, unsure if I want to talk. He moves around quietly, slipping into the ensuite. I hear the soft ratchet of teeth brushing, then the running of the tap. I close my eyes. The door creaks, and I feel his presence. I lie still, expecting a kiss. Nothing. I wait. The bedroom door closes with a muted click, then distantly, the car revs and crunches down the drive.

I lie on my back and stare at the ceiling for a while, studying its decorative cornices and ceiling rose. The room is large and the carpet soft; the bed is king size. I could stay horizontal all day.

My phone buzzes.

'I'm sorry —bout last ni—,' James says. His voice cuts in and out.

'Don't worry about it.'

'I jus— say —ave good day.' The whirr of the truck's engine and other cars on the road crowd the spotty line.

'What time will you be home?'

'Arou— five.'

A fat earwig tracks its way across my blanket, aggressive-looking pincers protruding from its behind. I flick it away and it sails through the air, landing somewhere out of sight. I put the phone on speaker and raise it towards the ceiling, as though this will magically improve the connection.

'What— you think— do today?' James says.

'I just woke up.'

'You don't— do anythi— physi—. Doctor said— recover.'

I have no plans to be physical at all. I run my nails gently but persistently across the scar on my stomach, bringing a sweet, momentary dampening of the tingling. It's followed by a burn.

'I'll get up and have a coffee.'

'I set up— fire has log—. Push— air vent closed— keep hot.'

I am relieved to say goodbye and end the patchy call. I put my phone on the bedside table. The light on the screen turns black, leaving the oil of my fingerprints visible. I shift my legs carefully over the side of the bed and sit, looking out of the window. The sky is clear and the mountains seem further away than yesterday; a blue-ish line near the horizon.

I get up and pull on a dressing gown, then shuffle up the hall to the kitchen. It's bright in the daylight: a bay window facing the view, beige walls decorated with white tiles, and wooden hutches displaying patterned dishware. There's a loaf of sourdough on the table, and a butter dish. I boil the kettle. James has left a mug and a jar of instant coffee granules next to it. No espresso machine. I tip the coffee into the mug and pour over the hot water. Warm my hands against the porcelain. Listen for sounds. No mice this morning; they save their activities for evening. Bird trills float in from outside, along with distant braying from the cows. Small cracks and creaks from the walls and roof of the house. Otherwise, quiet. Undisturbed. The day stretches ahead.

I sip the coffee and meander through the rest of the home. The layout is totally different to anywhere I've lived before: when I entered yesterday into the large central foyer, I saw the back door immediately opposite me, and the narrow hall stretching away on both my right and left. To one side of the foyer, steep stairs lead up to a small landing with a closed door – presumably an attic, given the dormer window I saw from outside.

Down the hall to the left is the homely kitchen, a formal dining room, a large living room and a study. To the right of the foyer is the master bedroom and ensuite, a family-sized bathroom and laundry, and two more bedrooms. Each bedroom features densely patterned wallpaper atop cream wainscoting: tiny cows, rabbits, flowers, spirals, shining suns, crescent moons.

I pause in the one James must have slept in when his parents were here. I want to know what he's like when we're apart. What does he do when I'm not around? I have my own routines: he doesn't know, for example, that on the days he was away I liked to sit on the couch, peeling my nails with my teeth and dropping the detritus behind the cushions. He doesn't know that I measured my waist, arms, thighs, calves, breasts and belly to make sure my weight was consistent. He doesn't know that I'm hopeless at push-ups, but I do them anyway to try and achieve yoga-toned arms without the yoga. He doesn't know I can't do yoga because I can't relax and I think saying 'ohm' sounds ridiculous. He doesn't know that I spent too much time googling *why am I unhappy* before I met him, and that it stopped when we started dating, only to resume a few months later: a lifelong melancholy I do not understand and that nothing, not even love, is able to fully dislodge.

The bed is unmade, the sheet and doona twisted together; one corner of the fitted sheet has come off the mattress. Two pillows slump against the wooden headboard. A pair of James's pants – brown cotton, gardening pants I guess – are lying on the floor. These habits are not new to me. I open the bedside tables, scrabbling through the items. Perhaps I shouldn't, but I once found an ex-boyfriend's hair-thickening and Viagra tablets; it pays to snoop.

There's nothing unusual here, though. Just old receipts, a comb, some mints. In the wardrobe, there's familiar clothing from his last visit: a wool jumper, checked shirts, jeans, belts. I pause and smell the shirts; I love the woody, dirt smell of James's worn-in country clothes. Then I finger the belts, stifling a laugh at one with a tarnished gold bull skull for the buckle: not a style suited for the city.

In the backyard there's no verandah, just a concrete path from the back door; beyond that, longer grass, plants and trees I don't know the names of, and a pile of hard rubbish against the garage wall. Wire, bricks, rusted tools, old whitegoods. I wander along the path to the garage behind the homestead. The door is open, but there's no vehicle inside. I'd hoped James's parents would leave us their spare car; it seems I'll be reliant on James's schedule.

I walk back through the house, noticing on this second appraisal how substantial – how *inherited* – the furniture feels. There's no pine or veneer; nothing from IKEA. The living room is furnished with velvet armchairs and an old-fashioned floral sofa. I sit on the sofa to test it out and it's still spongy, still comfortable. There are two cedar cabinets with lead light glass doors, and I pause to peer at the tchotchkes inside the first display case. Patricia must be a collector: there are porcelain plates with blue and white flowers, silver cups, and trays and vases, all lined up. The vases are unusually shaped. Each vessel has a bulbous bottom and a top that stretches into two handless arms reaching skywards. I count seven of them, in different sizes, colours and finishes. One looks like it was hewed from an old, pockmarked stone. All antiques, no doubt. Another is shaped like it has two breasts protruding from its chest; others have a swirl pattern engraved on the front.

I've always felt immature – lacking in something vital – when visiting houses where people display art and knick-knacks collected over a lifetime, or several lifetimes. Houses with Middle Eastern rugs and expensive cabinetry and linen presses. Families that pass down objects of sentimental or monetary worth. It indicates a stability I've never experienced; that people have lived long enough in a home to display their memories, their history. I've moved often enough that I don't collect possessions, just clothes I can throw into a suitcase. Even in my Coogee apartment, the place I thought might be a long-term home, my belongings are minimal. Permanence is not something I've lived.

I wander back into the kitchen and put my empty cup on the wooden table in the centre; it's slightly too big for the room, and uneven, like the planks have been warped by moisture. The counters are busy with appliances. Yesterday, from the outside, I assumed it to be an open-plan home, but in fact the interior is labyrinthine, with rooms and walls everywhere. Overhead, light bulbs flicker; they'll need replacing soon. Some of the door handles are loose. The back door has no lock. I've found little agitations everywhere.

Tiring, I go to the bedroom to collect my painkillers, then return to the kitchen and fill a water glass. Swallow the Targin. As I consider what to eat, there's a knocking sound, and with a mild start, I understand it's not a developing migraine but an actual noise. The sound makes no sense at all: I'm in the middle of nowhere. There are no neighbours.

'Anyone 'ere?' A male voice.

I'm confused, standing tense and motionless. More rapping.

'Okay, I'm coming,' I mutter.

I cross the foyer and look through the spyhole. A broad man with a dark beard and ruddy skin is standing there. He's wearing a khaki shirt and pants; his sunglasses look like the kind you buy from a petrol station. Atop his head is a crumpled suede Akubra: the brim flops down on one side of his face.

'Hello?' he calls. 'I can see your feet under the door. Open up.'

'Hang on,' I say. I clear my throat and firm my voice. 'Who are you?'

'Sorry love, it's Matt,' he says. 'Matt with the cows?'

For a moment I pause, but he's not a stranger, not technically. I crack open the door. 'I didn't expect to see you.'

'James didn't tell ya I was coming by?'

I shake my head, but let the door ease open further.

'Huh. Well, nice to meet you anyway.' He takes off his sunglasses and sticks his other hand out, which I shake briefly. It's knotted with calluses and the skin is dry. He doesn't make a move to come inside. He's probably fifty or so, though it's hard to tell. His eyes crinkle even though he's not smiling; his stomach betrays a fondness for beer.

'I come and move the cows to a new paddock every week or so. If you need any jobs doing about the place while I'm here, I'm happy to help.'

I force a smile and thank him, moving to close the door.

'I brought Rusty, too.'

'Rusty?'

'I took him in for the Crawleys for a few nights. Just until you and James arrived.' He gestures behind him, and I peer past his shoulder. Lying in a sunny spot on the verandah pavers is a toffee-coloured dog with dark brown eyes and a bushy tail, which flaps slowly. A bit larger than a cattle dog, but with longer hair.

'He'll keep you company.' Matt gestures to the fields. 'On your own all the way out here. 'Cept for the cows.'

Discomfited, I say nothing. He must read my face because he adds, 'I didn't mean anything by it. Just that it's nice to have some company during the day. Trust me, you'll want someone to talk to.' Matt offers his hand again. 'Right, if you need me, I'll be down in the front paddock.'

I give his hand another squeeze and watch him lope back to his truck. He gets in, revs it, and waves through the windshield. I wave back. Rusty pricks his ears and stands, watching the truck leave. When it's no longer in sight, he turns and cocks his head at me.

'Come on, Rusty,' I say, opening the door, and he trots inside. I reach down and pat his head, and he nuzzles against my palm. His coat is silkier than expected. 'You can be my new friend.'

I stand for a minute, watching the slope of the driveway to make sure Matt's ute doesn't return unexpectedly. It's a habit from my younger days: in stillness, ears tuned to the sounds of the house, I would wait by my window until I could confirm that my mother's boyfriends were properly gone before leaving my bedroom to get ready for school. Watchful like a hunter; vulnerable as prey. I didn't want to meet them in the tiny hall, to have to slip past their gaze, their thin attempts at small talk.

Once silence resumes, I know the vehicle has departed and I walk back down the hallway. Rusty follows, his paws clicking and echoing on the hardwood floors. It's a comforting sound. I step into the bedroom and Rusty's clicks stop abruptly. When I turn, he's standing at the door, his tail down.

'You can come in, Rusty.' I soften my voice. 'Come in.'

Rusty sniffs the air, then drops his head and lets out a small whine. He backs away and clacks down the hallway. I hear a heavy flop and a deep sigh. In the bedroom, I look at the suitcases and slowly, carefully, unpack.

—

After putting away my belongings, I turn the shower taps on in the ensuite. Pipes rattle in the wall and water streams out of the showerhead.

Removing my top, I stretch my arms gingerly over my head, careful not to pull at the scarring any more than necessary. Although it's considered healed, the scar is still furious, bright red and raised, an incongruous smile drawn under my belly. Steam rises from the shower cubicle and I take off my tracksuit pants, resting them over the towel rack, and draw in several deep breaths.

The hot water on my body cuts through the fog of the pills and everything feels lighter, like a layer of muck is being removed. I lather on body wash. When my skin is stripped clean, I turn the tap off and reach for the towel, quivering in the sudden cold. As I pat myself down, an odd noise snakes through the house: the kind of noise that, once heard, makes everything feel out of place. It's like an echo of a high-pitched sound, but I can't make it out. I turn off the bathroom fan, but the sound is gone. Perhaps it was a sudden snatch of howling wind, or a squalling bird. *Tinnitus*, James would joke.

I get dressed in the bedroom. One foot in my underwear, gripping the chest of drawers for balance, then the other foot. I put on a singlet, then a soft jumper and step back into my tracksuit pants. I bought them a size larger, with gentle elastic to ease the pressure on my stomach. By now I'm so tired, I sit on the bed to drag them up my legs, breathing harder than I'd like. The fatigue frustrates me, but I know getting upset about it will only exhaust me more. I breathe, and take my time. It's a small win each day to shower and dress myself. I slide my feet into slippers and walk into the hallway.

'Rusty?'

There is a snort in response: Rusty pokes his head through the living room door and looks at me. We move towards each other and meet in the middle. He stands, tail wagging.

'Sit.'

Rusty lowers his rear to the floor, tail sweeping the rug. I'm impressed and relieved that he already knows this command,

and that he acquiesces to it. Coming of age before the advent of cavoodles and groodles and labradoodles, I thought dogs were dirty and rough. The only dogs in my neighbourhood growing up were muscular pit mixes leashed to fences, foaming with rage at being contained.

'Good dog,' I say, briefly leaning down to scratch him behind the ears. Rusty holds my gaze, his big eyes unblinking. 'Let's find something to eat. You hungry?'

He falls in beside me and we enter the kitchen together. I open the fridge: there are vegetables and salad ingredients, a whole chicken, a lamb shoulder, ham, bacon, milk, yoghurt, steaks, and an array of different cheeses, including my favourite, a strong blue. James can't stand it, won't even kiss me when I've eaten it. On the bottom shelf there's a stack of shiny plastic packets with a picture of a German shepherd and a bowl of pinkish-coloured meat balls. *CHUNKIES*. James must have known Rusty was coming. I take it out and Rusty taps his front paws repeatedly.

'Is this your food?' I ask and he spins a few times. 'We need to find your bowl.'

It's not in the kitchen, or on the front verandah. I go to the back door. Outside I notice two bowls, one filled with water, the other empty. Rusty dashes to the empty bowl and waits. I read the feeding instructions and estimate Rusty's weight, then err on the side of overfeeding him, pouring a third of the packet into the bowl. He wolfs it down; I don't think he stops to chew. Then he slurps from the water bowl, splashing it all over the concrete. I can see why he is fed outside. I laugh, and he pauses and looks up at me, cocking an ear, water dripping from his lips.

'Nothing, Rusty,' I say. He trots over to me, and I open the door for him. 'You're perfect.'

I put the dog food back in the fridge then slice off a piece of bread, spread butter on it and take a bite, leaning against the counter. Rusty nudges my knee with his wet nose, and I swallow and admonish him: *You've just had your food.* Then he taps his front paw on the floor and the realisation is swift – it's not food he's indicating, but a sound. His ears are straight and stiff. We watch each other for a moment. The noise is almost identifiable now, perhaps a little like whimpering, or – no – it is whispering. The words are indecipherable, and I can't tell if it's because I can't quite hear them or because it's an unknown language. It's coming from behind me, diminishing as I strain to listen, but not disappearing.

'Do you hear that?'

I walk into the foyer, stopping at the base of the steep, narrow stairs leading up to the small attic room. There's no whispering now. I close my eyes. Listen again. Do I hear squeaking up there, footsteps perhaps? Is that sound any different to the creaks the house has been making all morning? I hold very still. It is silent, though a familiar anxiety ripples through me – the feeling that I'm not alone, not the only presence in the home, that I might be surprised by someone or something. I tell myself that there there's no reason to believe there is anyone else here – no rational reason. I watched Matt drive away.

Just like when I was young, listening intently for evidence of men in the house, sometimes I simply imagine things that aren't there. As I take in a small, tense breath, I'm reminded that my body doesn't always know the difference.

'Leila?' Somebody twists the bedroom doorknob and I open my eyes. The room materialises but it's out of focus; a figure moves close to me and sits on the mattress. A hand rests on my thigh. 'You been in here all day?'

James's voice. James's face. I ease myself up and look around. Rusty stands in the doorway, his brown eyes fixed on me, but still he won't come in. Beside me on the bedside table is a half-eaten slice of bread.

'I fell asleep,' I say.

'You slept all day?' James picks up the plate.

'Yesterday knocked me around.'

'Did you eat anything other than this?'

'I don't think so.'

He leaves the room with the uneaten food and Rusty and I regard each other. It's cold, and the skin on my arms is pimpling. I pull the doona up to my shoulders and try to wake up, to be on the ball, ready for conversation. Instead, my eyes flutter closed.

'I squeezed this.'

James proffers a glass with orange liquid in it.

'You need some vitamins in your body.'

I gulp down the juice; it's thick with pulp.

'You didn't tell me you have a dog.' I nod at Rusty.

James turns to look at him. 'Well – family dog. He was meant to herd cattle for Mum and Dad, but he was useless. Probably because they were sold a mix instead of a pure collie. They're happier being retired anyway.'

He goes over to Rusty and gives him a long scratch, all the way down his back. Rusty drops to the floor, belly squishing on the cool wood, head on his paws. It's clear he doesn't possess working dog mettle. James kneels and roughs up Rusty's ears, flipping his head left and right; the dog licks his lips, and ducks away.

'How old is he?'

'Six or seven.' James stands, removes his blazer and hangs it up in the robe.

'And now they let Matt run cows here?'

'Yeah. He leases the paddocks. Good bloke.'

James unbuttons his shirt and takes off his pants and drops them in a little pile on the floor. He's lean from consistent farm work, a sinewy body that I've touched every inch of. Even now, I stare. His skin is white, and busy with moles and freckles;

the spots run all the way up to his cheeks. When he sleeps, I love looking at the little marks, counting them. They make him seem boyish, innocent somehow. My skin is a pale brown from my Lebanese heritage, smooth and clear; I feel alien next to his body, a body so clearly built in the outdoors. I'm made of circles; he's made of angles. And yet we come together. He stretches, then rummages through the chest of drawers and pulls out a wool jumper and tracksuit pants.

'It's bloody cold in here,' he mutters. 'Did you close the air vent?'

'I thought I heard something earlier.'

'Heard something?'

'I wasn't sure if I heard something in the attic.'

'In the attic?'

I meet his eyes; they are as brown and unblinking as Rusty's. His brow is furrowed. His technique of repeating my statements has the effect of chastening me; when he says them, I hear how they sound.

'I thought maybe I heard creaking, like footsteps.' I do not mention the whispering. 'It made me a little nervous, that's all. Especially when Matt turned up out of nowhere.'

He visibly relaxes, shoulders dropping. 'It's an old place. You'll hear all sorts of noises. The foundations were built in the 1800s, they're cracking and moving all the time.'

His logic releases a tightly held breath from me, the fear I had rolled up inside that I might have heard something strange. 'Makes sense.' I nod and nod and nod, and he watches me. After a pause – perhaps a moment of consideration – he says,

'Drink?' and I agree. I follow him down the hall, and we pause by the attic stairs, crane our necks, stare upwards. I notice how high they reach, they're not much more than a ladder, really. At the top, the door is closed.

'Wait here,' he says. He climbs the stairs easily, balancing on the balls of his feet, the smooth movement based in repetition, familiarity. When he reaches the door, I hold my breath. He grasps the handle and swings it open. I cannot see into the room, but I watch him walk inside and out of sight.

'Nothing in here,' he says. He pokes his head back through the doorframe. 'You want to come up?'

A dizzy feeling comes over me, and I grip the bannister. Rub my forehead.

'Are you all right?'

I shake my head as I say, 'I probably just need to eat.'

James descends the steps. 'I'm coming.' When he reaches me, I'm shuddering, and he pulls me into him and holds me. I murmur, 'Thank you,' and, 'I'm sorry,' the words muffled by his jumper. Above us, there's a slow creak and then a click as the attic door shuts.

'See?' He kisses my hair, speaks gently into my ear. 'Shifting foundations.'

We stand that way until Rusty comes over and bumps James's leg with his nose. He releases me, leaning back and looking over my face.

'Perhaps—' He cuts himself off.

'Perhaps what?'

'Never mind.' He walks into the kitchen.

I follow him and tap him on the shoulder so that he stops and faces me. 'Perhaps what?'

'You seem highly anxious,' he says, his voice dropping to an even, professional tone. 'Your medications could be causing some minor hallucinations. If you take too many.'

My mouth goes dry.

'It's a common side effect. You could think about cutting them back.'

I swallow, trying to find saliva, to find sound.

'James,' I say, in a low voice. It's all I can get out and I intend it to be a warning, but he seems unaffected by it and turns away, speaking over his shoulder.

'Or it was just the house. Forget about it. Let's eat dinner.'

—

Rusty lies under the table, lured into the kitchen by the smell of food, but then falls asleep. His paws wiggle as he lets out tiny barks, chasing something in his dreams. Behind me, a wood-burning oven and a gas cooker line the wall. Initially, I had hoped to cook a traditional roast for James in the wood-burner, but the instructions, detailed as they were, turned me off, so I took the easier option – grilling steaks on the modern stovetop. The setting sun first hovers and then sinks in front of us: we watch through the huge bay window as the afternoon glows pink, and then a brilliant orange. Once it is black outside, the glass acts as a mirror: our reflections captured, warping as we move about the room.

'This woman, she has five children, one with behavioural issues,' James says, sitting at the table. 'There's an eldest girl, eighteen, and an eldest boy, sixteen. Then a fourteen-year-old boy, and another girl and another boy, both under twelve.'

I bristle at the way he calls their mother *this woman*. James has always shared his work with me, and I told him early in our relationship that he sounds dismissive. He explained he can't use their names for confidentiality, and I was chastened. Yet something about it still feels wrong. I can't help but picture the doctors and social workers who treated my mother going home and saying to their loved ones, *This woman, you should see her. She needs so much help.*

'Everything they do is designed around not upsetting the fourteen-year-old. Everything. They can't go outside after three pm or eat certain foods in front of him, they can't watch certain TV shows or listen to music he doesn't like. He acts out, throws punches. The other day he picked up a knife and threatened his mother with it.' James swigs the wine in his glass then sets it down. I quickly refill our glasses, but he pushes his away and gets up, opening a cabinet and rooting around. He pulls out a bottle of whiskey and uncorks it, gives it a sniff.

'What's causing the violence?' I ask.

'Likely to be trauma in childhood,' James says. 'It'll be something to do with when their father left. The fourteen-year-old boy was at the most vulnerable age.'

The steaks hiss in the pan, and I flip them over, causing a crackle and sudden release of steam. The smell rouses Rusty, who rolls onto his belly and inches out from under the table, looking at me with a hope-filled expression.

'I need to reach the oldest brother.' James pours himself a shot of whiskey. 'He needs to step up for his mother and change the routine. Counselling isn't going to do a thing if he doesn't step up.' He taps the table as he speaks, then takes a long sip.

'What about the oldest girl?' I ask. 'She could help.'

You should see this woman's daughter. It's so sad.

'No, no. It's the dynamic of it. It's two boys. The oldest girl can't do it.' James refreshes his glass. 'It'd be better if she moved out altogether.'

And the house! It's barely fit to live in.

'Move out?' The steaks spit. 'She's only eighteen. She'd feel a responsibility to her mother—' my voice breaks off, and for a moment, we do not speak. I focus on the potatoes bubbling on the stovetop.

'Sometimes it requires a man,' James says.

I stick a fork in a potato to check if it's soft enough. I mustn't jump on everything James says. Whether it's his opinions on his own work or on my medication, I can't always oppose him. I remind myself that he grew up in a traditional household. On a farm, no less.

'We can talk about her, you know,' James says.

I put the steaks in the oven to rest. 'No need.'

'Perhaps—'

'I don't want to talk about her.' I pick up the pot of potatoes and pour them into a colander. 'I don't even want to think about her.'

There's silence while I take milk and butter from the fridge and a masher from a drawer. Instinctively, I go to shove the drawer back in with my hip, but a sharp abdominal pain forces me to abort the attempt. The drawer is stuck, hanging at a skewed angle. I can't see James with my back turned but I know he's sure to get up and fix the drawer. Like clockwork, he does, giving it a jiggle and sliding it in. *Sometimes it requires a man.*

I mash methodically and the potatoes surrender into a creamy paste. Behind me, the thud of plates and cutlery: James is setting the table. The noise is amplified in the soundlessness of our surrounds. In Sydney, there were buffers everywhere: the television on with news to discuss, music playing, mobile phones vibrating. Updates from friends and stories from work, my roommate buzzing around, until she moved out so James could move in with me. Outside the apartment, the romantic ambience of restaurants and the attentions of wait staff. Tonight, it's just us: our relationship is laid bare in the remoteness of the farm.

The clinking of the crockery stops, and James leaves the kitchen. I ponder that I haven't spoken to any friends for weeks. None of them knew I was pregnant because I never reached the magical thirteen weeks, so I didn't tell them about the miscarriage, either – it was easier to burrow my head in the sand and send benign texts: *I'm fine! Just busy! Catch up soon xx*

I scoop the mashed potatoes into an old blue and white porcelain bowl – small chips on its perimeter create tiny parapets – and set it on the table. Pull the resting steaks from the oven and place one on each plate. Crack salt and pepper over everything. Music filters into the kitchen, followed by James holding a small speaker. He smiles; I soften and yield, just like the potatoes. He sets the speaker at the end of the table and sweeps me into a hug.

'Give the farm a chance,' he says. 'I've planned so much for us.'

I let him hold me for a while. Our breathing falls into rhythm after a few moments, and then we break apart. He kisses my forehead, then we sit at the table to eat. I pick up my glass and take a deep slug of wine.

'The house is a little different to what I expected,' I say. 'Do your parents have anyone to help them maintain the place?'

James scoops up mashed potato and swallows it the same way Rusty does: in a gulp, like he hasn't been fed in a year. 'Other than me? Nah. The house is fine.'

'The back door doesn't have a working lock,' I say. 'There's hard rubbish, out the back?'

'And the wonky screen door.'

'Well, yeah.' I shouldn't say anything; the house I grew up in was nothing.

'We don't lock the house. Matt's the only person who comes out here.' James grins. 'Growing up, we'd leave the place unlocked even when we went away on holidays.'

'That's weird,' I mutter, slicing into the meat on my plate, somehow cutting against the grain.

'It's a country thing. And maintaining the house comes second to maintaining the farm. If it's between a screen door and a broken fence, you fix the fence, every time.' He groans.

'And I have a few to fix while I'm here. Matt needs the extra paddocks.'

'Matt would probably do it, if you asked him.'

'Dad told him I would.' James waves a hand. 'It's okay. Mum and Dad are older now, they spend less time at this place. They're probably disappointed that I'm not living here with my wife and kids already, doing more work for them.'

I say nothing to that and swallow more wine.

'They did add a bathroom to the attic room twenty years ago, and the ensuite to the main bedroom, but those are the only changes from the original house.' He reaches over and grasps my hand. 'Maybe if we moved in permanently, we could renovate?'

I look around the kitchen, trying to picture myself here long term, imagining Patricia's disappointment in me being replaced with pride, or at least, satisfaction, or at worst, relief.

I can't conjure an image of the kids; no names, no faces, no personalities. I've learned from last time.

James doesn't wait for a response. 'But I think you'll get used to it and love it for what it is. Tradition's important. Just because something's old doesn't mean it needs to change.'

I nod. After a few drinks, James tends to wax lyrical about tradition.

'You grow up all the way out here, you don't throw stuff out until you're sure you're not going to use it.' He releases my hand. 'Most times, you put in a bit of effort, you can fix things.'

I eat while he talks himself back into not changing anything about the way he and his parents live. James has a lot of affection for his family's country ways. It was romantic when we were first dating; I loved hearing about his bucolic upbringing. Horseriding, wood-chopping, swimming in the river. It sounded like paradise.

'We could at least throw out the rubbish near the garage?' I ask. 'Snakes could hide in there.' For me, romance is limited by practicality.

'I'll dig a hole for that.'

'And should we bait for the mice? It's strange hearing them in the walls.'

'No point.' James gets up and grabs the whiskey bottle, sloshes some more into his glass; sits heavily. 'They'll die in the walls, and that smell will bother you a lot more.'

He's smiling, relaxed from the whiskey and the food, a dot of pink blushing in both cheeks. A happy man in his little empire. He cuts into the last of his steak and, while chewing, says thoughtfully, 'You should start writing soon. You could check out the library in town. If you cut back your medication, even by one pill a day, you'd be powering. Sleeping all day isn't good for you.'

For a moment all I hear is the tinny music from the speaker: Jeff Buckley is crooning 'Last Goodbye'. I grasp my glass of wine tightly, tingling all over, and resist the urge to storm out of the room. Like so many corporate professionals I know, I'd love to write a book – a long-held, impractical notion confessed over many wines on early dates. After the miscarriage and the surgery, James suggested a year at the farm, not just for recovery and a reset, but as an opportunity to kickstart a creative epiphany, to become the writer I've dreamed of being, the one he believes I can be.

But there's something of the pious in James, a rigidity: a belief that there's a right way and a wrong way to be, and it's clear to me which side I'm on. To him, men are the problem-solvers and here I am: the problem. He thinks my pill-taking and sleep schedule is delaying recovery. I know he had some kind of religious education alongside his schooling, but he's never elaborated on it, and I have no understanding of belief systems anyway. I went to public school and smoked at lunchtime around the back of the dunnies, before realising I needed to pick up my act if I was going to get out of there and make a life for myself. James doesn't expect me to be like him — we couldn't have come this far if he did — but I notice the discrepancies between us now and wonder how conservative he is, underneath it all. The differences express themselves in ordinary moments; in these uncomfortable little reveals.

I calm myself with deep breaths. He's not telling me what to do, just making suggestions. And he's encouraging my ambitions, something I've always wanted from a partner. Besides, moving into someone else's established home was always going to feel strange. Regardless, I agreed to be here, I must make the appropriate amount of effort.

'What kind of childhood trauma can lead to violence?' I ask, steering the conversation back to safer ground.

'You'd be surprised,' James says. 'Pretty much any kind.'

I stand at the screen door, canvassing the landscape. Rusty is at my side, waiting. He sits with his head raised, watching me, ready for the moment I might let him out.

In the ten days since we arrived at the farm, the dog and I have become a pair. His clicking paws follow me as I move about the house; a soft head nuzzles at my knee when I'm still. We sit together on the couch in the living room while I watch television and stoke the fire, Rusty's head plopped in my lap. The house is draughty, and the cold currents drift around us no matter which room we're in. Rusty squishes as close to me as possible, twisting onto his back so I can scratch his warm belly, and he holds perfectly still to ensure I don't stop. Under my hand, his heart beats.

He sheds silky hairs with every huff, sneeze and scratch; my clothes are covered in him. While eating, I occasionally pull dog hair from my mouth. I cup his face with both hands and stare into his eyes, wondering how much he understands me when I speak to him. I've tried to coax him into the bedroom when I nap – I'd have let him on the bed and just not told James – but he looks at me, disheartened, and treads away.

So far, I've spent every day at the farm inside: listening to the chittering mice in the walls at night, eating the bare minimum so I can take my pills, and sleeping when they come into effect, despite James's opinions on my prostrate habits. He doesn't understand that I'm often exhausted from the act of getting up and showering; that I'm cold all the time in this old house and need to be swaddled up and next to the fire to stay warm. Unbeknownst to him, I've been using the key that usually hangs next to the front door; I lock it when he leaves, and push a chair against the back door so that when I'm dead to the world in medicated sleep, no-one can get in. Not Matt; not anybody. Before James gets home, I remove the chair and unlock the door.

At night, I cook dinner and listen to him talk about his day. I'm making a considerate effort not to snap at him, not to pick at his every word. He seems happier, kissing me often, his hands trying, unsuccessfully, to find me at night. I'm not ready; I roll away. My stomach burns.

I turn the handle, and Rusty backs up to let the door swing open. We step onto the porch, eager for fresh air, and Rusty leaps past me and clatters down the stairs, his tail wagging like it's in fast forward. He dashes back to me, licks my knee, then bolts away again and waits, front paws tapping the grass, sneezing in excitement

'Just a short walk,' I warn him, and he spins at the word *walk*. I sit down on one of the patio chairs and squeeze the toes of my gumboots to check for lurking spiders before putting them on.

The hills and mountains are smothered in white morning fog. The autumn wind is sharp and cool, and it prickles the skin on my exposed face and hands, the sensation bracing and disconcerting all at once. Rusty trots ahead and we walk around the back of the house, heading south.

We reach a metal gate to a paddock, and I grasp the lock. It's a simple one, it just takes squeezing a loop for the lock to slip and the gate swings open. I usher Rusty through, and then close and secure it. The gate is worn, and the wire fence is bent in different places from age and weathering. There are holes in the links stretched as big as my head, where animals have pushed their way in. I like the idea of a chunky wombat battering through like a ram, ignoring the purpose of that particular obstacle.

The paddock grass stretches as high as my boots, meeting my calves. I can't see the earth, and my first few steps are clumsy. Then I stomp through the brush to ward off any snakes, the movement yanking on my stomach each time. Snakes are the most dangerous thing I can think of on a farm, the most threatening thing. I know there are snakes in the city, but they're hidden; you don't see them sunning themselves on apartment balconies or slithering across roads. Before we moved here, I shuddered reading stories of women living in rural towns who found red-bellied black snakes mixed up in their laundry baskets or brown snakes headbutting screen doors, trying to get in. Though now that I've experienced my own body as dangerous, sometimes I wonder what's more frightening: the venomous, unpredictable wildlife, or the fact that my body is capable of killing its parts at whim, indifferent to my feelings or pleadings.

We walk in silence, save for our respective panting. After a while, we reach a slight incline, and at the top I need to stop; I'm breathing harder than I ever used to, my lungs burn and my body aches. I turn back to what I think is the direction of the house, but I can't see it; I've gone too far. I defer to Rusty. 'You know how to get home?'

The dog ducks his head, unwilling to return just yet. He heads to the right and trots in a direction that I think runs parallel to the house, but I've lost all sense of place. Grass seeds cling to my tracksuit pants as we trudge through the fields. We come across fallen gum trees, the trunks dried almost to white, half-obscured by grass and swarmed by ants. The mist in the distance has lifted from the mountains, and the sun lights up the green peaks. Rusty stops and sniffs every few steps, slowing our pace, and I'm grateful for it. When we stop, I look around in all directions, surrounded by paddocks and sky, a distinct departure from the beige and grey architecture of Sydney's CBD. Then, we keep moving. Always forwards, no matter how slow.

A breeze wafts towards us, and just as Rusty whimpers, I smell it: something rotten. The dog doubles back and presses against my legs, staring straight ahead, his nose twitching. I pull my shirt up over my nose, breathing through my mouth. The scent is thick and cloying and rancid. It smells worse than anything I can think of – and I thought I'd experienced the worst of it with Mum. But I'm reminded I'm in a different place, a place with animals, their by-products, and dead things in the wild. What creature could smell so dreadful, out in an open field? I look around, but the long grass obscures every-thing. Rusty grumbles and turns right, scampering away. He turns to look at me and barks once; I follow the dog and hope he knows where he's going. The smell slowly recedes.

After about twenty minutes, the back of the house comes into view, and I expel a sigh of relief. The smell is completely gone, and I question myself: perhaps it wasn't that bad. Perhaps there was nothing dead, nothing rotting.

We go around the side to the front verandah. I open the door, let Rusty in and pull off my boots, leaving them next to the welcome mat. Lock the door from the inside. Fetch an Endone. My body is throbbing all over and I'm sweating; the walk was longer than I'd planned. The recovery sheet the gynaecologist handed me after the surgery suggested ten-minute walks three times a week, building up to once a day before increasing in length. I check the clock; we walked for nearly an hour. Before the operation, that was nothing. I've done ten kilometre runs; I didn't even consider walking exercise.

I sit for a while on the bed, hand pressed on my surgical scar, trying to quell the stabbing pains bouncing around from the lacerated nerves. Creaking sounds filter through the house; the roof shifts and moans, the doors vibrate in their frames. The joints are swollen, the skeleton of the house holding the weight of the walls is under strain. Everything still works, but it's old and rasping, like me.

—

I tremble a little as I step into the shower, my feet unsure on the slippery tile. I grip the arm of the shower head, safely fastened to the wall, and close my eyes, willing the tremors to stop. Maybe it's the smell of the soap or the fact that I feel unwell, but the top of my mother's head comes to me. She's in the bath, and I'm standing over her, washing her, trying to rinse all the shampoo bubbles from her hair. She sits unmoving: angry with me for being her carer, angry that she is vulnerable. Angry that she is dying. I strain but find no better memory and wonder if I might cry. Then the feeling passes. It is only a brief flare. I straighten under the scalding water and wait for the rest of my skin to become as red and hot as my scar. Then I dry off and get dressed in the bedroom.

I check the fires in the kitchen and the living room: both need stoking. I sit in front of each fireplace, open the door and blow on the logs for a while, until the flames seem strong enough to manage without me. The trick, according to James, is to let the logs begin to burn, let the large, blue-tinged flames develop, and only then push the vent closed before the wood disintegrates into embers. The embers, glowing orange, emit a warm, sustained heat, but despite doing this every day, I'm cold. In the study, I find a small electric heater, grey and dusty, but it might work. I drag it back to the kitchen, give it a cursory wipe down and plug it in. It clicks and makes a thudding noise. The orange light flickers on. Rusty watches me from underneath the table; he's a furry incarnation of the Mona Lisa, his eyes following me no matter where I am in the room.

I fill the kettle, and it whirs and puffs steam from the spout. Crumbs dot the kitchen table, collecting in the wooden grooves. I open my laptop and connect to the wi-fi. The kitchen has the best internet reception in the house; something to do with the location of the Telstra poles. But because of the poor mobile reception, the Crawleys have kept a landline in the study: another thing that's not used, but kept *just in case*, like the collection of junk out the back. Rusty gets up and rearranges himself so he is lying on my feet, keeping them warm. From here, through the kitchen window, I'll be able to see anyone approaching up the driveway.

I spend some time googling *rotten smell* and *farm* and *cattle property*. I learn enough to reassure me that what I encountered was normal, even mundane, but still, none of the potential sources of the smell were good, and there were a few possibilities. First and most worrisome: that the septic tank was leaking, or the lid had been pulled off in a storm. The latter would be even more problematic; heavy rain can dislodge septic tanks and send them moving, spilling sewage as they go. A question to pose to James when he arrives home. Until now, I hadn't even considered where the waste from the kitchen sink or the toilet went. Gas leaks were another possibility. And dead animals: a fox, wombat or kangaroo could be large enough to smell that terrible as it decays.

Unable to explain the smell, I open a new tab and google the Bathurst library. The photo gallery on the website shows the interior to be brightly lit with reflective laminate counters. I'll borrow James's ute one day and get a membership; I just need to think of a good novel idea first. There's no rush.

I make a cup of coffee and take several sips, then open Instagram to check in on my friends. My old flatmate was out at a bar last night. She's tanned, her mouth open in a posed laugh, champagne glass raised. My high school friends in Brisbane are posting photos with their babies: soft bodies and even softer filters. I post *Looking hot!* for my flatmate and *So cute!* for the babies. Both comments are low effort. I no longer fit in either of those scenes; it's who I used to be.

A private message comes through from my flatmate: *How are you?? How's the farm?* I stare at it for a while; type and then delete the letters each time I try to form a response. The green dot next to her name persists; she is waiting for my reply, enticed by the three blinking marks coming from my end. I don't know how to answer. I don't know how I am. And it occurs to me, as I type, that James has access to my phone. We agreed this would be a good idea should I stop being functional again. I can't say anything negative about the house in case he reads it. I leave the chat.

I keep scrolling and then pause to look closely at a photo of an old school friend snuggling her third baby, taking in the serene smile on her face, the casual mussed-up hair. She's the picture of joy, but that's not all I see: there's fear hidden in that image, because there's horror in bringing life into the world, too. 'Oh god,' she said to me once, 'I've been reading these online forums about mothers whose children have died. It's awful.' She did it, she said, the same way people gawk at an accident; once she stumbled across it, she couldn't look away. I told her to stop, that she was torturing herself.

Now I know that must have been the point, because here I am, exiting Instagram, searching for miscarriage websites, trawling comments about how long it took to expel the foetus and how big the clots were. I click on fuzzy pictures, pixelated to protect viewers from seeing such graphic images without intent. When the photographs sharpen into the expected red tissue, I recognise my own. All of us, millions of us, bonded by death.

I read about women who suffered stillbirths.

I read about women who have had miscarriage after miscarriage, finally reaching twenty-six weeks and allowing themselves to feel hope, only for the baby to die.

I read about a woman who suffered a miscarriage while on holiday in Crete. The local authorities refused her a dilation and curette until she became septic, and she only just survived.

I read about hundreds more women in the United States, dying preventable deaths from miscarriages or ectopic pregnancies, all refused medical help because *Roe v Wade* was overturned and their states have banned abortion.

Then I read the stories of women whose children made it out of the womb alive. I read about women whose babies suffered a lack of oxygen during complicated births, or perfect deliveries where the infants were later diagnosed with terminal diseases.

I read about a woman whose child is only twelve but is already taller than her, who hits her and spits on her. She's tried everything and is at her wits end.

I read about women who have multiple children, whose spouses leave or die, who cannot find an affordable rental.

I read about women whose children have died from drug overdoses, from car accidents, from violent boyfriends.

I read all this and tell myself I'm lucky. I'm so lucky. My suffering is singular. It can be stuffed in a box, it can be swept under a rug. It can be solved with a sweaty run on the beach; obliterated by plunging into a cold sea.

———

Someone is trying to get in. There's a loud, violent rattling; angry grunts. I shake with adrenaline as my eyes cast around the darkened room. I fell asleep watching a nature documentary, swaddled in my dressing gown, with Rusty lying next to me so we both stay warm. The only light is the dying fire: behind the glass, orange embers glow through powdery ash.

A bang follows the next rattle; someone is hammering on the back door. I freeze. Rusty stares up at me, his chin resting on my chest, his shining eyes sweet but not particularly useful.

'Who is it?' I whisper to the dog and he sniffs. The noise stops and I hear footfalls – the sound is unmistakable – around the side of the house. I can't look out the window because I drew the curtains earlier, so I lie motionless, arms gripping Rusty, hands buried in his fur, while the footsteps pass by the living room window. Then there's a loud whack on the front door and I twitch.

'Leila? You there?'

James. I shuffle underneath Rusty, and he reluctantly rolls off me. I sit up as quickly as my stomach pain allows, calling out, 'I'm coming.' My feet land on the wooden floor, my knees and ankles stiff. I reach the front door and shove the key into the lock. *Shit*.

'I'm here, I'm here.' Turn the lock. Open the door.

James stands in front of me, cheeks flushed, his scarf askew, glaring.

'You okay?' I'm bewildered by his appearance.

He shakes his head and stalks past me, heading down the hall.

'It's cold out here,' he snaps over his shoulder. 'Why'd you lock the doors? I don't have a key. The back one doesn't even lock, what did you do to it?'

I follow him silently into the living room and he groans.

'You let the fire go out?'

I'm groggy from waking up too quickly and sit on the couch, breathing slowly. I say sorry, but he doesn't acknowledge it. A headache is coming on – my skin is tight, sensitive, with a deep pounding underneath. I reach up to rub my head, but it hurts to even touch my hair.

'I was out there for twenty minutes, trying to open the doors. I called out, didn't you hear me?' He jabs at the fire with a poker. The embers crumble and ash flies into the air. He closes the fireplace door with a clang.

'I was asleep.'

'Not just asleep.' He picks up my Valium packet from the coffee table and tosses it. It lands in my lap. He's right, the fire is close to being out: the log basket next to the hearth is empty, too.

'I'll get some wood,' he says, pulling on a pair of gardening gloves.

I shuffle into the kitchen, fill the kettle and put it on. Outside, wood is dumped into the wheelbarrow with heavy thuds, and James is panting. Then the creaky wheels turn, and he passes by the kitchen window. He walks back and forth, carrying in logs, filling the basket, and then there is the crunch of wood being shoved inside the fireplace.

The sun disappears over the mountains, and the kitchen loses the last of its amber glow from the bay window. I flick on the light. When James appears at the kitchen door, I say, 'Coffee?' and he assents. I spoon the instant granules into mugs, fill them with steaming water and add milk. I bring the mugs to the table and we sit, facing each other.

'I'm sorry.' He grips the mug. 'It was a long day.'

I nod, my gaze on the window. There's no moon, and dusk has settled quickly, the blue-purple light masking the mountain line.

'You don't need to lock the doors out here. I've told you, it's perfectly safe.'

I stare down at the table. 'I'm not used to leaving doors unlocked. If I'm asleep, someone could get in.'

'No-one is coming out here except Matt, and he's a gentle giant.' James takes a long sip of coffee.

'Sure.' I raise my head and look directly at him. 'But *I* don't know him.'

There is silence between us for several moments.

'It's all right,' he says finally, rubbing his temples. 'It'll be better when you're not sleeping as much during the day.'

I pull my dressing gown tighter across my chest. He notices, and reaches over to grasp my hands.

'You're too cold,' he says. 'If you do nothing else, keep the fire going. The house loses heat really quickly if you don't.'

'It's cold all the time anyway. The electric heater is busted.' I'm not lying. The entire house is draughty; I never feel warm, fire blazing or not.

'It's only cold because you haven't kept the fire on.' He's insistent, and his voice, pleading but directive, is grating. 'Forget the heater, it's useless. The house isn't getting a chance to hold any heat. You're from the city, I understand this isn't natural to you. But by July, it's going to be colder than you've ever known. We need that fire.'

I don't argue. I could remind him that I lived in London — a rather cold place — for two years, but I don't have the energy. Valium does knock me around, but what other option do I have? To never sleep?

'So.' His tone lowers, his manner more conciliatory. 'What did you get up to today?'

'I went for a walk with Rusty,' I say, hoping he'll be pleased. 'But there was a terrible smell, right up the back. Away from the house. Shocking. Could it be the septic tank?'

James takes a sip from the cup. His eyes are glazed, and underneath, his sockets are lined. Finally, he says, 'Could be.'

I wait for him to explain further, but he doesn't. He drinks his coffee in silence.

I take my cup to the sink, rinse it out and then say, 'I looked up the library like you said. I'm keen to check it out. Once I know what I'm going to write about.'

I feel arms circling me from behind and a kiss on my ear, and I'm relieved.

'Sounds great.' James squeezes me, a little too hard for my stomach, and I wince and grab his hand, moving it away from my abdomen. 'I'll drive you when you want to go.'

'I could drive myself, I think. If we had a spare car.'

He kisses my neck. 'There's something I want to ask you.'

'Okay.' I wriggle out of his grip and turn to face him.

'We've been invited on a camping trip, and I'd really like us to go.'

My shoulders clench. 'Camping? With who?'

'My mates – Adam and Dave.' He adds quickly, 'Don't worry. I'll organise everything we need – a tent, food, sleeping bags. An air mattress if you want.'

'I don't know those people,' I mumble, struggling to find an excuse not to go.

'You'll really like their wives. We've all been mates since uni.'

I don't say anything. James takes my hands and pulls me closer to him. He kisses my forehead. 'We haven't been camping together yet.'

James loves to camp. He had pictures on his dating profile of sitting in front of a tent, and the dreaded 'holding a large fish' photograph, too. When we lived in Coogee, I agreed I'd try it one day, blithely, because I didn't think I'd have to make good on the promise.

'When?'

'In June. You'll be feeling better by then. And it'll be cold enough that there won't be any snakes, no flies or mosquitos. We'll have a big, warm fire. Fall asleep under the stars.'

I get it. It could be fun.

'Can we bring Rusty?' I don't think I could be away from the dog now.

'Is that a yes?'

I nod under his chin, and he hugs me again. I catch a whiff of his body odour and cologne. I've always loved the smell of him, even when he's unshowered and a little funky. I relax into the embrace.

Our first date was at a Hunter S. Thompson inspired bar in Randwick, a grubby place decorated with plastic-feathered chickens. A bartender in a floral shirt served us strong Old-Fashioneds and we chatted giddily for hours. James was so much better looking than his online profile suggested: his thick dark hair, brown eyes and angular face married together handsomely, anchored by his intelligence, his keen interest in me. He looked like the perfect country boy in a checked shirt and jeans, a brown leather belt and shoes. I turned in the minimum of effort – it was just another online date – and wore a plain tank top and denim shorts. It didn't matter. At the end of the night, he hugged me for a long time, and I felt immense comfort. My mother rarely hugged me, and if she did, I knew something was wrong. But James hugged me to make me feel good, not the other way around, and I was deeply intoxicated by it, the power of just being held.

'We'll have the best time,' he says now, arms around me. I press my head against his chest so that my nose squishes and all I breathe is him.

I sleep late into Saturday morning, and when I wake, I feel heavy, as though I completed an intense gym workout yesterday instead of a simple walk. Outside, James has begun restoring the patches of damaged sandstone on the side of the house using traditional masonry tools. I go outside to kiss him hello, then flee his attempts to share his knowledge of the tools with me and retreat to the kitchen.

I stare at my laptop trying to figure out what to write. Rusty snoozes in front of the fire, his lips flopping open. Drool spills on the floor and little grumbles blow through his nose. I look at creative writing textbooks and novelists' blogs and manuscript courses; I read about narrative arcs and story structures, the hero's journey and man versus nature; but not a single story idea comes to me. I save all the website tabs, counting it as research, and call it a day. The library will wait; a book idea will come. I settle down with Rusty in the living room and switch on the television.

In the late afternoon, the weather grows overcast, so James abandons the sandstone and suggests we go to the pub for dinner. Rusty leaps up from the floor at the word *dinner* and shakes, releasing a flurry of hair. While James feeds him, I get ready. Shower. Brush teeth. Pull my hair into a ponytail. I open my make-up case and scrabble around, find concealer, an eyebrow pencil and lipstick. Cover up the dark circles, brighten the lips. Thicken the brows that are becoming sparse in my late thirties; I regret the regular waxing appointments in my twenties.

From the wardrobe I pull out a black knit dress, nice and loose. It was a perfect dress for the office in winter, showing off none of my body, but put together enough. I sit down and add ankle boots. The effort of getting dressed and putting on make-up leaves me puffed and headachy. I take a few deep breaths, steady myself, then get up and meet James in the foyer. When he sees me, he whistles. I wave it off because he's just being polite, though perhaps he is relieved that I appear human again. He helps me into my coat, then takes my hand and we step out onto the verandah, leaving Rusty alone and disgruntled inside.

'Guard the place for us, mate,' James calls as he closes the front door, and we hear a hacking cough in reply, which I take to mean Rusty will do no such thing.

'We can't bring him with us?'

'We'll be sitting inside,' James says.

In the car, James cranks the heat and flicks on the headlights, and we head slow and steady down the drive. The night is pitch-black, and every so often the lights catch on gleaming eyes for a brief moment before I blink and they disappear.

'Foxes,' James says with distaste. 'Just can't get rid of them.'

He takes the bumpy drive slowly and I layer both palms against my stomach, between the wool of my dress and the plasticky seatbelt. The warm air issuing from the vents has a stale smell at first, of dust and rust and dirt, but then it clears. When we reach the gate, James gets out and opens it, and then we drive through. He doesn't stop to close it again. I don't mention it, but can't help but think of the unlocked front door, and now a wide-open gate.

We head down the road and drive through the stretch of tall, ghostly gums, with their chaotic, reaching branches, on both sides. The trunks of the trees flash in the headlights, leached of colour and ethereal. Then we turn onto the two-lane road, in the direction of Bathurst, and the gums thin out, and paddocks appear. After a while, James points.

'See?'

There are lights ahead, the long, low shape of a building, and cars parked in front. We pull in.

'Busier than I expected,' I say.

'Yeah. Locals love it.' James pulls the handbrake on. 'It's the original pub, been here since 1865.'

We enter a hallway with a low roof, the walls decorated with black and white photos – flocks of sheep crowding the road near the pub, the smiling faces of owners and licensees, and framed newspaper articles. Inside the main bar, the flooring is old terracotta tile, uneven and rustic, and the heels of my boots click against the hard surface. There's delicious heat from a crackling fire. I remove my coat, wishing the fire at home felt like this. James leads me over to a round table.

'Wine?' he asks.

'Beer,' I say.

He heads to the bar. There are some older men scattered about the tables. The bar is polished wood, atop a dark-brown brick wall; the bricks are misshapen and charming, not the blonde mass-produced material of 1980s Brisbane. The roof is pitched at an angle, made of nestled-together wooden planks with beams that look like whittled tree trunks; they still have whorls and bumps and aren't perfectly straight. Carved into a beam above the bar are a series of odd shapes – some look like letters, others like the patterns on runestones. Affixed next to each is a gold plaque, but the writing is too small for me to read. Mounted high on the far wall is a twisting, fibrous pair of black horns. Out the back, through broad windows, I can see strings of festoon lights and glowing heaters under a tin roof, and more people gathered.

James sets down a pale ale for me – it's brewed locally, he says – and a dark beer for himself. I point to the horns.

'Are they from a bull, too?'

'Yeah. Beautiful, aren't they?'

'And those shapes above the bar?'

'Old cattle brands. Each farmer had his own back in the day. Sometimes it was his initials, other times, a symbol. If cows wandered off, you were able to identify them.'

A man sitting at the next table with two other blokes looks over.

'Jim.' He holds out a creased, sun-spotted hand.

'Rich,' James says, and they shake hands; the older man's fingernails are shadowed with dirt. 'Good to see you.'

'And you. Who you got with you?' He nods at me. The other two men stare at us.

'This is my partner, Leila.'

I smile and hold out a hand. The man takes it and gives it a squeeze; then he bends down and kisses it, his wrinkled lips pressing against my knuckles. The surprise of it and the wetness of his lips glazing my skin feels unfairly intimate. I should pull my hand away, but I freeze momentarily. He raises his head and grins at me.

'Lovely lass.'

I take my hand back, tucking it away under the table, rubbing the moisture on my skirt.

'That she is,' James says. 'How's the lambing this year?'

They discuss stock numbers and prices, the weather, and how the feed is going. The other two men join in. I shrink back in my seat and study the menu. Steak, parmi, chicken breast with bechamel sauce, beef pie. Lamb cutlets. *Proudly local*, it proclaims. Another man approaches our table, then another and another; some are old like the first man, with thinning grey hair, dressed in slacks, checked shirts tucked into leather belts and Driza-Bones; others are younger, in a uniform or high-vis vests, with thick beards. They crowd around us, shaking James's hand and asking where John and Patricia have gone. Each man is envious of their sojourn to the coast to avoid the bitter winter expected this year. The men look at me and give me a nod. I don't offer my hand again. After a while, one of the younger men standing next to me notices my beer dwindling and offers to get me another.

'I'm okay,' I say. 'Thanks, though.'

'No trouble.' He points to the bar, where people have begun to form a line as they come in from outside. 'Shortest bar of any pub in Australia, mate. If you go up, you always order a round. Stops a big line up of everyone tryna get served at once.'

'Shortest bar? You mean literally?'

'Yep. Even if it's the least of something, it's the most of something, know what I mean?' He stifles a burp with his hand, then wipes his palm on his uniform, uncomfortably close to his groin. The logo on his shirt says *Aurum*.

'So where do you work?' I ask him, pointing at his shirt.

'Gold mine outside Orange. Just came off a twelve-hour shift. You work out here?'

'No, no. I'm here with James, for a sort of . . . holiday. In Sydney I'm a consultant.'

'Aah.' He raises his eyebrows, jabs the table with his index finger. 'You'll find this interesting. We've been tryna attract women out to the mines, but we can't reach the quotas. You know why?'

I shrug.

'Women aren't applying for the jobs.' He says each word with emphasis, like he might clap in between, if he wasn't holding his schooner.

'Perhaps they find the culture or work practices unappealing, or unsafe.'

'Nah, that's the thing. The company brought in some *consultants* to find out why.' He makes air quotes with his stubby red fingers, liquid spilling over the lip of his pitching glass as he does. 'Turns out, *women* are the problem. Women won't hire other women. As for the women already there, they bully and push other women out of jobs. Crazy, right?' He gulps his beer, foam clinging to his moustache.

'That is crazy,' I say.

'Totally. They're their own worst enemies.' He skulls the rest of his drink and then turns and calls to James, nodding at me: 'She's a good chick. Beer?' A few of the men around us nod, and he joins the line at the bar. James turns to me.

'What do you feel like eating?'

I choose the lamb cutlets. James goes to order, and the men disperse from our table. Rich looks over at me a few times, but I study my phone, even though the wi-fi in the pub is slow. James returns, and while we wait for our food, he reads me the gold plaques for the cattle brands, pointing out his family brand, a spiral.

'You didn't use initials?' I ask.

He stares at the brand. 'It's an old family symbol. Like Catholics wearing crosses, or families with crests.'

I wonder again what church he went to. 'Do you all go to church in Bathurst?'

His eyes refocus on me. 'Not a specific church. We practise religion at home. It's more private. God just means . . . nature. It's part of living on the land.'

I nod, though I have no idea. 'Sounds kind of nice. I've always wanted to believe in something. Just never knew what.'

'Mum and Dad will be happy to hear that. They're a little bit traditional.'

'Yeah, I picked up that vibe,' I say, thinking of Patricia's unceasing interest in babies.

The food arrives. The lamb is tender and moist, and the gravy nice and fatty. We eat quickly as more people arrive, looking for inside tables.

Outside, as we head to the car, we pass a man smoking and James says, 'Hey, mate.'

'Jim,' the man says, dropping his cigarette on the ground and stamping it out. 'Missed you the other day.'

It's Matt. He's holding a schooner of beer and looks a little worn. He smiles at me. 'Hello, love. How you goin' with Rusty?'

'Good,' I say. 'He's such a lovely dog.'

'Yeah, a great little companion. Hope I didn't frighten you when I dropped him off.'

James looks at me but I avoid his gaze.

I smile. 'No, you didn't. I'm sorry I wasn't friendlier.'

Matt shakes his head. 'You were fine.'

'You having dinner?' James asks.

'Nah. Been helping a mate paint his house in Oberon all day, I'm buggered. Just a beer and smoke before I head home to the missus. I'm allowed one ciggie, long as it's not at home.'

James pats him on the shoulder. 'Thanks for looking after Rusty.'

'Not a prob. I should be out sometime next week to move the cows.'

We nod and smile and say goodnight. In the car, James says, 'Told you Matt was harmless.'

'I know.' We bump along for a bit and then I ask James why Rich felt he could kiss my hand.

'Old Rich is fine too,' he says. 'Useless sheep farmer though. We called him Bo Peep, because he let his sheep wander off. Wouldn't pay to fix his fences.'

'Well, the kiss was unwelcome,' I say. 'And that other, younger guy? Telling me women are the reason why women don't get jobs?' I snort.

'Oh really?' James says absently as he navigates a tight turn into a lane. 'Did he say that? I wouldn't worry. They're good enough blokes.'

'I just don't know why they think they can say those things to me. Or kiss my hand out of nowhere.' I try to blot out the memory of Rich's lips on my skin.

James rubs the steering wheel. 'Out here, tolerance goes a long way.' A bug splatters against the windshield. 'For Mum and Dad's sake.'

I notice a rabbit leaping across the road, its silver fur lit up by the headlights, springy legs propelling a plump body.

'My mates aren't like that,' James says. 'You'll like them and their wives a lot more.'

'Did you see the rabbit?' I say excitedly, enchanted. 'He was so cute.'

'Shame I didn't hit it,' he says.

'You're terrible.'

'They're such a pest. As bad as rats. Dad used to set traps for them. I found one stuck once, when I was a kid. It wasn't dead, so I wanted to free it and nurse it back to health. Keep it as a pet.' James steers around another corner. 'But Dad made short work of that.'

'What did he do?'

James glances at me briefly. 'He killed it.'

I don't ask any more questions.

—

On Monday, with James at work, Rusty huffs until I let him outside so he can roll around in the grass, scratching the spots he can't reach himself, and snoozing in the gentle sun. But by Tuesday, his patience has run out, and he bops me with his nose every hour. He is desperate for another walk. James said there's a pretty part of the Fish River flowing through the eastern section of the property that he wants to show me, but I'm sure Rusty can find it. The thought of a natural body of water to lower myself into, to numb the aches and cramps, is appealing. I miss the beach.

At midday, the sun reaches its warmest point, and I say to Rusty, 'Walk?' and he sneezes and prances to the front door.

Outside, I say, 'River?' and he stares at me unblinking. I try: 'Swim? Do you wanna go for a swim?' He turns east and trots ahead. After fifteen minutes, we reach the river. It runs further than I can see, a serpentine stream banked by sandy clay, disappearing into thick trees. The water is clear, and I see shimmering rocks, mottled plants and sticks beneath the surface. The sound is gentle as the water laps against and plops over the rocks. To reach the bank, there is an incline peppered with stones and quartz. I hesitate while Rusty bounds ahead, as sure-footed as a mountain goat, but I don't want to be left behind, so I look for natural steps and pick my way down tentatively, walking sideways for better balance. Loose rocks dislodge under my feet and tumble down, dust rising. The grip on my gumboots is average at best, but I persevere, sweating from effort, and eventually reach the river's gritty bank.

The water gurgles, and some of the larger rocks direct it into little pools that reflect the sky. The opposite bank is lined with reedy grass and enormous she-oaks that dapple the space with shade. Black cockatoos fly from tree to tree, squawking and eating seeds from the branches. Rusty sniffs his way to the water, then trots in deep enough to wet his belly. Soon, he is swimming, his face above the surface, his nose twitching. He paddles in a wide circle. When he returns, he shakes his body all over, sending droplets flying into the air. He lowers himself onto his side in the clay dust, serene, his eyes resting on me.

'You're not the only one who can do it.'

I look upriver and downriver, checking my surroundings, but glimpse only more water and more trees. I smell dirt, pine needles and mist; it's clean and natural. I remove my shirt, gumboots, socks and trackpants and fold them up, shivering in the chilly air. The mossy stones leading into the water are slippery, and my feet curl from the cold. Gingerly, I lower myself down, clutching at the stones for balance, gripping hard. I slip into the water, into a shallow pool that drops down far enough to leave the larger rocks as a wall I can lean against. My body tenses in the cold, but it's soothing: the numbness eases the irritation of my scar and for a moment I can't feel my body at all. It's an overwhelming relief.

The water pools around my shoulders, and I listen to the sloshes and spits as the current continues its path downstream. The sky is blue and cloudless, and the she-oak leaves, swaying from a light breeze, are a dehydrated green: the silvery glint of native plants used to conserving water. I squint and count at least twenty black cockatoos in each tree, watching us. Every so often, they shriek at one another, or perhaps at me, and flap wildly to another branch. There are probably a hundred sets of eyes on me. The birds must be unused to seeing a person in their patch of the river, but, unlike the diving plovers of my childhood, they don't seem aggressive, just watchful.

My exposed upper arms pimple up. A surge of feeling, the same one I felt at the house – that I'm not alone – arises suddenly, though there's nothing around but the birds and the crackling trees. Inexplicably, I feel I should leave. I look back at my clothes, and they're exactly as I left them. I glance at Rusty. His eyes are shut, head resting on the bank, ears down. There's nothing to fear. Then, all grows quiet: the air turns still and the birds simmer down into silence. Returning my gaze to the stretch of river in front, I seize up, hard, and then let out a gasping cry.

There is a face. Eyes. A beard. Between the conifers, *I saw it.* The face retracts, and I watch a shadow – human, there is no doubt – slip away. I cover my body with my arms, stuck in place, and strain to see where the man went. But there's nothing. The cockatoos, perched around me in every direction, are unmoving.

My heart thuds painfully. Rusty is now on his feet, nose trembling, looking downriver. He whines. I reach behind to grasp the river stones, willing the slick mossy surface to hold under my hands, and slowly pull myself up. My stomach stretches and throbs from the effort. I drag myself into a seated position on the rocks, too frightened to look behind me, shuddering in the cold, then rise slowly. Out of the water now, feet clinging to the rocks, I am completely exposed, sodden bra and underwear on display, surgical scar bright red against blue-tinged skin. My slowness increases my panic; my breathing grows ragged. *Move carefully. Don't fall.* I make my way back to the clay sand, my body stiff, desperate to reach the safety of my clothes.

How long was he watching me for? Where did he go?

I dress, trembling, putting buttons in the wrong holes, and Rusty and I walk upriver as quickly as I can manage. We find a flatter slope to ascend, heading in the general direction of the house. Sopping wet underwear leaks through my dry clothes, and everything sticks in the wrong places, chafing against my skin. I regret stripping down, allowing myself to be bare. I confused the isolation of the property with it being private. Anyone could walk onto this land. And there I was, a sitting duck.

—

I lock the front door and barricade the back door and wait for James to come home. When I hear the rumble of his ute, I open the front door and wave at him. He gets out of the car, carrying grocery bags. As soon as he steps onto the verandah, I say:

'I saw someone watching me down at the river.'

His expression alters instantly into worry, and I know this isn't concern for me, for my physical safety, but rather that I'm making things up – that the pills are making me believe things that aren't true. He kisses me on the cheek and I stand aside to let him in.

'Give me a second,' he says, putting the groceries on the kitchen table, then disappearing down the hallway and into the bedroom. I lean against the foyer wall and wait. When he emerges, he's in warm, comfortable clothes. He reaches for my hand.

'Let's go to the kitchen.'

He pours himself a whiskey and I have a glass of water.

'Okay,' he says, sitting down. 'Tell me again?'

'Rusty and I walked to the river,' I say. 'I undressed and took a dip. I looked up and I saw a face, watching me, from the conifers.' I hate that it sounds hard to believe.

'A face in the conifers?'

'Yes, a man. He had a beard. And then he disappeared – he saw me looking and he disappeared.'

James drops his shoulders and rolls his neck. 'Probably Matt. He was coming to move the cows this week, remember?'

'It didn't look quite like him,' I say.

'What did he look like?'

I try to picture the face again, but it is already fading. I only caught a glimpse.

'I think his face was smaller,' I say hesitantly. 'The beard was different. But even if it was Matt, that's not okay. He shouldn't be spying on me. I was nearly naked. I shouldn't feel afraid to be here.'

'You're right.' James pauses. 'So, what do you want to do?'

I'm uncertain of his meaning. 'I don't know.'

'Do you want to report it? Call the police?'

'Should I?'

'If you want to. Can you describe the face in more detail?'

'A dark-ish beard. Small eyes.'

'Clothes?'

I begin to feel hot. 'I can't – I can't remember.'

'Okay.'

'I didn't imagine it.'

'I'm not saying that. But I think it's more likely there wasn't anyone there, if I'm honest.' He studies me, twirling the glass around on the table. 'There's a documented phenomenon humans experience where they see patterns in nature. The most common pattern they see is a face.'

He pulls his phone from his pocket and types something, then shows me the search result. It says: *Pareidolia: humans can interpret patterns of light, shadow or inanimate objects as faces.* I shake my head.

'Just for argument's sake,' James says. 'You've been through a tough time. You're not used to this environment. Is it more likely that you saw a pattern that looked like a face, or that someone trekked all the way out here on the off chance they might see you in the river, undressed?'

'Well—' I stop, unsure what to say.

'And you've said he didn't look like Matt, so we know it wasn't him, accidentally coming across you.' James tilts his head, searching my face. 'Baby, you're also still taking strong meds.'

'It's *not* from the meds.'

'Okay, okay. Calm down. I'm just asking questions, trying to get all the information.'

'I am calm.'

'You said you feel afraid.'

I go to snap, *So what? That doesn't mean I'm wrong*, but pull myself up short. Sullenly, I scrape back a chair and sit down, resenting James's tendency, since the miscarriage, to direct me to a conclusion I don't know that I agree with. But his expression is relaxed; he's meeting my eyes, and there's compassion in his. Perhaps he's not judging me. Perhaps he really is worried about my adjustment to this place.

He's always been attentive to every detail, asking questions, caring about even the little things – early on in our relationship, this habit manifested in him wanting to know everything about me, so he could make sure I was always comfortable. If I was ever too cold, he'd offer his jacket; on weekend mornings, he'd run out and get us coffee, so it was there when I woke up. On our second date, we went to the movies; I offered to buy the tickets if he bought the snacks. When I met him outside the cinema, he held up a bulging grocery bag full of savoury and sweet options. 'I didn't know what your needs were,' he said. 'So I tried to meet all of them.'

At the time, I was charmed. Most men I'd dated wanted the benefit of regular sex but had no interest in me or my desires; they were uncomfortably like the men my mother clung to. When I reached my mid-thirties, I stopped sleeping with men I didn't care about and who didn't care about me. Meeting James felt like the reward for dating with intention, for weeding out the time-wasters and the non-committal.

When we began trying to conceive, his level of interest in me increased again: tracking my ovulation cycle with me, planning my food intake, suggesting visits to naturopaths for herbs and supplements. He prepared endless cups of sour, herb-spiked tea for me, intended to boost my fertility; I took iodine, folate, and vitamins daily. It became clear just how invested he was in me, in us. It was exciting, feeling like someone's sole focus; in fact, I told myself, it was amazing, because that's what healthy, functional people do in relationships. I wanted to reach this adult milestone. Our life was easy and purposeful and, until the miscarriage, nothing unexpected had happened to us. Once I emerged from that blinding grief, getting away from the apartment seemed like the right thing to do; I didn't want us to be cooped up there with our loss. But I hadn't considered that being with James out here, alone, could be just as difficult; that in bringing my pain with us, the farm might intensify its effects. And, unlike our life in Sydney, we no longer have those predictable days apart, days that perhaps acted like a valve letting off steam. Here, that valve is gone.

'I promise if you see this person again, I'll check it out.' He scoots his chair in closer to me and grasps my hand. 'Leila, you're safe here. You believe me, right?'

I nod. Of course I do. I must.

He gets up and unpacks the groceries animatedly, showing me the Lindt chocolate and specialty ice-cream he bought for me, alongside blueberries for their antioxidants and kale for folate. Sometimes I'm so grateful for his kindnesses that I want to cry; I feel I will never measure up to him, that I do not deserve such attention. Other times, I feel numb; that I am a woman he is making over, he has diagnosed me as a damaged model that he has committed himself to repairing.

Friday is clear and cool, as it has been all week. At the kitchen table, I try to type, but the indoor chill renders my fingers stiff, and the lack of dexterity impedes any meaningful progress. I tap away for a few moments, stopping to warm my hands on my coffee mug. James set the house fires before he left for work but, as usual, I'm still cold. Rusty lies over my feet, a mess of hair and warm skin folds I'm grateful for.

The surgeon told me people experience all sorts of things while recovering from a procedure. Depression, anxiety, brain fog. Unexplained joint soreness. Unusual sensitivity or responses to temperature. I drag my feet out from under Rusty, who doesn't move an inch, exhaling a light snore with his breath.

Outside, the sunshine is bright. I pick up my laptop and mug and push my chair back, rousing the dog. When I open the front door, I move aside to let Rusty out first; it's something he seems to love, darting out the door and assessing the land for danger or adventure. I sit down at the little table on the verandah, right in the path of the morning sun. It's warmer outside than in. My skin prickles pleasurably from the heat, and I take a long sip of coffee. A rosella alights on a rose bush and pecks at the flowers. Everything in my body loosens.

Rusty sniffs his way along the paddock fence. Beyond the property, the mountain range is clearer than it's ever been. Without the haze of fog, the brown ridges are visible and the masses of trees that protrude from the slopes are distinct. Sunshine. Green hills. No roads. I tell myself firmly, *This is a beautiful place.* Despite the seclusion. *Submit.*

I return to my laptop and review the document I've started. With no other brilliant ideas, I've found myself writing about my mother.

The persistent smell of Winfield Blues and a fermented undertone of alcohol greeted me every afternoon after school. We lived in a Housing Commission block, a small, square house in yellow render with a patchy grassed yard enclosed by a chain-link fence. The property market being what it is, those houses are now privately owned with lush front lawns. The Housing Commission stigma is mostly gone, schools have been erected, and the neighbourhoods are family friendly, but I couldn't ever live there again. Once I was accepted into university, I moved into a weatherboard share house, the kind of Queenslander standing high on stilts that I'd always wanted to grow up in, with polished floorboards and wooden slatted walls. The memory of our old brick house, the knobbly rendered ceiling and its sickness-stained insides, makes me ill.

I'd long grown used to the smell of smoke and cheap vodka, so when the newer smells supplanted the old ones, I had no blueprint of how to cope. The antiseptic of the hospital ward, the whiff of bleach, was repellent when I first encountered it, our own house being only – at its best moments – tidy and the rubbish bin emptied. Never disinfected.

It was the smell of the cancer, though, that frightened me to my bones. At first sickly sweet, then mouldier; an unremitting scent of decay. The more she deteriorated, the more I wished for the old days of cigarettes, booze and a new male cologne each month. My mother withered during the treatments like a cut flower starved of water, and I learned to clean like a nurse: I cleaned her body, surfaces, bed and linen. All day, every day, school being the only reprieve.

Something in my peripheral vision makes me look up. Rusty is standing stock-still, his bushy tail raised and stiff, staring at the paddock directly ahead. I squint and then gasp in delight: a mob of kangaroos. There are at least twelve of them. They're a brownish grey, some standing tall with developed pectoral muscles like bodybuilders, others hunched over, their curved backs sliding over into thick tails.

Rusty starts towards them, and when I call his name, he pauses and looks back at me. Insolent, he runs a few steps in their direction and I call again, firmly. He drops his tail and turns, trotting back to the deck, then nestles under my hand and whimpers while I watch the kangaroos eat the grass, hop languidly about and occasionally lift their heads to look around. He's desperate to give chase, to protect his patch, but I won't let him. Not all our instincts should be acted upon.

I pick up my phone to take a photo. Something from the farm to post on Instagram, a declaration: *Look at my new surroundings.* Perhaps if I post that the farm is idyllic, it might start to feel that way. I pull on my gumboots at the stairs and tread softly across the front lawn. As I get closer, I marvel at how big the kangaroos are. Their front arms dangle, claws for fingers on each paw; eyes large and round and framed with the longest eyelashes. Their ears stick up as straight as television antennae. So many gathered in a single group, like a family.

I'm halfway across the lawn when they move in formation, huddling in a straight line. They stare at me, unmoving, and as I raise the phone to take a photo, a long scream rents the air. In unison, they leap away. My mind takes several moments to catch up. I fumble my phone and whip around to face the house. My eyes run over every window, every door, but there is nothing and no-one to see. Rusty, however, is standing at attention, his eyes focused on the attic window, sniffing the air furiously. Trembling, I snap a photo of him. He's fixed in place, every hackle on his neck raised.

A hot wave comes over me and I break out in a sweat. I enter the house, hesitant, shaking, looking for any clue to explain the noise. Wind? Can wind do that? Did a window shatter? The house has made strange noises before. But, but, but . . . This one was different; it was loud and clear, the keening of someone with nothing left to lose. A human noise. *A person made that noise.*

Confused, damp, I pause in the foyer. There's creaking from the attic stairs. At the very top, the wooden door with its burnished gold handle is slightly ajar. It swings open a little further as I watch, groaning as it inches back and forth. I can't see anyone, not even a shadow. My skin prickles and I'm aware of nerve pain in my stomach; it fucking *hurts*. Is someone up there? That man from the river? I grasp the stair rail. Do I confront him? Does he think I'm weak, out here alone? *Fuck him.* The steps are very narrow; I'll have to go up on my toes. As I take a furtive step on the first stair, the attic door flies away from the doorjamb and then slams shut. I jump backwards, feet scuttling to find the ground behind me. I stumble and trip, landing on the floor, and cry out from the jolt to my stomach.

Thoughts flood in, unrestrained. *Someone screamed, someone is in the house, what am I doing here?* Black spots spatter my vision. I crawl away, lean my back against the wall, panting. No. This cannot be real. Not real. Nothing there. My mother's voice, exasperated, rings in my ear. *Stop it, Leila. Stop crying.* I'm practised at this part. I can make it go away. Keep breathing. Slow it down. Close my eyes. Everything is black.

What did James teach me? Rub the outside of my arms. Feel my feet firmly on the floor. Picture a sticky substance – bright yellow, easy to see – in my body, then roll it all together in a ball and throw it far away. These are intrusive thoughts. I need to remove them.

A wet nose against my elbow. Trembling, I open my eyes. The spots are gone. Rusty is at my side. Shakily, I stand, glance through the open front door. There's no sign of anyone outside. There are plains reaching the mountain range and nothing but hills between them – no houses are nestled in the crevices, there's no view of the road. Inside, the house is quiet. Nervy and stiff, I approach the attic stairs, stand and listen, but hear nothing. I wait there for a long time. There are no creaks, no footsteps, no shadows, no noises. It must be empty. It must be.

No-one can see me from out there. No-one is in here but me.

—

I go to bed and lie down. My abdomen is burning; I need emptiness, a reset, blankness. I plead with Rusty to come into the bedroom but he refuses, standing guard at the entrance, his ears pricked, head turning in every direction. I close the door and drag the dresser halfway across it, until I completely run out of strength and cannot ignore the stomach pain any longer. I take two Valium and one of my emergency Endone tablets and pull the doona up tight around my neck.

When I wake, it's afternoon. I slowly push myself up. The stomach pain has dulled, just an ache now, and I practise the behaviours of normalcy. A shower, washed hair, and comfortable, clean clothes. I prepare a fresh salad to go with a pasta bake for dinner. Eye bottles of wine, but don't drink them. Jostle some small logs onto both fires and fiddle with the air vent. Moving from room to room, I turn on all the working lights and eliminate the shadows.

When James arrives home late, I am on the lounge, laptop in hand, serene. I greet him with a smile, tell him I had a productive writing day, that his dinner is in the oven. He eats gratefully, shares anecdotes, pats my knee. Swallows his food quickly, to get more words out. He gestures widely, describes his progress, enjoying his audience of one. And all the while, I think, *You have no idea what's going on here.*

—

While James sleeps, I lie tense, facing the bedroom window. A low moon emits a small amount of light, just enough to see blurred trees and fuzzy mountain lines. Rusty remains stationed at the open door, half asleep, ears still raised. The protective instincts of the dog are comforting. Every so often, his nose wiggles; he can smell even while sleeping. Unless it's a shadow twitch, a muscle memory initiated by his dreams.

I re-live the scream over and over – the wail reaching fever pitch and then falling away into a despairing moan. Each aspect of the sound was distinctive. It was surprise, then panic, then grief. Though it was only a few seconds long, it played like a song, telling me that someone had been caught by surprise, only to realise their circumstances were dire. I'm well-versed in the different expressions of pain. The sounds Mum made were longer, lower. The moans of someone in unrelenting agony. Those types of noises were not made in shock, nor to obtain help; they were submissive, uttered unconsciously, in the knowledge that the pain would not end.

These thoughts, unable to be deterred, interfere with the Valium – nothing will send me to sleep tonight. I consider waking James and confessing to hearing the scream; but dismiss the thought almost immediately. He didn't believe me about the man watching me from the trees. I'm sure he knows of a psychiatric phenomenon for noises, too. And if I insisted, what then? Would he take away my meds? Would he admit me to a hospital?

For a few moments I wonder if that's what I need. The farm, despite some elements of beauty, is not what I expected. It feels like the land owns us, that we live by its grace – and this, I suppose, is the truth. The fences are coming apart. The paddocks are swarmed by grasses and weeds. The animals observe us carefully. The wide space is oppressive; the isolation of the house smothering. The absence of the sounds I'd grown used to in the city – traffic, the ocean, meetings and conversation, public transport, the beat of music at the gym – is a layer of skin ripped away. We're not meant to be here.

But it's not just that. I expected something restorative, that being in nature would help ground the grief I feel; help it all make sense. I've lost a pregnancy, a potential child and perhaps even the possibility of having one in the future. I understand why James was so insistent that we come out here: he expects that I'll discover the joy of nesting, that I'll recover, and we'll try again. Everything in life has a season; that's what he thought nature would teach me.

And I agreed, hoping for the same.

Instead, I look at this landscape and think, how unnatural. I don't belong in this house, and this house doesn't belong on this land. And our baby didn't belong in my body. These are things we ignore. We just keep trying and pushing and fixing.

If I talked to James about this, he'd tell me that I'm giving in to anxiety, to catastrophic-style thinking. He'd say – and I would agree – that change is harder when it happens *to* you, even if my specialty at work is helping others deal with change. He'd say there's no rational reason to think I don't belong here, and besides, don't I belong wherever he is?

Rusty stands in a rattle of nails on the wooden floor and repeated huffs. He whines, and I roll over to see what he's doing.

'You okay?'

Rusty huffs more, turning to face down the hall, his tail raised, the hair along his back standing to attention. Then he barrels away, barking, and disappears from view.

I reach over and squeeze James's shoulder.

'Wake up.'

He murmurs and burrows deeper into his pillow. I push him harder.

'What is it?' he says, half asleep.

'Rusty's going nuts. Can you check the house?'

'He can probably smell a fox.' He exhales back into a drowsy sleep. I stare at him.

'Fine, I'll do it.' I get up and put on a dressing gown. I cannot let James know I'm scared, or he might feel justified in not helping. He protests faintly, but I walk out of the bedroom and down the hall. Behind me, I hear him grumbling and moving about.

Rusty is at the front door, hitting it with his paw, agitated, jumping at the handle. I rub his ears to placate him, but he jerks away. I open the wooden door and peer through the screen but can't see anything, just the usual shadows following the curves of the land. He headbutts the mesh urgently. Maybe he needs to go to the toilet. I open the door and Rusty bolts onto the verandah, halting near the top of the steps, barking madly. I flick the outdoor light on; it illuminates the verandah, the rose bushes in front. I take a few steps outside, blink and then I see it: a long, thick shadow, undulating up the stairs and onto the verandah.

I scream, I know I do.

'James!' I back away inside and barrel into him as he appears at the door. 'It's a snake!'

'Shit. I'll get a shovel.' James turns and hurries back into the house. 'Keep an eye on it.'

'Fuck, Rusty, inside.' The words come out weak; I'm breathless, and Rusty's barks are insistent. He's frothing from the mouth, his stance unyielding. The blunt, triangle-shaped head of the snake is raised high off the ground, swaying in a way that seems particularly angry. Its back half is slung across the front steps, its front half on the verandah, banded in dark brown and yellow. Rusty is too close; he makes a faux attack on the snake, jabbing his head forwards, which doesn't deter it. It starts to hiss.

'No, Rusty! Get over here.' Rusty ignores me, and I take in a deep breath and shout, 'Now! *Rusty!*'

The dog stays, growling; he won't leave his post. *Shit.* I slip outside again, legs quaking and, trying to give the snake a wide berth, reach out and grab Rusty's collar, pulling him back. I keep my eyes trained on the snake; it's hissing, the head oscillating, but no closer to us. Every nerve in my body is buzzing, my legs feel like jelly, and I yank Rusty back as hard as I can. He bucks and suddenly howls, and I lose my grasp on him, stumble backwards a few steps, feel a stabbing pain in my stomach. The snake rises higher and lunges at Rusty. I scream again.

'I'm here.'

Behind me, footsteps, and then James pushes past. He reaches the growling dog, shovel raised, and stares at the ground.

'Where the fuck is it?'

He paces, turning on a torch to peer down the steps and from side to side.

'Did it make it onto the verandah?'

I say nothing, struck into dumb silence. James walks carefully up and down the porch, checking every plank, every corner.

'It can get in the house through cracks in the walls. Did you see where it went? It's probably looking for a place to wait out winter. Fuck, I should have finished the sandstone earlier.' He continues to mutter, frustrated, as he stomps around, shovel at the ready.

My body shakes. I can't speak. The snake didn't go anywhere. I watched it. Did I watch it? I saw it rise to bite Rusty, I was sure it would strike. Rusty comes back to me, and I run clumsy, shaking hands all over him, searching for a bite. Did it strike? I couldn't see it. I screamed, and then the snake was gone. Did I close my eyes? I grip Rusty's face, my fingers white and bloodless. No bite. He wriggles away. No bite.

It can't be me. It can't. Did I see it slither away? I don't know, I don't know. I don't know.

Blankets are a fort. Underneath them I can't see. I curl up, refusing to wake. Hear my name being called, in a vague sort of way, and close my eyes tighter. If I open them, I don't trust what they'll tell me.

—

The whisk of curtains pulled back and the clunk of a cup placed on the bedside table. I smell the coffee aroma, sense a person standing by the bed. I'm motionless and unresponsive. After a few minutes, footsteps recede, and the bedroom door clicks shut.

—

Lying on the couch, Rusty stretched out in front of me. I hold him from behind; he is the little spoon, so small, he is the teaspoon. I scratch his belly and he falls asleep, snoring and farting. I'm watching a documentary on the ocean. The male Japanese puffer fish is undertaking a courtship ritual to attract a mate. He uses his fins to burrow in a seabed, back and forth and around, until he has created a stunning circle made up of dozens of ridges and canyons. From above, it looks like a sun, a decorative shell, or a sunflower. It is grand. It is art.

It doesn't last. The display is temporary, a tactic to attract a female. Once this is accomplished, currents wash the sand sculpture away. Like it never existed at all.

—

James tells me things. That I'm regressing to the dark days when I lay in bed and said nothing, or at least, nothing that made any sense. That this is too close to what I did after the miscarriage. That I must get up, talk to him. I would, of course I would, but I'm so tired, and I'm so cold.

—

'I can't get warm. I see and hear things. My stomach is still painful.'

The office is small, covered in posters, many of them cartoons for young children. A jar filled with colourful jelly snakes sits on the corner of the doctor's desk.

'I struggle to do basic things. Shower. Walk. Concentrate. It was never a problem before the surgery.'

The GP appears to be in his sixties, small round glasses, a nice quality suit. His watch looks expensive. Thick grey hair. Dr Stewart: the best in Bathurst, James says.

'What sort of things have you seen, or heard?' He pushes his glasses up his nose, gives the impression that he's listening intently. Penetrating blue eyes.

'I heard a scream at the house a couple of weeks ago.' I falter. 'And someone was watching me near the river.'

He waits in silence.

'I think there's someone in the attic. Maybe the person who screamed.' I genuinely want to see how he will respond to this. His expression doesn't change. He rolls his chair back to his desk and faces the computer.

'Your partner heard the scream too?' He starts typing.

'I was alone.'

He stares at my medical file, impassive.

'And tell me about the stomach pain.'

I try to think of the right words. 'It twists. Crampy. But also – it aches. And my scar hurts, like a nerve pain.'

'Frequency?'

'Every day. Morning, afternoon. Whenever.'

His chair squeaks as he turns towards me.

'What are you doing to manage the pain at the moment?'

'Sleep. Hot water bottle. I take Valium.' I don't tell him about the temazepam, Targin and emergency Endone. He *tsks* and I bristle.

'The pain is a signal left over from your surgery. Your central nervous system is still on alert and sending false pain messages to your brain.' He leans back in his chair, satisfied he has solved one mystery. 'It's a protective mechanism. The best thing you can do is get some gentle exercise and cut back on the Valium.'

I don't say anything, and fidget with the handle of my bag. *The pain feels real.* I'm not deluded. I look at the floor.

He softens. 'Leila. You've been through a lot of changes. Moving is a big adjustment for most people, and you've also had some quite serious health complications. It's understandable you might be feeling unnerved. And the Valium could be contributing to what you're seeing and hearing. Benzodiazepines can cause delirium. I'm not suggesting that's what's happening here, but auditory and visual hallucinations can occur in some people.'

I wonder if this is how women felt a hundred years ago, when their ailments were diagnosed as hysteria.

'How are you settling into town?' He studies my face.

'I don't really come to town. I don't have a car.'

'Are you in touch with your friends from Sydney?'

I wonder what I would even say to them. My friends at work were great for a wine and debrief after a challenging day: *That stakeholder was an arsehole*, or, *Can you believe that team has no documented work processes*, and, *All right, let's get one more glass.* We vented: our bonds were built on the frustrations of corporate politics, peculiar to the particular viper's nest each of us worked in. My boss was the only one who knew I had been pregnant; we agreed to say I was taking a twelve-month creative sabbatical.

'Do you want to see a psychologist?' Dr Stewart asks. 'I can refer you to someone in town who is very good. Talk therapy can be helpful.'

I shake my head. 'My partner is a psychologist. He helps me.' Pause, then: 'I just need a new prescription for Valium. Thank you.' I didn't tell James I was going to ask for more. He insisted I come and get checked out, so I might as well take advantage.

'I'll give you a prescription for twenty-five tablets but no repeats. Come back and see me when you've finished them, and we can discuss what to do next.'

'Fine. Thank you.'

Dr Stewart leans back to the computer, clicking buttons, activating the printer. He signs the prescription form and hands it over; he's given me the lowest possible dose. He prints a second form and makes incomprehensible notes on it: U/S RS ABDO/LS ABDO/UTERUS.

'We'll get your abdomen checked out, too, all right? There's a radiology clinic right next door, you can have these as soon as you're ready. I'll copy the results to your specialist.'

He double checks the name of my specialist, then my phone number and address. I fold the papers and put them in my bag. As I stand to leave, he says, 'The Crawley house? Your partner is James Crawley?'

I nod.

'I thought I saw him in the waiting room with you. Lovely family. I went to school with his father.'

'It's kind of John and Patricia to lend us the house,' I say.

'It's an historic property. Do give James my best.' The doctor holds eye contact for a moment and then adds, 'Think about the exercise. A lot of our pain is just in our minds. You have no idea how powerful the mind can be.'

I zip up my bag. I'll fill the prescription at the chemist before returning to the farm – I'll tell James I need to duck in for tampons or something. I stand and reach out a hand, re-establishing formality; we are not friends.

'Thank you, Doctor.'

—

The appointment doesn't help; I fall back into gloom as soon as we return to the farm. I refuse to attend the radiology clinic and undergo the scans. Getting out of bed, eating, even talking to Rusty; it's all too difficult. My body aches. James brings light meals and an array of juices to the bedroom. I stare at him with my hollowed-out face and pallid skin, and he grasps my hands, encouraging me to eat like you would a small child. I block out all the noises of the house, ignoring the scratches and rumbles and groans like they do not exist.

The end of May brings driving rain and storms. The roof cracks and shrieks from stinging hail. Lightning splits the sky. Worms escape the drenched soil only to die on the front verandah instead of drowning in the mud. Matt moves the cows up to the top paddock, right in front of the house, where there is more tree cover. From bed, I listen to their low grumbles. I watch them through the window; they collect in groups under the trees, huddled together, tails flicking. I wonder how much they hate the wet.

Rusty keeps a close eye on me from his position at the bedroom door.

Finally, sun. Remembering Dr Stewart's advice, I reluctantly put on gumboots. When I rattle the front door, Rusty bolts in from the living room where he'd been comatose by the fire; mostly I'm doing this for him, but I want to know if I really did smell something rotten weeks ago. It's one thing I may be able to prove to myself. Perhaps after all this rain – and time – there'll be nothing, but if it was the septic tank, I can get someone to come around and check it.

Rusty's tail wags so intensely that his entire backside swings from side to side. I walk down the front steps, keeping a careful eye out for any reptiles, and point south. I love that Rusty understands me so easily: I point, say 'this way' or 'stop', and he does exactly that. If he gets too far ahead, he turns to look for me and waits. When I catch up, he stares at me, ready for the next command.

The chilly air pinches. When I expel breath, it swirls in front of me. It isn't long before I begin to pant. The ground is rocky and uneven, slightly uphill. My stomach pulls and I start to feel clammy, but I push on. Rusty needs this. He has slowed, his nose bobbing ahead of me occasionally, but otherwise we're in step.

We venture right, and ahead there's a loose circle of dead trees. They appear stark and desolate; the bark is smooth and grey, not a single leaf or hint of green. Then again, this might be normal in preparation for winter. The trees rise high into the sky, their trunks solid and firm, morphing into skinny branches that reach upwards like swirling smoke. Within the ring of trees, there's lush grass instead of paddock weed and, surprisingly, it seems to have been mowed or at least whipper-snipped. Outside the ring, the usual long grass and weeds abound.

Could it be a natural formation? Something about it seems constructed; there by design. Then again, who would plant trees in a circle, all the way back here, and keep the lawn curated and cut? The trees themselves must be generations old to have reached that size, planted when the house was built. I move to take a closer look, but Rusty barks. The sharp sound surprises me; when I look at him, his hackles are up, his front legs shaking. He barks again and pushes his head firmly against my hand.

'What's with you?' I mutter, but he's already turned and started trotting away. I look again; there's nothing else to see.

Catching up to Rusty, I scratch his head and point back in the direction where I think the smell was.

'Let's head down a little bit.'

It isn't much longer before we find the smell. It's worse than I recalled, despite the rain; I pull the hem of my shirt up over my mouth and nose, but it doesn't do much. The smell is so thick. There's no visible animal carcass. Plenty of long grass, tussock and weeds, eucalypts all around in varying stages of growth and health, but nothing unusual.

'Come on.' I follow the smell as best I can, battling an innate desire to get away from it. I sniff every few seconds, gagging each time, and head to where the smell is thickest. Rusty dashes off again, ploughing through knee-high grass and disappearing completely.

'Don't go in there,' I scold him, but he's gone. My orientation is all messed up. I turn around a few times. Which direction is the house? I strain to hear the river, but there's nothing. I spin around looking for landmarks, but there are none. Just paddock and trees in all directions. I should have taken note of the landscape. *Idiot*. I've never been lost walking in the major cities of the world, but here, on a single property, I need Rusty to lead me home.

Rusty. My ears tune in and I hear the dog barking incessantly; I stomp my way through the grass until I reach him. He's standing next to a round stone structure overgrown with weeds. I take a hesitant step towards it, my feet sinking into the still-gluggy mud.

The structure rises a few feet above the ground. It has a concrete lid weathered with old dirt stains and dotted with bird shit. Grass creeps up the sides, along with a lichen or moss. This must be the septic. Looking at it, it's unclear how the tank works – how it connects to the house and where it empties. Edging forwards, holding my breath, I examine the lid closely, but I don't know what I'm looking for. The top of the lid has a small symbol or logo etched into it – a circle with a small crescent atop it, like a precariously balanced hat – but there are no handles or screws.

Despite using my shirt as a makeshift mask, the stench is as powerful as a punch. The clammy feeling I've been fighting off intensifies. I raise a hand to my forehead and it's drenched in sweat. My skin is hot, my stomach roils, and I vomit, a splash hitting the side of the structure. The heat dissipates, and a chill rolls through me.

'Shit.' I sit on the concrete lid and breathe through my mouth. I swallow hard to suppress any more bile and kick some mud over the contents of my stomach. Hopefully a plumber will know what to do with this – there must be a malfunction somewhere. I wave to the dog. He meets my eyes, and I nod my head away from the septic. Rusty takes off ahead of me and I follow gratefully. As we get further from the tank, the damp air becomes neutral again, tranquilising me as the rotting smell recedes. The sky is a vivid blue, and every footstep results in a satisfying squelch.

Perhaps the doctor was right; getting outside and moving around might help if I keep it up and increase my strength.

After vomiting, there's barely any pain in my stomach. As each foot finds the mud, I listen to Rusty's panting in rhythm, and all my muscles are warm. I feel almost like my old self. The woman who did everything on her own, and did so perfectly.

FOLLICULAR PHASE

(fol·lic·u·lar) *noun*
the follicular phase starts on the first day of
menstruation and ends with ovulation. The ovary
produces around five to twenty follicles. Each
follicle houses an immature egg. The growth of
the follicles stimulates the lining of the uterus to
thicken in preparation for possible pregnancy.

Usually, only one follicle will mature
into an egg. The others die.

For the camping weekend, we will spend three nights away from the farm and drive sixteen hours for the round trip. James has been regaling me with stories of his old jaunts, the kind of camping where you need only an esky and a swag, where you catch everything you eat. In his retelling, the rivers were thick with yabbies, and he'd hold a piece of meat to the water's edge, wait for a yabby to approach and then grab it with his other hand and pull it out. To eat it, he boiled it alive.

Other times, he and his mates raced the yabbies. They'd set up their plastic table and dump the crustaceans on it, and the first yabby to fall off was the winner. James said yabbies are so primitive, they'd panic and clutch at each other with their claws, getting stuck together. He and his friends would wait, watching, until they figured out how to untangle themselves and escape.

I pack a bag with fleece track pants and jumpers and thick socks. I add pyjamas, and a small toiletries case with a hairbrush, toothpaste, a toothbrush and my pills. I pop two small travel cushions on the passenger seat – one for behind my back and one to buffer my stomach from the squeeze of the seatbelt. After some indecision, I include a woollen throw blanket.

When James comes home from work, he starts packing the ute with a tent, air mattress, pump, fridge, our pillows, fishing rods, bait, a case of water, some cartons of beer, two sleeping bags, headlamps and several bottles of wine. I watch him through the kitchen window as I prepare dinner, impressed by his effort to make the trip comfortable for me, even though it's only a few days. If I weren't around, he'd certainly rough it. He spends a couple of hours packing and re-packing until everything is just right. Then he pulls a tight tarp over it all and fastens it to the tray.

We will drive to a place called Warrego River. James says it's 'out the back of Bourke', so I suppose Bourke is the type of place that is the last known destination on the map.

———

We get up at sunrise, usher Rusty into the back seat of the ute. The June morning is cold, the proper start of winter, and Rusty is reluctant to leave the house, but he trots to the car when I ask him to. Mist envelops everything. We drive through the country lanes and then take the road to Bathurst. This early, there are only a few cars and a couple of trucks on the road. By the time we get into the town, it's brighter and clearer, and I take note of the buildings for the first time: they have a quaint, historic look about them. Bathurst is the oldest inland city in Australia, but I'd never thought of it as anything but a place with a racetrack. The light posts are cast iron and they stand proudly in the main street. There are Victorian-era terraces and a gothic looking church, spires rising to meet God. Rows of deciduous trees line the streets, giving up the last of their red and orange leaves. We turn into the main street and park in front of a cafe; James jumps out to get us coffee. I twist around and scratch behind Rusty's ears until James returns, and then I guzzle the creamy, nutty espresso. So much better than the instant coffee at the farm.

We drive down William Street and stop at a red light. Directly in front of us, facing the main intersection, is a large billboard; the face of a young woman stares out from it. Immediately, from the image alone, I can tell the girl is missing. She's brunette, with a wide smile, big hoop earrings and a black tank top. Glittery eyeshadow. She appears to be holding a drink, but her lower half is cut off. It looks like a photo taken straight from social media, from a night out with her friends. On either side of her, I can see their cropped shoulders.

HAVE YOU SEEN RENEE BRICE? MISSING 12/10/2009

The words are simultaneously aggressive and mournful. Fifteen years. Surely the young woman is long gone. The car behind us bips; the traffic light is green. James turns onto the Mitchell Highway. I stare down the road and think of how many kinds of loss there are. How terrible each one is.

We play music from James's Spotify, and I wonder about this woman's mother. Whether she pays for the billboard each month, in a transaction that has become routine, or whether the community lets it pass. Does anyone still mention her daughter to her? Do her friends come round for coffee and discuss every topic but the one that matters? Do they mark Renee's birthday? Wrap presents and leave them in her room, untouched? Do they release balloons, light candles, visit a particular site? I try to imagine the funeral, held without knowing whether the girl was alive, but the mother needing to make a decision. To take back control.

I picture a woman with a grandmotherly air about her, the loss of her child having accelerated her into old age. I never knew my own grandmothers, on either side. There'd been no birthdays with extra presents, no hugs from women who smelled like floral perfume or Cussons Imperial Leather soap. When a friend lost her grandmother during university and went to pieces, I was confused by the intensity of her grief. I accompanied her to the funeral and was stunned by the sheer number of people, the amount of emotion in the room. Would Renee's have been similar? School friends, university friends, work friends, relatives, an outpouring of anguish. A particular type of grief, tinged with fury, with confusion. With my own mother, it had been just the two of us, the funeral company, and the priest. We hadn't been in touch with any of Mum's relatives in years. I'd not asked my school friends to go; even then, I felt a distinct embarrassment about who she was, and what that meant I was.

Outside of Bathurst, on the country roads, it's dull and foggy. Beyond the car's headlights, I can't make out much. Again, I feel the remoteness of this country. I still can't quite believe I exist here, in this vast and alien place. The quietness allows in too many thoughts, too many memories. Ones I don't want to revisit. I hadn't thought of my mother's funeral in years. Her coffin was so small.

There's a pant, and hot air hits the left side of my face. I turn and see Rusty's nose wedged between my headrest and the window, his tongue out, puffing, his breath clouding the glass. He's unfairly squashed in the back seat, an esky pushing up against his bum, but he's managed to get as close to me as he can. I jiggle until I'm on my side and can pat him in longer strokes. Our faces are close together and I breathe in the mild scent of his coat. It's thick and soft, and he gives off a reassuring smell. The aroma of something alive: skin, hair, earth.

—

The terrain becomes rockier, with scattered evergreen trees. The fog lifts and the air is voluminous. I peer through the car windows and think that, if not for the car, we would roll around the hills like skittles. We talk about the freedom of being on the road, but more important to me is the hemming. Lines to live within.

—

We stop at Nyngan. There's a statue called The Big Bogan. The base is a reddish brown, and his face and body parts are drawn in white strokes. The statue has a hat, a beard, stubby shorts, a Southern Cross tattoo, thongs on his feet and a fish hanging from his rod and reel. His thumb curls up. This man has everything he needs. On his singlet it reads, *Nyngan, NSW, Aust.* Singlets like that were called wife-beaters when I was at school. We thought it was funny. We get out of the car and open the door for Rusty. He leaps to the ground and trots to the closest tree, urinating for at least a minute. James poses in front of The Big Bogan, pulling his shorts up to mimic the statue; his muscular thighs are pale, reflecting the sun. I snap photos on his phone.

'The boys'll love this,' he says, winking at me. I laugh and call him a dork and we let Rusty sniff around for a bit before we all hop back in the car and drive on.

The road is mostly straight, which is somehow more tiring than one with a lot of bends. Each pothole – every uneven layer of bitumen that's been dissolved by rain and patched once, twice, twenty times – bumps the car, and my stomach responds to each one with an aching pain. Uncomfortable, I rearrange the pillows every few kilometres. We drive on and on, yet the horizon cannot be caught. It is a wavy line always out of reach. We pass towns that seem like an afterthought, slipping into our rear-view before I even notice them, and dusty petrol stations that must bake in summer. Rusty whines and we roll down the back window for him. I watch him in the side mirror, his hairy little face pushed back by the wind, eyes blinking in the dust, nose twitching with the new smells. When we stop again, Rusty coughs in disappointment.

In the public restroom, I hold my breath and hover my bottom above the seat because the entire cubicle stinks of shit, and the toilet and walls are covered in remnants of every kind of human fluid. James walks out the back behind a tree and pisses there. Men and their dicks, it's so much easier for them. When we get back in the car, he proposes a driving game to pass the time and I suggest counting the dead animals instead. He snorts, but indulges me. I have eight wombats and five kangaroos when a feathery brown hump with stick-like legs dashes across the road ahead of us. I shriek and James laughs.

'Never seen an emu before?'

'In the wild?' I turn to see it disappear into the scrub.

'Heaps of them out here. Gundabooka is full of emus.'

I imagine them roaming, their long throats fighting gravity, their humpbacks bobbing with their legs. A ridiculous animal. How do their necks not get sore? How do they sleep?

'I can spot one ages away,' James says. 'Same with roos.'

'What do they eat out here?'

'People,' James says, and I scoff.

He laughs and then points, and before I know it, he has slowed the car as another giant bird zigzags across the road, its small head low, in line with its hump, as if to reduce wind resistance. And then it's gone.

'We're getting close to Bourke,' James says. 'It's unsealed after that. Might be bumpy.'

'You didn't tell me we'd be driving unsealed.' I reach into the glovebox and pull out some Endone. I'm exhausted, and my stomach feels like everything has been given a vigorous shake.

'Yeah sorry. I forgot.' He squeezes my knee. 'But you're doing much better now, right?'

'Just go slow,' I say, and swallow the pills. We pass a green sign: *Girilambone 43*; *Coolabah 73*; *Byrock 124*; *Bourke 202*; *Brewarrina 208*. I wind back my seat and close my eyes, waiting to be knocked into nothingness.

—

I hear a thump, followed by a gritty squelch. I open my eyes. The sun has lowered, sitting squarely in my line of vision.

'How long was I asleep?'

'Couple of hours,' James says. 'We've just left Bourke. On the way to Warrego now.'

I rub my eyes, adjust my seat and look out the window. The bitumen is gone. We're driving on orange dirt and rock, surrounded by gnarled trees.

'Can you slow down?' I say, watching the speedometer. James shaves five kilometres off and I frown. He ignores me.

'This is a weird place to camp.' I point out the plain-looking trees and he says, 'Mulga scrub,' as though I know what that means. I shift my pillows, pulling one all the way under my bum.

We don't speak; James is concentrating on the road, peering through the sun, and so I hold my stomach and my resentments to myself.

—

There are four people – two men and two women – in a small, cleared site close to the river when we pull in at three o'clock. Both men are dressed in singlets and flannels. One of them, wearing a cap over long curly brown hair, trots to the side of the truck and throws his arm in the window, clasping James's hand and shaking it in a mock victory gesture. 'Yeahhhhh maaate!'

The women stand together near a struggling fire and watch us as we park. I give them a small wave and one, a brunette, waves back. The other, a blonde, turns back to chatting with the first woman. The other bloke finishes hammering a tent peg and yells out in a gravelly voice, 'Get a beer already,' and James shouts back, 'On it,' then leans over to give me a dusty kiss on the cheek.

'I'll have a drink and get the tent sorted.' He's out of the car before I've even unbuckled my belt. I take my time. The breeze is colder here than at the farm. Chilled air floods the gap between my collar and my neck, biting through the mesh of my runners. The dirt underfoot is soft. The sun is still up, but probably only for another hour or so. It'll be frigid later. I toss the travel cushions onto the back seat and open the door to let Rusty out. He immediately disappears into the bush to urinate. My ears feel hollow from the cold.

I wander over to the women. James and his two mates are off near one of the tents, whooping and laughing.

'Hi,' I say, and they look up, wide-eyed, like they forgot I was here. Both of them are dressed in jeans, knee-high Hunter wellies and woollen jumpers. The blonde woman has a long puffer jacket draped around her shoulders, and wears large pearl stud earrings and a heavy gold fob chain around her neck: signs of country wealth. The brunette has three wedding rings on her finger, and all are encrusted with diamonds. I'm wearing loose tracksuit pants and a hoodie, didn't bother with jewellery or make-up; being unwell has stripped me of the ability to care how I look, for the most part. Until I see other people and remember, this isn't normal.

'I'm Leila.' I stick out a hand and the brunette shakes it. There's tattoo ink visible on her wrist, half-hidden by her sleeve.

'Nice to meet you,' she says. 'I'm Charlotte.'

'Hi Charlotte.'

There's a brief silence while the other woman looks me over – my trackies have crumbs on them, I realise, and I brush them off quickly – and then Charlotte says, 'This is Emma.' I nod at her; she gives me a thin smile. Her eyebrows are tinted and feathered into perfectly matching arches.

Charlotte points to the man with the cap. 'That's my husband, Dave, over there being a dickhead, and Emma's husband, Adam, with the tent.'

'Great.' My mouth is dry. 'You guys know James already.'

'Sure do,' Emma says. We all look at James: he's saying to Adam, 'You can't peg a tent to save yourself.' He leans down and pulls one of the half-submerged pegs up; a quarter of the tent dips over and they laugh uproariously.

'You guys on fire duty?' I ask.

Charlotte glances down at the bundle of kindling that has turned ashy and grey. 'Oh shit,' she says. 'Yeah, we are. Clearly doing a crap job of it.'

'I'll get you more kindling.' I'm pleased to have a reason to leave them.

'Thanks,' Charlotte says, squatting down and poking the barely lit coals with a stick. 'Anything'll help.'

I head back past the truck and up the dirt road. There's foliage on either side of the track, and I take my time gathering sticks in different sizes. I look up at the sky and see streaks of cloud in pink and orange. The sun is getting low. I can't hear any birds, but the rustle of lizards – or perhaps snakes – is all around. I focus my eyes on the ground as I trudge back to camp.

When I get there, Adam and Dave have taken over the fire, trying to restore it to health, while James is setting up our tent. Rusty is lying by camp chairs that have been set up near the smoking fire.

'Where'd you go?'

I hold up the bundle of sticks. 'To get kindling.'

He points. 'Just drop it over there.'

I dump them. 'I need a glass of wine.'

'Yep. I'll get it in a jiff.'

I stand by him, handing him pegs and watching him hammer them in. He's precise. He kneels, and I admire the muscles in his back, his jumper draped over the ridges of his shoulder blades and deltoids. The hammer drops evenly – once, twice – and the peg slides into place. It's a cliché that a man doing something practical for a woman is a turn-on, but I've always been turned on by anyone doing something nice for me.

'Happy?' He stands back, admiring the tent. I lean into his shoulder, and he puts an arm around me.

'So, red?' he asks after a minute, and I nod. He returns to the ute and rummages around, pulling out a long-necked bottle and a large plastic cup. He fills it all the way and I smile; he winks as he hands it to me. As I take a soothing sip, he grabs another beer and we walk over to the fire. I sit in one of the chairs and slide my wine into its netted cup holder.

'What did you do to this fire?' Dave pokes at it, the kindling smoking heavily.

Charlotte sips a white wine. 'I don't know – I supervised it.'

Dave pulls the visor down on his hat and mutters and pokes around, breaking off smaller sticks and holding them to the tiny orange sparks, blowing on them. Small flames build up and lick the kindling, then recoil as though they dislike the taste. James picks up a few sticks then pushes Dave aside and positions them around the fire, blowing on the flames gently, encouraging them to increase their heat, the base of each finally showing blue. With a loud crack, a tower of kindling collapses and flames run over the pieces of wood. James balances two small logs on top. I smile at this display of capability. Nothing is too difficult for James. The logs catch alight, and he stands, clapping debris from his hands.

'Smart arse,' Dave says.

—

The men are gathered around Adam's barbecue, frying sausages and steaks, a fatty, smoky smell sweeping over the camp. Rusty sits at James's side, staring up at him, never blinking. Every so often James cuts off a bit of steak and tosses it to him, and Rusty catches it with a snap of his jaws and swallows it whole.

Charlotte sets up a trestle table with a plastic bucket for dishwashing, a chopping board, knives, cutlery and tea towels. Emma produces a silver catering bowl and I throw in pre-mixed salad and drizzle over packet dressing. A dozen white bread rolls, nestled together like sleeping puppies, sit in a plastic bag alongside bottles of tomato and barbecue sauce. LED lamps are set around the site so we can see what we're doing. I keep the wine bottle handy.

'Ready?' Adam calls and Emma says, 'Yeah,' and sighs as though he's a toddler asking for ice-cream. So far, Emma has mainly said *yeah* and rolled her eyes a lot, and drunk a lot of white wine. Charlotte is the welcoming one, patting me on the back, shoving a plate of cheese and crackers towards me when the salad is done.

We fill our plates with rolls, meat, cheese, salad and sauces, combining them in a variety of ways. I mush the sausage, sauce, cheese and salad into the roll and chew hard; Emma picks at a steak and some green leaves; Charlotte eats everything separately, slathering her roll in butter. The men make steak and sausage rolls and ignore the greens, leaving them to wilt on their plates. We gather around the fire, a crackling entity that hisses welcome heat at our faces.

I sit between James and Charlotte. He leans over to the blokes, so I ask Charlotte how she and Dave met.

'Uni,' she says. 'We were all in the same psych class. Emma and Adam ended up doing medicine. Dave and I did teaching.'

'You've been together that long?'

'Yeah. Crazy. Dave drives me nuts.' She takes a big bite of buttered roll and shrugs. 'But I love him.'

Emma cuts in. 'How did you meet James?'

'Online.'

Emma glances at Charlotte but doesn't respond.

'I was working all the time,' I say. 'Hard to meet people.'

'What do you do?' Charlotte asks.

'Consultant. I work on transformation projects, mainly.'

'Work,' Emma says with a little groan. 'I'm so glad I don't have to think about that anymore.'

Charlotte snorts. 'We can't all be doctors' wives.'

'Aren't you a doctor, too?' I ask Emma.

'I did the degree.' She clicks her nails against her wine glass; they shine in the lamp light, an unnatural shade of pink. 'I started training, but I wanted to stay home once I had kids.'

'God knows why,' Charlotte says. 'They'll send you bonkers.' She puts her plate down next to her chair and gestures broadly. 'Dave camps a few times a year. I mean, look at this place. It's a wonder anyone finds this habitable, but he insists. Probably to get away from us.'

'So does Adam,' Emma says.

'They come here a few times a year?' I ask.

'Don't worry, you won't be invited every time.' Charlotte sips a beer. 'We ladies stay home to look after the kids. Did you say you have kids?'

The men's chatter and laughter clutters the air; I can't think of an answer.

'They don't,' Emma says for me, slipping off her coat as the heat of the fire intensifies. She is slim underneath the jacket; both she and Adam are blonde and tanned, and I imagine their athletic blonde children, playing sport, winning awards, growing up to become doctors, too.

'We tried,' I say, and then find there are no more words. Charlotte is sympathetic.

'That's rough,' she says. 'I'm sure it will work out.'

That's what everyone says; that's what I used to say about lost pregnancies to friends and colleagues. *Not to worry. It will work out.* Only when you haven't experienced it do you say that. In the ensuing silence, we listen to the fire crackle and spit.

'It's okay,' I say finally. 'I saw on Instagram that dogs are the new kids and plants are the new pets, anyway.'

'Oh, you have a green thumb?' Charlotte asks.

'Not at all,' I say, and we both laugh. I'm pleased by the hint of camaraderie.

'How are you finding the farm, then?' Charlotte says.

'Fine.' I pick up the wine bottle by my feet – it's my second – and fill my cup. Drinking pinot noir from plastic doesn't taste the same.

'Finding winter pretty cold?' Emma prompts.

'It's an adjustment. Especially when I forget to stoke the fire.' I gulp down the wine. 'I'm learning a lot, I guess.'

'It's quite isolated at James's place,' Charlotte says. 'You get into town much?'

'Not really. We only have one car and James takes it to work.' I pause and, in the silence, Dave shouts, 'I hate white rabbits!'

I look over at him. The fire smokes heavily and James gets up, fiddles with it. It whooshes, sending orange flames skywards.

'Thansss mate,' Dave slurs when James sits back down.

'White rabbits?' I ask Charlotte, and Emma scoffs. 'Sorry,' I say. 'I don't know.'

'No, it's fine,' Charlotte says. 'It stops a fire blowing smoke in your face. Old country superstition.'

I take larger sips. We're slack in our camp chairs, loosened by alcohol, bodies heavy from the long drive. Charlotte's profile blurs in the orange light. She stares at the fire, small blue eyes gently creased by smile lines, hair cut in a sensible bob, resting her hands on her soft belly. I say: 'I've seen some weird things at the farm. Smelled something terrible.'

Charlotte sits up. 'What have you seen?'

The men fall silent opposite us and I regret sharing. 'Just . . . I don't know. Someone down by the river. I think I heard some noises at the house. And there's an awful smell out the back.'

'A smell?' Dave asks, from across the fire.

'Way out the back, behind the house. Maybe the septic.' I look back at Charlotte. 'But it really smelled like something dead.'

'Yeah, nah,' Dave says. 'If it was dead, you'd know it.' He grabs a beer from the esky and drags his camping chair between James and me, pulls his cap off and jiggles his curls. Shadows dance on his face, chased away by the firelight.

'You're from the city, right?' He doesn't wait for me to answer. 'Maybe you've smelled a dead mouse, *maybe*. But out here – you wouldn't believe what something dead smells like.'

I want to tell him there's lots of different ways a dead thing can smell. Sometimes it smells alive and like blood and like failure, too.

'The worst thing I ever smelled, my god it was terrible, was a dead sheep.' He chugs his beer. 'Growing up, we had sheep die all the time. Usually from being pregnant, of all things. They get toxemia – it literally poisons them.'

Charlotte looks at him, horrified, and goes to say something; I shake my head at her, and she sits back. James makes a joke to Adam that I can't hear. Dave is energised.

'The sheep all go into shock. There's nothing you can do. They get lethargic, then all twitchy' – he rolls his eyes back and wriggles in an impersonation of the wretched sheep, and Charlotte puts her head in her hands – 'and die. One year, we were cleaning up the dead ones, but there was a sheep we couldn't find. I walked everywhere looking for the corpse. Finally got a whiff of something terrible down by the dam. Went down and looked in the run-off pipe. There she was, curled up. I grabbed her legs and tried to pull her out and she came apart in my hands. Nothing but maggots left. The *stink*.'

I focus on Rusty, all spindly limbs and fluffy hair, stretched out by the fire. His coat appears even more orange in the glow.

'Now that's a pong you never forget,' Dave says. A breeze flings smoke into his face and he chokes out, 'White rabbit!' I feel pleasure as he coughs and gags.

'She's a city girl,' James says. 'Back off.'

'Gotta break her in, mate.'

'Your house is haunted,' Charlotte says, cutting off her husband. She nods at me. 'Don't worry, you're not crazy. There are ghosts.'

James cocks his head at her. 'You seen one? Anybody in particular?'

There's a long silence, and then James bursts into laughter so forceful that beer spurts out his nose. 'Shit.' He rubs his face. 'Now I've lost my beer.'

Charlotte says nothing further. She slumps in her chair and Emma leans in to whisper something in her ear, patting her leg gently.

I stand up. 'Rusty.'

His head pops up, one ear pricked, the other floppy. Our eyes meet and I nod at him. He gets up slowly, stiff and tired from the long car trip, stretching first his front legs, then his back.

'I'm off to bed,' I say. I pick up the wine bottle and wave goodnight. James walks me to the tent and gives me a kiss and a tight hug. The group at the fire is silent, waiting out my awkward departure. Once I'm in the tent, I hear the men start talking, and laughter ricochets off the dry trees. James has, thankfully, already pumped up the air mattress. I crawl into my sleeping bag and pat the ground next to me. Rusty curls up alongside me, his face perched on the bed. I feel the cool wet tip of his nose by my hand, and then there is nothing.

The first sound I hear is James's heavy snore, then Rusty's scuffling. My right arm is dead, and I sit up and rub it; it prickles as blood rushes back in. Air has fled the mattress, and I feel hard ground beneath my tailbone. Rusty sniffs under my chin; I scratch his neck then push him away. I crawl onto my hands and knees and reach for the tent zip, pulling it up and around. Rusty escapes through the flap into the morning light.

I glance back at James. He had a late night and a lot of beers; his face looks ruddy. I pull on a hoodie and thongs and leave the tent. My toes and my nose react sensitively to the cold air; I grimace and it morphs into a sort of smile. A pain smile. Whether I'm running or frustrated at work or at the gym, the ends of my lips have always turned up, like I'm enjoying it, as if it's what I want. My mother resented it, but she hated it even more if I frowned, if I cried, if I complained. Always look like you're smiling, even when it hurts.

Rusty is just up ahead, peeing by a tree and then sniffing all around. I walk to the makeshift toilet, a hole dug by the men, hidden behind a sheet. I pee as quickly as I can manage and then return to the campsite. The fire has been put out, but it still smokes. The smell reminds me of dry autumn days in Brisbane, when the council would burn off tracts of forest; the smoke haze entered every room of the house and hung there, stifling and hot, warming the air so it felt like summer.

I think I'm alone until I hear the crunch of twigs and leaves. I turn and Emma approaches, a lit cigarette in her hand.

'Morning,' she says. In the daylight, I can see deep lines across her forehead and cheeks. Her hair is thinner than I thought. 'Bit of a late one last night.' She takes a long draw on her cigarette.

I back away from the smell. 'You pull up all right?'

She shrugs. 'I'm up earlier than this for the kids anyway.' She blows out smoke and inhales another draw. 'Boys'll be up soon. Fishing today.'

'Fishing, great.' Not one part of this camping trip has been designed for me to enjoy.

'You been fishing with James before?' Emma asks. I shake my head. She exhales more smoke and then a high-pitched whistle.

'He's very competitive,' she says with a firmness that states quite explicitly that she knows him far better than I do. She drops her cigarette and crushes it beneath expensive sneakers.

'I haven't noticed,' I say.

'Last year, oh my god.' She laughs, her long-nailed fingers clasping her cigarette pack and lighter. 'The boys wanted to use a net, just relax a bit and drink some beers. James fired up and went to fish for cod on his own.'

I look around for Rusty. He's sitting outside our tent, staring at me. Our eyes meet and his tail thumps against the ground; he wants a walk.

'You know what net fishing is?' Emma says.

'I should walk Rusty.'

'It's a gill net. You put it across the river on both banks, tie it off and wait for fish to swim into the net. Their gills get caught. Then you bring up the nets and you get whatever fish have swum in. James hates it.'

'Why?'

'He says there's no skill in it.' Emma turns and I follow her gaze. Adam has emerged from his tent, in last night's singlet and shorts. 'James always wants the biggest fish, the best fish.'

I smile at Emma and try to appear grateful for the conversation. As I'm about to turn away, she says, 'So you're nervous up at the farm, yeah? Hearing noises and all that?'

I pause only for a jerky second and then turn and walk away. I crawl back into the tent and see James sitting up, rubbing his face.

'I'm going to take Rusty for a walk,' I say, slipping off the thongs and pulling my joggers on.

'Don't go too far,' James says in a thick voice.

'Have a sleep-in,' I say and pat him on the leg. When I emerge, Rusty sees my shoes and starts to spin, his tail whipping around with him.

'Come on,' I say, my hand grazing the top of his head. He falls into step with me, and we head up the river, away from the camp, from the traps I could fall into.

———

We leave the river and turn inwards, following a rabbit path on a mild elevation. It's cloudy with no breeze; some sun pokes through the cover. Walking is a generous term for what Rusty and I are doing. He stops every few steps to sniff. About half the time he lifts his leg, even though he's out of piss; the other half, he sniffs for a few seconds and then runs ahead as he picks up a newer, more exotic scent. I keep an eye out for snakes. We move slowly, walking higher and further into trees and scrub. Sticks, stones, bits of glass and weeds crunch under my shoes.

Rusty limps back to me, holding up a paw. Between the soil-caked pads is a sharp pebble. I prise them apart, and he butts my hand with his nose, but doesn't pull away.

'I know it hurts,' I say, angling my finger between the pads, which are usually black, but are now a reddish brown from the dirt. I catch the stone with my nail, digging my fingertip underneath it. He whines and then *pop*; the pebble falls away. Rusty stares into my eyes. Impulsively, I kiss the bridge of his nose. He dashes off, the discomfort already forgotten, and I wish my memory of pain worked the same way. A flush of feeling, of care, envelops me. I keep the excited dog in my sight, yearning for him though he's only a few yards from me.

What makes a parent? It must be more than pregnancy, more than the act of birth. More than the keeping and the feeding, the educating and the punishing. Parents talk about unconditional love, say they'd love their children no matter what. Even if they killed someone. I can't imagine that. It's a dimension of emotional life that I've never reached: the level where love is constant, love is eternal. It is the province only of parents – though I don't believe my mother ever reached that place either. Her love seemed entirely conditional. I watch Rusty, his nose close to the ground. The curious snout disappears under bushes, prods through long grasses. I'm rigid with concern for his safety. This little companion. Would I love Rusty if he bit someone? If he killed someone? Does it depend on who, on the context?

Rusty howls, suddenly and furiously. All the hair on his back stands up; his tail is raised and stiff. A metre or two ahead of him is a long brown thing, a branch; no, it is a lizard. The head is narrow and sharp, and a forked tongue jabs into the air. I try to see how big it is, but it's like a funhouse mirror: the raised head links to a body, and when I follow the body to the ground, it disappears, camouflaged by speckled scales in the dirt. For a moment, I don't believe it's real; it's another hallucination, a product of my medications.

Rusty barks and jumps forwards, but it is a test stance, pure bluster. It fails, and the lizard hisses and rises to its hind legs, and I take a sharp breath, because it's enormous. It is not my imagination. This isn't the lazy, blue-tongued lizard of my Brisbane childhood. It's a goanna. Its belly is fat and pale; its front legs dangle with pointed claws. Rusty backs up, and the goanna drops to its front legs again, hissing louder. We are the trespassers here.

'Rusty,' I call, frozen in place. His ears prick, but he is shaking and doesn't move. He growls, long and low. *'Rusty. Come. Come now!'*

He wants to fight, but here is something I can teach him: if you want to escape danger, you don't attack. Don't confront. Be quiet. Tread lightly. Go around. Make yourself so very small. These are the steps to survival. Avoid, avoid, avoid.

I call him again and he runs back to me, his mouth foaming. He shudders and makes to run at the goanna again, but I grab his collar and drag him with me, down, down, away. I don't look behind me.

We pick our way back down, more cautious now. I reach out to pat Rusty every few steps. I miss the simple colour of flowers. There's not a single petal here.

———

The campsite is awake. Bacon and eggs sizzle on the barbecue, manned by James and Dave. They are each drinking a beer. Rusty belts towards the food and I follow behind. James waves at me and I smile. Charlotte is putting together more rolls, squirting BBQ sauce on the already-hardening bread.

'Hey,' she says. 'Bacon and egg roll?'

I accept the offering and stand with her, chewing on the bacon, a dribble of sauce escaping to my chin.

'Sleep all right?' Charlotte says.

'Pretty well. Woke up early so I took Rusty for a walk.'

'Not much to see around here.'

I agree and don't tell her about the goanna. 'Don't suppose there's coffee?'

'Girl, *yes.*' Charlotte plops the rolls down on a plate and points to a large French press. 'Just push that down and we're good to go.'

The press has a thick layer of ground beans crowded at the top. I push the lid down, nice and slow, and thank any god there is that Charlotte is on this trip. I pour the liquid into two plastic cups, breathing in the aroma. There's a packet of UHT milk and I splash some in. I hand her a cup, and we sip and moan with pleasure simultaneously. Charlotte laughs.

'Gotta have a vice,' she says.

'I have more than one,' I say. 'But this might be my favourite.'

'It's definitely mine.' She sips again. 'Once, I told Dave that coffee is better than sex. He's never forgotten it.'

'You're not wrong.'

'Hey, I'm sorry about what he said last night.' Charlotte rubs my shoulder. 'He's an idiot.'

'He didn't know.'

'Still.'

We stand together in comfortable silence, chewing and slurping. Kookaburras fly overhead. A curious magpie lands near the barbecue, its head bobbing up and down like a piston, pecking for food. Rusty waits by the table, eyes alert for scraps.

'James is lucky to have you,' Charlotte says as she swallows her final bite. 'How long have you been together?'

'Just over a year.'

'Well, it must be serious,' she says. 'He hasn't brought a girlfriend camping in ages.'

I want to ask her about James's previous girlfriends. When we met, I quizzed him about this, and he said he hadn't had a proper girlfriend for years. *You've just been sleeping around then*, I'd joked, and he laughed. I remember feeling relief: no exes to worry about, no baggage to navigate.

'Maybe his other girlfriends just refused to camp,' I say.

'All right, girls.' James joins us. 'You'll be manning the rods. We're going out in the tinny.'

Dave shouts, 'We're gettin' the cod!' and I nod, trying to share his enthusiasm. James must have talked them into it.

'Where's Adam and Emma?' I ask.

'Down with the lines,' James says. 'You'll need water, food, a book. You'll be there all day.'

I want to bite at this, at being told what to do, but Charlotte is watching me. I realise James and I have been more like the happy couple we used to be since we arrived at the camp. His tendency at the farm to focus on me, analysing my care and recovery, has been diverted to the tasks of camping and fishing – so I agree instead.

'Looking forward to it.'

—

The muddy bank stretches a long way, disappearing into scrub. Murky water pools at the edge. Currawongs investigate the line between earth and water, searching for worms. They look at us as we approach, their yellow eyes darting and inquisitive. They don't move on or fly away; as with all the wildlife here, we're on their turf.

Emma sits on a camp chair, reading a book and smoking, and Adam sets up the last of the rods. They are stuck in what looks like a stumpy black pipe shoved into the sand. He baits the end of the last rod, tosses it back and throws the line into the water, then wedges the handle into the pipe. There are five lines and three camp chairs. James grabs my hand, pulls me over to explain.

'They're secure in the pipe,' he says, 'but when you see the line tugging, get up and reel it in.'

We're fishing for yellow-bellies, or golden perch. He pulls out a rod to show me how to operate it, but it's all clicking and whirring and pulling and I don't pay attention; I just agree when he says, 'All good?' He kisses me hard on the lips and squeezes my bottom, pleased with my participation in this thing he loves. I wave him off. Charlotte sets down an esky and takes her spot a few feet away. She opens it and hands me a beer. I sit down in a chair with my book, beer and water bottle, Rusty at my feet. Here we are, in a row, watching assiduously: gathering food while our men go out to hunt.

—

It's two hours and four beers later that a line starts twitching. I'm a little drunk so I pat Rusty and tell him to alert Charlotte; she'll know what to do. Charlotte is asleep with her mouth open, sunglasses askew. Rusty licks her hand and she sits straight up, waking the way I imagine a mother does, ready to respond.

'The line,' I call, and point at the rod.

Emma lowers her book and looks over but doesn't move; Charlotte rises and stretches. 'Oof, I was *out.*' She picks up the rod and the line tugs harder. As she spins the wheel, I walk over to watch her.

'Heavy bugger,' she says, and her arm ripples as she pulls the catch in. The fish emerges from the water, slimy in the sun, suspended by an invisible line, glinting and twitching. Charlotte grunts.

'Carp,' she says. She steadies the rod back in the pipe and unhooks the fish, drops it on the muddy bank. It gasps with its tubular sucking mouth and flaps about on the ground. Its eyes seem to bulge, but perhaps all carp look like that. I stand by the fish, feeling I should witness its passing, but Charlotte taps me and says, 'Takes a while. Carp last a few hours. Bloody pest.'

I retreat to my chair and stare noiselessly at the mucky russet water, the flailing carp in the corner of my eye, thudding repetitively against the dirt. Rusty sniffs the fish, trots back to me and puts a paw on my knee. I nod. 'We can go.'

—

I'm in the tent, lying on the mattress, the tent door open to let in air. There is no breeze but it's cool, even with Rusty lying on my feet. His head faces the open tent flap, ears occasionally pricking up at a noise, then deflating again. I take an Endone. His eyes stay open while mine grow heavy, and I fall asleep.

There are voices, the patter of conversation. It's settling into dusk. I sit up, groggy. The dog is not with me now. My back aches, my stomach burns; I scrabble in my handbag for another pill. The air is freezing, and I grab fresh socks from my duffel. No-one has come to find me, which is mostly a relief. Being just on the outside of something is where I've lived my entire life. I can't imagine the pressure of being in the middle. I think of Emma and her standoffish attitude and realise I don't like her much, and at the same time, that she is very much like me. We separate ourselves deliberately. I wonder what made her that way. You'd think it would bond us, but we dislike ourselves too much. We gravitate to the Charlottes: the easy, relaxed personalities who fill the silences, the voids we create.

I duck out of the tent and stand up slowly. Emma is sitting in a chair, drinking white wine; Charlotte is directing the men. She holds a large metal pot, blackened at the bottom. Dave tips a generous amount of salt into it, then Charlotte picks up a large bottle of water and pours that in, too. She adds a lid and wedges the pot in the smouldering batons of the fire. She sees me watching and calls out.

'Drink?'

I walk over. She opens a bottle of red and pours me a glass.

'The boys did well today,' she says.

'They caught the cod?' I ask, and Dave turns from the table and says, bitter, 'Fuck, no.' I tense up.

'No, they're too useless for that,' Charlotte says. 'But they did manage to get a bunch of yabbies.'

Adam and James bring over some plastic bags, bulging with catch.

'Hey baby,' James says and gives me a kiss.

'No cod,' I say, and he grunts. 'There's still tomorrow.' He shrugs and turns to the esky.

'Don't mention the war,' Adam says. 'Check this out.' He opens one of the bags and I see a horde of hard-bodied crustaceans, blue-brown in the dying sunlight, rustling against each other. They have long, mottled pincers and I take a step back.

'Like giant prawns,' Charlotte says. 'The pot should be good now.'

'Are they alive?' I ask.

'Not for long,' Charlotte says. 'We're going to boil them. I've made thousand island dressing.'

Adam and James empty one of the bags into the pot. Charlotte gets plates for everyone and an empty bag for the yabby detritus. I grab a lemon quarter and wait. The first yabbies to come out have turned bright orange.

'Here,' James says. He twists the head off the cooked yabby and throws it in the bag and then peels the shell from the body. He hands me a body the thickness of two fingers. I dip it into the dressing then squeeze some lemon over it and take a bite. It's firm but not chewy; it has an earthier flavour than the sweet and salty ocean prawns I'm used to.

'Like it?' James asks.

'You can peel me a few more,' I say and he laughs. We eat instead of talking, peeling shells, passing the smaller bits of flesh to Rusty and sharing the thicker morsels between ourselves, dipping them in dressing and listening to bird calls in the quiet dusk.

Adam throws more yabbies in the pot whenever we run low. Finally, Charlotte drops her plate on the ground, kicks out her legs and exhales a contented sigh.

'That is the only reason I come here,' she says, turning to Dave. 'No yabbies, no Charlotte.'

—

The evening passes in units of beer. I count them: five, six, seven; after James has drunk fifteen, I stop tracking. Charlotte pulls out more and more bottles of red and white, who knows from where, and keeps filling up my glass. I don't stop her. Nor does Emma. I'm so drunk that when Rusty nudges my knee to go to bed, I gasp. I forgot he was there. I stagger to the tent as he follows by my side, his head bumping my knee. When I unzip the flap, Rusty walks inside, his tail down, then turns back to look at me, his eyes reflecting the blue-green camp lights.

'In you go,' I mutter and drop the flap. Walking back to the campfire, I step on uneven ground, lose my balance, and fall in what seems like slow motion. My hands hit the ground first, then my knees. I grip the cold dirt. There's no pain, and after rolling onto my left side, panting for a while, I stand up and return to my camp chair, brushing dirt from my trackies.

'Leila,' Adam calls from the other side of the fire, 'how well do you really know James?'

'What do you mean?' I cast around for my cup of wine and pick it up. It sloshes over the lip and trickles down my hand.

'Can't understand how a wanker like James picked up a city woman, that's all.' His cheeks are bright pink, eyes red and glossy.

James gives him a half-hearted shove. 'I can show you, mate, if ya want.'

They jab at each other, batting insults away with either a guffaw or derision. Emma and Charlotte spark up a quieter conversation between themselves.

Dave turns to me. 'James taken you hunting yet?'

Adam looks up. 'You're not a country girl until you've been hunting.'

'I don't think anyone wants me hunting,' I say.

Dave whoops, an ear-splitting noise. 'You're coming tonight,' he says. I stare at him, too drunk to laugh, to protest. I think of appeasement, I think of playing pretend. Yes. I will hunt. Sure. Let's do it. But they cannot force me, when the time comes.

'We're shooting roos,' Adam says. He burps, releasing a percussion of compressed air. 'You can sit in the back.'

'Nah, I'll drive,' I say, and all three men burst into fits of laughter. I join in as though I'm part of the joke. Then I drink more, kick my legs out straight so the fire warmth rolls over the top of them, and stare at the stars. The Milky Way swirls above and I see bright, juddering shooting stars, but it's just me rocking in my chair, jittery from the booze.

—

The truck is swerving but still hits every bump and hole. I don't want to be here, but I can't say so; this is where I must prove myself to James, because I've failed everything else. I swallow acid and clutch my stomach.

When the time came for the men to leave, I stood to go to bed, but James held my elbow and guided me to his ute. I felt malleable, unconcerned with what might happen to me, so I let him push me up into the back seat and tuck my legs in. My head lolled and rested against the cold glass window. The vehicle lurched as Dave jumped in the tray. Adam took the driver's seat; James in the front beside him, a rifle secured in one hand across his lap.

I'm hurled from side to side every time James says he spots something and Adam turns the wheel. In the tray, Dave mans the spotlight. Somehow, he moves it with precision despite how drunk he is.

'Over there!'

Adam eases off the accelerator and shifts into a lower gear. The engine drops into a low rumble. I grab the handle above my head and close my eyes. I can't see much of anything: it's all black, and while the spotlight on the truck lights up the land in front, mostly I see only the back of James's and Adam's heads. Then James is leaning out of the side window, the ute slows to a roll and there is a loud crack. The car stops and the men jump out, rushing to inspect their prey. I lean forwards and see gold shining eyes facing the headlights. They're small; smaller than Rusty's.

'Fuck.' James storms back to the ute. 'Just a fox,' he says.

'Did you hit it?'

He snorts. 'A hole in it the size of your fist. Intestines everywhere.'

I don't react, not at first, then I curl my fingers together and stare at my hand.

'You can do better than that,' Adam says to James as he gets back behind the wheel. We bounce through more scrub, more darkness. My stomach churns and I try to stem hiccups by pressing on my wrists; an old high-school trick taught to me before exams. I push harder and harder. It feels like we're driving in circles; everything in the spotlight looks the same. I don't know how we will find our way back.

We hear a faint tap on the back window and Adam slows down. There is complete silence in the cab as we inch forwards, the spotlight glancing off gnarled trees and tiny, white eyes that the men ignore. Then we see it; a kangaroo, standing stock-still, frozen in the hope it will be invisible. James leans out of the window; there's another crack. The animal falls with a thud and the men cheer, the sound filling the ute; Dave slaps the roof of the vehicle. Adam and James throw the doors open and James puts the gun on his seat. He peers at me.

'Come out and see.'

I walk to where the men stand, their heads inclined down. The kangaroo fur looks more silver than brown in the bright light; it lies with its face away from us and I'm thankful not to see any injury. But then James leans down and rolls the animal towards us, and there's blood, a mass of split pink tissue and chunky meat across the abdomen. I go to speak, to say, *I don't want to see that*, when what I mean is, *You've already killed him, leave him alone*, but I can't move, can't form words. I see James reach into the animal, his hand disappearing, and when it comes out, I still can't see it. It's like he's wearing a furry glove and that's when I realise the kangaroo was female and this is her joey, her baby. James hands it to Adam, who walks to the ute and slams the tiny thing against the bull bar.

I stare at the blood spattered on the grille, my teeth suddenly chattering, as Adam tosses the joey into the tray and Dave and James pick up the kangaroo and pitch her in the tray, too. Adam drives us home, Dave sitting in the back seat with me now, the men talking and fabricating, enhancing the story. The hunt becomes bigger, grander, with each re-telling, their parts in the action inflated. Adam's driving becomes that of a rally driver; Dave's eyes are as sharp as a hawk; James's shooting is better than a military sniper, even while shitfaced. They bray about the following night's hunt, how a roo that size will attract pigs. I think of Charlotte and Emma, whether they've seen their husbands this way, and I wonder why James sought to include me. I assume he thinks I'm soft; that I need toughening up.

When we exit the car, I cannot look at the tray. I walk to the tent and see Rusty pushing his nose through as I brush aside the flap, his nostrils flaring. I grab hold of him tightly to stop him running out, but find I can't quite release him even once I close the tent. I nuzzle against his silky neck. *You don't belong out there.*

—

I wake. I sit by the fishing lines. I drink. I take my pills. We eat. I drink more. The men leave again at night to hunt pigs, bags of yabby scraps in hand, stinking dead roo in the tray.

—

James wakes me early to pack the car. I stumble around, being of very little help. The eskies are wedged into ute trays, the tables and chairs folded down. Uncooked yabbies are packed in fridge bags, the tinny hauled into the scrub and left there for their next trip. The tents deflate, are shaken out and rolled up. I pack my small bag and place it in the back seat of James's truck. Rusty sits next to it, having rushed to the vehicle, lest we forget him. I avoid the front of the ute and the tray and climb into the passenger seat. Leaning over, I jostle the key in the ignition and start the truck, pushing the heat to high to warm up the cab.

Charlotte pauses by the window, and I roll it down.

'Nice to meet you,' she says.

'You too,' I say and then add: 'And Emma.'

'Do you have your phone? I'll give you my number.'

I reach for my bag. 'I don't think it's charged.'

'Don't worry.' She pats herself down and pulls out an old receipt. 'Got a pen?'

I find one in the glovebox, and she flattens the paper against the side of the car, scratching her number on it.

'If you feel like a coffee, or just getting out of the house,' she says, and then she leans in and gives me a brief kiss on the cheek.

'Thank you,' I say, touched by her kindness. Then I ask: 'Charlotte, do you really think there's ghosts at the farm?'

She winces. 'I'm so sorry about that. I hope I haven't worried you.'

'It's fine. I just wanted to know if you meant it.'

'Well.' Charlotte leans on the car door and a smaller ute pulls up beside us and honks. Dave leans over to the passenger window.

'Come on, Lottie,' he says. 'Stop gossiping.'

She waves him off and speaks quietly. 'I don't know. But look, the house was built during colonisation. So, I mean, at least in that sense it would be teeming with them.'

Dave honks the horn again and calls out: 'Come *on*, Lottie! Haven't got all-fucken-day.'

Charlotte rolls her eyes, but moves to the ute, calling to me, 'You did good!'

Emma waves from inside Adam's four-wheel drive, and I wave back. James gets in the car. We exit first, the other cars trailing behind us. We move as a loose convoy until we leave the unsealed road and reach the highway. Then we separate: our speeds vary, trucks intercept us, and we choose different routes home.

—

When we reach O'Connell, I say: 'I thought the camping trip was just hanging out. Fishing.'

'Too many beers?' James says.

'The kangaroo.'

'Oh, that.' We trundle on for a few moments.

'Why did you make me come?' I ask.

He blows out air. His face is lined from dehydration and dirty from dust. 'I thought you wanted to come.'

We drive up the road towards the front gate.

'You never told me that you hunted.'

Rusty bumps my ear from the back seat, and I squirm around, reach back and press the button to roll his window down. He sticks his head out into the rushing air.

'Sydney people don't hunt,' James says.

'Still,' I say. 'The joey.'

'We had to kill it,' James says frankly. 'It'd starve without its mother.'

He pulls into the farm driveway and stops at the gate; then he turns off the car, gets out, walks around to my door and opens it.

'I want to show you something.'

I get out; Rusty whines in the back seat, but James says to leave him. He opens the gate, and we walk along the fence line. The grass is messy and straw-like. We continue for a couple of hundred metres, and then I see it and pause.

Hanging upside down on the fence is a brownish grey form, its small head almost touching the earth, two feet bound together on the wire of the fence. Further down is a smaller animal, orange and brown. In the distance, I see more bodies dotting the fence that marks the perimeter of the land.

'Foxes and roos,' James says. 'They're a pest.'

'You do this?' It seems the work of a sadist.

'Dad and me. You have to keep the numbers down.' Hanging them on the fence deters the others, he explains. He has a responsibility to Matt's livestock. 'It's part of life,' he adds, irritated by my silence. 'They'd hunt us, if they could.'

I sit at the kitchen table with my laptop, looking out the bay window. Drizzle spatters the glass. Outside, Matt is visible in the distance, shifting cows to a paddock further away. Closer to the window, a pair of crimson rosellas alight on the rose bushes, searching for insects to eat. They seem completely at home. One flies to the ground and walks along the grass, poking its beak among the blades. It is not bothered by the rain.

Rusty is inside with me, stretched under the table and over my feet; he's lying on his belly with his face resting on his paws, a position I now understand to mean, *I'm happy to lie down, but if you want to go somewhere I can jump up in an instant.* When I look down at him, his eyes meet mine and the tip of his tail flickers, then his lids flutter into a light doze. He is not interested in the birds and their activities. Even if he was, I suspect most would be too quick for him; they can be in the air in a second or two, while land animals can do nothing but look into the sky. None of the birds I've encountered here are scared or fearful. They watch, they are occasionally inquiring, but they are not afraid. They do not second-guess themselves, do not question their instincts. If there is a threat, they launch off the ground, spread their wings and go.

I open Google and search for articles about why people hunt. The culling side of it, the wildlife management, makes a type of sense on a theoretical level, but that wasn't what I witnessed on the camping trip. I saw thrill; wild abandon; a chase for the largest prey.

I read some research that insists hunting is a primal instinct for humans, and that bringing home the most dangerous animal is a display of virility, much like the vibrant feathers on the male peacock. A hunter who can provide the most food for their offspring is the safest bet for a family. Regardless of whether they live in cities or not, men have an instinct to kill and protect. Other experts are less encouraging of this idea. One article is scathing of what it calls 'trophy hunting': the kind where the hunter poses for a photo with his kill. A study found that the smiles in these photographs exhibit more pleasure when the prey is large and carnivorous, a type of pleasure that mimics sexual satisfaction in the brain. The thought makes me feel ill. I recall the photograph on display in the foyer of James with the dead pig, and feel relief that he was not smiling at all.

I change my search terms to *animals hunting*. Is hunting so unusual? After all, humans are just animals, when you get right down to it.

I find a National Geographic compilation on YouTube. A sombre narrator explains the tactics of an orca hunting a penguin in Antarctica. The orca springs up from the water through holes in the ice, after tracking the penguin from beneath. It appears ahead of the scuttling penguin, one eye fixed on the small creature. This seems a taunt, somehow, torturing the little bird that cannot fly. The icebergs are diminishing, and the penguin has fewer and fewer options – the only escape is into the water, but then what? It cannot outswim the beast.

I get up, inching my feet out from beneath a sleeping Rusty, and wrap my dressing gown around me. Fill the kettle, then stand at the bench waiting for it to boil. My eyes glaze over as the water churns and bubbles. Steam hums as the heat increases, the sound joining with the rain on the tin roof and forming a tonal buzz. It reminds me of the morning radio growing up. Mum would get up at five am and turn on the news. I'd hear the flat newsreader's voice and the program's synthetic jingle wafting into my bedroom, the words droning but unformed, and I'd wonder why Mum wanted to spend more hours awake, more hours being unhappy.

When I'd enter the kitchen, she would always be standing at the sink, drinking coffee; I'd sit at the small dining table, eating cereal or finishing up last-minute homework. The news would invariably frustrate her, and she'd spit swear words in Arabic. It was easy enough to ignore. But once, I came into the room and saw her mouth moving, yet there were no words. She began slamming dishes and cups into cupboards, crying uncontrollably. I said, quietly, *Mumareyouokay*, all the words running nervously together, and she turned and pointed a stabbing finger at me and yelled something I couldn't make sense of. Her face was slack, her eyes saw through me. I shrank back, and in that moment a dish flew at my face, hitting my forehead. It tumbled to the ground, cracking on the floor, and I *ran*.

The bruise took a week to fade. That kicked off a new phase of her wrath: violence. She'd insist afterwards that she just snapped, but I knew it was purposeful, or at least premeditated, because she hurt me in less visible places: arms, legs, stomach, places covered by my school uniform. There was no way to escape it. I couldn't launch into the air, fly away from her. Mum and I danced through icebergs for most of my life, she with one eye on me while I swam in her waters, trying to survive.

Depleted, I lean down and look at Rusty; his eyes are closed now, and his lips twitch. He shudders and lets out a little whimper, and I hope he is not dreaming of being chased by some predator, larger and cleverer than him.

—

Rapping echoes through the house, and Rusty jumps up and runs to the front door. I take a final sip of coffee and save the document I'm working on. I tried to write down the memories of my mother's rages – perhaps there was a way to understand them – but instead found myself googling her type of cancer.

I was angry to discover multiple experimental treatments for pancreatic cancer, but then remembered they weren't available twenty years ago. I walk slowly to the door – the rough driving from the camping trip and my drunken stumble bruised my legs and jumbled my insides. I'm taking more painkillers than James would like, I know that, but he's not around to see.

A tall, broad outline is visible through the spyhole. Matt must be finished. I open the door.

'Hey, Matt. How are you?'

'Good, love.'

I look closely at his face; compare it to the face from the conifers, what I can conjure of it. As I told James, the beard was cut differently. Matt seems larger, somehow, and thicker; his features are stronger. It couldn't have been him. Even from a distance, the face did not match his.

'Come in. Coffee?'

'Nah, that's all right, I've had me coffee today. Just letting you know I've finished moving the cows. I'm just gonna separate the steers and then I'll be off.'

'Has the rain stopped?'

'Near enough.'

I'm relieved; the cows are a noisy bunch. Despite feeling unsettled by the quiet, the foghorn blaring of the cows has somehow been worse. I gesture for him to come inside anyway and he gingerly steps into the foyer, removing his hat. Rusty sniffs his shins and shoes excitedly and Matt reaches down to scratch the dog's head. 'Hello, mate, I've missed ya,' he says, and Rusty taps his front paw on Matt's knee.

'I have a favour to ask you, actually,' I ask, smiling, hoping to build a rapport with him. Enough that he forgets my initial reserve, at least. 'There's been a pretty bad smell, way out the back. James said it's probably the septic. I'm not sure if that's part of your job, but I wondered if you could look at it for me.'

Matt shakes his head. 'Septic out the back?'

I pull on gumboots, discarding my dressing gown. 'If you go up along the river and then cut in parallel to the house, it's there. We could walk straight up the back too, I just don't know if there's a decent path through, and it takes about half an hour.'

Matt rubs his chin. 'That's not where the septic is. No septic is half an hour from the house.'

'Maybe it's quicker if we find a more direct route?'

'Nah. I've been around this property for a while. I'll show you the tank.'

He opens the front door for me, Rusty bolting out like he's never seen daylight before, and I follow him round the side of the house, where Matt points to a small garden bed running alongside the wall.

'Can you see the manhole there?'

I squint; there is a smooth, black shell, flush with the ground. We walk over and Matt taps it with his foot. It has one large round lid secured with screws and two small caps on either side. Rusty sniffs around it and then trots away to piss in the grass.

'This is the septic. They planted flowers either side to help with the smell, but it's fully sealed. Did you say there was a leak?'

I stare at the lid. 'This is the septic tank?'

Matt nods.

'This tank looks fine.'

'Yeah, it is. The drain field is over there.' He points down-hill. 'With the rain lately, it might be saturated. Step back and I'll check it for you. Any gurgling in the pipes inside?'

I shake my head, and he settles onto his knees and unscrews one of the smaller lids. 'You can take these off without a screw-driver. It's easy to check the levels.'

I stand uncertainly. 'Thank you.'

'That's all right.'

The sewage smell hits me the moment the lid's off and I try not to gag. Matt seems unaffected and peers down the hole.

'Nope, you're fine. Come and have a look here.'

Hesitant, I step forwards.

'Come on. Don't be a bloody city girl.'

I laugh and cop another round of the stench. He gestures to the hole, and I look down into an unholy sight. Scum is spattered over a wide tube, and water is visible. Toilet paper floats in the mix.

'See how the water is close to the top, but the tank isn't full? That's how it's supposed to look. If you take this lid off and it's fuller than that, then you've got to worry. But on the other side, there's another outlet – hang on, I'll show you.'

I try to look appreciative as he screws the second small lid off.

'Check this out,' he says. 'The waste comes in here, so check this side too, in case it's blocking the access into the middle tank. It goes from here, to the middle, to the far side, then out into the drain field. If your drains are full, always check this. Sometimes it's just a basic blockage. Get a big stick and unblock it.' He screws the lids back on and stands up, brushing his hands on his pants. 'Saves a couple of hundred bucks on a plumber.'

I stare down at the tank, trying to remember if James told me the septic was up the back. Didn't he tell me that?

'Thanks, Matt. I really appreciate it.'

'No problem at all.'

'Do you think you could come up the back with me and look at the thing I found? Where the smell is? It smelled different to this. And the tank I found was stone and concrete.'

He blows air out of pursed lips. 'I've got to move the steers and get to town. Half an hour's walk, you said?'

I nod.

'Let's drive it.'

The seats in Matt's ute are leather and cracked from sun exposure; the vehicle feels like it's held together by paper clips and tape, but that doesn't stop him from driving at a breakneck speed through the back paddock, bashing through metre-high grass, hitting potholes as we go. Rusty is bouncing in the tray. I can see his face in the side mirror; he's facing the wind, his mouth open, tongue out, thrilled. I grasp my stomach and grit my teeth; I'm in no position to ask Matt to slow down. This is why James drives as he does: one hand on the wheel, the car rattling over every piece of debris, braking heavily at the last moment. It's just another country thing. Matt chatters away, pointing out the shed he wants to fix up for the Crawleys, when they let him.

'So many jobs I could do around this place. Make it even nicer, 'specially the landscaping,' he confides. 'But they're private. Old school. Now James is here full time, he might let me make some changes.'

'I'm sure he'd like that.'

Matt pulls up. 'This the tank?'

I look ahead. The concrete disc is there, visible above the ground. We exit the car and draw nearer; there's no rotting smell now, just the scent of grass.

Matt walks around the structure, his boots squelching in the mud. 'Wet enough.'

'What do you think it could be?'

Matt doesn't say anything; he circles it a few times, looking back towards the house, frowning. He leans over the tank, feeling around the edges.

'There's no way to open it,' he mutters to himself, his thumbs running along the side.

I stand next to him and point at the marking on it. 'Is that a logo for tanks or something?'

His eyes flicker over to it and then he shakes his head. 'I don't recognise it. But this is old. Looks like a well that's been sealed up.'

'A well?'

'Yeah. It's basically a bore.' He gives me a swift smile; I can tell Matt loves explaining things. 'But without the electricity.

They all switched to bores with pumps once they could. You said there was a smell?'

'An awful one. Could an animal have crawled in there somehow and died?'

'It'd have stone walls all the way down. I don't know how an animal could get in.' He slaps the concrete with an open hand; it's so thick, it swallows the noise. 'And they go down for hundreds of feet. Even if there was something dead at the bottom, there's no way you'd smell anything.'

He stands with his hands on his hips, and we both stare at the well.

'There you go,' he says, finally. 'Bit of a mystery for ya!'

I laugh. The way Matt speaks takes the confusion away. It's a well. Maybe there was a smell, maybe not. Bit of a mystery, that's all.

'Thanks Matt,' I say. 'I'm sorry to waste your time.'

'Not at all, love. Happy to help.'

We get back in the truck. When Matt starts the engine, Rusty leaps up into the tray and pushes against the side, ready to face the wind. Matt spins the wheel, and the ute turns around, leaving muddy skids in the ground.

'Do you go hunting?' I ask.

'Hunting?'

'I went camping with James and his mates on the weekend. They were hunting kangaroos. And pigs.'

'Oh yeah? Where'd ya go?'

'Past Bourke. Warrego River.'

'Popular there.' He scratches his chin, and we hit a massive pit, the vehicle vibrating. 'I'm not too into it meself. But I didn't grow up here, I moved here after school.'

'James said he has to cull kangaroos and foxes here a lot.'

Matt nods. 'Gotta protect the livestock. Roos can be aggro. You don't want 'em around the cows. Or Rusty, even. And foxes are a bloody pain.'

'Right.' We bump along. 'So, people grow up hunting, here?'

'Hunting, fishing. Would've been their main entertainment,' Matt says. 'They probably didn't get TV until late, who knows.'

'Maybe it was better for them, being outside. I grew up in front of the TV. Don't think it did me any favours.'

'You're all right, love.' Matt turns the wheel, and the vehicle swerves sharply and comes to a stop. I flop around under the seatbelt and wince at the pain.

'Here we are.' Matt points past the house, down to the front paddock. 'You see the calves drop?'

'Calves?'

'Yeah, didn't ya notice?'

'We got back late yesterday.'

'Go take a look, I only moved 'em one paddock over. If you go down the driveway you'll see 'em. They're beauties.' He's smiling like a proud dad.

I assure him I will, thank him again and get out of the ute, walk around the back and drop the tray, so Rusty can jump down, which he does reluctantly.

Matt peels away, waving through the driver's window, the truck heading towards the front paddock. What he said about the hunting makes sense. It's something James was brought up with, not something he nurtured in secret because he likes to hurt animals. It's community out here; it's how men bond. And James has shown me, over and again, how caring he is. How much he cares for me. There's nothing to worry about.

I pull off my gumboots and clap them together to dislodge the mud. Then I scoot Rusty inside, the dog sulking, tail down, and close the door against the chilly, wet air.

—

When James walks in the front door, I call out, 'In the kitchen!' He enters to a table set with a roasted lamb leg, spicy, crunchy potatoes, and a salad. A small ceramic jug is filled with fatty gravy. The smells are glorious: lemon, garlic, rosemary. The lamb skin, stippled with fat, is crispy with a rich tamarind hue. I have a whiskey poured. All of it was an enormous effort and I feel like I could double over from cramps and exhaustion, but I want the feeling of the camping trip, that we are a couple in love, to last.

'What's this?' James is impressed, and I hand him the whiskey and give him a kiss, something I haven't initiated in a long time.

'You deserve a tasty meal,' I say.

He sips the whiskey and pulls me in close for a hug. 'This is more than that,' he says. He releases me and removes his tie, hangs it over his chair, then unbuttons his collar. I look at the slightly sunburned triangle at the top of his chest. There's something attractive about it, primal: the freckles, tough skin, the cleft between his collarbones.

We take our seats and serve up. Rusty rests his nose on my knee from under the table and I slip him a piece of lamb surreptitiously. Something about seeing his eager, jabbing snout tickles me.

'Delicious,' James says as he pours gravy over the meat.

'I love lamb,' I say. 'But I feel guilty eating it.'

'Me too. It took me a while to get over the fact that we were eating my pets.'

I fumble with my fork, dropping the meat on the plate. 'Pets? You didn't name them.'

'I did. God, what did I call them?' He rests his chin in his hand, looking embarrassed as he pushes meat and potato together. 'Fluffy. Snowy. Curly. I didn't know they were the same thing as the meat on my plate.'

'When did you first twig?'

'When Dad took me to kill one.'

We eat in silence for a bit.

'How old were you?' I ask.

James squints. 'Six or seven, maybe?'

'Jesus. That seems young.'

'Not out here.' He crunches on a potato. 'I was the only kid too, so I needed to be able to help. Sheep are a pain, there's always so much work to do with them. We mostly had cattle.'

'How did he tell you that's what was going to happen?'

There's a lull then; a pause long enough that I think James doesn't want to answer. He is looking down at his plate. Rusty nudges again at my knee; I slip him a potato and wince while he noisily crunches and licks his lips.

'He told me it was time I learned.' James takes a sip of whiskey. 'We went and picked a lamb. Hung it up. Slit its throat. Left it in the kill shed for a day or two to relax the meat.'

I look down at my plate.

'Don't feel bad,' James says. 'It's fairly humane. And we ate every part of the animal. After a while it felt natural, in a way, part of nature. Dad's attitude was the same no matter what we were doing on the farm. Whether it was butchering or hunting or culling or rinsing. Just: *Get up, it's time you learned.*' James's expression is distant. 'Fixing fences, taps, emptying the grease trap, snaking drains. Dad taught me everything.'

I can't imagine having a father so involved with day-to-day activities. A father who not only teaches you skills but also about life and death. My father left as soon as my mother told him she was pregnant. She'd rant about him, then turn her fury on me, enraged that I wasn't the thing that would make him stay.

'You must really look up to him,' I say, thinking of John's austere manner, seeing it now as an air of discipline and practicality. Solidity. 'It must have been great having your dad guide you like that.'

'It was hard. He and Mum relied completely on me. They ran a tight ship. I couldn't afford to fuck up.' His expression takes on a boyish look, and I feel the need to comfort the sudden appearance of this child.

'I'm sure you never have. They'd be so proud of you.'

He finishes the last potato on his plate. 'Baby, that was amazing.'

'You look tired. I'll clean up,' I say, getting up and gathering the cutlery, the plates. Rusty scrambles out from under the table, looking at me, tail wagging.

James scrapes back his chair and stretches. He comes over to me and gives me a kiss. 'I'm going to lie on the couch. I'm cooked.' He points at Rusty. 'Don't give the little beggar any food.'

I wait until he's out of the kitchen before I cut off a chunk of lamb and feed it to Rusty. I stare at him while he eats: *Don't tell anyone about this.* The tip of his tail quivers and he dips his head, then trots to the living room. I stack the dishes in the dishwasher and wipe down the bench. When I go into the living room, Rusty is asleep, stretched out on the rug; James is snoring lightly on the couch. The fire is stoked, casting a soft orange light over the walls. I pick up a throw and tread quietly to the couch, lie down next to James and sling the blanket over us.

The next day, I rise late. Rusty follows me from room to room as I make toast and then put on a load of laundry. He bumps my knee with his nose repeatedly. Walking together has become a routine he depends on, but I'm still aching from camping and yesterday's drive with Matt. Every so often a twisting cramp stops me, and I lean against the wall until it passes.

But Rusty doesn't know about muscle soreness or stomach cramps or tiredness. He only knows that I'm here and we should walk together. I say, 'Just a short one today,' and he skitters to the front door, sneezing, tail flapping. I open it, and he trots to my muddy gumboots and taps them, then looks at me.

'You're too clever sometimes, you know that?' I tell him. The rain from yesterday has eased, and thick, dark grey clouds hang low in the sky. The colour somehow makes the paddocks look greener. There's been more rain than I expected out here, and James comments favourably on it each time, checking the rain gauge enthusiastically. *Twenty-five mil today,* he'll say. *Not bad.*

Gumboots on, I click my tongue and point to the driveway; a new direction for us. Rusty looks towards the river but I shake my head and he relents. When we reach the drive, the wet grass turns to slick gravel. Going down the rise is tricky, and I take it slow. Rusty is a patient companion; though I know he'd love to pick up the pace, he prefers to walk together.

We reach the flat after five minutes and continue on. I can see the cows in the near distance and crane my neck, hoping to spot the calves. The June day is cold, chilling my nose and ears, but I relish the feeling of warmth in my muscles and coolness on my skin. We pass by gums and eucalypts and conifers; on the ground, clutching at the fence wire, are little purple flowers atop a weedy base.

We round the corner to reach another straight, and a gentle moo kicks off a cacophony. We're near the paddock fence now, and a cow has caught sight of me. A few of them wander over to stare at us, tails flicking. More cows join them, blinking. Rusty prances in front of them, head up, sniffing. And a few metres away, with their mothers, I catch sight of the calves: little brown bodies with white heads and chests, tangled up in their mothers' legs. One cow lowers her head and licks her calf; another calf catches sight of us and extricates itself, galloping towards the fence. Its bum bucks in the air as it goes, landing goofily on all four hooves.

'Oh my god,' I mutter as more calves follow. They're fluffy and excitable, like overgrown puppies. They jump around and wag their hairy tails. Their mothers watch them, and me, coming closer to the fence. The calves' big round eyes roll between Rusty and me, drinking in our strangeness. Rusty walks up and down the fence, sniffing every cow and calf.

I lean forwards. 'Hi,' I say, unable to keep the wonder out of my voice. 'Hi, babies, you're so beautiful.' I feel intensely guilty for not being a vegetarian. One calf pokes his pink nose through a hole in the fence wire and I restrain myself from patting his snout.

'How old are you?' I ask him, entranced. 'Are you a big boy now?' His mother gives him a warning moo and he retreats. The rest of the calves lose interest and trot back to their mothers, and Rusty follows along the fence, barking; he wants to play with them. The cows bellow in response, and Rusty dashes back to me, tail between his legs, ears flat. A calf latches onto his mother's teats and drinks, and the mother cow stands and stares into the distance. I can't help but anthropomorphise the look of weary duty on her face, and a surge of feeling – of respect and empathy and recognition – engulfs me. Rusty coughs.

'I know, I know,' I say, scratching behind his ears. 'They're not as cute as you.'

Satisfied, Rusty turns to walk back the way we came. I follow him, looking back at the animals, sad to leave them. The cows wander away from the fence and return to their loose group, surrounding their babies; protecting them in this unusual world they've been born into.

—

Back at the house, it's quiet and lifeless. Charlotte's words – *There are ghosts* – come back to me. What seemed outlandish among company doesn't feel so crazy alone today. The house feels to me like another dimension, an unnatural place. Inside its walls, it's harder to breathe, to relax. Yet I haven't experienced any strange events for a while. Maybe it was always me.

I hang out the laundry and feed Rusty and do some basic cleaning. After that, my stomach cramps badly enough that I move to the sofa, stuffing cushions all around me so everything is spongy. I open my laptop and type, recording the events that have bewildered me. The whispering from the attic. A long-sealed well that smells horrific – but only to me, and not all the time. An unknown face watching me at the river. The scream. The attic door. The snake, which may or may not have disappeared. Black letters fill the white page on my screen. I read them back. Do I believe these things happened just as I experienced them? Is that rational?

But they did happen.

'Hey.' James leans against the living room doorframe. He's slightly dishevelled, and the bags under his eyes are dark. There's a prickly shadow on his face; he needs to shave.

'You look tired.'

'Long day. And Dad called to check on progress with everything.' He squeezes his eyes shut and rubs his temples.

'With the farm jobs?'

He crosses his arms. 'Yeah, a few things.'

'Did he put a bit of pressure on or something?' I've not seen James look this tired before.

'It doesn't matter.' He falls silent.

I check the time. It's after six. 'Dinner?'

'Please.'

We walk into the kitchen, and I take yesterday's lamb leg from the fridge. I shave slices of meat from the bone and heat it up quickly in the microwave, then toss it in some salad and drizzle some olive oil on top. James takes the plate and inspects it, then slowly eats.

'Hey,' I say. 'Remember what Charlotte said? About this house being haunted?'

'Mmmm?' James sticks his fork through a pale cherry tomato.

'Well, I had an idea for a book, finally. Maybe weave in some history about the house.'

'A book about what?'

'A sort of mystery novel. About a house that's haunted – or at least, the people in it are.'

He sniffs. 'Don't you think you should focus on something lighter? Less macabre?'

His reaction disappoints me; I expected him to be supportive. My mouth opens and closes a few times as I struggle to work out how to respond.

'I thought you wanted me to write.' I glance down at my plate and mutter, 'Isn't that why we're all the way out here, anyway?'

'I do. Just not something so depressing.' He looks at me and says, with a sudden heat, 'You *know* why we're out here.'

I look down at my plate again. I run his reasons for moving out here through my head. I could recover. I could write. He could work full-time in his hometown. What makes him angry about that? We both fall silent. The intimacy of last night's dinner is gone. I think of the book idea I spent the afternoon pondering, the odd events I've experienced here and feel tempted to believe that maybe I am crazy, but I'm not going to take James's side against myself. I'm not in the wrong here. I'm not being difficult.

I feel my blood pressure increasing, thudding in my ears. I want to push for a confrontation, find out what's pissing him off. I'd rather know; but I hold back, telling myself he's tired from work, under pressure with the farm, and I can't litigate everything he says and feels. Did I always do this? Was he always this moody? It's difficult to remember. When we met, in those heady early days, we'd debate and argue and persuade, and he seemed to love those qualities in me. He'd been so much more agreeable, or at least, we seemed to agree much more often.

Try again. Get this right. Fix it.

'It won't be depressing. I promise. And I'm making friends. Charlotte gave me her number.' I reach for my bag where it sits slumped on a dining chair and pull out the scrap of paper to show him. He'll be pleased I've forged a connection with his mate's wife. I won't be so dependent on him; one less thing for him to worry about. I won't be stuck inside all day. I won't be depressed.

His fork clatters onto his plate and he wipes his mouth with a paper serviette.

'So, is it true?' I ask. 'Do people really think this house is haunted?'

'How could it be true?'

'I don't know. It's just that Charlotte said –'

'I know what Charlotte said. Bloody hell. She was drunk. She's an idiot.' James stands and scrapes his food into the bin. He hasn't eaten much. I stifle a twinge of panic at the waste. I've never let edible food go into a bin. I wouldn't have survived my years at home if I had.

'I thought she was your friend,' I say.

'Dave's my friend.' His back is stiff, his tone flat. 'Charlotte's just his wife.'

He rinses his plate in the sink, and I'm taken aback by this characterisation of the ebullient woman he introduced me to. *Just a wife.*

'There's nothing to it, then?'

James opens the dishwasher and groans. It's stacked full; I forgot to run it last night. He jostles items around, the crockery clinking loudly against the glassware, finds a spot for his dishes then shoves the door closed.

'This house is two hundred years old. One of the first properties here. My family practically founded this place. People gossip; you shouldn't listen to it.'

He turns on the dishwasher. 'Listen, I've got more work to do tonight. I'll be in the study.'

I watch his back, straight and tense, as he leaves. Rusty whines from somewhere beneath the table, and I lean down and see his glossy brown eyes peeking at me. I open the bin and pull out the lamb James threw away and hand-feed it to him, piece by piece. He sniffs the meat carefully, then licks it; satisfied, he swallows each morsel whole.

'That's it, that's all I've got,' I say, showing him my palms.

Rusty clambers out from under the table, tail wagging, and stares at me. He trots to the bin and sniffs, then to the fridge and sniffs. He's already had his dinner but must be desperate for the taste of real food. I grab my phone and search *safe food for dogs recipes*. I go to the fridge and pull out the lamb bone, still with plenty of meat on it, and place it in a saucepan. I grate in some carrot and broccoli and apple, then add some rice. Fill the pot with water and let it simmer. The fat from the lamb forms globules on top and the smell overpowers the room. Rusty lets out an excited whine, his front paws tapping the floor.

When it's ready, I take out the bone and pull the soft meat away. My fingers feel gummy from the tallow, a thick coating that reminds me of cooking with my mother and my aunts, before she fell out with them. My mother's sisters taught me how to roll lamb and rice into vine leaves, how to season and cook shawarma, how to make spinach pastries. Lamb was our favourite meat, until it became too expensive. One time, a meal – shredded chicken, minced lamb, buttery vermicelli noodles, chickpeas and rice, a memory that still makes my mouth water – turned up on our front step, but whatever my mum did, my aunts never reached out to us again.

I add the lamb meat back into the rice and vegetable mixture and then spoon some into Rusty's bowl. He circles it, impatient for the food to cool. I seal the rest in Tupperware and put it in the fridge. Finally, the hot steam dissipates, and Rusty gobbles the meal in seconds. I pour dishwashing detergent on my hands and scrub to get them clean.

—

In the morning, Rusty and I move about the house, slow and lazy. Wet weather turns Rusty off walking, and I'm tired and sore from the past couple of days' activities. After breakfast, I forage in the bedroom for pain pills, pop them from the sleeve and carry them to the bathroom. I scoop water into my mouth with the pills, swallowing hard. They scrape the back of my tongue, leaving a sour flavour. I sit down on the bed again, breathing gently, my hand pressed on my surgical scar.

The doctor might say the pain could be all in my mind, but the pills work. I stay motionless on the bed for some time as I wait for them to blunt the burning cramps. Then I pick up the hot water bottle from the end of the bed and make my way to the kitchen. Boil the kettle, then pour steaming water into the bottle. The rubber warms up instantly and I hug it to my chest. Rusty is already there, curled up under the table. I nudge him with my foot, and he immediately rolls onto his back, exposing the silky white hair on his belly. I drag my foot back and forth on his chest, which he loves, then wedge the hot water bottle between my stomach and the table and launch Google on my laptop, waiting for it to slowly load. The house is bloated with silence.

I delete the tabs on pancreatic cancer and hunting, and search for the history of the O'Connell region instead. It's part of Wiradjuri Country, one of the largest First Nations. In 1813, white settlers arrived to colonise the region, and Bathurst was established in 1815. By 1824, the colonisers' refusal to understand Indigenous customs – and their desire to own what cannot be owned, to conquer what did not belong to them – led to violence, cruelty and death.

The O'Connell hamlet was used as a thoroughfare between Bathurst and Sydney, with housing built as early as 1822. The pub was erected in 1870. Over time, many of the farming families subdivided their land, sold the blocks for expensive sums, and affluent city people moved in to build their country homes.

I search the address of the Crawley property next. A database listing its proposed value is the first result. I comb further, finding a site listing the owners of local property titles. Only the name Crawley has ever been attached to the house; the only other results are stock records from the 1900s. I search *Crawley surname meaning* and *Crawley ghost stories* and Google tells me the name means 'crow' and 'a clearing in the woods', and that crows can be portents of death, or just about anything. The ring of trees and its cleared grass does make me wonder.

I pause, not entirely sure what I'm looking for. A website that neatly explains Charlotte's comments would be perfect, though wholly unrealistic. It could have been drunk gossip. But her reaction by the campfire still bothers me; she was emphatic before she quietened down. In the sober morning before we left, she blamed the age of the property, but she didn't take it back. It's the *why* of it all; why did Charlotte think ghosts were attached to the farm? Did something happen when they were building the house?

Picking up my phone, I scroll through my messages, stopping when I reach James's mother. I click on her name and open our message history. There were a few messages sent to me in Coogee when we decided to move to the farm: information on local attractions and businesses she recommended, including general practitioners and gynaecologists she'd worked with before retiring. I'd acknowledged each message with a heart emoji, staring down at them in the dead of night while I couldn't sleep. But nothing since then.

I could call Patricia. Taking a keen interest in the house would surely be something approximating her main interest of family, and it could give us some common ground. It would give her the opportunity to teach me something; besides, the best stories and most useful information always come from people. It's the most effective strategy when you're working to change a business or roll out a project: to find out what's going on, or how things are done, you talk to someone. People contain a complex assortment of history, memories and small details that you can't find on a desktop, things that help you work with them rather than against.

And perhaps I could reassure her and John that James was doing his best, despite the long list of farm chores that were still to be completed. I press her name and put the phone on speaker. There are a few clicks and then nothing. I look at the coverage – no bars today. I go to the study and pick up the old landline on the desk.

'Hello?' Patricia's cadence is measured and stately; if she'd been British, I'd have described her as posh.

'Hi Patricia.' I shift in the desk chair. 'It's Leila. I'm sitting here in the study, enjoying the view. How are you?'

We exchange pleasantries, Patricia inquiring about James and the house, and I tell her my favourite Rusty idiosyncrasies: the way he loves resting his nose on my feet, and how he follows me from room to room, and nudges me at the same time each morning to ask for a walk. She says, 'Oh really, he was a terrible working dog, such a disappointment,' and I change tack and ask about the weather on the South Coast.

'Is the hot water holding up?' Patricia ignores the weather question, seeming to assume I'm masking a maintenance call with small talk. 'That main shower head could use replacing. The hard water leaves so much calcium that it blocks the holes.'

I wonder whether this is a hint to install a new one. 'Everything seems to be working.'

'You can always scrub it with a mix of bicarb and lemon juice. Very effective.'

'Great. I'll try that. But actually, I was calling to ask you about the history of the house.'

'The history of the house?' Patricia's voice rises slightly.

'I thought you'd know a lot about it.' I hope the flattery isn't too transparent.

'Why would you think that?' Patricia's voice fades slightly and I waver; her altered pitch conveys a boundary overstepped.

'I just mean – you've lived here for so long and know so much about the region. One of James's friends mentioned that the house has a lot of interesting old stories attached to it.' I force a laugh, try to lighten the conversation. 'She mentioned a ghost or two. I was thinking of writing a novel.'

'What an odd thing for her to say, and, if you don't mind, a very odd thing for you to call and ask me about.' Patricia's voice has returned to normal volume, but her tone has changed. I'm struck; she's offended

'Oh, I'm sorry. I just—'

Patricia cuts me off. 'Nothing to be sorry for.' She is brisk. 'I have to go, Leila. John and I are about to meet friends for lunch.'

'Well, it was nice to talk to you. We really appreciate you lending us the house.'

'You're welcome. Remember, bicarb and lemon.' Patricia ends the call. I stare at the phone for a moment, then laugh. There it is. All the bottled-up resentment of our not-quite mother–daughter relationship spilling out in one call.

I wriggle my shoulders to shake off the annoyance. I'm no closer to understanding what Charlotte was talking about.

Don't founding families like the Crawleys usually have a proud lineage? One they're keen to share? I have the uncomfortable feeling that perhaps Patricia no longer considers me one of them, and so their history isn't my business. My prior reserve has burnt a bridge. If Patricia was a leader in a business I was working with, I'd try again; failing to win her over would bottleneck the process. But it appears her problem lies with me, so backing away for now is the best option, until an opportunity arises to gain her trust once more. For now, I'll have to go around her.

—

The next day, more rain. I rummage in my handbag while James showers, the water in the ensuite beating a rhythm into the bedroom, out of sync with the rainfall outside. My fingers scrabble in the pockets and folds, grasping medication packets, keys, wallet, lip balm, tissues, random bits of paper, a roll of mints. The taps shut off and the shower door closes with a muted clang. I upend the bag, the leather sagging as I shake everything out onto the bed.

James walks to the dresser and pulls on underwear.

'What are you doing?'

'Looking for something.' Spreading the contents of the bag over the bedspread, I pick through it all. Nothing.

James disappears into the walk-in robe for a few minutes and then returns, dressed, sliding a belt through the loops of his trousers.

'Did you see where I put Charlotte's number? It was just a scrap of paper.'

His expression is blank; he shrugs and looks around. 'No. Have you seen my wallet?'

'Your bedside.'

I wait as he slips the wallet into his pocket and then slings a jacket on.

He looks at me. 'What is it?'

'I had the paper the other night. I showed it to you and then I thought I put it back in my bag. It's gone.'

'You can never find anything in that bag. It's got too much in it.'

The bag was my work bag in my former life. It fit my laptop as well as everything else: tampons, wallet, phone, keys, lunch and any other random purchases. The downside is that everything is engulfed by it. Suddenly I feel that perhaps he's looked through my bag before. If he found the zippered pills I keep in it, he didn't touch them. But I don't like the idea of him knowing they're there.

'You really haven't seen it?'

He shakes his head. 'Not since you showed it to me. You're meant to put your important things in one consistent place.'

I know he's right. We discussed that well before we came to the farm, because after the surgery, the fog that descended on my brain made me confused; I'd lose my keys, my purse, my phone.

'I'll get her mobile from Dave for you,' James says. 'Don't worry.' He kisses me goodbye.

Even though it's probably too soon to get in touch with Charlotte, I'm annoyed with myself for losing her number. I can't shake the feeling that nothing in this house is mine. Even the relationship I wanted to build with Charlotte; the house swallows it all.

I lie awake for the fifth night in a row in what has become routine: the Valium I take doesn't work, James's deep breaths indicate he's asleep, and I ruminate about everybody's bizarre responses to this house: Charlotte's, Patricia's, my own. Rusty wanders between different rooms – though never our bedroom – and then chooses a place to sleep, flopping on the floor, snoring instantly.

To pass the time in the darkness, I'm crafting a mental list of jobs I can ask Matt to help with. I can't bear the dangling door handles, the lack of security. The back door needs a proper lock installed. The attic room needs checking – there could be dead rodents up there, or something else. At night, on top of the scratching of the wall mice, I've heard slithering and clicking in the ceiling. When I asked if it could be the snake from the front steps, if perhaps it made its way inside after all, James said it was more likely to be a lizard coming into the roof cavity, away from the cold. He said not to worry, that it would chase away the mice. The notion of using wildlife for natural pest control seemed normal to him, but peculiar to me.

There are yard jobs too; not just repairing fences, but removing general junk, the hard rubbish piled up and left to rot against the garage. James's plan to dig a hole on the property for the junk – a sort of private tip – hasn't come to fruition, even though he's had two months to do it. I'd thought these were the regular jobs he did while he was out here on weekends, but maybe he just enjoyed Patricia's hospitality. Weeds have to be poisoned. The yard needs mowing and whipper-snipping. The grass isn't growing much now that it's winter, but it was tall to begin with. When I ask James about this, he says the ride-on mower needs a new tyre and battery but doesn't mention any plan to fix it. He is always at work, spending long hours in Bathurst, and on the weekends, we cook together, watch movies and he chips away at restoring the sandstone while I search for something new to read in the study's bookshelves.

I look at James's face. He looks so restful; in the morning he'll be restored, able to go to work, make a difference. What will I do? Sit in the kitchen, stoke the fires, and stare out the window, aimless. Annoyance flares with every minor house offence as I go about my mornings: an uneven floorboard catches on my socks, the old kettle shows new copper stains from the hard water, the water pipes rattle when I shower. The cold air pinches: my nose, feet and hands are never warm. I should have acclimatised by now, but I haven't. The logs for the fire leave splinters in my fingertips as fine as dandelion seeds, too small to remove. I wait, enduring the stinging red dots, until my skin pushes them out.

Am I bored? Is it as simple as that? I'm used to chasing praise, results, outcomes: existing has never been quite enough. Being alone with my thoughts is something I've avoided since my mother died. Distractions – a share house, boys, study, side jobs, weed, alcohol – were more than enough to propel me away from the silent, tense young girl of that home.

It's unfair that James has his purpose here and I don't. It's unfair that I'm not healing – physically or emotionally – like I expected. That I'm not falling in love with the farm, like we both hoped.

Everything, on both sides, seems unfair.

I'm spiralling, my chest tightening, heat rising. *Calm down.* I lean over and flick on the bedside lamp; James doesn't stir. I've come to believe an earthquake wouldn't wake him. I've collected a stack of books from the study, the oldest being *The Castle of Otranto*, filled with old English language, medieval curses and desperation to continue the familial bloodline. Reading it requires absolute focus, which usually tires me enough to sleep. I'm not sure if that's a compliment to Horace Walpole or not. I open the tome and squint down at the type.

There's a shifting noise and I look to the open doorway, expecting to see Rusty hovering there, but I don't see anything. I lean forwards, eyes trained on the hall in case he appears, his lean body swaying in line with his back hips. Sometimes he trots all the way to the door in the middle of the night, surging with a puppy-like energy at the worst possible time, wagging his tail and staring at me expectantly, like a walk might be forthcoming. But tonight, nothing. I return to the book.

Footsteps. My head shoots back up. That's not a Rusty sound. I sensed the weight in that sound. The floorboards creaked. It wasn't the gentle squeak of the house shifting at night, either. The boards were groaning under pressure. I call out.

'Hello?'

Running. *Running steps.* My skin prickles. The steps were distinct, loud, impossible to ignore. From wherever he is in the house, Rusty barks. It's enough for me. I shake James.

'Wake up.'

He murmurs but doesn't open his eyes.

'There's someone in the house.' I push him harder.

'What?' He sits up.

I point to the doorway. 'I heard someone. I called out, and they started running. You promised you'd check.'

He's out of bed. 'I know. Stay here.'

I watch him disappear down the hall. Barely breathing, I clutch at my phone, checking it for battery and coverage. One bar for both.

'Fuck.'

I plug it in to the charger and listen intently. Banging doors, lights switched on. James is checking each room. My every muscle clenches. Who would be in the house? That man? The person who screamed? Someone else?

Exasperation floods my body. This wouldn't be happening if the house was properly managed and secured. The tension from waiting pushes me into standing, and I stride out of the bedroom. Down the hall, light streams out from the living room. When I reach the doorway, I see James on the couch, patting Rusty, speaking to the dog in soothing tones. The animal is standing alert, stiff tail raised.

'James?'

He looks up at me briefly, then returns to massaging the dog. 'I didn't find anything.'

'You checked every room? Including the attic?'

I could swear he rolls his eyes, but it's hard to be sure with his head angled down.

'Not the attic, but everywhere else.' He taps Rusty on his flank and says, 'In your corner.'

The dog reluctantly trots back to the corner of the room, sitting upright, not quite letting go. I feel he's on my side, and I'm gratified by the loyalty.

James pats the couch. 'Sit with me.'

I perch next to him, straining to hear any further noise.

'I know this is hard for you, baby.'

I'm surprised by his softness. I experience a flash of memory: this is how he was when we first met. Compassionate. Understanding. Before the miscarriage, before this house, changed us. I've almost forgotten why I loved James in the first place; I keep telling myself it must be me, it's my fault, but he has been different, too.

'I didn't expect you to love being here, not straight away.'
He's gearing up for a pep talk; synapses flicker behind his
eyes. 'What you went through was traumatic. I don't claim to
understand, but I'm here for you. You need time to recover. Be
patient with yourself.'

I begin to shake; but not from cold, oh no.

James talks about the pregnancy loss gently, quietly. He tells
me he's proud of my strength, proud that I've come here, that
I'm coping as best as anyone could after such a disappointment.
That he's sorry for the loss of our baby, what we'd hoped and
planned for; and for the loss of my body, the failure I feel.
Then he tells me how sad he's been, how losing the pregnancy
affected him too, and how he's always pictured us as parents.
That he has hope, that things are not dire, that we can still
have what we planned for: a family.

'It will come back, Leila. You won't always feel like this.'

Gratitude seizes me unexpectedly, and tears roll down my
cheeks. He hugs me, tightly, and I bury my face in his shoulder:
the safest place I'd known, for a time. His arms around me
are stabilising, neutralising. I feel calmer, feel an echo of his
hope ripple through me. Then he is kissing me: first my forehead, then my cheeks. And then, with a little more force than
usual, my mouth.

I let it go on a while, searching for the intensity I'd once
marvelled at, striving for the attraction that bound us together.
I think of his skin, his neck, his broad shoulders and strong
hands. But nothing in my body responds. I try to conjure
memories of him inside me, the heat and need I once felt for

him. Instead, it feels like target practice; his tongue pushes further into me, and I can't help but notice his breath, the mildly fetid taste of unbrushed teeth. His hand reaches down to my vagina and I stiffen; undeterred, he paws at me, rubbing me in a way that makes me want to slap him. My lack of defence seems to convey enthusiasm to him; at the moment it crystallises in my mind that *I don't want this*, he pushes me down hard on the couch and climbs on top of me, panting. I stare at him for a moment in shock. He thinks this is good? Do I just let it happen, would that be easier?

His eyes are glazed, his cheeks pink. A flash comes to me: the trophy hunters, excited to dominate their game, the limp bodies of their kills at their feet; and everything screeches to a halt. I squeeze my legs together, push his chest with both hands, but he is far stronger than me, and he barely notices, his mouth wet, sucking on my neck.

'James.'

Nothing. The pantomime continues, and when he slides a knee between my legs, I react instantly.

'Get *off* me!'

He sits up and backs away, down the couch. His face is flushed, his hair mussed, his expression bewildered.

'Couldn't you tell I hated it?' It comes out before I can temper it; we both hear the revulsion in my voice.

He stands, his hands raised in surrender, and he lets out a sharp breath. 'I thought – you seemed to want to . . .' He trails off. He considers speaking again, his mouth opening, but then closes his eyes and shakes his head. I'm confused, and hot, the instinctive reaction of my body when in danger. I try to breathe slowly, to tamp it all down, remind myself, *There's no danger here.* Try to think of something to say to reverse the irreversible; to explain what even I don't understand. But each time I look at his face and go to speak, there are no words. James looks like he might cry; his face is flooded red. It's at this moment that I'm sure the next thing he says will be that he can't go on. That we're finished. And so, I wait, half in hope, half in terror, thinking he might finish this for the both of us.

'I'll sleep here tonight.' His voice is gruff, and he doesn't look at me. I wonder for a moment if I should offer to take the couch, as penance, then realise he doesn't want to hear my voice. I walk slowly to the door. Before I leave the room, I can't help but say something.

'I really am sorry.'

Not just about tonight, but about all of it. Ours is a sorry relationship, bound by an immovable grief, and I don't know how to steer in the change we need. We love each other, I think, but love can only take you so far. Maybe, sometimes, it takes you nowhere at all.

A week passes: a week of small talk and space. James doesn't touch me. He spends the weekend outside, chipping away at sandstone, patient as ever, trying to find the diamond amid all that rough.

—

There is a cloying scent: a spicy vanilla, almost as twee as the fragrance my schoolmates once washed themselves in. Impulse-branded deodorant infected every school bus trip, the girls spritzing themselves liberally before the ride home, in anticipation of the private school boys clambering on. The mix of smells made my head ache, fostering a lingering aversion to perfume.

This vanilla is familiar, but before I can grasp the memory it evokes, I feel a hand on my knee. A bearded face swims before me – it is a man, but I don't know who he is.

'What do you want?' I try to lean back, but the face follows; I look down and see a skinny leg poking out from a cotton skirt, a broad hand resting on the knee. The hand on my leg grips harder. I open my mouth to scream but my chest is tight, so tight.

My mother's voice tells me to shut up.

I'm in the farmhouse now, the vanilla smell stronger than ever. I run up and down the halls, opening every door, searching for a way out. Each door opens to a blank wall. I hear footsteps behind me, drawing closer. Seeing the steps to the attic, I bolt to them and begin to climb. My breathing becomes laboured, every inhale is a struggle; I'm suffocating, I realise, my body powering down. A hand grasps my leg and pulls me back and I shut my eyes, certain my pursuer has me, that this is the end. My body convulses, and then James's face appears before me, framed by streaming daylight.

'Leila? Leila, wake up.'

I open my eyes, the fragrance still strong in my nose. With consciousness comes the knowledge that the smell was my mother's favourite perfume, sprayed on before every date, every visitor. Why did I dream of it?

'You were trying to scream in your sleep.' He gets up from the bed and turns his back to me, fiddling with his tie in the mirror.

'Sorry.' I watch him straighten his shirt and shrug into a jacket. There's still no warmth between us, and even less to say.

He seems to know it too. The door slams behind him. I lie back down, exhausted, everything aching. Try not to think how our mornings used to be: entwined naked together, tugging on each other, each begging the other not to leave the bed.

—

Another morning. I wake early, earlier than James. Pour a glass of water and stand with it, staring out of the kitchen window, attempting to practise mindfulness. I absorb the mountains while I try to meditate. The sharp blue winter sky and streaks of white cloud are expansive, a message from nature that there are things bigger than me and my problems. Today, however, the ceaseless landscape feels smothering, like I'm deep under-water, being crushed by the pressure.

I need something to do if I'm going to stay here. Something to distract me. Spending hours in a cold farmhouse, waiting for James to come home, is objectionable. This isn't a life. These empty hours spent sleeping or staring at my computer or walking around the property with Rusty are going to drive me mad. I've seen what madness looks like. I know how it feels when it's flung at you.

When James wakes and enters the kitchen, I ask him to drive me to the Bathurst library. I have to get out of this house.

—

In reality, the library is different from its appearance online: its exterior is more charming, the red brick and white windows are well maintained, and there is a small pergola with a wisteria vine entwined around it. Inside, however, it's the same bright orange decor, grey carpet and patrons boasting a median age of seventy-two.

I approach the main desk. A woman clacks away on a keyboard, thick black glasses on her face, neck adorned by a busily patterned scarf. Her hair is threaded with silver and she wears bright red macrame earrings. I'm in skinny jeans, sneakers and a leather jacket, and I suddenly feel immature and underdressed. Until now, I dyed my hair on schedule. What for? Who for? James?

The woman looks up and gestures for me to step forwards.

'Good morning, how can I help?' She seems composed and in command; the library is her little territory. Her name tag reads *Amelia*.

'I'd like to join, please.'

'Absolutely.'

She asks the usual questions – name, date of birth, phone number, email, home address. Her eyebrows rise when I tell her where I live.

'Is that okay?' I ask. 'Am I too far out of town?'

Amelia gathers herself. 'You're in a different shire to Bathurst, technically. Not to worry. We welcome everyone.' She runs a plastic card through a reader and then hands it over. 'Are you looking for any books in particular?'

I glance quickly around the room. There are a few computers and plenty of bookshelves, but I don't know the most efficient way to begin.

'Actually, I wanted to research the property I'm living on.'

This time, Amelia can't contain her expression. Her mouth presses into a tight line, her eyes widening. She might be uncomfortable but I've no idea why.

'Do you know the property?' I ask.

Amelia nods her head and says simultaneously, incongruously, 'No, not really. Well. It's an historical property, so everyone knows of it.' She pauses. 'What sort of information are you after?'

'Older information about the people who lived there. Closer to when the house was built. So maybe marriage records? Or birth records?' I'm too nervous to ask about death records.

Amelia checks there's no-one in line behind me. 'Come to the office. Depending on the year, there are a few different places you can look.'

She lifts the counter next to her and gestures for me to walk through to the other side of the desk. I follow her into a tiny back room with two desks, a computer and a small fridge.

'Pull up a chair.' Amelia sits down at one of the desks. 'We can access the databases for births and marriages. We'll start with the microfilm.' She clicks her tongue as the first portal loads on the computer. I settle in next to her and wonder if Amelia enjoys working at the library. Was it always her dream to be a librarian in a small town? Every day would be the same, just with diminishing returns. Fewer and fewer people are reading.

'Here we go.' Amelia types the names Crawley and O'Connell into an archaic-looking search bar. Rows of headlines appear, surrounded by metadata; she clicks on one and a white box appears with tiny print.

'Edward Crawley, married to Harriet Crawley nee Avery, 1841,' Amelia reads. 'I suspect these were your founding relatives. The house was built in 1840.'

I stare at the names, but they mean little to me.

'Oh,' Amelia says, pulling up another record. 'He married again. In 1868. To a woman called Caitriona Byrne.'

'Could you do that back then?'

Amelia snorts. 'I think men could do whatever they wanted back then. If she wasn't meeting expectations.'

I like her cynicism. 'I suppose.' A thought strikes me. 'Or did his first wife die?'

Amelia executes a search for Harriet Crawley. 'No – her death notice is decades later.'

I feel strangely relieved for Harriet, a woman discarded but at least alive.

'A birth record here,' Amelia says. 'Francis Crawley, 1878.' She looks at me. 'Keep going?'

'Yes please,' I say. 'I'll just make a list of them all.' At least it gives me a place to start.

Amelia logs in to other databases, switching between programs with ease. She's like a human archive, knowing exactly where to look and how to bring up the records, these small collections of data that mark lives now long past.

A baroque font loads up; it is a small notice marking the marriage of Francis Crawley and Mrs Catherine Crawley in September 1908. James's great-grandparents. I nod for her to move to the next item. It's an October 1918 christening notice for William Crawley, announcing his mother as Mrs Catherine

Crawley and his father as Francis Crawley. March 1947 is a marriage notice: the little boy was grown and married. June 1955 brings another notice: the birth of James's father, John. September 1978 is the marriage notice for John and Patricia. And then, in February 1988, James's birth. I calculate the numbers in my head. For generations, the Crawleys only ever had one child, each of them years in the making.

'Well, there you go,' Amelia says. 'Does that give you what you need?'

'It does,' I say, though it doesn't really. Nothing here explains Charlotte's comments. 'What about death records?'

Amelia dutifully searches for the records and checks them all. 'They all seemed to live quite long lives.'

'Right.' I sit back. No unusual deaths. Nothing unusual at all, really. 'Well . . . is there a way to look at any news reports from back then?'

'We have the microfilm of Bathurst newspapers back to the 1840s,' Amelia says. 'Not every country library can say that.'

'Brilliant,' I say.

'Yes, well, we are Australia's oldest inland town.'

'I didn't know that,' I lie, smiling as Amelia peers at me through her glasses, her eyes magnified.

She's pleased. 'People forget that.'

'I won't.'

Amelia pauses to check the live security feed; there is no-one new at the front desk. She turns back to the computer and logs into another program, adds in the farm address and family name. A row of results come up from *The Bathurst Times*:

articles on stock sales, mostly. It seems the Crawley family were very successful at breeding cows, and occasionally sheep. Then Amelia says, 'Oh!' and clicks on an entry. A scanned newspaper clipping appears slowly on the screen and my eyes take a moment to adjust to the tiny rows of text.

'*Death at Crawley Farm.*' My heart flutters. I lean in closer and Amelia edges her chair away to give me more room.

'Is this what you're after?'

'I think so. A friend mentioned something and . . . I wanted to know more about it.'

Amelia zooms in and the text becomes clearer. In September 1918, Tilly Johnson, aged twenty, was declared dead, attended to by the local doctor in the bedroom at the front of the house.

'That's the main bedroom,' I mutter.

Amelia looks at me. 'Sorry?'

'Nothing.' The notion that there was once a dead body in the bedroom I'm sleeping in chills me. 'Who was she? A relative of the Crawleys'?'

Amelia points to the article onscreen. 'The housekeeper.'

'A housekeeper died in the main bedroom?'

Amelia pushes her glasses up on her face. 'Mm-hmm.'

'Why would the housekeeper be in the main bedroom?'

'Perhaps she was cleaning.'

'Miss Tilly Johnson, twenty, unknown cause. Farmer Mr Francis Crawley said they found her passed in bed when she failed to rise and prepare breakfast.' I point at the screen. '*In bed*. They've made the distinction.' I keep reading, but there's no further detail. 'She was so young.'

'Let's check other articles, in case there was a follow-up.' Amelia seems to be enjoying the activity; no doubt a welcome respite from dusting books and reading aloud to local pre-schoolers. But there's nothing else of interest.

'Did that help?' Amelia waits, her hand resting on the mouse, right index finger raised above the button, ready to click.

'I think so.' Given I had no idea what I was even looking to find, Amelia has helped immeasurably.

'It's an interesting property.' Amelia's voice softens and she clicks the mouse several times rapidly.

'People keep saying that to me,' I say. 'It's just difficult to get the history. I mean, I don't need to know everything, but I was sort of hoping to write a novel.' I feel I need to articulate my motivations, to justify her time. 'Maybe a story inspired by the place.'

'Was there anything else you wanted? More recent information?'

'No, this is great, thank you.'

Amelia gestures for me to stand. 'I've printed everything for you. We'll get them from the front.'

I sling my handbag over my shoulder and we shuffle out of the small space. Amelia stays behind the counter, while I cross to the public side. She picks up the printouts and hands them over.

'Thank you, Amelia.'

Amelia gives me a professional smile, no teeth. 'Pleasure. I'm always happy to help you with any research.'

I nod and smile, clutching the pages. Outside, I stand on the pavement and read over them again. *Death at Crawley Farm*. I stuff the papers in my bag, zip my jacket and walk up the street. The wind is frigid, and I regret not dressing more warmly. I pause at a coffee shop window: it's kitschy with mismatched chairs painted in bright colours – turquoise, yellow, fuchsia – and it looks warm. Inside are mums with prams, and sprightly, chatty retirees with white hair. A waiter comes past with a plate of enormous pancakes. I think of sitting in there, warming up, but my stomach is aching. I suddenly feel very tired.

'What are you doin' here?'

I start and turn around. It's Matt, but I struggle to recognise him without his hat and away from the farm. It's as if he only exists when he's at my front door.

'You being a sticky beak or you goin' in?' He grins and gestures to the coffee shop.

'I'm not feeling great. I think I need to go home.'

'You look a bit pale,' he says. 'How you getting home? Need a lift?'

I was supposed to call James, but I know he's busy. 'A lift would be great. Are you sure?'

'Yes, no trouble.' He points across the road to his truck. 'I was just in town to see the doc. Apparently, my gall bladder can't handle any more KFC. I was heading home anyway.'

I realise I don't know where Matt lives.

'Brewongle, love. Not too far from your place.'

We get into his truck and he starts it up, the engine straining in the cold until it finally turns over. Matt pulls into the street without indicating, without even a glance in his side mirror. He takes a series of back streets to avoid traffic lights, and when we get a green light to drive on to the highway, he whistles.

'Running the green,' he says.

'Well done,' I say. 'I have no idea how you timed that, but well done.'

'Not my first rodeo.'

Once we're on the road to O'Connell, I ask Matt how long he's lived out here and he says he moved up from outside Canberra after school to do a trade, and then met his wife and stayed.

'Four kids,' he says proudly. 'And one grandkid. I think she was a bit of a mistake, my boy was only twenty-one when he had her, but we all love her.'

I tell him he doesn't look anywhere near old enough to be a grandpa and he laughs, but I can tell he's pleased all the same. I've worked with many Matts on projects that involved infrastructure. They're plain-speaking and mostly helpful. They might make the occasional casually sexist joke, but they don't mind if you throw a bit of shit back at them. I've always enjoyed knowing what level I'm on with somebody.

'You and James will have to get on to the baby making, I s'pose,' he says, steering around a flat bend. 'You'd be a terrific mum.'

He means it kindly, but it takes the breath from me. I wonder what he's noticed that would even make him think that. He doesn't know me. I shrug and smile. Then I ask him whether he's still keen to do some handyman work at the farm. He responds with enthusiasm, and we haggle over an hourly rate, with me trying to make it higher and Matt refusing.

As we pull into the driveway at the farm, Matt tells me about his plans to one day own a property with acreage, run sheep and cows and have his own chickens, be more self-sufficient. His wife wants a donkey and he's not sure about that, but he hasn't said no. I nod along.

'Here we are.' Matt pulls up slowly in front of the house and parks. He gives me a little business card with his details on it and a cartoon of a muscular handyman.

'Looks just like you,' I say, tapping the card, and he snorts. I thank him and hop out, then wave while he backs up and turns the truck around. A flash of something catches the corner of my eye – James's truck is parked around the side of the house.

I open the front door. 'James?'

No answer. I enter the kitchen and drop my bag on the table.

'Leila.' He's standing stiffly in the doorway.

I jump. 'Don't scare me like that. Why are you home so early?'

'Because you didn't answer your phone, so I went to the library to pick you up and you weren't there. I was worried.'

'Matt drove me home.' I check my phone; James called me ten times.

He enters the room. 'We need to talk.'

'I know.'

'Did you call my mother?'

I blink, startled; this isn't the talk I was expecting.

'Your mother?'

His mouth is a hard line. 'Why did you call her?'

'I wanted to ask about the house. What Charlotte had said. For my book. It was a couple of weeks ago.'

'What gave you the right to do that?'

I realise now that he isn't just serious, he's furious. His neck flares red and he's glaring at me, his hands clenched into fists. I turn away from him to the kettle.

'Do you want a coffee?' I ask.

'You called my mother and upset her with Charlotte's nonsense? What were you thinking?'

I haven't encountered James like this before; I need a moment to process the conversation – the fight – he clearly wants to have. I shake my head, weighing up what I want to say *Who gives a fuck, James, it was just a question* – against something more conciliatory.

'I thought she might enjoy having someone to talk to about it. I thought she might be flattered that I asked.'

'Sit down.'

I put the kettle on its hob and flick it on, then sit at the table.

'Dad called me, absolutely pissed off. They'll turf us out of here if we don't respect the house. They're doing us a favour letting us live here, you know.'

'How is asking disrespect—'

'What's in the past is past. They don't want to dredge up small-town shit, and frankly, I don't know why you do.'

I bristle. 'Me?'

'Charlotte says one thing and you're off trying to write a book about it? About our lives? You didn't ask what I thought about it. You didn't stop to consider how that might affect my family.'

The kettle whistles loudly and shuts itself off. Neither of us rises.

'I'm sorry.' I grab the papers from my bag and push them across the table. 'I just wanted to know more about your family history, that's all.'

He scans the papers one by one until he reaches the news article. 'This is exactly what I mean. It was a hundred years ago, Leila. A housekeeper dies, and the town gossips for generations.'

'Is it gossip if it's reported in the paper?'

'Being in the paper makes it worse. She probably died from influenza or an infection, but everyone in town wants to make it something nefarious.' He shoves the papers back to me. 'My great-grandparents copped it; my grandparents copped it; my parents copped it. We're done with it. Write something else.'

I fold the pages and stuff them back in my bag, a vessel holding ever more items abhorrent to James.

'James.' I can't ignore it any longer. There's so little warmth between us, no shared humour, neither of us cares what the other does with their day. The aborted attempt to have sex was nothing short of disastrous. I'm nervous; I don't want to say it aloud. Saying it would mean this relationship I put my faith in was the wrong decision; a waste of time; further evidence of my fundamental failures. Yet there's little sense in pretending we're solid. He must know, too.

'We should talk about what happened,' I say. 'With us.'

He waits for me to say more; a psychologist habit. I blunder on.

'I – I didn't mean what I said.' *Yes, I did.* 'We're obviously going through something.'

'The transition has been harder than I expected,' James says. 'But I'm happy to wait.' He looks at me, firms his chin. 'I can wait. I know this has been a lot for you. I know we want the same things still. That's okay.'

I'm lost for words; this isn't the outcome I expected. James, once again, putting his needs last, making a show of supporting me, supporting our relationship. But that's the thing: it's *all* a show. The farm has brought our differences into stark relief. This isn't the life we believed we would have: childless, resentful, being exposed to each other's weaknesses. Not this quickly, anyway. When we met, we seemed to have endless common ground: professional careers, lifestyles, aspirations. Now, I fear those pillars were – have always been – cracked, resting on unstable foundations. I wanted what he wanted – a family – only in the abstract, I think; in the sense of gaining this mysterious thing that has always been missing from my life. He wants a woman like me – educated, hardworking, independent – in name, but not in practice. Really, he needs a woman like his mother: traditional, nurturing. Turned on by domestic duties.

'Leila,' he says. 'We love each other. Don't we?'

I nod. *There is that.*

'So, then. We'll get through this.'

I shake my head, tears welling. 'I don't know.'

'Well, I do,' he says, reaching for me now, pulling me to him. 'And until you do, I'll get through this for the both of us.'

He holds me tight, cradling my head to his chest as I cry, and whispers soothing noises to me, words I can't make out. He's not angry anymore and I'm intensely relieved; he strokes my hair. After so many days without affection, the physical touch warms me, releases tension in muscles I didn't know I was clenching: my jaw, my shoulders. It strikes me that this is a comfort I never received when I was young; despite everything else, maybe it's something I can't give up.

———

James reminds me I still need to go to the radiology clinic in Bathurst for my next round of abdominal scans. I put him off, telling him it's too early, that I want to give my body more time to heal, and he accepts this for a fortnight. I walk with Rusty nearly every day, clean and cook, read and do not mention the house. I reduce my painkillers to only twice a day.

In July, he asks again, and this time he persists until I have no viable excuses left. He insists on coming with me for support, but there is no support he can provide me; he sits in the waiting room while I undergo the scans alone. I cry helplessly during the ultrasound and the sonographer plonks a useless box of tissues next to me. The wand feels like an assault this time. When I get back in the car, I scream at James that I'm not enduring another medical procedure, ever. Then I sob hysterically, collapse onto his chest, and he holds me tightly and murmurs that he loves me, that I'll be all right.

When I lived in Sydney, a lawnmower was one of the worst sounds I could imagine; waking with a mild hangover from too many glasses of wine, I'd curse the retirees who were so were gung-ho of a Saturday morning, cutting their grass to a precise inch, and whipper-snipping the Council-owned nature strips.

How things change depending on context: today, the sound ignites a deep satisfaction. Matt is here to do all the things James doesn't have time for and I physically can't. He fixed the ride-on mower in less than an hour and has been mowing for two. The rough buzz makes me feel like I've accomplished something; when James arrives home, the grass surrounding the house will be cut and the front path edged.

The roses also need attention. Left to their own devices, they've grown halfway to the roof, twisting up the verandah poles. While beautiful in their own way, I want to try and manicure them to see if James prefers it. The leaves that haven't yet dropped also show signs of black spot, a fungal affliction. I watched a few YouTube videos and asked Matt to find me a pair of secateurs; my goal is to eventually create bushes that are perfectly round orbs, a lofty ambition. Writing about the house and the mysterious events here is on hold, probably permanently. I've determined that, while at the farm, it's not so much about interrogating or resisting the surroundings as it is working with them. Finding my place in them.

Ironically, the only door on the entire farm that had an actual lock was the shed. When I led Matt over to it, we found a padlock and chain sealing the doors shut. Matt said this was common – farm equipment is expensive – but it was frustrating nonetheless. We peeked in the dusty windows and saw the ride-on mower inside, among other clutter. The lure of cut grass was enough for me; I convinced Matt to break the chain. I have months to replace it. Reluctantly, he grabbed a hammer from his ute and made short work of it. I gathered the padlock and the rusted links and took them inside, leaving them on the kitchen bench. When we entered the shed, it was so full that it made the house seem almost minimalist in comparison. A strong smell emanated from inside, somewhere between rotting food and wet dog.

'Some dead rats in here,' Matt said cheerfully. On a bench covered in tools, he located a large pair of shears and a dusty pair of gloves, and then handed them to me. 'Don't worry, I'll clear 'em out.'

We took a quick look around, me holding my breath in a grimace, and agreed that Matt should come back with a trailer and remove the hard rubbish. I trust him to discern what that is. He whistled, excited; he'd been wanting to get into the shed for years and sort it out. I left him to it and went to tackle the roses while he ventured further in to find the mower. Thirty minutes later, I heard it roar to life and smiled to myself. As the cut-grass smell carried on the air, I felt a surge of energy. Imagine if I adjust to farm life after all, and even become useful while I'm here. Not as useful as Matt, but at least as a body with something to do; something to offer.

The shears are old and a little blunt, but they still outperform the woody rose stems. I clip away every extraneous part, even the pretty, twisting vines. Leaves detach and fall as I burrow into the heart of the bushes. The videos said to clip them all the way back to stumps and that July is a good month to do it. It encourages the plants to regrow healthier stems in the spring and summer. They'll rebound with bright green leaves, more roses, and I'll be able to shape them as I desire. It amazes me that the stalk can simply regenerate an entire bush; cut away the diseased parts, the overgrown and unnecessary parts, and it will start again, stronger than before.

I sweat, despite the daytime temperature only reaching eight degrees. My shoulders ache from clipping roses above my head. I keep going. My lower back burns from squatting down to cut off new shoots. I keep going. Every so often, I feel a sting in my hands; the thorns penetrate the gloves, scratching the skin, and need to be removed. I keep going. Then, my stomach radiates a pulse, a nerve pain prickling behind my scar, warning that stomach cramps are not far away.

There are eight rose bushes, and I've completed three when I hit a wall. I stumble to the patio chair and sit down, breathing heavily. I watch Matt's cows in the distance, wandering in a loose herd, drinking from the dam, walking slowly to find more feed. They moo the way a school of fish swims: one starts, and they all join in, a collective bellowing. The sound rolls through the air, muffled by the stretch of land separating us.

Matt appears briefly from the side of the house driving the mower in a straight line, the machine shooting out grass clippings. Sunglasses protect his eyes from twigs or pebbles; his head is covered in a cap secured by earmuffs. When he reaches the driveway, he executes a sharp turn and drives back, disappearing once more behind the house. He's already completed the front lawn: the area from the house to the paddock gate has been transformed from a tufty mess to velvety green grass.

I push myself to stand. I have a wheelbarrow ready: I must pile the clipped rose stems into it and dump them somewhere along the conifer line. Bending down is the hardest part, but I want so badly to complete one task: to show James I can be depended on out here. The rose bushes aren't perfect yet like I imagined, but they are, at least, tidier, and when I finish, each plant will have more breathing room.

I gather the green matter, pushing it together with my feet. When I have a big bunch, I take a breath deep into my belly, squat down and scoop it up, a voluminous mess of vines, leaves and thorns held firm against my chest. Too late, I realise my mistake: the rose thorns scratch my face, neck and arms. By the time I reach the wheelbarrow, I'm moaning, eyes half shut; I lean forwards and drop the rose matter into the vessel, but a good bunch of them hang from my shirt, thorns plugged into the cotton, setting off stinging pain as I pluck them off.

'Fuck.' When I'm free of it all, my hands and forearms are covered in bloody pinpricks; my chest and neck will be the same. Leaving the rest of the clippings on the ground, I enter the house and scurry to the main bathroom. I rifle through the mirrored cabinet: nail clippers, combs, mouthwash, floss. No Band-Aids. I go to the ensuite and look around. Nothing. I find my mobile in the kitchen and hold it in the air: three bars. I dial James and put him on speaker.

'Hey.' His voice is faint; I can hear him typing.

'Hey, can you talk? Just for a second?'

'Yes, but I have an appointment in five minutes or so.'

I'm relieved there's coverage. 'I was doing some gardening and, ummm . . . I scratched myself pretty badly. Clipping roses. I need some Band-Aids. There's none in the bathrooms. And some antiseptic? Does the house have a first-aid kit anywhere?' I check myself in the mirror – I look a wreck, there are even scratches on my chin. None of them deep or worrying, just unsightly. The ones on my arms are worse; quite a few are bleeding. Others have started to swell.

'You were gardening?' James's tone is bemused; the typing pauses.

'And some other jobs.' I frown at my reflection. 'It's a surprise for when you get home.'

'Well, well,' he says. 'Okay. Uh . . . there should be a first-aid pack in the attic.'

My gut drops.

'But the stairs are pretty steep,' he adds. 'I've only got one appointment left. Can you shower and then I'll get the kit for you?'

'Sure, probably—' I'm on fire with itching; I look down and see my skin reddening.

'My client's here. I'll see you at home. Love y—.' The phone cuts out.

The scratches are so hot. I check back in the mirror. The marks on my neck, chest and chin are swelling too. I need antihistamine cream.

I walk to the attic stairs, debating whether they really are too steep. I stare up at the attic door. After the scream, there's been no more noise from the attic – if there even was any at all. Warily, I step onto the tiny stairs, grip the rail, and take each step slowly. I hear a small whine and look behind me. Rusty is sitting at the bottom of the stairs, staring at me, ears pricked.

'It's all right.'

He drops his head to the side. I take the next few steps, panting already, and hear Rusty's paws click away into the kitchen. The air grows thicker; it's hard to fill my lungs. Beads of sweat roll down my temples. Confronting my physical limitations time and again is demeaning. The doctor said the pain is all in my mind, so I'm not going to stop now. A few more steps. I hold the rail tighter, compensating for the slick of sweat in my palms. The effort required to get enough air staggers me; my throat feels like it's closed altogether.

The top. The door. I grab the doorknob and try to twist it. Nothing. It's so stiff it doesn't move. I wipe my hand on my pants and try again. The knob resists. I try rattling it; perhaps the door is stuck in the wrong groove. It doesn't move. I stare at the innocuous round knob. A delicate pattern is etched into metal of the sphere. I try to take in a breath, but I can't get enough in. My diaphragm is stuck; my lungs won't open. I'm dizzy and too high up. I could fall and snap my neck. I turn around on the small landing, reaching for the railing. I miss. Looking down, the floor begins to blur. There's not enough air.

I sit heavily on the landing, my hands on the floor. I move down the stairs on my bottom as gently but quickly as I can. About halfway down, my lungs fill more easily and the confusion and panic subside. After several breaths, the dizziness dissipates, and I stand and descend the rest of the way on my feet. At the bottom, I look up at the attic door. It doesn't creak, doesn't move. I can breathe easily again. What is wrong with me?

I go to the ensuite and dampen a hand towel and pat it across my face, chest and arms. Soothe the heat from the cuts, rub away the sweat and pinpricks of blood. Then, in my room, I take an Endone from the packet, tell myself I've earned it, and hope it deals with both the stomach aches and the itching.

Making my way into the kitchen, I pour a glass of water and swallow the pill quickly. Then pick up my phone and WhatsApp James. *Can't get into the attic room. Can you please pick up antihistamine cream?*

The mowing noises have stopped. I fill another glass of water and venture out to the shed, scratching my neck and chest. Matt is inside, lugging twisted metal out to the front.

'Water?' I proffer the cup, and he downs it in seconds. There's a deep V-shaped sweat stain down the front of his chest.

'Love, you need a long-sleeved gardening shirt,' he says, looking at the scratches on my arms.

'Now you tell me,' I say, taking the empty glass from him.

'Amateur,' he says, and we laugh.

I glance at the shed interior. 'There's a lot of rubbish.' I spot broken mattocks, shovels, other tools and piles of cracked tile.

Matt nods. 'Plenty to do here.' He points to the metal. 'This stuff is no good, but I won't throw out anything that looks like it could be useful. If something's broken and I can fix it meself, I will.' He ducks inside and returns with a plastic tub. 'I was going to give you this, if you want it. I checked some boxes but haven't been through them all yet. This stuff is in good nick.'

He rests the tub on the ground and opens the lid. Folded neatly, with mothballs to prevent holes, are baby clothes. Blue onesies, pyjamas and bibs. I stare at them a moment, then kneel and sort through them gently.

'Figured you and James might want 'em,' Matt says. 'Or you could sell 'em. Once I get this shed cleaned out nice, I'll put in proper shelving and sort everything out. I can install lighting too.' He points at a switch near the shed door, flicks it up and down a couple of times. 'Electricity's here, just needs a new fitting.'

'Great, great.' I'm struck by the baby clothing. It isn't old enough to be James's; besides, these items have never been used, they still have the tags attached. I can't discern exactly when they would have been purchased. I feel a stone in my stomach. Baby clothes. The Crawleys have clearly been hoping for grandchildren for some time. Matt pulls the shed door closed with a clang.

'Thanks, Matt.' I pick up the tub; thankfully it's light. 'Appreciate it.'

'No worries.'

'Coffee?'

'That'd be great, love.'

I leave the box on the verandah table and we amble inside to the kitchen. I make instant coffee for us – 'Builder's coffee?' he says, aghast, when I present it to him – and we sit and sigh deeply in unison. The heat and itch from the scratches are building up again; I try to ignore them.

'Is landscaping and farm work always this painful?' I ask.

'Oh yeah. I slipped a disc years ago. Back hasn't been right since.' Matt goes on to tell me his entire history of work-related injuries and I gasp at every single one.

'But I keep workin',' he says. 'I don't like sitting around. It's me gallbladder that's the problem. They were worried it was cancer, but it's not.'

'Thank god.'

'Yeah. But they told me to eat healthy food now.' He frowns. 'I hate vegetables.'

I laugh. 'You'll have to suck it up, princess.'

He guffaws. 'Yeah, yeah. Careful, city girl, you still need me to finish the job!'

We laugh and chatter about inconsequential topics from weather to Rusty to Matt's missus wanting to take a trip to Port Macquarie. Once he drains the coffee, he stands.

'So, I'll come back tomorrow. Bring the trailer and get rid of this stuff and the stuff behind the house. I'll go through the rest of the shed, pull out anything I think James or his folks might want to keep.'

He scratches Rusty behind the ears, the dog having found a sunny spot by the kitchen window. Rusty opens his eyes and stares up at Matt, then at me. The dog stands slowly, stretching out with his bum in the air and his head down to the ground, then shuffles alongside us to the door. Matt gets in his truck and I wave him off, walking along the verandah to the box of clothes as he heads down the drive. He brakes abruptly and backs up; James's car appears. Matt eases off to the side and they pause next to each other. Matt gives James a thumbs up and then he zooms away.

I wait at the front door, itching, while James parks in the side garage. Unsure, I hold the box of clothes in front of me. As James approaches, he says, 'What do you have there?' He leans in and gives me a kiss on the forehead. 'You did a number on yourself,' he says, checking over my face and arms. I don't say anything, and he lifts up the lid of the box. When he sees the clothes, he appears dumbfounded. We're both silent for several moments before he gathers himself and takes the container from me.

'Here, you shouldn't be carrying that.' He walks inside and I follow him to the kitchen. He sets the box down and notices the broken padlock and chains. I speak up quickly.

'I thought I'd get Matt to do some jobs – mowing, keeping the garden nice.' James doesn't respond so I add, quickly, 'I'm paying for it.'

'Matt was in the shed?' He looks at me.

'I asked him to clear it out, put in new shelving, some lighting . . . to surprise your parents when they move back.'

He rubs his temples; I can see he's trying to contain his reaction.

'I'll talk to them about it.' He takes a tube from his trouser pocket and hands it to me. 'You need this.'

I accept the antihistamine cream gratefully. He picks up the broken lock and chain and leaves the kitchen; I hover at the door and listen as he ascends the attic stairs. He opens the door easily, his steps echoing down into the hallway, and returns holding a first-aid kit.

'Do you need help with these?' he asks, handing me some Band-Aids.

I shake my head. He sits down at the kitchen table and faces the bay window. I take the Band-Aids and go to leave, but then stop.

'James. Who are the baby clothes for?'

I can only see the back of his head. He doesn't move, and then he says, softly, 'I'm not sure. I'll move them to the linen cupboard.'

I wait a little longer, but that's it; there's no other explanation forthcoming, and driven by the unrelenting itch of my body, I head for the bathroom.

—

James retires early. After taking the baby clothes to the linen closet, he went and lay down on the couch, immediately falling asleep. I tiptoed around the house and prepared dinner before waking him. We ate quietly, both of us subdued.

I clean the kitchen and turn the dishwasher on while James showers and goes to bed. Then I fetch a fresh towel from the linen closet, ignoring the box on the floor, and head to the main bathroom down the other end of the house. I shower and dry myself, then spend a good deal of time applying fresh layers of antihistamine cream to each puffy scratch on my hands and arms.

When I finish, I lean closer to the mirror to lather my neck and face. I've mostly avoided mirrors since the surgery; now, with my hair wet and slicked back, the scratches crimson on my skin and my face under the bright lights, I can see every detail. My eye sockets are concave, with deep black circles around them; my cheeks are gaunt, my chin pimply, pores stretched. There's a streak of grey in the front of my hair. Wrinkles are deepening, especially around my cheeks and mouth, and I look sick. Worse: I resemble my mother.

We share a nose that dominates our faces, and mine looks even bigger thanks to my sunken cheeks. Some stubborn black hairs poke out of my chin. They remind me of Lebanese relatives in photos Mum used to show me. Women I never met, women from 'the motherland'. Ageing women with moles and thick, curly hair, heavy bottoms and full breasts. 'Our stock,' she'd say, tapping the photos. 'Be proud.' I wasn't. At school and at work, I called myself 'L' and let people think it was Elle. I didn't wear religious icons like the Greek Orthodox students, and at work I didn't bring cultural food to the office for potlucks. I straightened my hair, wore neutral colours, hoped to blend in. Still, I can't outrun my body. Unlike the roses, I can't clip off the ugly parts and expect to grow new, desirable ones.

A flash of something catches my eye. Not in the mirror. Just to the left of it. I blink and gaze out the window, a small pane of glass divided by wood in a French door-style. It's difficult to discern anything; it's pitch-black outside and there's no illumination from the moon. Seeing only my own reflection, I return to the mirror, daubing on more cream.

Another flash. A streak. I turn back to the window and scream; I drop the tube. There's a woman, her pale face pressed against one of the panes of glass. I freeze, my eyes locked on her. There's a swollen bruise on her cheek near her eye, and violent marks around her neck. Her mouth opens wide, wide, in a desperate shout, but there is no sound; her lips move, her eyes beseech. We stare at each other. Suddenly, there's a *slap*, and I jerk away at the sound of the woman's hand hitting the window. Her fingers scrape the glass as she is pulled backwards, and she disappears into the blackness.

'Wait!' I grab the window handle and winch it open, cold air rushing inside. 'Do you need help?' I shout into the blackness, hearing nothing in return.

There was no mistaking the woman's face; whatever help she needed, it was urgent.

I rush into the foyer, pull on sneakers and throw open the front door.

'Are you there?' I'm shouting, then gasping in panic. I bend over to get air, then straighten and yell again: 'Do you need help?'

Nothing. I grab the car keys. Race around the side of the house and unlock the ute. The lights flash and illuminate the surrounds briefly; still no-one. I hear my name behind me and turn. The verandah lights are on. James stands on the patio in a t-shirt and pyjama pants, hair mussed.

'What are you doing?'

'There's a woman. A woman needs help.'

He rubs his eyes and looks around. 'A woman?'

'I'm going to look for her.' I don't want to babble but can feel it coming on. 'I saw a woman, in the window, in the bathroom.' I count these facts on three fingers. 'She was saying something. I couldn't make it out, but she needs help.' I stop, panting from alarm and adrenaline. 'Look with me?'

He approaches me and pats my shoulder, reaching down and taking the keys from my hand. He presses the button and the car lights up again. Locked.

'Come inside.' He takes my hand and walks me back into the house, closes the door and flicks off the patio lights.

'What are we doing?' I ask. A flash of inspiration. 'We should call the police!'

'Leila.'

God, I hate it when he says my name like that, like I'm a child. 'What?'

He steers me away from the foyer and into the living room, sits me down.

'We need to hurry,' I say. 'She could be anywhere by now. Someone might have her. We need to call for help.'

His hand is on my knee, slowly applying pressure.

'Leila.' His face is lined. 'There's no-one here. We're miles from anyone. Remember?'

I stare at him, trying to think back to our first day, arriving at an unmarked gate in the middle of nowhere; a driveway that is several kilometres long.

'Yes, but—' I stop, trying to find a thread of logic.

'So, a woman, on foot, couldn't be on the property. She'd have to cross pine forest, paddocks with grass up to her head, a river, and then find the house. In the dark.'

I blink rapidly, trying to process what he is telling me. He continues: 'She didn't drive here, because the ute is the only vehicle here.'

'Maybe she escaped to the road.' There's all sorts of possibilities he's not considering. 'Maybe she walked up the driveway.'

He nods, humouring me. 'Yes, she could have. But why would anyone do that? If she was on the road, she could have run to the pub.'

'I don't know.' My voice wavers. This house, this house. I can't think straight. I saw a woman. The woman needed help. There was pure distress on her face; I recognised it instantly because I tried for years to ease that expression from my mother's face, before I realised, I realised, I realised, I couldn't do a thing.

'There was a woman,' I mutter. 'Desperate.'

'There is no woman.'

'It's the house. This house.'

'The house is fine,' James says, low and firm. 'You're going through something.'

He moves his hand from my knee and grasps my hands; for a moment I think he's going to ask me to pray.

'Breathe with me.'

We sit like this for some time, breathing in and out together.

'Things keep happening,' I say. My chest is still too tight. I consider telling him everything from the beginning: the sounds, the rotting smell, the face in the woods, the wretched, shrieking scream. Things I can't explain.

'Keep breathing.' He unclasps my hands and wraps my arms around myself, then holds me. I close my eyes, breathing in, out. In. Out. I feel him pull me into a standing position. I'm light-headed and open my eyes to see James assessing me with deep concern.

'Let's go to bed,' he says. 'You've had a big day.'

I let him take me to the master suite. He helps me climb into bed; gently lifts my feet and tucks them under the blanket and fluffs my pillows like I'm a hospital patient or a resident of an aged care facility. I stare up at him, watching every move he makes, every action slow, deliberate, tender, intended to calm me, quiet me. He pulls the blanket up to my chin and then smooths it out like wrapping paper; he kisses my forehead. For the first time in a while, I don't remember falling asleep; there is simply James's face, watching me.

I sleep long and late; only the direct sunlight proves enough to pierce through a heavy slumber. Waking up feels like the gradual removal of a tight bandage. A feeling of blood rushing in, a swell, takes over my head as I open my eyes. The ceiling comes into focus; a dust web dangles from the light fitting. The curtains are open, and I can see straight out. A ute, not James's, is pulling down the drive slowly, a trailer attached to it. I feel a total lack of comprehension; then remember Matt promised to remove the rubbish he pulled from the shed. I'll have to call him later and find out how much I owe him.

My next thought bulldozes in like a charging hippopotamus: *Who was the woman?*

Breathe, breathe. Lie on my back. Follow James's instructions: in, out, in, out. Watch my belly fill with air. Flatten as it expels.

Must keep my heartbeat in check; I can't let panic overwhelm me. I used to handle complex issues, manage huge projects. No problem was big enough to make me react like this. Now, something as small as a sound, a smell – a face – and I'm cut off at the knees.

It isn't wrong of James to be worried. I imagine if our positions were reversed: James on painkillers and downers, unemployed, negative and moody. Hallucinating. If I'm honest, wouldn't I have left him a long time ago? But he's here, caring for me, still trying to make me better.

Is that love? Is it something else?

I'm so unwell.

I don't believe in ghosts or spirits or energy, so it must be the drugs having an effect. Maybe it's a kind of sleep paralysis. Or a fugue state. Waking dreams. Pareidolia, like James told me. A documented condition, physical and fixable, with the right help.

There's a woman, I remember insisting. *A woman needs help.*

Is that woman me?

There's a vibration on the bedside table next to me, and I pick up my phone. Three bars. The screen shows a number I don't recognise.

'Hello?'

'Leila Haddad?' The line is fuzzy, but I can make out the voice.

'Yes?'

'It's Dr Wong's offices. We saw you in March for your myomectomy.' The meditative breathing halts, my chest seizing immediately. Like many healthcare workers, trained in detachment, the woman's voice is bureaucratic.

'Dr Wong has looked at your latest scans and feels your surgery result wasn't as adverse as she first thought.'

'I'm sorry?'

'She wanted me to ring and see if you can come in to discuss it. She mentioned you and your partner were open to IVF, is that right?'

The woman is typing as she speaks, no doubt doing three things at once, even if one of them is influencing a stranger's fertility.

'We were, yes.' A box we ticked on my medical forms; a numb nod to the gynaecologist's stream of questions before the surgery. After, when Dr Wong told me I'd been lucky not to lose my uterus, the idea of IVF was so far from my mind I'd forgotten we even talked about it.

'I have a cancellation for the day after tomorrow, so Dr Wong could see you at eleven in the morning. Otherwise, it's a three-month wait, which would bring us into October.'

I think of James. 'I'll take it.'

'Okay, you're booked in. We'll see you then.'

I hang up the phone and consider for a moment; this is, factually, good news. With some effort, and some expense, perhaps we can return to where we were before I got pregnant and miscarried; a return to the days when we understood each other, when our plans lined up like dominoes.

I try not to think of our failed attempt to have sex, our

co-existence like that of roommates – but there was a time, wasn't there, when I loved him. And he insists he loves me still.

I carry a sleeve of Targin to the kitchen, swallow one and then dial James's number. He answers quickly.

'I just had a call from the gynaecologists' office.' I picture him sitting up straighter, his eyes focusing intently.

'Oh? And?' His voice gives him away; he is lured like a fish to bait.

'Things may not be as bad as they initially thought. She wants us to go to Sydney the day after tomorrow. Friday. At eleven. Thing is, the next appointment isn't for three months, so I took it. I wasn't sure about your work, but I can go alone.'

'No, no, no, no, no.' The *no*'s are dashed off in rapid succession; he's thrilled. 'I can rearrange my appointments. You can't drive alone, anyway.'

'Okay. Thank you.' I fall silent.

'This is fantastic news.' There is something slightly more eager in his tone than just excitement. It's relief. Hope. He wants a return to before, too.

'It is,' I say. 'Unexpected.'

'You're cutting out. Gotta go. I love you.'

'Love you, too,' I say reflexively, surprising myself.

—

James is doting on me again, the way he did when we first began dating. He offers me foot massages. He cooks dinner and then, while I'm in the shower, he cleans the kitchen. Brings a herbal tea to the couch for me.

He makes these little efforts and does not mention them, unlike so many men who declare their household achievements as if deserving of a gold star. James has always been less obvious. In Coogee, he used to wait for me to notice and then humbly accept my delighted thanks, my insistence that I'd never met a man so considerate. Unwittingly, I realise now, I'd thanked him for doing things that any adult should do.

This time, I don't accept the foot massage. I notice the clean kitchen and say nothing. I'm not where I used to be; I feel an unspoken debt between us too keenly and can't afford to add to the ledger.

I drink the bitter herbal tea, slumping on the couch, then drag myself to bed and sleep long and late into Thursday morning. It's midday before I wake, and even later when I manage to get up.

On Thursday night I retire early again, feeling fatigued and nervous. James brings me a hot water bottle, an extra blanket and a glass of freshly squeezed orange juice. I wait for him to leave, and then use the juice to wash down a Valium.

On Friday morning, I wake to the sound of James's alarm. He is already up, his side of the bed empty. I shower and dress, pull my unbrushed hair into an elastic; I don't care how it looks. Wrap myself in a black wool coat. I make coffee and transfer it to our travel mugs, then usher a sleepy, resistant Rusty outside. He looks at me resentfully and curls up on the verandah. The air snaps and burns, and fog surrounds the house. There's no noise, not even the distant morning moo of Matt's cows. The fog swamps every visual and auditory cue. I'm worried about being able to see the road – it's thick and white in every direction – but James promises he could drive with his eyes closed and in the dark. Still, every bump jolts me; every pothole announces itself with a sudden rattle. All we can see is a metre or two of white line on the road ahead.

'Fog in the morning means a sunny day,' James says.

I sip coffee. 'I don't see how.'

Once we pass the peak of the Blue Mountains, visibility returns and I'm thankful.

When we arrive at the fertility specialist's office, we're ushered into an artificially warm room with cushioned seats. It's all beige soft furnishings, no grey plastic chairs or cheap carpet; there's money in this waiting room, in failed fertility. Black and white framed photographs of Paris and Venice hang on the walls, a subtle message that travel is a solid consolation prize for childlessness.

Soon, my name is called, and we follow Dr Wong into her office, a markedly more sterile room. We exchange pleasantries while she turns to her computer and brings up visuals of the ultrasounds and the accompanying report.

'I was pleased to see these updated scans.' She prints a piece of paper and hands it to me: *No evidence of fibroids, uterus normal, ovaries normal, fallopian tubes normal.*

'Given the extensive removal we had to do, your reproductive organs look surprisingly healthy. Now, bear in mind that the report doesn't show where your scar tissue is from the last surgery. We simply can't see it on the scans. However, I can go in and have a look and remove any that's on your ovaries or fallopian tubes.'

I sit numbly, shaking my head. *No more procedures.* But James says, 'That sounds great. Yes. What would that entail?'

'Just a day visit to hospital. Lap procedure. I'd be able to do it in . . .' She turns to her computer and clicks rapidly. 'I have one gap left for surgery in mid-September. Eight weeks from now. Otherwise, October.'

'Excellent, let's book that in.' James squeezes my hand.

'Wait.'

They both look at me.

'No.'

James looks at Dr Wong, then back at me. 'What do you mean?'

'No more procedures.'

Dr Wong leans forwards. 'It's a very minor procedure. Very little pain. Nothing like the last one.' She tries to mimic reassurance; she thinks I'm being silly.

Once again, James jumps in before I can respond. 'Can you think about it? Before saying no?'

I look down at my hands. They're trembling. The room feels very clinical, and very small. It's too warm in here; a sweat breaks out over my forehead.

'I want to know . . .' I break off, conscious of the size and display of James's intent, his resolve to convince me to continue. It's not just his presence, his hand on mine. His desire takes on a manifestation all its own. He'd say yes to any procedure to give me a chance of conceiving. *Any* procedure. I clear my throat.

'If I do this . . . lap surgery . . . what happens after that? What's the next procedure? And the one after?' James stiffens next to me. His hand finds its way to my knee.

Dr Wong nods. 'After removing the scar tissue, you'd go home and recover. After that, when you're ready, you'd start hormone medication to stimulate your ovaries. You can do that at home. If you don't fall naturally, after six months we'd have you back in the surgery to extract your eggs. You can freeze them; you don't have to undertake IVF right away.'

'And IVF? What does that involve?'

Dr Wong rummages through her desk and pulls out a brochure. *Fortem Fertility.*

'Read through this at home. People are nervous of IVF, but it's not that invasive. We combine your egg with James's sperm, and if we get a viable embryo, we insert it into your uterus.'

I'm nauseated; what she describes is the very definition of invasive. I lean over and cradle my head in my hands. 'I need air.'

I hear James and Dr Wong murmur to one another, then Dr Wong says, 'Leila, do you want a glass of water?' I nod, keeping my eyes shut. She leaves the room. James says nothing until she returns. I open my eyes and take the tumbler she offers, gulping down water. Dr Wong pulls up a chair on the other side of me and sits down.

'How are you holding up after the last surgery?'

'I'm exercising. I walk the dog.'

'And what medications are you still on?'

I brace. 'Just some painkillers. And Valium for sleeping. Temazepam for anxiety.'

'Which painkillers?'

I feel tears well up. James watches me intently.

'Targin in the morning. Endone if I'm really . . . desperate.'

'That's okay,' Dr Wong says. 'It's easy to feel a little bit too dependent on these medications. We probably over-serviced you with them, given how serious your surgery was. I'll give you a script for melatonin for sleep. It's much safer than Valium.'

Dr Wong stands and walks back to her desk. I look down at the linoleum floor and there is a long period without any conversation, just the whirr of the printer and a flutter of paper.

'Leila.'

I look up, eyes wet, blinking furiously. Dr Wong wears a concerned expression and holds a wad of papers.

'Here's the script for melatonin. There's paperwork here for the laparoscopy, if you decide to go ahead. And I've given you a sleeve of the hormone medication to start you off, with a script for more.' She hands it all to James, then casts me one more sympathetic glance. 'You don't have to do the lap surgery if you don't want to. It's just a cautionary look. You're probably fine. If you'd prefer to reduce the number of procedures, you can just go ahead with the hormone therapy and try to conceive naturally for six months. Cut back your pain medications over the next few weeks, okay? And no more Valium. It's addictive. We don't want you suffering any side effects.'

—

The traffic in Sydney is gridlocked and I wonder if it was the same when I lived here. The long, open country roads are what feel usual now. Leaving the city, we take every tunnel poss-ible, and the beep of the e-toll is the only sound above James's muttered frustrations when cars cut in front of us: 'This is why we moved.'

Once we reach the M4, my anxiety grows. Sydney had its problems, but it's a place where I managed to make a career and a home, all on my own. The eastern suburbs felt safe to me; the beaches and bays a cornerstone of carefree weekends when I didn't feel so *tight*. Before I allowed myself to be wrapped up in this new compromise of a life: a life based on collective decisions rather than my own.

I think back over the appointment. I don't recall asking James to come in with me to see the doctor. His agreeing to medical procedures on my body was a shock. My expectation was that he would be involved only to the point of my consent; he is just one voice to be considered. But it's clear he feels ownership over me. I don't think he means to, but there's no other way to describe it.

When I was in my teens, the federal government was trying to ban what they termed an 'abortion pill'. A federal represen-tative – one from the regions, not too far from where I'm now living – insisted abortion was against God's will and, somehow, akin to slavery. Ensuing conservative governments were no more libertarian about reproductive rights. For a time, if I needed a simple morning-after pill, I had to be 'counselled' by the phar-macist. In practice, I only experienced this once, years ago, in Brisbane; I ventured into the pharmacy, and the pharmacist ushered me into a small, airless room.

'I'm supposed to ask you if you have considered keeping a possible pregnancy rather than taking this,' the woman said. Then she shook her head. 'But honestly, you don't even have to answer me. Would you still like the medication?'

No wonder James feels ownership over my body; after all, the highest powers in the country have declared it a thing to be owned.

'You're quiet.' James taps the steering wheel. 'I thought that was good news today.'

He pulls the car off the freeway and parks at a McDonald's.

'I guess.' I focus on a spot outside my window.

'You don't think so?'

We turn in our seats to face each other. His expression is one of genuine confusion; I search his face for irritation but can't find it.

He repeats: 'You don't think this is good news?'

There must be a way to explain how I'm feeling. I pull out my phone and google old news results about the banning of the 'abortion pill'.

'There was a time when the government tried to have the RU486 pill banned.'

James purses his lips. 'Uh . . . okay.'

'It was back in 2005. There was a pill the prime minister tried to ban called RU486. It meant women who were less than eight weeks pregnant could terminate their pregnancy at home. But some politicians fought against it. Because they thought it would lead to more abortions.'

'Well, it's probably good they did, then.'

The punch of disappointment at his response hits hard.

'You don't see what's wrong with that? The government making decisions about women's bodies; *my* body?'

James throws up his hands. 'Why are we talking about abortion when we just found out you can get pregnant?'

'Because it's *my* decision! Mine. Not yours. Not Dr Wong's.' I take in shorter and shorter breaths and turn away from him, my body shaking.

'Okay, okay.' He reaches for my hand, and I yank it away. 'Calm. Breathe.'

'I don't even have a car at the farm,' I snap. 'I'm alone, all the time. You won't let me write what I want. You have me in this *grip*. I'm not just a petri dish to make a baby in.' I punctuate this with closed, shuddering fists. It feels good to express my feelings, tossing them at him to deal with. See how he likes it.

There's a long silence. I turn further away from James, curl up and rest my head against the window. I hear him unbuckle his seatbelt, rummage for his wallet. The door opens, closes, and then he is gone.

Outside the window, four kids mooch in the car park, taking turns on a skateboard. One attempts a jump and promptly overbalances, falling. The other boys laugh loudly, a honking, antagonising sound.

'Idiot,' one snickers.

'Fuckin' you try it then!'

I blanch at the cursing, despite being fond of the word *fuck* myself. Their hair is styled in rat's tails – shaved underneath – and they wear baggy shorts and t-shirts. A picture of indolence.

The car door opens, and James passes me a brown paper bag. The smell of McDonald's is intense: tacky meat and reconstituted oil. I peek in the bag. He's bought me a grilled chicken salad. Of course; he remembers all my preferences.

I pick out the least grainy tomatoes and swallow dry chicken while James inhales a burger and fries. As I eat, I feel calmer. The silence provides a reprieve, and my hackles deflate. James crumples his rubbish into the paper bag and holds it out to me; I hand over my plastic container and fork.

'Listen.' He clears his throat a few times. 'You've asked me not to analyse you, and I don't. But the grip on you isn't me.' He scrunches our rubbish into the paper bag and tosses it into the back seat. 'It's your mother,' he says.

I shake my head.

'It's whatever happened with you and her. Growing up, and when she died.'

I press myself against the window, trying not to punch it with my fist. The reprieve is over. The intensity of this rage is new to me; I don't know where it springs from. I want to punch *him*.

'I love you, so much that I want to create a life with you, a baby who we'll love even more. Of course, it's your decision.' He leans over and rubs the nape of my neck, slowly but deliberately encouraging me to turn and look at him, and so I do.

'And whatever your decision is, we'll live with it. I'm not leaving. Just know that I think you'll be a wonderful mother. You don't have to repeat history if you don't want to.'

Defeated by his reasonableness, I nod. He's right, he's right. He's always right. The fury and the adrenaline drain away; it leaves me exhausted. Where do my outbursts come from? James turns the key in the ignition, releases the handbrake, and we pull slowly out into traffic, his hand steadfastly on my knee.

James was right about one other thing: the weather driving back is glorious. The clearest of blue skies, not a single streak of cloud; a gentle, golden sun. It's as though the fog never existed, the way sleep doesn't exist once you're awake. We settle into a companionable silence. James chooses an eighties Spotify playlist, providing enough background noise for the tension of our argument to subside.

As we near the farm, I let out a long exhale, relieved to be far from Sydney and the fertility doctor. From the decisions placed upon me. On turning into the driveway, I notice a little posy of flowers set just in front of the fence. It's a colourful mix of gerberas: pink, orange, purple, white; tied with twine.

'What is that?' I lean forwards to see more clearly. The flowers appear fresh.

James stops the car and jogs over to the bouquet. He examines it and then tosses it away, into the paddock grass.

'Why would they be there?' I ask as he gets back in the car. 'Whose were they?'

'No card,' James says, shrugging. 'There are plenty of car accidents along these roads.'

'We could have kept them.'

James drives through the gate, gets out, locks it, then resumes driving. I twist back to see the abandoned flowers, but they're out of sight. Soon, we lose mobile reception and Spotify becomes patchy. I shut off the music and we listen to bird trills, the sound of pebbles hitting the underside of the ute, and the crunchy squish of the tyres on the rocky drive.

'I can't wait to see Rusty.' I say it mainly to myself, picturing his brown face, his serious eyes set in an expression of curiosity or anticipation. We wind our way up the driveway. Then a new sound; one I strain to catch.

'Do you hear that?'

James frowns as though he doesn't, but to me, it sounds like sickness. Sickness doesn't just present visually; it isn't just a smell. There are specific noises associated with being ill: the vomiting, the crying, the moans. They're familiar to me. Often, the sounds are the most harrowing part of dying.

This sound is long and low, unnatural, unwell. I think of the cows, but their insistent and sociable moos are nothing like this. Rusty and I have trekked down to the wire fence where the calves cluster multiple times, their heavily lashed eyes focused on my hands. They always want food, but we never have any and so we walk on. The cows sputter and groan and blow air out of their noses; the calves buck and prance, and Rusty scampers past them, no doubt showing off his relative freedom.

There! Something else, too. A shout? A curse, definitely.

'Is Matt here?' I ask.

'I don't know. Maybe he's moving cattle between paddocks.'

The car rolls on, the noises growing louder. I look at James and we exchange a worried glance.

'You hear that, right?' I say.

'Yeah. Mind if I speed up?'

I nod and grasp my stomach to fortify it as James squeezes the accelerator. We hit potholes and bumps at speed, dust billowing behind us. As we near the final rise before the property, I catch a glimpse of the paddock beyond.

'Do cows lie down to sleep?' I ask.

James looks over to the paddock and says, quietly, '*Fuck.*' He hits the throttle aggressively and we jet up the last section of drive, then veer off the marked gravel and go straight over the front lawn. James brakes hard next to Matt's ute, which is parked haphazardly, the driver's door still open. Next to the ute is a white van I've not seen before. The decal reads: *Bathurst Animal Services.* A float is attached to the back.

James jumps out of the car. 'I'll be back.'

I unclip my seatbelt, panicked by the loud, gargling moans and shrill, blaring cries. I walk to the paddock gate; James is belting down the hill to where Matt and another two men I don't recognise are crowded around an animal that's bellowing intermittently. I stumble forwards a few steps, then stop. Look further afield. Brown lumps, port-wine shapes, tawny colours. I watch for the flick of a tail, a raise of the head, but there's nothing.

Dead. The cows are dead.

I begin to jog, navigating the uneven earth as quickly as I can, my feet landing awkwardly. The men are bent over a brown cow that's lying on its side. I stop when I'm close enough to see the animal's face. Red mucous clusters around its wide nostrils. Foam escapes from its mouth. The eyes, usually clear and glossy, are half closed and red. The animal's entire body judders forcefully, then flops into momentary stillness. A leg twitches; the head lolls back and forth. I swallow a cry. The animal is in agony.

One of the men sits back and rubs his hands on his thighs. The other stands and walks over to Matt, says something in his ear, shaking his head. Matt grasps his head in his hands and bends over halfway, then he staggers a few steps away and screams. The sound echoes around us, and we drop our eyes to the ground. Matt returns to the cow, leans down and strokes its head tenderly. James turns around, looking for me, and we lock eyes: he holds up his hand, *don't come closer.* I watch as Matt retrieves something long and black from the grass next to him – a rifle – and the three men stand back in unison while Matt aims it at the cow. A *clap!* hits the air, and I press both hands to my mouth to stop my scream. I look at the innocent creature, I can't help it. All that's left of the head is ragged red tissue, white bone and brown hair.

We stand unmoving. After a moment, Matt drops the rifle and lurches to the paddock gate, grasping it as he bends over to take in air. I take furtive steps towards him, my legs feeble.

'Matt.' I'm near tears. I don't know what to say.

'Poisoned,' he says bluntly.

'I don't understand.' I can't compute the word.

'How many?' James is with us now.

'Dunno.' Matt's eyes run over the paddocks, the cogs in his brain struggling to engage. His ruddy face is tear-streaked. 'The cows by the dam are dead.'

'And the steers?' James asks.

'I'd already moved the steers to the river, they're alive. And the bull's with them. But, about seventy dead in here.' He nearly breaks down; he hiccups to suppress a sob.

One of the other men calls out. 'Mate, there's some down there still moving.'

We all look down the paddock; he's right. Several black and white cows are up and wobbling; one buckles, the legs crumpling like they all broke at the same moment. Another dips its head and begins to heave.

'Shit.' The man is urgent. 'We gotta get them in the float now.'

Matt nods and turns away from us. 'I'm going with the guys.'

'I'll come,' James says, but Matt doesn't seem to hear him.

They all jump into the van and drive roughshod across the paddock, bouncing over wombat holes and quartz rocks. Before long they're leading the cows into the float, closing the door. Driving slower back up the hill.

They stop to open the van door and James jumps out. 'Don't worry about this,' he says, nodding to the paddock. 'I'll shoot the rest.'

Matt is hunched in the van, eyes on the floor. James slides the door shut and moves to the driver's side window.

'And I'll pay for the treatment. Send me the account.'

The man nods and James slaps the van and steps away. We watch them disappear down the drive. When they're gone, I survey the paddock once more. I can't look at James; I know I'll cry. There's a small cluster of dead cows by the dam, and then dark shapes spread out over the paddock. Even worse: I can pick out every calf, even from a distance. They are half the size. James reaches over and takes my hand.

'What could have happened?' I say, not moving. 'Why did Matt say they were poisoned?'

'Probably they were.' He is so certain, so matter of fact.

'Who would do that?' It's nonsensical; I think of black widows, or diabolical Agatha Christie novels; a villain spiking a drink.

James rubs my back. It's intended to be comforting, but I'm confused and scared and irritated, so I move away.

'This isn't uncommon,' James says. 'Back when this was a working farm, the cattle dip Dad and Grandad used had arsenic in it. Killed the ticks. Farmers don't use it now, but they buried the barrels all over the paddocks. We've had rain. One of the barrels probably split and leached into the dam.'

I stare at him.

'It happens. It's a farm.' He grimaces. 'Things go wrong.'

Something is missing. Rusty. I turn back to face the house but can't see him anywhere. Normally he'd be lying on the verandah; normally he'd have come to meet us. I run, grabbing my stomach to steady it.

'Rusty?'

I reach the verandah and ascend the steps as quickly as I can manage. I pant from fear and effort, swinging my head in both directions. The verandah is empty, no clicking of paws. I throw open the front door, even though I know he cannot be inside. I let him out this morning.

I curse myself.

'*Rusty?*' There's no response.

James calls out to me. 'It's okay.'

'What if . . . what if . . .' I can't get the words out.

'He's in Matt's ute.' James points to the vehicle, still parked off the drive. Rusty is sitting in the passenger seat, no doubt having jumped in when Matt left the door open. I call him and he moves into the driver's seat and waits for me, wagging his tail. I rush to him and we nuzzle together, my face buried in his soft neck, breathing in his comforting smell. His hair tickles my face and pokes up my nose; I don't care. His wet nose is cool on my clavicle. Finally, I lean back and hold his face, staring into his eyes.

'Don't ever drink that nasty dam water, okay?'

He seems amenable. I click my tongue and he jumps down from the ute and spends a good minute sniffing my jeans and shoes. Then we walk, side by side, to the house. James appears from the garage, carrying a large knife and a bucket.

'What are you doing?'

'Told Matt I'd finish off the cows that can't be saved.'

'They didn't take all the live ones?'

'No.' James hitches the knife into a cover and loops it onto his belt. 'There's three that are going to die. Didn't want Matt to have to shoot them himself.'

I eye the knife. 'Where's your rifle, then?'

'I forgot I've run out of bullets. Have to buy more. I'll slit their throats. Just don't tell Matt.'

I gape at him.

'It's the quickest way.'

'And the bucket?'

He pauses, then takes a deep breath. 'Look. They're still alive so their hearts are beating. I can't get them into the kill shed where the drain is. Just something Dad and I used to do if an animal was immobile in the paddock. Collect the blood and tip it into the drain. I don't want to attract more wildlife.'

I swallow hard and back a few steps away. Gesture to the inert bodies. 'And then . . . what happens with the dead animals?'

'Burn them.'

'What?'

He scans the scene, considering. 'But the damage to the paddock . . . too much wood and feed to lose. Safer to bury them.'

I don't know quite what to make of a mass burial. I head to the front door. James calls out behind me.

'There'll be a smell when the wind blows up until we work it out.'

I linger in the foyer, watching as James gets in his ute and drives down into the paddocks. I drop to my knees to pat Rusty and focus on his face, his warm, loving face, so I don't have to see the scale of death stretched out behind me.

—

Matt, prompt and productive as ever, returns at dawn the next day with several men and a truck towing a bulldozer. James answers the door and I eavesdrop on their conversation from the kitchen. They don't say much; just agree to bury the dead cows and arrange a time for the removal of the living steers and bull from down by the river. Matt doesn't want his remaining cattle on the farm. He's already found somewhere else.

I feel a deep disappointment. Matt, while sharing absolutely nothing in common with me, has been a welcome visitor to the house. He turned up to check the cattle, but I felt like he was really checking on me. We planned a lot of jobs for the property together, jobs that will now go ignored. Part of me hoped that if I could improve the house and its landscaping – the shed, the roses, gutters, lawns – I might have achieved something, might have started to make the place a home. But this landscape isn't made to be controlled.

I pour myself a glass of water and pull out the sleeve of hormone medication: letrozole. There are five pills. One per day, starting on the second day of my cycle. I was surprised last night when my period came on aggressively, the heaviest it's been in months. It's three days early.

I swallow the letrozole and cough a little. James calls out from the foyer, 'I'm going to help the guys with the cows,' and I yell back, 'Okay,' over the slamming of the front door.

James is so rough. No wonder the doorknobs are hanging by a thread.

———

James wasn't exaggerating about the smell; the wind blows the rancid scent directly to the house. As the sun rises, the bulldozer excavates a series of pits. The men loop a metal chain around each dead cow's neck, attach the chains to their utes, rev the engines and drag them into the holes. At this point, the wind picks up, and though I'd been watching from the verandah in a show of moral support for Matt, I go inside and observe from behind a window instead.

It doesn't take the men as long as I thought; I assumed days, but it's all done in a matter of hours. By the afternoon the men pull out, and James is showering, scrubbing himself down vigorously. I gaze out the bedroom window. The paddock is utterly changed: where once it was rolling green, feed and some pesky tussock, it's now upended. Everything that was underneath is now on top: deep brown earth, haphazardly razed, the occasional lump rising above the flat ground. It's a huge cemetery, now.

Tears prick my eyes. The paddock wasn't the only thing transformed: Matt looked a different man. His posture was slumped. I watched him nod and issue short instructions during the burial, pointing to different cows. Even from a distance, I could see that none of his enthusiastic, larrikin charm survived their deaths.

James enters the bedroom, rubbing himself with a towel, and opens the chest of drawers. 'You okay?'

I sit on the bed, watching him dress. 'Matt looked broken.'

'He'll be right. It's farming life.' James sits next to me. We both face the window, the brown paddock looming ahead. 'He'll get through it,' he says. 'My grandfather and Dad . . . the animals they lost. Matt's got all his steers and his bull still, which is a big win.'

A win seems an odd way to describe the events of the past twenty-four hours. 'How?'

'He only lost the cows. The females.'

I blink at him.

'He's still got all the males.'

I bend over; I feel sick. 'God.' All the female cows, dead; all the calves they bore, dead. And it doesn't matter, because the males are alive. Succession continues. Tears roll down my cheeks and James puts his arm around me. The feeling of fitting together perfectly is gone; I shift.

'All the calves. All the mothers.'

James makes a clicking noise. 'I didn't think. I shouldn't have said anything.' He squeezes me tighter. 'Just didn't want you to worry about Matt. He'll start again.'

I hiccup, straining to keep the crying at bay. 'Why would he want to? He had to kill the animals he loved.' I can't get the image of Matt tenderly rubbing the head and nose of one of the dying cows out of my mind. What it must have taken for him to step back and shoot her dead.

James strokes my head and says softly, 'It's mercy.'

I wriggle backwards, fumble at the sheets, put space between us. My vision blurs with the image of my mother, bone-thin, jaundiced, lying on her bed, gasping for air, her skeletal hand squeezing mine. There had been begging. There had been entreaties. Enduring pain to stay alive is not mercy. Alleviating pain through death is not mercy. There is nothing merciful in illness or dying. What a lie we like to tell ourselves.

—

I'm rattling a doorknob so hard, my fingers are frozen in a kind of arthritic spasm. I can barely breathe; something is blocking my nose and mouth. Opening my eyes, I stare up at an unfamiliar ceiling, a raked timber roof I've never seen before. The rattling continues, though it isn't me grasping at the door anymore. I'm lying down, immobile. Trapped. Air leeches out of my lungs. Dots swim in front of my eyes and I fade away.

My mother's face appears. Gaunt, with big eyes – so much white around the irises. They bulge in a face yellowing from pancreatic cancer. Her body is systematically shutting down, organ by organ, and it shows in her skin, her eyes. Her hand is gripping something. I look down; her brittle, bony fingers are wrapped around my broader, fleshier hand. Then, the moaning: the low hiss of my name, and eventually, just grunting and fitting.

There's a giant clang. I look up. I'm cold, wet, and there's a thin sliver of light metres above me, like the crescent of a moon. It disappears with a scraping sound, and then there is complete and total blackness. I reach out blindly, my hands scrabbling to find purchase; I turn in a circle and find only stone.

Day five, another letrozole pill, the final for the month. James seems lighter and happier now we have a plan for conception. He breezed out the door after giving me a particularly wet kiss this morning. I rub my fingers over my lips, still feeling phantom saliva even though I wiped it off straight away. We'll have sex soon; he's thrilled by the idea.

I swaddle myself in a wool blanket and step outside to the front verandah. The winter sunshine is beautiful and clear. I don't look away from the paddock, but with Rusty at my feet and protected from the chilly air, I tell myself there is still the possibility of renewal: there has to be. At least for James and me. I've made efforts to look after the house; I keep the fire stoked all day; I plan and cook dinners. I even finished clipping the roses, wearing a long-sleeved flannel shirt of James's.

I needed to do something.

I hear a dull whirr and a crunching noise and look out the kitchen window. Matt's ute rolls into view, rattling over the stony driveway. I feel immense relief to see him again and wave wildly. He raises two fingers – the country salute – in response. Following him is another truck with a huge trailer; it pulls over to the front paddock gate. Matt exits the ute, and I gesture for him to come over.

He waits at the bottom of the stairs, stamping his boots on the ground as I walk to the top of the steps. Rusty trots to him, sniffing at his legs.

'Matt.' If I hadn't been wrapped in a blanket, I'd have given him a hug.

'Yeah, g'day.' He fidgets and doesn't look at me, grabbing the waist of his jeans and pulling them up.

'Can I get you guys a coffee or a water? Do you want to come in for a minute?'

'Nah. No. Thanks. We're just here to get the bull and the steers.'

'Okay.'

'We won't be long.'

I shake my head. 'Please. Take as long as you need.'

He gazes at the paddock; I hope he isn't reliving the discovery, the awful choices he had to make. The paddock is still brown and grey and lumpy. I can barely remember what it looked like before, and it doesn't matter anyway. This is what it is now. The aftermath of a seismic event.

'Stop by when you're finished.' I want to delay the inevitable; I can't fathom not seeing him again. 'Come and say goodbye.'

He nods and trudges away. The men from the truck are standing beside it, smoking and pointing down the paddock, plotting a course to the river. They speak briefly to Matt and then they open the paddock gate and rumble through. The procession eventually disappears; Rusty sits on the front lawn watching long after I can no longer see the vehicles, his ears pricking at sounds I can't hear.

I get up to retrieve my laptop from the living room and return to the verandah. Keeping watch. I don't want Matt to just leave.

Two hours later, I hear crunching as the vehicles make their way up to the paddock gate. Rusty stands, tail erect, sniffing the air. He runs to the fence and I call him back. Chastened, he clambers up the stairs and sits, peering up at me earnestly. I tell him, 'No, stay,' and he whines and huffs, then dramatically flops on the ground. I don't know what mix of breeds he is but I'm certain I don't want to let him loose around a truck containing a bull.

The truck and trailer roll on, straight to the driveway and soon disappear. The ute parks in front and Matt rolls down his window.

'That's it,' he calls to me. 'We're all good. Got 'em in the yards and up the ramp no trouble.'

I walk down the steps to get closer to him, telling Rusty to stay.

'Matt, I just want to say I'm so sorry.' I don't want to make things awkward, but it was too big a thing, too terrible an experience, not to acknowledge.

He shakes his head, glances at the miserable paddock. 'Thanks.'

'I wish it had never happened. I feel – we feel – utterly responsible.'

Matt gives a dry laugh. 'Don't think James does.'

'What do you mean?' I try not to sound prickly.

He shrugs. 'I got the vet bill the other day. I thought James was going to pay it.'

'He is. I heard him say that.'

'Well.' Matt taps the steering wheel and shrugs.

'I'll make sure he does.'

His face falls suddenly, the bravado gone. His chest deflates. 'Thanks. I mean, it's not about the money.'

I recall his expression when he comforted the dying cow; the grief etched into his face when he pointed the gun. 'I know it's not.'

'It was definitely arsenic.' He finally looks at me.

'James said there's old barrels buried all over, from his grandfather's days or whatever.'

Matt regards me for a moment. 'There are arsenic barrels in the shed. I found 'em when I was cleaning it out.'

The relaxed look he wore when we first met is gone. He's firm, and the frown lines I'd never seen on him seem permanent now. I shake my head, but I don't know, I don't know.

'My cows died in a couple of days,' he says. 'That ain't leaching. There's a lot of arsenic in that dam.'

He sticks out a hand and I shake it numbly. Then I hold his hand with both of mine and look into his eyes. But I can't say anything. I need him to know, without betraying James, the man I'm trying to have a baby with, that I feel what Matt feels. That I'm devastated, too. His hand is rough and warm and solid. I find it hard to let go. All I want is to rewind the clock. I should have been better at noticing things; maybe I could have done something to change it. He waits until I'm ready to release his hand.

'Be safe out here, okay,' he mutters.

He pats me on the shoulder. His car window slides up, he rolls down the driveway and is gone.

—

At dinner, I ask James directly if he's paid the vet bill. He's confused.

'For the cows?'

'What else?'

'No, Matt would pay that. They're his cows.'

'But you said you'd pay it. I heard you.'

'Did I?' He chews his lip, frowning. 'I don't think so.'

I excuse myself to the bathroom, closing the door and standing against it. I text his number furiously: *Matt, we'll pay the vet bill. Send it to me. Leila.* I press send. A line of green appears at the top, slowly loading, the text in telecommunication limbo. *Please,* I pray, *once, just this once, give me decent service somewhere other than the kitchen.* For a moment it seems it will send, there's half a bar, then it disappears, and a red exclamation point appears: *Your message was undeliverable.* I look his number up on WhatsApp, but he's not there.

I go to the study to use the landline instead, but when I reach the desk, I pause. The phone is gone.

———

Snow arrives at the end of July. I wake one morning, go to the kitchen to make coffee and see white flakes floating to the ground outside. I rush back to wake James and he says, sleepily, 'It's just frost, it won't settle.' But it does. It's the first snow in five years. It continues well into August.

James drives to work the same as always, no chains. It's light snow, but I get up early each day and sit in the kitchen and watch, enraptured. I've never seen snow fall before, not even in the time I spent in London: climate change rendered that year's Christmas unusually warm. Rusty whines and I take him outside to walk, but he doesn't like the icy wetness and returns, defeated after each attempt. I wander around the front yard, listening to the squeak and crunch under my gumboots, feeling the tickle of snowflakes on my upturned face. The curves of green and parcels of crops and mountain haze and army of trees are gone, everything is blanketed in white; we are a tiny outpost in the cold, and, to the land, we may as well not exist.

OVULATION

(ov·u·la·tion) *noun*
the release of a mature egg from the surface
of the ovary. The egg is funnelled into the
fallopian tube and towards the uterus by
waves of small, hair-like projections.

Unless the egg meets a sperm
during this time, it will die.

Winter is over and when I'm alone in the house I feel it move, speak, exhale. When I see or hear incomprehensible things, I acknowledge to myself that these experiences are mounting evidence of my emotional instability: the result of my pills and my stress about my health. They are not real.

So, I let it all wash over me. When I feel an unusually cool draft, I place another log on the fire, don another jumper. At night, when I feel a presence, hear a creak, or glimpse a shadow in the corner of my eye, I merely roll over. When I am struck by intense waves of loss, grief, shame and anger, I remind myself that these are my own feelings, to be processed, not externalised. The house is not a person. The house does not have feelings. I must not blame the house.

I'm not pregnant. This is my third cycle with the hormone tablets and my body has changed. I'm spongier, weightier; my breasts are larger, and my stomach stippled with fluid. My hips have widened. My face appears more swollen. James and I had sex three times during my first month's ovulation period. During the act itself, I smile up at him and make the noises he likes: I moan and squeal and scratch my nails down his back; he is elated. Red-necked and sweaty, he clutches at me like a koala to its mother, coming with a shudder, and then he falls asleep while I lie awake, sticky and numb, trying to decide if the house is sighing or if I am.

I swallow another pill. The third for this round. September, month three. The doctor recommended six months of the letrozole. Six months of planning when to take medication, when to have sex, waiting each month to bleed, or not. Avoiding alcohol, soft cheese and caffeine. I'm not even pregnant and I'm the only one making the sacrifices. *That's just being a woman*, my mother would snap, if she were here. I set my water glass down roughly. Everything shitty is excused by womanhood.

I walk to the verandah and sit on the chair, pulling on walking boots.

'Rusty?' I call. I can't see him, but he's outside somewhere. 'Walk?'

There's a whoosh of displaced air as the dog rounds the house, panting, paws thumping. He dances on his back legs, tail wagging in anticipation.

'You want to go for a walk?' I ask him a few times, pretending confusion. He leaps in the air and turns as if to take off, then runs back to headbutt my knee. I lean down to tie my laces and he licks my nose, then as I get up he zooms away again; I jog to catch up. Despite having complete run of the farm, Rusty's never more excited than when I walk alongside him. Dogs are community animals, I realise. They need to be part of a whole.

Without Matt, the grass will grow tall again, and the weeds will go to seed. I haven't mentioned the mowing to James. Already I feel like a non-contributor in my role as a stay-at-home partner; I'm not inclined to add nagging to my position description.

I did go to the shed to see if the arsenic barrels were still there, or if they were gone. It had a new padlock on it. I'm reluctant to speculate about that, though I know James was unhappy about us poking around in there to begin with. I think back to the baby clothes Matt found and imagine there could be other personal items stored away.

Besides, what James told me simply makes more sense. If Matt's right, it follows that James poisoned the cows on purpose. That isn't rational; Matt was, understandably, very upset. I'm wary of irrational thoughts these days. I can hear James say, *For argument's sake, why would I poison Matt's cows and ruin an income stream for my parents? Why would I hurt Matt like that?*

James would tell me to ask myself: *Is this a sensible thought or a silly thought? If it's silly, forget it. Put it in the bin.*

I follow Rusty to the river and we head upstream. I step heavily, hoping to ward off any snakes sunbathing to warm their cool bodies. The sun glows, picking out the scruffy yellow dandelions. Tiny black insects dive around me and cling to the front of my shirt; butterflies flit across my face and spirit away. Spring in the country is a glorious mess of green growth and animal noise. Birds call incessantly. I'm grateful for the sounds, but miss the cows' moos and bellows, something I didn't think possible when I first arrived here. Thankfully, they've been replaced by new noises, new life. James reckons we'll see lizards around the farmhouse as their babies hatch. I thought briefly of checking under the front steps to see if there really was a snake huddled in there; even worse, if it had reproduced. But the thought of getting on my hands and knees, and poking my head into the dark, made me hesitant. Instead, I enjoy visits from the benign animals: a pair of ducks have taken to wandering across the front yard each day at dusk, picking out worms and earwigs to eat. Cockatoos roost in the trees. Grey bush wallabies hop along the conifers; I hope James doesn't see them.

Something thick and buzzing whizzes past my head. I see a tree husk ahead of us, a hollow stump of a thing, close to the ground. It's heaving with activity. A swarm of bees hangs around the stump, treading air, humming in unison. Inside the stump is a round grey hive that extends into the hole as far as I can see. The insects wear distinct black and yellow stripes; a few plunge past my head.

'All right, all right.' I whistle to Rusty and steer him away. I wonder if there's a way to extract the honey; to harvest something from this land, something sweet, able to be shared. I feel a glimmer of motivation. I could leave some bottled for

James's parents, take some home to Sydney. Something tangible produced from this year away.

On our way back, we pass the ring of dead trees. I'm happy enough to see it; a decent landmark to help me circumvent the old well and its inexplicable smells. The white gums rise in their usual formation, fingers stretching to the sky, but they are no longer lifeless. Silvery green leaves sprout from various spots on the trees. Little tufts sit on top, like a baby's initial shock of hair. Not enough to make a canopy, but a start.

The bark is dappled with another colour too. I walk inside the ring of trees and see slashes of brown on every trunk. It can't be natural, at least I don't think so, although I have little knowledge of gardening or horticulture. It looks like it's painted on. Does sap leak in this fashion? I lean in closer to look at the stains: they're rust-coloured and I rub one with my thumb. Some of the brown flakes off. I sniff it; there's a faint tang of metal. Stepping back, I look from tree to tree. The pattern of the slashes is familiar: full at the bottom, arms reaching to the sky, a spiral in the middle of each figure. They must have been painted on deliberately.

Rusty whines. He's standing outside the ring of gums, tail stiff. Our eyes meet and he ducks his head, front paws tapping impatiently. I step outside the ring and he dashes off, back in the direction of the farmhouse. I follow, stopping again to consider the cluster of trees, but he bounds away ahead of me, so I must give chase.

When I reach him, he's rolling in grass and dirt like a maniac, pink tongue half out, grunting. His eyes loll back in his head. He pauses when he catches sight of me, then sneezes and canters over, panting heavily, tail flapping madly. He looks like he's grinning, and I smile back and go to pat him, but instantly recoil. He's covered in shit. Mixed through the scruff of hair on his neck, on the back of his head and all down his back. I don't know if it's fox or kangaroo dung, but the stink is overpowering.

'God, Rusty.'

He looks up at me, excited, not understanding that I want no part of him. I stand, hands on hips, wondering how to discipline him, when he leans forwards and licks my knee, then sits down as though anticipating a treat. I laugh; it just slips out. The dog is only obeying his instincts. No doubt he's wondering why I don't want to roll in the shit with him.

'Let's get you home and wash you.'

When we reach the farmhouse, I tell Rusty to stay on the concrete path while I go inside through the back door. I grab detergent from the laundry, a bucket that I fill with warm water, and a scratchy old towel. Select a fresh scrubbing sponge from the kitchen drawer. I cast around for something to protect my clothes and settle on a bin liner, punching holes through it for my head and arms. Add some dog treats to my pocket. I carry the bucket out first and set it down next to Rusty, who sniffs it but doesn't try to drink from it. Then I return with the towel and detergent.

'Stay.'

I squeeze detergent over him, from his head down to his tail, then soak the sponge in the water. I press it into his head and scour back and forth, working my way through his scruff and down his back, pausing only to rinse the sponge in the bucket. The water becomes murky. He whines, but I tell him to stay, and he obeys, his back legs wavering only a little. I kneel to get closer to him and he tucks his nose under my armpit. When I'm satisfied there are no clumps left, I leave the sponge floating in the brown water and walk over to the hose. Rusty shivers, smothered in white bubbles, ears flattened against his head. I twist the tap on and unravel the hose. Gently, I squeeze the nozzle and water streams out, rinsing the suds from his body. He shirks the hose, ducking away, only tempted back by the dog treat I offer him. He crunches on the dehydrated beef stick and watches me intently.

'We're nearly done.'

Quickly, I hose him down again, looping my arm under his neck and gripping him so he can't move. Once the water begins to run clear, I let him go and he shakes vigorously, his ears making a satisfying wet rattle. I give him a second treat, then wrap him in the towel to rub him dry. He likes the massaging and stands close to me, relaxed. For a moment, I stop and simply hug him. His nose tilts up and touches mine, and I know I'm forgiven.

I go back to rubbing him down, but he darts off; he's had enough. He taps at the screen door and I open it for him. The moment we're inside, the damp dog smell attaches to the walls, part lemon detergent, part dirt, part bitter. But underneath all that is his natural mild scent, the whiff of his skin and hair and oils. He collapses on his side on the living room floor, one eye closed, the other watching me. Rusty makes me feel protected in a way I've never experienced before. He makes no demands, but is concerned about me always. He asks for nothing but love, and the simplicity of it, this easy reciprocity, makes me feel safer than I ever have before.

—

Here are the things I will gain if I have a baby with James: admission to mum's groups, both online and at the local park; the right to complain about low milk production; guilt over using formula; a newfound ability to prop a living creature over my shoulder and pat it firmly on the back until it burps; a vagina that will either be torn up and stretched to infinity or perfectly fine, depending who you ask; saggier breasts; diastasis recti; insomnia; an emotional equilibrium finely tuned to my child's level of happiness; endless discussions over when we plan to have another; tears on the first day of school; carpooling; sports days; a shared household calendar; pride every time my child reaches a milestone or achieves anything; wonder at my child's first word; the worry of my child's first heartbreak; despair at my child moving overseas; unbridled happiness when they move back home; and hugs – so many warm hugs.

My child will experience none of the following: a mother lying in bed all day, refusing to answer any questions, including, *What's for dinner?*; strange new men every few months, with nothing in common but a swift exit; an overflowing kitchen bin that's home to a growing cockroach family; the panic of being forgotten in the school car park long enough that the sun turns orange and evening beckons; stiff, unbending hugs; empty bottles in the sink and vomit in the bathroom basin; stealing money to buy lunch from the tuckshop; and later, stealing money to buy weed; the certainty of being unwanted; the responsibility, at seventeen years old, to care for their dying mother; the resentment of not having a chance for the relationship to heal in later years, because there are no later years.

—

James is gently shaking me awake. At first, I see only his shoes, then cast my eyes up to see him squatting, his worried face looking down at me. Tucked close to me is Rusty. My arm is around him, and he's snoring. I blink a few times and slowly sit up.

'Why are you on the floor?'

Rusty stirs and swings his head backwards to look at me, as if to say, why are you moving? I scratch under his chin, worrying a stubborn hair, and he rests his head back on the living room rug.

'Sorry. I fell asleep.'

'Why are you so tired?'

'The hormones, I guess.'

There's a quiet moment between us while James looks me over. He seems to battle with himself briefly, and then he says: 'What about the painkillers? Are you still taking them?'

The baldness of the question unsettles me. 'No.'

'Okay.'

He lets out a long breath and then offers me a hand. I take it and we stand up together. James collects me in a conciliatory hug; I pat his back while he burrows his face into my neck. After a while, I pull out of the embrace and walk to the kitchen, James following, a little tension released. I fill the kettle and switch it on, pulling out mugs. Coffee for James, decaffeinated herbal tea for me.

'How was your day?'

He launches into a detailed recount: government funding not renewed, a psychiatrist who didn't review a medication report correctly, and the failures of the Office of the Public Guardian. I listen intently. His work is interesting, and I miss my own. I sit down, sip my drink and make the appropriate facial expressions. After he finishes, he asks me how my day was.

'I took Rusty for a walk. He rolled in shit, so I washed him.'

'He hates baths.'

'He was all right. We found a beehive. Do you think we could extract the honey somehow? It would be nice to leave some bush honey for your parents.'

'A hive? Where exactly?'

I describe it as best I can. The half tree stump with the buzzing insects, the grey fingers of hive filling the hollow.

'A grey hive? What did the bees look like?'

'Yellow and black.'

'Furry? Or smooth?'

I picture their bodies. 'Smooth.'

James pulls open my laptop and quickly types, then swings it back around to show me. On the screen are black and yellow insects exactly like the ones I saw.

'Are these the bees?'

I nod.

'Those aren't bees. They're European wasps.'

'Wasps?' I stare at the image. Black and yellow, hovering. Like bees. 'But they didn't try to sting me.'

'It's pure luck you didn't get stung. Not to mention—' he breaks off, rubbing his temples.

'What?'

'Rusty. European wasps can easily kill a dog. They start stinging you, or Rusty, and they won't stop. If you run, they'll chase you. Jesus.' He's frustrated with me, pushing his mug away. 'You need to be smarter than this.'

'I didn't know. I've never lived on a farm before.'

'Research something for once!'

I draw back when he snaps at me, struck dumb by familiarity. The specifics of many of the memories are hazy, but that tone, the contempt, is the same one my mother used. For a moment, I'm frozen while a roll call of my mother's exasperated insults echoes through my mind. I won't let them harden into actual words. I just remember the feeling: of being stupid and worthless, the reason her life wasn't what she'd expected. I've always remembered the violence, the slapping, whacks with a wooden spoon, the flying objects and whippings with a belt, but in the end, it wasn't the physical stuff that really hurt. Besides, once I reached my teens, she couldn't touch me anymore; I was taller and stronger. She relied on her most powerful weapons then: words. Every single one chipped away at me until I believed them. I was *a bitch, a whore, a stupid slut, a failure, a fat cunt.* They come to me even though I try not to think of them. They're ugly words. I ran from those words for years, but here in this house, they've found me; they pile up around me; they will not be ignored.

James is trying. I'm trying. We speak to each other nicely; we eat dinner together and talk about our days. He kisses me often. I have sex when required. Being our third month on fertility medication, we don't want to waste it. He tries to forget that he's irritated by my presence and my inability to adjust to the farm. I try to forget everything.

We're going into town for the Bathurst Spring Festival. James's colleagues will be there, and I badly need someone to talk to other than James. We need reminders of our old life: drinks, restaurants, laughter, conversation. Squeezing each other's hands under the dinner table, exchanging understanding looks across groups of people. We did have it all. Until I changed. I'm the one who messed things up. He doesn't say that, but I know it. Would I have stayed with someone who spent weeks at a time in bed? Who refused to speak half the time? I'm not sure I would have. I force myself to see our situation clearly. James has stood by me.

Our drive into town is scored by James's favourite Spotify playlist, a mix of acoustic covers and ballads: Diesel is crooning 'Fifteen Feet of Snow'. Rusty is secured in the tray; I couldn't bear to leave him at home alone. His face is turned gleefully to the oncoming wind. He's in heaven. It's early dusk and the sun is setting, casting a brilliant orange and pink glow. The trees lining the O'Connell roads have burst into blossom; white and pink petals are everywhere.

James is excited to show me the glasshouse at the festival, which promises an impressive array of tulips. He's determined to develop my green thumb. I'm looking forwards to the local gin distillery's signature cocktail: a blue gin that turns purple, spiked with a sprig of fresh rosemary. I haven't had anything alcoholic while we've been trying to get pregnant again, but tonight I've ruled an exception, and James hasn't fought me on it.

Undulant hills and soaring poplars pass by as we drive. I tell James he was right all those months ago: it really does remind me of Tuscany, and he's pleased, though I can tell he doesn't quite believe me. I don't say how lush Italy is and how the farmhouses are more charming, with their old stonework and small turrets. I don't mention that I drank my weight in sangiovese and chianti in San Gimignano, that my friends and I wandered around the vineyard, drunk and full of bread and cured pork. One of those friends moved to Canada and we've lost touch; another moved back to Brisbane and has three children under five.

We're on the Western Highway now, which is crammed with more cars for Bathurst than I've seen before. We all inch forwards together, P-platers weaving in and out of lanes unnecessarily. I ask about parking, and James says there'll be plenty, it's just a bottleneck until we get off the highway. As we approach the town centre, I stare up at the billboard for the missing local girl. Renee Brice. I rub James's knee and point.

'Terrible.'

He glances up. 'Awful.'

'Did you know her?'

'She went to my school.'

We pull into Bentinck Street and park in the undercover car park that services the Woolworths.

'Happy to go from here?' James asks.

'Yeah. Rusty will be glad of the extra walk.'

James unclips Rusty from the tray and fastens his lead. As soon as the dog hears the click of the lead around his collar, he leaps to the ground and takes off, yanking James's arm. I tell James I'll take him, and he hands the lead over. I mutter, 'Walk with me,' and Rusty pulls back to my side, matching my pace.

'Got him well trained,' James says.

'We walk together a lot.'

James takes my other hand, and we join groups of people all walking in the same direction: couples old and young, but mostly families. Parents younger than James and me, with three or four kids, holding juice poppers and Freddo Frogs, wearing warm coats and beanies, because the night air in spring is still cool. The kids in front of us push each other and snicker; a little one gets upset and his mother picks him up swiftly, positioning him on her hip and giving him a firm pat on the back. He hiccups a couple of times, his face on her shoulder, his hand gripping a jelly snake. His eyes meet mine and he scowls.

The park is lit up like a wonderland. There's a huge Ferris wheel covered in lights flickering from green to pink to blue to white; people are queued down the street, waiting for their turn. The trees in the park are illuminated and their foliage filled with fairy lights. An ice-skating rink has been erected in front of the town hall; it's festooned with lights, and the city hall has swirls of colour projected onto it. Children skate with varying degrees of success. The bold ones crash into each other, screaming with laughter; the nervous ones grip the hoarding and look about for their parents. On the far side of the park, food and drink trucks are parked side by side, with people milling about, holding hot chocolate, fairy floss, popcorn, hot dogs and drinks. I spy the truck I'm after: *Whisky and Gin!* I tap James on the shoulder and lean into his ear.

'I'm going to get a drink.'

He looks over at the trucks. 'I'll get it. You stay here with Rusty. Gin cocktail?'

'Yes, please.' I watch him enter the crowd. A little girl nearby catches sight of Rusty and squeals: she runs to him, and her tiny hands grab at his face and ears.

'A doggy!' she cries and presses her face against his nose. Rusty bristles, moving slightly away from her. I lean down.

'He likes gentle pats. Like this.' I show her how to stroke his head and scratch behind his ears.

'Wow.' She's spellbound.

'Evie!' The girl turns and I see a woman walking towards us. 'Sorry,' she says to me, scooping up the child, who says, 'Mum, can we get a doggy? Pleeease?'

I give her mother a sympathetic smile as they leave. I watch them until they blend in with other families and I can't make them out anymore. The way the families move is chaotic: the kids wander off, distracted by twinkling lights, and the parents reach out quickly, jerkily, to grab their hoodies or their upper arms. In families with multiple children, the kids amble ahead of the parents in a loose group, laughing loudly or shoving each other, the mother staring intently at them like her eyeline has the power to hold them, the father looking into the middle distance, slack-jawed and exhausted. It's hard work now, I want to tell them, but imagine when they're adults and you're all together for birthdays, and Christmas, and everyone's finally grown up enough to be friends, to forget the grievances of childhood. You'll have the bond of shared memories, you'll say, *Remember when we used to go to the Spring Festival and ride the Ferris wheel and eat curly chips on a stick,* and everyone will murmur their agreement and share a funny story of when it all went wrong but it was really all okay.

I feel a squeeze on my shoulder and turn around. James holds out a clear plastic cup filled with lavender liquid, a rosemary sprig poking out jauntily. I take a long sip. There's a couple close to James, looking at me.

'Hi,' I say.

'This is Nick,' James says, 'and his wife, Melanie.'

I reach out and shake their hands. 'Lovely to meet you.'

'Nick's my boss,' James says, and Nick, looking bashful, waves a hand.

'Not tonight,' he says genially. 'I've been trying to organise dinner for the four of us. We've heard so much about you, Leila. We've been looking forward to meeting you.'

I smile, though I immediately feel uncomfortable; has James said good things or bad things? Will I live up to either picture he's painted of me?

'I hear you're taking a break this year,' Melanie says, moving closer to me. 'You sounded so busy in Sydney; you must be enjoying it out here?'

The men start their own conversation, and Melanie leads me to a cluster of bar tables and stools.

'It's different out here,' I say. 'I'm still adjusting.'

'Nick stole me from the city too.'

I realise Melanie is delighted to find someone with whom she thinks she has something in common.

'He did?' I say, feigning surprise.

'Yes! Years ago, now. I was a bit younger than you, though. I was nursing, at Westmead, and Nick was the psychiatrist on the ward, and . . .' Melanie continues in great detail, and I nod at the appropriate intervals, draining my drink rather quickly. James notices and fetches me another. I clutch Rusty's lead and he sits wedged under the bar table, head on his paws, ears pricked, his eyes looking up at me as if to say, *What are we doing here?*

—

James and Melanie have gone in search of food. The lines are long, so they'll be a while. I'm warm from four gin and tonics, feeling slack, and less anxious than before. Nick is as talkative as his wife, so I don't have to contribute much. I've learned their entire life story, up to Nick establishing the first holistic mental health practice in Bathurst, where James now works.

'We manage everything from aged care to youth to disability, to everyday people who need help,' Nick says proudly, and I nod enthusiastically, because he should be proud; he's making the community a better place. I know James feels the same passion about his own work, too. It's one of the things that attracts me to him. He's committed to making life better for the adolescents he works with. Behind every second door is a family in crisis; I know that well enough. I longed to be part of the functional fifty per cent. It's a desire that never truly goes away.

'I hope you don't mind,' Nick says. 'James has shared a little of what you're going through at the moment.'

I'm too struck to respond. It's worrying that he could be referring to a long list of problems and I don't know which one.

'Anyone would be hearing noises, or having fears, after such a big transition.' Nick smiles, cheeks dimpling. He has a sympathetic face. 'What I find in my practice is that, after an emotional or physical trauma, sometimes our brain gets stuck on high alert. We experience dangers where there aren't any.'

My mouth is opening and closing but I can't get a single word out.

'And fertility treatments are a difficult experience. Melanie and I went through the same, ten years ago. We're lucky to have our two now, but we understand how isolating it can be.' He pauses and reads my face. 'I hope I haven't said too much. But if you need someone to talk to, Melanie or I would be happy to lend an ear.'

I stand and stack my four empty cups, but I don't balance them correctly and they tip over. Melted ice spills out across the table and I gather the cups, turn on my heel and storm to the bin. I throw them in and then stand still, breathing hard, trying to contain the fury and humiliation I feel. *What right does he have*, I think. *What right?* I'm frozen, too angry to return to the table and make nice. I'm embarrassed, too. The years spent building resilience, building a career, blocking out the misery of my upbringing have failed suddenly. Moving here has somehow taken apart each of these achievements, exposed their innards and poked around to find the holes.

'Leila!'

I ignore James's call. I walk, haphazardly, looking for the way out. There are so many people now, I can't see where we came in. I bump and graze past them, trying not to trip on people's feet. I'm clammy and need space; I need quiet. Someone grabs the back of my arm; their grip is too firm for me to pull away.

'*Leila.*' James swings me around, and I'm crying now, taking in breaths too fast. 'Calm down, calm down,' he says. 'What's wrong?'

'You – you—' I can't get words out.

'Listen. Calm down. Do you know where Rusty is?'

I stop breathing and a hot, sick feeling rushes over me. I look down at my hand. I'm not holding his lead. When did I drop it?

'The table,' I cry. 'He's back at the table.'

'He's not. I thought he would be with you.'

'Oh my god.' I shake James off and look around wildly. I can't see Rusty anywhere. It's properly dark and all I can make out under the garish lighting are people in hoodies and beanies. I take off down the path; maybe he's gone to the food trucks. James is behind me, calling, but I ignore him and start asking people in the food lines if they've seen a reddish-brown dog; they haven't. I push to the front of the lines and ask the food purveyors, but they ignore me; too busy pulling together Greek gyros wraps and Brazilian barbecue trays. I check around the back of the trucks where the wheelie bins are; maybe he's looking for scraps. Nothing. I run around the outskirts of the park, feeling pain and cramping start up in my belly. I see cavoodles, kelpies, the occasional German shepherd and husky, but no Rusty.

'Are you all right?'

A hand reaches out and takes my arm. I look up and see a woman in a red puffer vest with a polka-dotted scarf around her neck. The macrame earrings. Amelia. The librarian. I stare at her wordlessly.

'Leila, isn't it? Do you need to sit down?' Her glasses reflect the colourful lights.

'I – I – have you seen a brown dog? Well – he's brown everywhere except he has a white belly, and I've lost him—' I stop and hiccup, then bend over, my stomach flaring with cramps. The gin has sloshed around in my gut and I haven't eaten yet. I shiver – suddenly and violently – and then I'm retching in the gutter, trying to hold back the bile with my hands, the wet mess splattering everywhere. I feel her holding back my hair and patting my back, saying, 'Are you alone? Can I take you home? Or to the hospital?' I stand up, panting, revolted by the grit between my teeth. I go to speak, but then James is there, thanking Amelia, his tone brusque. I want to explain to her, *It's me he's mad at, not you,* but he leads me away before I can. I turn back to look at her and she watches us with a deep frown, shifting from one foot to the other, her hands wrung together.

——

James takes me to the public bathroom and cleans me up. He speaks quietly, soothingly, while I cry hysterically for Rusty. When we walk into the restroom, a group of teenage girls glance at us and hurry out, eyebrows raised. James collects some paper towel, wets it and wipes my face down. I lean down to the sink and gargle some water. Once I've calmed down, I tell him I'm going to the toilet. He says he'll make our apologies to Nick and Melanie and meet me back here.

I sit on the toilet seat and shake, trying to figure out how I let go of Rusty's lead, how I could possibly have forgotten to keep an eye on him. The gin flavour has mixed with vomit and the thought of drinking flushes me with shame. I let Rusty down. I let everyone down. I'm thirty-seven years old, crying in a public toilet after getting too drunk and throwing up. I look at my hands. They are wrinkled and dry, skin peeling from the knuckles, which have broadened over the years. 'I don't recognise myself,' I say, and the words echo in the empty brick building. 'I don't recognise myself,' I say again, and with it comes fury and I clench my fist and start hitting my leg. After a while it hurts and I enjoy that, but I tire easily, so I stop and just sit, panting.

'Leila?' James's voice carries inside the building.

'Coming.' I get up and flush the toilet, even though I didn't use it; the ritual is important. I need to be put back together. I meet James in the doorway. He takes my hand, and we walk silently though the festival crowd, my eyes on the path, James navigating us. When we reach the street, there is finally air, and I look up and down the road, praying for Rusty to appear, but he doesn't. We keep on, and I realise we're walking to the car; we're going to leave. I'm trying not to cry, but pressure builds unbearably behind my eyes. I can't bring myself to even look at James. Rusty is his family's dog.

We enter the car park, breathe in petrol fumes and walk over oil splotches. We weave around cars entering and leaving and walk to the pylon marked 8C. As we near our parking space, I look down at the ground, barely able to believe we're just going to get in the ute and go home. I hear James say my name but can't look up, I'm starting to tremble terribly. He says it again and pulls on my arm. I look at him; he is pointing to the ute. There, in front of the vehicle, is Rusty, sitting at full alert, tongue out, tail wagging. At first I think it's an halluci-nation, that I'm dreaming, but then I rush forwards and throw my arms around the dog. He props his front paws up on my shoulders and sticks his wet nose into my neck. I hold him tightly until he squirms away and trots around to the back of the ute, where James has opened the tray. I meet James's eyes and for the first time, nothing, absolutely nothing, passes between us.

—

When we get home, James empties my handbag onto the kitchen table, everything scattered about. He unzips the pockets and pulls out every last pill. I'm stunned by the invasiveness of it; how demeaned I feel. I should be able to argue against this, snatch the bag back, but I don't. He arranges the packets on the table and reads them out. I don't need this. I know what I have and that there's more: in my bedside table, tucked under my mattress, nestling in my boots. I have prescriptions rolled up and stored in my coat pockets. I guess I always knew this day would come.

'That's enough now,' James says. He pops each individual pill from the foil and dumps them in a bowl, then fills the bowl with water. The pills start to disintegrate. Part of me wonders at this level of distrust between us, but another part thinks of Rusty slipping from my hand, so quietly and perfectly, and I cannot call James unreasonable. He sits opposite me.

'You're not coping.'

'I've been looking after Rusty,' I say automatically, before I realise I shouldn't even speak Rusty's name.

'You're taking medications you promised to stop.'

I don't remember making any such promise.

'You don't talk to me anymore.'

I laugh: sharp, machine-gun laughter. His face is ashen.

'I'm going to ask Matt to take Rusty for a while,' he says.

I begin to protest, then he slaps the table and I jump.

'You put him at risk!' he shouts. 'First the wasps, now this!'

'Matt won't take him,' I say.

"Course he will.'

'Not after the arsenic.'

There is a moment after I say this where I really don't know what will happen. I expect James to explode, perhaps I want him to. Perhaps I am goading him; I want to yell and scream all the hateful things I feel and think, I want this relationship to be torn apart. I know I can do it; I watched my mother perfect this routine for years.

Instead, he is weary, quiet, perhaps even sad.

'I'm going to get you well,' he says.

He empties the bowl of watery powder into the sink, then offers me his hand. I take it, and he leads me to bed and tucks me in. He gets in next to me and rolls over; soft snores rise within minutes. I wonder how he can sleep when I am so embroiled with rage, when he is taking from me the only thing I care about in this fucking place. Once I'm sure he won't hear me, I get up, push my hand under my side of the mattress and scrabble around until I grasp a foil packet. I pull it out and pop a Valium from the foil, then shove the remainder back under the mattress. I swallow it and go to the living room. Rusty looks up from his corner and I beckon him to the couch. He leaps up and I wrap myself around him tightly, the scruff on his neck brushing my chin. He nestles into me, claiming a cushion for his head, and I marvel at how human he seems, or perhaps I have made him this way, and then my muscles go slack, my eyelids heavy. Everything is dark. I have no memories, I have no thoughts.

—

I sense movement and resistance. Light streams into the room: it's morning. I open my eyes to see a hand reaching out. Rusty is a dead weight and James is trying to pull him down off the couch. He won't move and nor will I; my arm is slung over Rusty's belly.

'Get down,' James says, and I'm proud when Rusty opens his eyes to a slit, then closes them again. James leans over us, loops an arm around Rusty's middle and tugs. I don't remove my arm. Rusty buries his nose in my shoulder.

'Can you help?' James says. I tighten my grip on Rusty and close my eyes.

There are a few seconds of further yanking and then I hear footsteps leaving the room. I raise my head and listen closer. There is a jangling noise; Rusty's head jerks up, ears pricked. Car keys. *Damn it.* Rusty jumps up and trots to the living room door.

'Come on,' James calls and Rusty disappears into the hallway. I leap up and follow, getting there just in time to grab hold of Rusty before he canters out the front door.

'Sit,' I command, and Rusty looks up at me, confused. He slowly lowers his rear to the ground, then begins to whine. I'm holding him back from riding in the ute. If only I could explain to him what this really is: a trick, a dirty, nasty ruse.

'Rusty, let's go,' James says evenly, rattling the keys. Rusty gets up again, and again I restrain him. He looks up at me and sniffs; I'm ragged from the effort to hold him.

'Enough,' James says and comes over to us, trying to disentangle my grip around the dog's torso. I latch on harder, and Rusty must think we're playing a game because he sneezes and flops to the floor, rolling onto his back for belly scratches. I lean on top of him, my knees giving way; Rusty huffs, excited. His tail thumps against the floor.

James says my name. Rusty's rear leg is jabbing into my stomach, which is painful, but I don't care. My breath shortens; I moan. James pulls on my arm, unspooling me from the wrestler-like position I've adopted over the dog. I grunt, pushing against him; it's a sad attempt at an arm wrestle, and James wins easily. He puts both hands under my armpits, lifting me to my feet. In my ear he says, 'Go back to the couch, please Leila,' and I start to scream between jagged breaths, 'No! No! Fuck you! Fuck you!' And then it is over. James's arms are wrapped tightly around me. He holds me from behind and says, 'Breathe with me: in, out, in, out,' and I collapse. My knees buckle, and he goes with me to the floor. I'm on my knees while he holds up my torso and I sob loudly and painfully. Rusty comes over and licks my ear. I attempt to struggle, reaching out for the dog, but it's farcical and James says over my head, 'Let's go for a drive, you wanna go for a drive?' Rusty stands still for a moment and then throws his head back and lets out a long howl. He turns and ambles out the front door, looking back at me, his tail down. I fall back on my heels and James lets me go. He kisses the top of my head and then crouches in front of me, his face a mass of downturned lines, worn angles.

'I'll be back in an hour.'

The truck revs and there is crunching as the vehicle spurs into movement. I lie on my side, clutching myself, wailing, the house and I now barren together.

Here are the things I will lose if I don't have a child: the ability to answer without social anxiety when people ask, *Do you have children?*; the notion of dying with someone who cares enough to bear witness; being able to brush away the hair on the top of my child's head and then smell the crown; buying onesies and cooing over my baby's feet enclosed in the fuzzy fabric; serving food at the school tuckshop with all my mum friends; smiling with pride at Dad as our child performs on stage; nagging my child to please put away their school shoes or please empty their lunch box; family road trips to the beach; playing the child my favourite music and having them deride it; mountains of laundry, apparently; saying *because I said so*; screams and fights and tears, and being told I just don't understand, all to be resolved with a loose hug from a sullen child; driving lessons; endless jokes at Dad's expense; a drink on their eighteenth birthday; being thanked in a speech at a wedding I'll pay for but have no say in; the sweet hope of grandchildren, and the opportunity to right all the wrongs I committed when raising my own child.

I won't lose these things, not really, because I don't have them now. Instead, I will miss them. I will yearn for experiences I can never have; I will imagine the person I might have been and mourn for her. I might have been a much, much better person than I am now.

———

James hovers outside the bathroom. He wants to know if I'm bleeding before he goes to work. He wants to know if I'm okay. I tell him I'm not pregnant and to leave me alone. I look down at my thighs, squished together, my feet on cold tiles. My skin is sallow; the deep tan I sported from living in Coogee faded. Dusky blue veins criss-cross my legs, larger than I've ever seen them. My mother had them, too; I remember seeing her in shorts, with these royal blue webs wrapped around her thighs and calves, and thinking, *She's so old.* The flesh of my thighs is pressed together; everything is pudgy and doughy. I stand and wipe, noting the blood clots on the paper. It's a heavy period. Five days early. Month three on the letrozole has failed: I've had periods in July, August, and now September. I pull a pad from the ensuite drawer and line my undies with it. Pull my pants up, flush, then drop the lid of the toilet and sit on top of it. James is still outside the door; I can hear his feet shifting, his throat clearing. Now that Rusty is gone, everything else is quiet. James always has to be the largest presence.

'Are you coming out?'

I sit still, waiting for him to sigh and walk out of the bedroom. Then I delay a while longer, staring at the bathroom tiles. They're white rectangles with pale blue patterns along the edges. The pattern is busy, and I took it for an old-style floral when I first arrived, but now I see it's different. It's a rendering of the female form – a simple line drawing of hips, arms and a head – and she's holding a moon above her, with a crescent on either side. The tip of each crescent meets the crescent on the figure next in line, even across the grout of the tile. It must have been quite a job to line them all up. Some of the patterns are faded or scratched off; another thing that needs rectifying in this worn house. The shapes remind me of the unusual vases in the living room.

I leave the bathroom. There's a packet of pills propped against the lamp on the bedside table. A sleeve of letrozole, ready for month four. A little note sits under it: *Fourth time lucky!* James has added three kisses, tight little *x*'s, and I rearrange them in my mind to create a face with two *x*'s for the eyes and one for the mouth. I open the drawer and sweep the note and pills into it, and slam it shut. Then I get into bed and look at photos and videos of Rusty stored on my phone. I press play on a clip and hear my voice saying, 'You're a good boy Rusty! Yes, you are!' as he cocks his head left and right, his silky, black-tipped ears pricking up, and the tip of his bushy tail flickering. My hand enters the frame and scratches behind his ears and I hear myself say, 'I love you.' The clip cuts out. I scroll through the camera roll. I took photos of him everywhere: curled up in the living room asleep, his short white eyelashes visible; jumping into the ute; sitting on the couch, wrapped in a blanket I took from the bed, his brown eyes staring directly at the camera; standing in the front yard, ears up, positioned beautifully in front of the distant mountain range. That was one I intended to frame. I swipe over and over, then stop on the first image I ever took of him: standing to attention, every hackle up, his face trained on the attic window, where I heard a scream that sounded like death.

———

I stand up, dizzy and nauseous. In the ensuite, I change my pad and throw out the blood-soaked one, then I go to my leather jacket and ferret in the pockets to find a single sleeve of Targin. I swallow one, and a flash of my mother comes to me: her body thin and wizened, her dark skin yellowed and papery. She tries to talk; I lean my head in closer and feel the heat of her breath, but I can't make out the words. Her mouth smells like a chemical burn and her lips are cracked and dry. I get some pawpaw ointment and return to her side, dabbing the cream on her lips. She pushes me away angrily. I haven't understood what she wanted. She rolls over, her back to me, a collection of bones barely in the shape of a person.

Instinctively, I go to the foyer where my runners are, then simply stand and stare out the front door. I hear Rusty's nails clicking on the hardwood floor and imagine him nudging my hand with his wet nose, desperate for a walk. Matt was right; I shouldn't be here alone. I walk aimlessly back to the living room. I sit. I can't focus on the television. I stand and wander. Up and down the hall, into the study, back into the kitchen. I'm the ghost, now.

Three periods of failing to conceive, even with hormonal boosters.

I go to the linen cupboard and open the doors, scanning for the box of baby clothes Matt found back in July. It's not hidden; James put it on the floor of the cupboard. I take it out and open the lid. Sort through each piece. Clothes for a baby aged zero to one. All different shades of blue. Summer onesies with the clickable gussets. Winter onesies that make the baby look like a tiny frog, their hands and feet clad in soft fleece. Tiny overalls. T-shirts. And the hardest to look at: shoes and socks.

I hold the shoes in my palm and cry. I hang my head, squeeze the little rubber shoe, and whimper like the trapped animal I am.

—

When the crying subsides, I re-pack the clothes into the box and push it back to the bottom of the cupboard. On the shelf above are photo albums. I pull some out. Generations of family memorialised in sealed pages. I want to see if there's something I like here, something I can be part of. James and I could be captured here too, one day.

The first album is all James: his baby photos, his early birthdays and pre-school pictures, and I close it with a snap:

I can't bear to look at those yet. I pull out more. Pictures of Patricia and John in the seventies, and more images of their wedding. Then new faces – James's grandparents. His grandmother wearing a floral shirtwaist dress, gloves and stockings, holding a baby. John. Even as a newborn, John looked serious. I flip through and watch John grow up, always with the same taciturn expression.

I swap it out for the last album. This one has notes and letters in the pages, but it seems to be mainly about the stock. There are some grainy black and white images. The years aren't listed, and I can't figure out whether they're of Edward and Harriet, or his second wife Caitriona; or whether it's the next generation down: Francis and Catherine. I turn the pages and pause. Look closely. A sudden nervy sweat comes over me.

It's a picture of people down by the river. There's a woman on the bank, fully dressed, unsmiling, sitting on a rug with a picnic basket. Standing on the rocks in the river behind her is a young woman in a swimsuit, arms raised, as if in victory. Her face leaps from the page. Even fuzzy, even gritty, the ridges of her nose, the planes of her cheeks, the slope of her neck: I've seen her before. Standing further away, near the trees, is a man looking at her, a beard visible in profile.

I peel back the plastic film and slide out the photo. Holding the picture, I walk to the foyer and inspect the framed photos one by one, but they are all James at various ages. On the other sideboard, the photos are historical. There's an older man standing in front of a herd of cattle, his thick beard familiar. He wears a button-up shirt and heavy jacket, a cigarette trailing from the side of his mouth. It's the man from the river photo. I hold them side by side; keep looking. There's the same man again, and the fully-dressed woman, standing in front of this very house. There are no roses, and the grass isn't manicured; they're standing in calf-high weeds and scruff. Behind them, a younger woman, carrying laundry, is mid-stride through the front door, her expression suggesting she didn't intend to be in the photo. She is the girl in the swimsuit.

I pick the image up, grip it tightly and bring it to my nose. This man's face is the face from the conifers; this young woman's face is the face from the bathroom window. I'm sure. I'm *sure*. Am I sure? I move away, intending to go to the living room to study the images under a better light. As I pass the first sideboard, James's senior formal photo flashes in the corner of my eye. I pick it up and study it, too. The girl – her hair is blonde, she's younger and her face is softer and rounder – but the girl's face, that face looks just like Renee Brice.

—

Dinner is ready nice and early, proof I am no drug addict. I've made lasagne and salad and even a small loaf of bread from scratch. The house smells delicious – the smell of cooked yeast, garlic, basil and melting pats of butter – and James smiles tentatively. I know he's wondering what kind of show this is tonight. Truthfully, I'm wondering the same. I pour red wine into glasses as James goes to get changed; I manage to quickly finish one glass and fill it up again before he returns. When he does, I'm cutting the lasagne into large slabs and transferring them to our plates. He comments favourably on the aroma and then sits heavily.

'I worried about you all day,' he says. I don't think this is true. If it is, he was concerned about the fact that we're still infertile, not that I was alone without Rusty.

'I was lonely by myself,' I say.

'I have a good feeling about this month. Did you get my note?'

I'm proven right and resent him for it. He leans forwards and pulls his plate closer. Picking up his knife and fork, he cuts into the layers of mince and tomato sauce. It's soft and it flops everywhere, red juice bleeding around the plate, running under the salad. He piles up a fork with pasta and mince and thick bechamel and eats it. I watch him chewing and swallowing, chewing and swallowing. I take sips of wine. Everything we do is repetitive. Pregnant? Not pregnant. Pregnant? Not pregnant.

'New client today. A pregnant teenager.' He looks at me and I meet his eyes. 'It made me think.'

'You want to adopt?' I ask. He's never mentioned this before.

'Not *adopt*.' He says the word like it's diseased. 'Surrogacy. Your egg, my sperm.'

I don't know what to say to that.

'It would take the pressure off your body, using someone younger. And the baby would still be ours.'

I top up our glasses, contemplating this notion of what's ours. Rusty was ours, for a short while. He was mine. We share no genetic material, but we were each other's in a way that I suspect James wouldn't understand. The hot prick of tears comes on and I blink them away. I wonder if Matt was happy to take Rusty. I wonder if James ever paid that vet bill.

'I was looking at your family photos today.'

'Mum loves her family portraits.' James cuts another bite of lasagne, his knife screeching against the plate.

I go to the living room and collect the photos, return to the kitchen, and show him the photo of the man and two women first. I point to the man.

'That's the face I saw in the conifers.'

James leans back; he must be thinking, *Oh here we go, the lasagne was just the warm-up.* Undeterred, I point to the woman in the background.

'That's the face I saw in the bathroom window. The woman in trouble. She was bruised.'

There's a long, long silence. James looks at the photos, then at me. I want to say, *Yes, I'm serious. This is not a joke.*

'That's my great-grandfather, Francis,' he says. He points to the older woman. 'My great-grandmother Catherine. And the other girl was the housekeeper, I guess.'

'The girl who died here. Tilly Johnson.'

James nods, his expression turned to one of puzzlement. I'm a Rubik's Cube he cannot twist into a logical structure.

'She died in their bed,' I say.

'Leila. That's a very old rumour.'

'I've seen these people. I've seen them here, at the house. At the river.' Babbling again. Am I surprised? Do I believe in ghosts?

'You've seen their photos before. You're imagining it.' He's almost at his wit's end, I can tell. His arms are crossed tightly. 'You're coming off heavy meds. You're confused.'

I laugh and he seems to think this is further proof that I'm erratic.

'It will pass.' He reaches out and holds my hand, rubbing my palm with his thumb.

I pull away and place his senior formal photo in front of him: shiny suit, pimples and gelled hair. Jab it with my finger, pointing at the girl.

'Why did you lie to me about knowing Renee Brice?' It's a gotcha moment, a smoking gun, but I don't yet know what I've caught. What prize I've won by proving him a liar. Once you turn the tables, where do you sit afterwards?

I don't expect him to cry; I don't expect him to bury his head in his hands and sob.

We sit for a long time as he sniffles and weeps. I do not comfort him, but I do feel a twinge of guilt. I've treated him as my enemy for so long I've forgotten that he's human, too. A human that I loved, for a good chunk of time. He's imperfect. He lies and has secrets and feels like shit, too. Just like me.

—

James hiccups and sits, crumpled, in the dining chair. I take his hand and lead him to the living room, guide him to the couch, then sit next to him. I return to the kitchen and collect the wine glasses and bottle, come back and place them on the coffee table. I drink and wait.

'It's nothing like what you're probably thinking,' he says.

'I'm not thinking anything,' I say.

'I had nothing to do with her disappearance.'

'You knew her.'

'When we were young,' he says, rubbing his forehead. 'A long time ago.'

'Why did you lie? When I asked if you knew her?'

He looks at me, bleary-eyed. 'How could I answer that? Anything I say, you look for a lie. You don't trust me.'

'You *did* lie.'

'We both do.'

He tells me their story. Renee was his first love – 'this sweet, girl-next-door blonde, she had this big laugh and loved animals, especially farm animals'. They fell in love in high school and dated for four years, and after finishing university, James wanted to get married.

'She did a vet science degree, I did psychology,' he says. 'I thought we could set up our clinics out here, buy a property. Start our lives, like our friends were doing.' Renee was more hesitant. She changed, just a little at first: she dyed her hair dark, got a tattoo, made new friends, ones James didn't know. Then they found out she was pregnant. It was accidental, but James was over the moon. He proposed immediately, just some cheap chip of a diamond, but Renee loved it.

They left their share house in town and moved out to the farm, living with James's parents to save money. Renee's parents were disapproving, thought they were too young and too impulsive. Renee became estranged from them during that time, James says. She didn't want to see them.

The months passed. Renee wanted to give birth at home – this home. She had read about home births and how much better it was for the baby to be born without drugs and without the risk of infection at hospital. James's mother, being a qualified midwife, encouraged this idea. They bought a small pool for the birth, made a playlist of Renee's favourite music. She went into labour weeks early but insisted on following her birthing plan. They put her in the warm water and stayed with her for hours, but suddenly she began screaming in pain. The baby was coming.

'Feet first,' James says. Patricia managed to get the baby out, but he was stillborn; the umbilical cord had wrapped around his neck, and he'd suffocated.

Renee was never the same. She was quiet with them, uninterested in James or Patricia, or even in burying the baby. She didn't want to see the baby clothes James and Patricia had bought, so they stored them in the back of the shed. Renee refused to talk about the birth or the baby again.

'It fell apart,' James says. 'She gave me back the ring. She wanted to be out with her friends, out with Charlotte and Emma, drinking and dancing. Partying like everyone else our age.' One night she never came home. James thought she'd gone back to her parents. Renee didn't answer his calls or texts. A few days later, her father, Bob Brice, turned up knocking on the door and said Renee had disappeared, wanting to know if she'd returned to the farm.

'That's how we found out she was missing.' James's voice breaks. 'And she still is.'

—

We sleep together. Slower, sadder and more vulnerable than before. I experience nostalgia while fucking; rediscovering how rough the skin on his hands is and how much I like it. The way his mouth gets wet when we kiss; how neutral he tastes. During the sex, I think of his expression when I handed him the baby clothes. I run back through his reactions to losing our baby and understand them now. He's not leaving me, will never leave me, because he knows the pain of being left.

The next morning, I get up first, make coffee and leave James a cup beside the bed. I dress and go to the foyer, pull on my runners and pour ginger tea into a travel mug. Rusty might not be here, but I still am. I leave the house and walk towards the river, my boots catching dew from the grass. I sip the tea: grassy and fresh. The liquid is thin. The heat opens my eyes wider, jolts my nervous system. I imagine Rusty trotting ahead of me, tail aloft.

It's not so bad to do things alone. It doesn't have to break you to remember the times when you weren't.

—

When I return home, James has left for work. I take my boots off on the porch and clap them together, walk inside in my socks and ditch the travel mug in the kitchen sink. Then I stand, a little aimless, wondering what to do next. If I could find Charlotte's phone number, I'd call and arrange a catch-up. I hear the crunch of gravel and immediately I think of Matt – returning Rusty, perhaps? Could James have called him this morning?

I fly to the front door, but don't recognise the car. It's an expensive-looking sedan, tinted windows, navy, highly polished, with a fine sprinkle of dust around the tyres and doors. I stare at it, curious. I see the feet first – clad in leather boots, knee high – and look up to see a woman exit the car. She straightens and I take her in: wool skirt, white blouse, pearl earrings. Heavy diamond and gold rings. She still wears a perm, her hair a mass of grey curls, beset by flyaways. I feel a note of empathy; flyaways were the bane of my high school years. No hairspray, silicone or straightening balm would defeat them.

'Hi, Patricia,' I say.

'Hello, Leila,' the woman says, pausing to assess me. She takes in my socked feet, ratty trackpants and oversized t-shirt. My hair is in a half ponytail, my eyes still ringed by dark circles.

'Will you help with my bags?' she calls.

I nod, pull on runners and walk down to the car.

'I can't lift very heavy ones,' I murmur, feeling disinclined to put myself out, and she tuts.

'We can all do more than we think, can't we?' But she leaves the smaller case for me. Out of stubbornness I pull out the handle and roll it to the stairs, grass getting stuck in its wheels. Then, hoisting it up, I ignore the faint nerve pain in my abdomen and walk up the steps to the front door. Patricia is already inside, her other case in the foyer. I hear her clattering in the kitchen and stand in the doorway. She's stacking the dishwasher, a Chux in one hand, a plate with food debris in the other. I watch her wipe dried food off the plate into the bin. Then she bends and puts the plate in the dishwasher.

'Can I make you a cup of coffee?' I want to ask why she's here but suspect the answer will be disappointing.

'I brought tea,' Patricia says.

I collect two mugs from the hutch on the far wall. Patricia hands me two black tea bags; I put one in her mug, and herbal tea in mine. I fill the mugs with steaming water and carry them to the kitchen table. Patricia lifts each mug and swipes her Chux beneath it, swishing crumbs off the table into her hand and brushing them into the bin.

'Any morning tea?' she asks, and I baulk. 'Not to worry – I should have some cake in the freezer.' She rummages and pulls out a slab of something wrapped tightly in foil and unpeels it, leaving tiny flecks of silver behind. She pops it onto a floral-patterned plate, saying, 'It shouldn't take long to thaw.'

I sip tea while watching this pantomime. Patricia finally sits, letting out a long sigh and says, 'It's a lot to take care of, isn't it? A house.'

'My apartment is a lot smaller. Fewer things.'

'How's the book research coming along?'

I shrug. 'I've stopped.'

She smiles broadly. 'I don't mind saying I'm pleased. This family has been through enough.' She picks up a butter knife and hacks into the half-frozen cake then offers me a shard, which I decline.

'Banana and walnut loaf,' she says. 'Homemade. Good for fertility. Especially the walnuts, they strengthen a man's sperm.' She giggles and I feel queasy. She pops cake in her mouth. Her lipstick has smudged onto the mug and bled around her top lip. I look away in embarrassment and gaze out the window instead.

'I'm sorry for any insensitivity with the book idea,' I say. Patricia nods, her mouth full. We sit quietly while she chews and swallows.

'More importantly, how *is* the baby making going?' she asks brightly, her sun-spotted hands gripping the mug. One of her rings has slid around her finger, the diamond clinking against the porcelain.

'With difficulty.' My tone is bland, but I'm offended at her presumption that I want to talk about this. There's silence for a while and I add, 'James should be home around five. Are you staying . . . that long? He'd love to see you.'

'Did he not tell you?'

I shudder internally; no, James hasn't told me. He never does.

'I'm staying for a while. Just to help you both. John thought it was a good idea.'

I don't ask what kind of help she has in mind. I smile widely and say, 'Oh – wonderful,' while my entire body clenches so tightly I can barely breathe. Patricia nods, maintaining eye contact, and we stare at each other, smiling stiffly, neither willing to look away first. Eventually, she gathers our mugs, even though mine is still half full, rinses them and puts them in the dishwasher. She walks to the hutch and inspects the glass; opens the pantry and looks inside.

'Bit of a smell in here,' she says. I simply watch her. 'All right, up you get.'

I sit, my expression blank. My hand drops to my side, searching for Rusty's head, but he isn't there.

'Leila, up! Let's give the kitchen a good clean. James would like to come home to that, wouldn't he?'

I stand as directed and open the cupboard under the sink, ignoring the jibe about my housekeeping skills – just another way I'm letting her son down. I take out sponges, sprays, bin bags and cloths and set them on the table.

'So, you do know where the cleaning supplies are,' Patricia says, laughing and winking at me. I smile and give her a gentle, *Oh yeah, I guess so*, and then start in the pantry, pulling out all the cans and bottles and glass containers and vigorously wiping everything down. She goes one better by lifting all the appliances from the benchtop and putting them on the table so she can wipe down every flat surface, removing all the dust. Then she sprays and polishes the appliances with a pungent lemon-scented chemical. At the back of the pantry, I discover two loaves of bread, unopened and covered in mould, and toss them in one of the garbage bags. Impossible to work out if she left them in there or I did. I get a dustpan and a torch from the laundry and carry them into the pantry, lighting it up with the torch. I kneel, uncomfortably, but this will be worth it. Looking under the shelving, I see the buggers – six fuzzy grey bodies, each about the length of my index finger, surrounded by specks of shit and smelling like rot. Holding my breath, I use the dustpan brush to wiggle them out, which is more difficult than it should be – the bodies roll around and away from me. Finally, I manage to sweep the mice and the crap onto the dustpan. Half are shrivelled, no doubt already dead when we arrived, but the others are plumper, their hair and eyes still intact.

Triumphant, I walk into the kitchen and begin to say, 'I found the source of the smell,' but trail off quickly when I see Patricia throwing my painkiller boxes into one of the garbage bags. She looks up and I realise she isn't even embarrassed; she isn't doing this behind my back. She wants me to see.

'You don't need these,' she says. 'Not while you're trying to get pregnant.'

I drop the dustpan, the mice, the shit, the brush, all of it, and with a clatter they disassemble on the floor, one hard little mouse rolling under the kitchen table. I dig through the bin bag, my hands catching on rubbish as I go, until I grab all the pill boxes. Patricia must have gone through my coat or the back of my bedside table while I was deep in the pantry; those are the easiest places for her to access, though they aren't the only places I hide medications.

I'm buzzing with anger at the violation, too furious to speak. I take the chemical bottle and spray them, wiping each box down with paper towel; I don't want any trace of Patricia or her mess on my belongings. I finish cleaning the packets and then shove brusquely past her. In the bedroom, I shut the door loudly and take all the foil sleeves from each packet. I hide them around the room, and in the pockets of my clothes, then pick up the pill boxes and walk back out. She watches me, one eyebrow raised, her jowly mouth drawn down to her chin, and I smile brightly at her and toss the empty boxes away. Even in the rubbish bin, they are distinct from her, from this house; they are the cleanest items in there. I won't be dragged down into this muck.

—

My ear is against the door, listening to James and Patricia argue about me. James sounds exhausted and conciliatory, saying, she didn't mean that, that's not what she's usually like, she's trying her best, over and over. Patricia's voice is lower and urgent, but I don't care what she thinks of me, so I move away and sit on the bed, staring at the wallpaper. Later, James comes to the bedroom and takes off his jacket and tie.

'I didn't know Patricia was coming to stay,' I say, striving for neutrality.

'It's her house.' He sits on the edge of the bed, taking his shoes off, then peels off his socks and drops them on the floor. 'Will you eat dinner with us?' His tone is pleading, and I nod. He kisses my forehead. 'Come out when you're ready,' he says, closing the door.

Dinner is quiet, or rather, I'm quiet. Patricia drinks sauvignon blanc and laughs like a squawking bird, her hand finding James's often, patting it like she's burping a baby. I listen to all the stories: James, the child prodigy who learned to speak at one and read at three; James, the chess champion who competed nationally when he was fifteen; James, an accomplished shooter who helped rid the region of problematic foxes when he was twenty-one; it's just such a shame it was no longer the done thing to sell the pelts. James smiles, his eyes flickering to me every so often, to check that I'm enjoying Patricia's performance. I smile regularly, and say 'wow' when appropriate, and it fools no-one, but we all pretend for politeness's sake.

'And then when he was twenty-five, he joined the volunteer firefighters,' Patricia says. 'I begged him not to. But our James wouldn't have it any other way.'

He's not our James, I want to shout. He's not even my James.

'Mum.' James finally appears faintly embarrassed.

'Dessert?' I offer, standing up and gathering the dinner plates.

'I didn't think there'd be any,' Patricia says.

—

The next morning, at James's insistence, I invite Patricia into town for lunch. Patricia drives, putting me in the passenger seat, with little say over our itinerary. We arrive at a small shopping centre. After picking up her own medications at the chemist, Patricia drags me into the bookstore, leads me to the cookbooks and points out *The CSIRO Diet*, telling me it's a good diet to follow for fertility. I carry it around for a while and then, just before we leave the shop, I stash it on a random shelf and tell Patricia I'll think about it.

She takes me next to a cheerful blue shopfront, the glass display window boasting a traditional wooden rocking horse, tiny farm boots and little Akubra-style hats. Inside, there's a pink section and a blue section, with racks and tables of clothes and toys. A sign hangs from the ceiling, the letters in childlike font: *Everything for your little bushranger!*

'Now, look at this.' Patricia picks up a onesie with pale blue stripes and bunnies plastered over the top.

'Cute,' I say.

'We should get it, don't you think?'

'There's a bunch of baby stuff at the house already,' I say.

'Oh.' She puts the onesie down. 'You won't be able to stop me buying new things once the baby is here.' She pats me on the arm. We continue to walk around the store while Patricia *oohs* and *aahs* and coos. I stand awkwardly at her side, quiet and worn out by her chatter. When she finally says, 'Let's get something to eat,' I smile widely and try not to say, *Thank fuck.* We walk past a few stores Patricia says we must go into after lunch: homewares, bedding, a shop with knick-knacks called *Sassy!* and a health-food shop – Patricia is out of ancient grains, and needs them to help stave off dementia for herself and John.

We find a table at a little cafe and sit. While I look at the menu, Patricia asks if I drink apple cider vinegar and whether I use turmeric in cooking; both help with reducing inflammation, apparently. I nod and then order a burger and chips, which will no doubt disappoint her. She fusses over the menu and finally orders a superfood salad, comprised of pumpkin seeds and broccolini which is, I'm sure, excellent for her digestion. We're both relieved when our coffees arrive, and she fiddles with the sugar while I sip mine stoically.

'There's so much to look forward to,' Patricia says, tapping her spoon on the side of her mug.

'There is?'

'When the baby comes.'

I shiver. 'I'm not pregnant.'

'You will be.' She is serious – she's not smiling now. 'Trust me.'

'It's not that.' James probably hasn't told her what happened to me in any detail. 'I've had some issues, fertility-wise. There were problems.'

'Problems, yes, but you'll fix them.' We both fall silent as the waiter delivers our meals. Patricia picks up her knife and fork and slices into the broccolini. 'There's nothing more important than family.'

There it is. I take a big bite of my burger.

'Listen,' Patricia says. 'I've had a hysterectomy. I know what problems there can be. You don't have them. Women like you get pregnant every day.'

'Patricia, you know that I had a miscarriage.'

She holds up a hand. 'We don't discuss ruptures in this family.'

I stare at her.

'We move on. Women, for years, have moved on. We don't fall apart.' She cuts another piece of broccolini. 'You've had quite a long lying-in period.'

'I'm trying to get well enough to manage a baby and go back to work . . .' I trail off, wanting to defend my position, but fall into silence and shame instead. I think about my struggle to move on, how many months I've failed at recovery; the months I've failed to conceive.

Patricia smiles, a fragment of seed stuck in her teeth.

'The career woman.' She shakes her head. 'This urge to do it all. To fight your biological imperative. Why? What's the point, dear?'

Flatly, I say: 'To forge my own identity. Not just a wife. Not just a mother.'

Patricia laughs. 'Once you have a child, you're always a mother.'

We eat in silence for a while, and I finish every bite. Patricia leaves half her meal in the bowl. The waiter comes and asks if everything was all right, and she nods enthusiastically, assuring him she just wasn't very hungry.

'We should go,' I say. 'Let me get this.' I go to the counter to pay while Patricia puts on her cardigan and picks up her handbag. I meet her at the door, and she turns to me, grasping my arm.

'You'll always be someone's daughter.' She leans in close enough that her perfume agitates my nose. 'Family means you belong to somebody. That you're part of something bigger than you. Just you,' she adds, 'isn't enough.'

———

We arrive home and I beg off, telling Patricia my stomach pains have returned. Before she can blame my dietary choices, I close the door to my room, feeling mildly guilty that Patricia is staying in a guest room in her own house. We offered to vacate the master, but she wouldn't hear of it. She's come in so regularly to locate clothing, or a bathroom item, I feel like she's moved in anyway.

I open my laptop and search the name *Renee Brice*. It disturbs me that Patricia, a qualified midwife, wouldn't acknowledge miscarriage. For someone who delivered a baby with traumatic results at her own home, she seems oddly intent on doing it all again. The thought of Patricia being involved in any potential pregnancy sends a shudder through me.

There are numerous articles. There's been no new information for nearly fifteen years. The reports from the time of her disappearance agreed that Renee was alive on 12 October 2009, but they don't reach a consensus about where exactly she was last seen or what she had been wearing. As I scroll through the newspaper articles, the case goes from fresh to cold: many cars of interest are ruled out, many sightings confirmed not to have been Renee.

Then, there's the video interviews. Bob Brice, her father, appealed for information repeatedly. There are several old press conferences preserved on YouTube, and I watch them all. He stood with the police and begged for news of his daughter, saying she was bright, hardworking, and loved her family. I check each clip for a glimpse of James, or any mention of the Crawleys, but there are none.

A few years ago, there was an in-depth write-up by a journalist at the ABC for the tenth anniversary of Renee's disappearance. Bob Brice had been dead for three years by then, leaving it up to his wife, Sheryl, and her sister, Amelia, to continue to raise public awareness. *Amelia.* The librarian.

'We believe we know where she is,' Sheryl is quoted as saying. 'But the police have never been able to confirm it.' I continue to read. This journalist is thorough and outlines a clearer sequence of events. Renee had been living with her fiancé, James Crawley, and was nine months pregnant with their first child. She was twenty-one years old. Initial reports mentioned sightings of Renee in a red car, then later in a white truck. Both turned out to be incorrect. Other reports that Renee was seen buying food downtown turned out to be another young pregnant woman, and a sighting of Renee at the local cafe was from weeks earlier; the person had their dates mixed up. Every lead was followed up, every tip. James reported Renee missing to the police three days after he said he saw her last. The police searched the property and found nothing, but Sheryl wasn't satisfied, calling the search 'lip service' and saying the police investigation was 'botched from the start'. She said Renee was only ever at the property; she believes whatever happened, happened at the farm.

There's a robust knock on the door. I close the laptop and get up slowly, resenting the intrusion. When I open the door, Patricia is there, smiling.

'May I come in?'

I step aside. 'Of course.'

She perches on the end of the bed, patting the spot next to her. I sit down and she takes my left arm and slips something over my wrist.

'A little gift,' she says.

It's a small gold bracelet with a round charm on it. I flip it over; there is a thin etching on the charm, delicate and quite pretty.

'This is so generous,' I say. 'Thank you.'

'It's a family heirloom,' Patricia says, looking pleased. 'It suits you.'

'Thank you,' I say again, lost for any other words. Patricia doesn't seem to mind. She turns my arm this way and that, watching the gold reflect the light.

'Such lovely skin,' she says, running her hand over my forearm. 'A little dark.'

'I'm sorry?' I say sharply.

'You've spent some time in the sun?'

The rush of blood to my head slows. 'Oh. I walked Rusty a lot when he was here.'

'Sunscreen, dear.' She points to her own face. 'I wish I'd known when I was your age.'

I laugh weakly.

'See you for dinner,' Patricia says. She leaves the room, pulling the door behind her, but leaving it open just a crack, like I'm a teenager up to no good. I look down at my arms; to me, they seem pale, though I'll always be a little brown from my heritage. I've barely been in the sun since Rusty left.

I wait until her footsteps are gone, then go to my handbag and tip everything out for a second time. Charlotte's phone number must be here somewhere. I can't spend every day with Patricia; I'll go mad. I dig into every pocket and unzip every section: nothing. I go through every coat in my wardrobe; I open James's bedside table to find old receipts for petrol and groceries, Panadol, mints, a couple of psychology texts, his passport. Back to the wardrobe. I search every pocket he has: jeans, shirts, coats. Nothing.

I leave the bedroom and go to the back door. Outside is a rattan basket holding random items: Seasol, more shears, an old lead for Rusty, a small trowel and a bunch of mismatched gardening gloves. I pick up each glove and slip my hand in. No.

I tell myself it's good that I can't find it. Not everything has to be a lie. I look at James's workboots, standing neatly next to the basket, and above them on a hook, I see his Driza-Bone. I walk to the jacket and stick my hand in the right pocket, then the left, and my hand closes over a small piece of paper. I pull it out and flatten it against my palm. I should be pleased: I've found what I'm looking for, I'm not paranoid or neurotic. Instead, it makes me sick. James took Charlotte's information from me, hid it from me, and never, not once, said a word.

I take my suitcase from the wardrobe and pack the necessities – underwear, bras, socks, pyjamas, jeans and t-shirts. I leave enough clothes that hopefully James won't notice items missing. Collect all the pills I've hidden under the mattress, in my bedside table, in all my coat pockets, then go to the bathroom and gather my belongings. Shove it all into a toiletry bag. Stop. Stare into the mirror: see the tile in the reflection. I look down at my wrist. The engraved pattern on the charm is identical. The soft curves of hips, arms and a head: the vase-shaped woman holding the moon; two crescents floating either side of her, and a spiral pattern on her stomach.

In the bedroom, I look at the wallpaper closely for the first time. Among the busy collection of flowers and suns and tiny birds, I see the spirals and curves of the same womanly figure.

Staring at it, I realise it reminds me of a uterus, the arms flayed out like fallopian tubes, the crescents hovering like ovaries. On the ceiling, the crown moulding repeats the pattern. It resembles the vases in the living room hutch, as well as the slashes of – blood? – painted on the trees in the clearing.

Opening my laptop, I google the symbol and read and read. I unhook the bracelet, leave it on the bedside table. Then I search for the cattle brand symbol – the spiral on its own – and for the symbol on the well, the round shape with a crescent like an upturned hat, or two horns.

And then, when I've finished reading, I take the suitcase and shove it under the bed. Tomorrow, I'm getting out of here, if I have to walk my way out.

———

Dinner is a quiet affair: James has had a long day at work, and Patricia is more subdued than usual. We eat bland food and engage in minimal conversation, and then Patricia and I clean the kitchen, exchanging only in practical communication: *Where does this platter go, Patricia? Can this saucepan go in the dishwasher? I'll take the rubbish out, don't worry!*

Afterwards, Patricia and James watch television in the living room, a gardening program. They invite me to join them, and we watch a segment about a thirteen-year-old boy who has become one of the most awarded orchid growers in Australia. From this, I conclude that people are either born with a green thumb or not; I'm definitely not.

I tell them I'm going to enjoy a cup of tea and a book in bed; they assent. I make peppermint tea and carry it to the privacy of the bedroom. Behind me, I hear them whispering to each other. I empty the hot tea out in the bathroom sink, then refill the mug with water and take two temazepam. I don't want to stretch this out any longer than I need to: I want to wake up when it's time to leave.

—

Turning in a circle again. Everything is dark. My hands are raw. I look up and see a crescent of light, that's all. There's screaming and I recognise it instantly: it's my mother, crying out for relief. I hold my breath, waiting for it to end.

—

The light is different. It's brighter than the bedroom usually is; I've overslept. I roll over to grab my phone from the bedside and slap something hard. I blink, snapping awake. I'm on a mattress, on the floor; my hand has hit pine floorboards. I don't recognise this room. A raked ceiling, a small window set high, two doors. The same wallpaper. I get up, woozy from the pills, and try the door. It's locked. I rattle it a few times and then lean against it and push; perhaps the latch just isn't connecting. It sticks, firm and resolute. *Breathe,* I tell myself. *Must breathe: in, out, in, out.* There's a second door. It opens into a tiny ensuite, just a toilet and handbasin. Back to the first door. I shake it as hard as I can, but it doesn't budge. Bang my fists against it. Nothing. I call out for James, for Patricia. My voice rises higher and higher. I stop, listening for a reply, but there's no sound, none at all. I check the window; there's no handle on it and no covering, just a smooth pane of glass. It's too high for me to see out of, and it hits me: it's the dormer window. I'm in the attic.

Scream. Scream. Louder. Longer. I keep it up until my throat gives out, then I crumple back onto the mattress.

—

It's been hours. I have no phone, watch or clock up here, but I can tell by the movement of the sun. The light is starting to settle into what I recognise as mid-afternoon, and my stomach is growling. I call out for James again. There are sounds now: the squeaking of stairs, muffled conversation. The doorknob turns and I watch in disbelief as James and Patricia enter the room, their expressions grave and resolute. Patricia locks the door behind her, even though I haven't moved. She juggles a plate with a sandwich and an apple and has a bottle of water wedged in her armpit. She places them on a side table. Then they stand side by side, like two kookaburras on a tree branch, gazing at me. James raises a hand as if calling for silence, though I haven't tried to speak.

'We're doing this to help you,' he says, and Patricia's head bobs up and down.

'I don't need help,' I say. Patricia *tsks* and I realise how much I detest her, have always detested her. 'You can't keep me in here.'

'We have to intervene.' James's tone is sombre. I search his face, his eyes, for anything suggesting this is a mistake, or a poorly executed therapeutic exercise, but there's nothing.

'I'm leaving.' I get up.

Patricia immediately steps backwards and stands in front of the door.

I laugh. 'Seriously, Patricia?'

'You're continuing to take a mix of prescriptions that is, frankly, dangerous,' James says. 'Targin. Valium. Endone. Temazepam.'

I knew he was still keeping tabs on me.

'We can't possibly have a baby with you addicted like this.'

'We're detoxing you,' Patricia adds. She almost has a spring in her body when she says this, that's how excited she is.

'Fuck you both,' I say. 'Let me out.'

They say nothing, but turn towards the door in unison, as though they are one brain split in two.

'Let me out,' I say to their backs. They ignore me and open the door. I race to them, grabbing the back of James's collar as Patricia steps onto the attic landing. James pulls my hand off his neck and spins me around, pushing his knee into the crook of mine, disabling me. I sink to the floor, dizzy and out of breath, and he lowers himself with me.

'Breathe, Leila,' he says quietly. 'Breathe.'

When I stop struggling, he lets go of me, leaving me collapsed on my haunches, chest tight, just as I felt when I tried to enter the attic months ago. It was a warning from my body; so many warnings I have ignored. James stands and goes to the door.

'Eat lunch,' he says. 'I'll bring dinner later.'

'No, please.' I'm breathless, panicked. Begging. 'Please don't, James, please—'

The door creaks. I refuse to look. I can't bear to see him lock me in here.

—

I don't eat the sandwich or the apple, but I do drink the water and take a long piss in the ensuite. There are fertility symbols everywhere in here too: on the tiles, on the wallpaper, etched into the moulding. The same shapes as the vases and the patterns on the trees. I'm furious I didn't notice and connect them earlier. The spirals and female form indicate fertility and new life; more worryingly, the symbol on the well was described as the horned god: a male fertility symbol and guardian of the underworld. A symbol that means whatever – whoever – is in the well has been shepherded in death to a holding place to wait until rebirth.

What is going to happen to me up here? I can't make sense of anything. Why is my educated partner, a professional psychologist, living in a house full of religious symbols and artefacts? Why has he imprisoned me in an attic in the middle of nowhere? He has my phone. I cannot alert a single person to what is happening to me. Matt has no reason to return here, and Rusty is with him.

I'm starving. And I really, really want a painkiller. I lie down and count the symbols embedded in the wallpaper, stopping once I reach one hundred. The sun disappears and I don't bother looking for a light switch. My skin is burning. I need to ask James for a fan. The room baked during the day; positioned at the top of the house and without open windows, it's stuffy, and there's nowhere for the air to go.

The doorknob squeaks. James enters with a dinner tray and a tall plastic cup of water, sets it quickly on the side table and locks the door. He flicks on the light.

'I want a fan,' I say. 'I'm hot.'

'Of course,' he says. 'Whatever you need.'

I prop myself against the pillows and he brings the tray over, hands it to me, squatting while I swallow a few spoons of soup. Pumpkin. The blandest of all the soups.

'I have to leave.' I plonk the spoon down into the bowl, spattering orange gunk up the sides.

He pulls a plastic sachet out of his pocket, and I groan in recognition. It's the fertility herbs, ground into a fine grey powder, the ones I took daily when we were trying to conceive back in Coogee. He takes the sachet, carefully tips the powder into the water glass, and stirs it vigorously.

'I'm not drinking that.'

'It will help with the detox.'

'Bullshit.'

He pauses and then says: 'We need to get your body back to a healthy state for pregnancy.'

I run cold, and I'm not sure if it's because I've been without my medications for eighteen hours or something else.

'James,' I say. 'We're over. I'm never getting pregnant.'

'Rubbish,' he says, proffering the cup. 'I'll help you.'

I take the cup and he's momentarily pleased, until I reach over and tip it upside down. Water spills out onto the floor. Swiftly, he takes it from my hand. We have nothing to mop the liquid up with, so I watch as the small pool of water runs back towards the mattress and delight in thinking of the mould that will develop under there; it will irritate Patricia to no end. James gets up and places the cup on the side table.

'I'll come back and see you in the morning.' He shuts the door and I hear it lock, a fastener sliding into a slot. Such a small thing, but I cannot find a way to undo it. I pick up the cup, take it to the ensuite and tip the rest of the contents down the sink. I rinse it out thoroughly and then fill it with water from the tap. It's cloudy and white, but after a few seconds it settles and turns clear. I take a swig and the smell of it – this water has a *smell* – makes me gag. All the water here runs off a bore, but the kitchen has a filter tap to improve the taste. This has a whiff of metal and sewage, the kind of odour that emanates from a pool of standing, stagnant water. I force it down, then go back to the mattress. Stare at the ceiling.

I think of Tilly and Renee, brought to this place and now gone. I may as well be gone, too. But then, perhaps I disappeared months ago.

—

Hot again. Don't know what time it is. Feels like the burning and sweating has gone on for days. James brought in a fan at some point, a white desk fan that barely generates any airflow. I'm drowning in stale air and perspiration. I'm nauseous. Not from withdrawal. It must be from swilling unfiltered farm water. I don't need a fucking detox. I don't. My head throbs and throbs as I scrabble under the mattress for a sleeve of pills, but of course there aren't any. Settle for more scummy water. Toss and turn on the mattress, trying to find a comfortable spot.

—

Light streams in through the windows. I didn't sleep. My head is so sensitive that I can't touch my hair; it hurts to lie on the pillow. A gurgle arises from my stomach, followed by a sharp spasm; I get a flash of the cramps I had during my miscarriage. Then – a burning heave. I get up as quickly as I can manage, black spots blurring my vision. I make it to the toilet and the diarrhoea hits immediately. I grip the toilet roll and grimace while my gut contracts and roils, waste coming out in a steady stream. The smell is god-awful. After a while, my left leg prickles, turning numb. I shift around on the seat, leaning my weight on my right leg instead, massaging the flesh under my left thigh to encourage blood flow. Another surge of shit and juddering and perspiration. My palms are slippery, my top lip wet, my forehead clammy. When I'm reasonably sure it's finished, I squat and wipe and flush. Then I wipe, and wipe and wipe. Flush some more.

I wash my hands thoroughly and look at myself in the small mirror. My skin is pallid, my hair matted and oily. More white streaks have appeared; there are so many of them now. My face seems lean, even though my body is swollen from fertility pills.

There are rolls on my stomach and legs. Who is this woman? What am I? Something made of fluid, pulp and bone.

I lie down on the mattress. Sometime later, the door opens and closes. James is here with breakfast.

'How are you feeling?' he asks.

'Let me out.'

'Here, eat.' He hands me a tray: toast with butter and strawberry jam and a cup of herbal tea. I'm desperate. I eat the toast, drink the tea. He stands by the door and watches.

When I'm finished, I glare at him and say, 'This is illegal. You've imprisoned me.'

James flinches. 'We're helping you. This is hard for me too.'

I pick up the tea cup and hurl it at him. It bounces off the door instead, cracks neatly in two. He bends to collect the pieces, and I get up and try to hit him, anywhere, but I'm slow and tired, and nothing connects. He grasps my clumsy hands, forces them down by my sides.

'Do you know what we've been through?' he says, gripping me. 'You had a breakdown.'

'No,' I say. 'No. I was grieving.'

'You had a breakdown.' He lets go of me. 'Don't you know how scared I was?'

I stagger back and sit on the edge of the mattress, try to remember the things I did. They weren't so bad. Everyone handles grief differently.

'You didn't care,' I say.

'You wouldn't get out of bed. You stopped working.' He looks like something collapsible that could be folded into a man half his size. 'You wouldn't speak to me. I'm your partner and I love you, and you shut me out. I'm a psychologist, I wanted to help you. You wouldn't even take anti-depressants. Just painkillers. Sleeping pills. You were a zombie.'

'My womb,' I say. It's *broken*. Does he understand this? Is it the same for men who lose or injure a testicle? It isn't, of course it isn't. They have a spare. Besides, they don't grow life inside them; their bodies don't burst open in the act of bringing life into the world. Their job is pleasurable, and mostly over in a few minutes. I wanted him to be in pain with me. If there was a void, I wanted us to fall headlong into it together. But he wouldn't. He didn't. It's easy to carry on when you don't feel the loss. It's women who suffer to nurture and sustain life. We suffer even more when we fail.

'I hoped the farm would be enough,' he says, turning to leave. 'I'll see you this afternoon.'

—

James brings soup. I ask him if the herb powder is in the food and drink, and he doesn't respond. I eat it anyway. We are quiet together. He sits on the floor next to the mattress where I'm propped up, eating as slowly as possible. I despise him, but I don't want to be alone. The sound of his breathing, the warmth from his body next to me. It's some kind of comfort.

—

The night is painful. Writhing. Vomiting now. My jaw aches, and my throat burns from bile. The diarrhoea continues.

I'm losing masses of sludge and filth from my body. Sweating out misery. I wash my face and armpits and vagina and arsehole, and wipe myself firmly with the towel. It's a damp, musty rag when I'm finished. I squash it into a ball and toss it on the ensuite floor. I feel a little cleaner.

—

I pull the sweat-soaked sheets off the mattress and ask for fresh ones. James gets them, and we make up the bed together. He jiggles the pillows into clean pillowcases and I fluff them on the mattress. He has brought a light cotton blanket too.

'In case you start to get cold,' he says. I ask for soap and fresh towels and clean clothes, and he promises to bring them later. Before he leaves, he kisses my forehead.

—

In the afternoon, I take the fresh clothes and towels and soap and toothpaste and toothbrush into the ensuite and peel off my sweat-stained pyjamas. James has brought my favourite sleeping pants. They are a soft grey marle with a smooth elastic waist. There are several t-shirts and a thin jumper. I take the clean washer and wet it with warm water, then lather it up with soap and rub it all over my body. I duck my head awkwardly into the handbasin and wet my hair, then lather it with the soap, scrub my scalp with my hands, then rinse it off. It's not a shower – Mum called this a sponge bath – but I feel fresher afterwards. Not as itchy. James is still sitting on the mattress.

I sit down next to him. 'My first bed was a mattress on the floor.'

'Mine was a single bed, on a wooden frame,' James says. 'I broke it jumping up and down one night. Dad wouldn't replace it.'

'Nothing of mine was ever replaced.'

'We've always had things in common.'

I pause. Shift over on the mattress, lie down and turn my back to him. 'I need to sleep.'

He gets up, walks to the door and closes it. I hear the lock turn. Then I close my eyes and, mercifully, the blackness of sleep arrives.

—

My eyes open. Sleep is finished and pain is here instead. I can't find a spot where my body doesn't hurt. My neck and shoulders are bunched into tight little rocks, even the backs of my arms ache. I put two pillows together, fold them over, but nothing works. My back spasms; my thighs are sore. I twitch and kick. I pull the sheet and blanket over me because I'm cold, but within minutes I'm too hot. Five minutes after that I'm shivering.

Did my mother feel like this, kept in her little room, on an uncomfortable little bed? I brought her the essentials and asked her what she needed. She tossed and turned and despised me. I cleaned her, fed her, watered her. In return she ignored me, spat at me, told me things I never wanted to hear. And I thought to myself each time: *What an ungrateful bitch.*

—

James comes with tea, toast and a fried egg. 'I thought you might be well enough to try it.'

I slice into the yolk and it runs, viscous orange spilling across the toast and onto the plate. The smell rises and makes me think of chlorine. I scrape the egg off the toast and eat the dry bread, drink the glass of water and then sip the tea.

'Still,' James says, picking up the plate. 'You're improving.'

'I can't sleep up here.'

'Your body is recovering. Sleep will come.'

The tea is sour. I assume they've put herbs in it. I go to put the cup down, then realise I have very little choice. I raise the cup back up to my mouth and swallow more.

'Why are there fertility symbols all over this house?'

James glances at the walls. 'You noticed them.'

I point. 'There's at least a hundred in this room alone.'

'I didn't notice them until I was ten.' He walks to the wallpaper. 'Then I saw them everywhere.'

'Like a magic eye painting.' I don't believe that he doesn't know more about them. 'Your mother gave me a bracelet with a symbol on it.'

James sits down next to me. 'Family tradition.'

'I guess it worked on Renee better than me.'

He doesn't answer, just laces his fingers together over his knees.

I want to ask about her, about where she is, because I think I know and part of me wants to hear him say it; but what good will it do to get the answer, to be certain? Where will it leave me? Instead, in a move that is more denial than desire, I lean over and rest my head on James's shoulder. It's terrible to need consolation so badly. To seek it from him.

He wraps his arm around me, and I shift over on the mattress. We lie down, my head on his chest, a place that used to feel safe and erotic at the same time. He still smells good. His breath smells like fresh coffee. Before – before the miscarriage, before whatever this is – we'd spend our weekend mornings just like this, lying in bed, drinking coffee, scrolling news sites on our phones, kissing, flirting, building up to morning sex. After, we'd be flushed and laughing, in a happy stupor for the rest of the day. On Sundays, he'd leave in the late afternoon to drive back to the farm and would call to tell me he'd turned onto the M1, whether the traffic was good or bad, that he missed me already, and he just remembered a show on Netflix I should watch.

In this moment, my eyes closed, our breathing in tandem, the scent of him so familiar, I wish to forget. To forget where I am and what he is doing to me, because even now, while it's happening, I can't believe it. It's like I'm watching it happen on a screen, where everything in life is these days, and I can't touch it to turn it off.

———

We kiss. We fuck. Afterwards, he wants to stay and hold me, but I roll away from him. When he leaves, I cry hard, ashamed of my lack of resistance, my need for care and affection. My eyelids puff up like an allergic reaction. In the afternoon, clouds creep in, blotting out the sun and casting a pallor across the room. I'm not vomiting anymore, but I am in pain. My skin hurts. My nerves hurt. I lie on my side and keep my gritty eyes shut.

—

Mum is thin and I think, *Surely it won't be long now.* I think that for forty-eight days straight. She gets yellower and yellower and still lives. It's all right; my job is to bring food, clean, empty the bedpan. At night I make sure she takes enough pills and drink so that I can study. At school the teachers regard me with concern, but no-one asks. I do well anyway; with my mother so ill and unable to speak as much, I actually do better. The quiet helps me concentrate. I finish my final exams and, as is tradition, run into the water at Southbank beach fully clothed with my friends. Our school uniforms swell with water, and we drag ourselves out, looking for ice-cream. I feel joy and freedom and hope she'll be dead when I get home, but she isn't.

When she finally asks me to help her end her life, I don't believe her. Then she begs and I'm angry. I'm so close to surviving her. I won't do it. Who would I be, if I were a daughter who kills her mother?

Later, when I'm older, I realise that's not the only reason I said no. I wanted to punish her. See, I do kill her. I *am* the daughter who killed her mother. I did it in stages instead of all at once; I protected her right to live. I cared for her so much and so well that she withered away in excruciating slowness.

I was satisfied, watching her die without a shred of dignity. And she knew it.

I deserve this; this is my punishment. Some things are meant to come back around.

The morning is still cloudy, the light still soft. I will my aching body to sit up and achieve it slowly. I pull myself back until my bum is against my pillow and my back against the wall and wait for James.

But when the door opens, it's Patricia. She holds a tray with toast and jam, water, tea. Orange juice as well today.

'Morning,' she says briskly. Without James, she seems less excited, more distant. 'Have you been to the toilet yet?'

I realise she isn't distant, she's midwifing. She sees this as healthcare. I'll be expected to thank her afterwards, no doubt. I don't answer her, and after a moment, she brings the tray over and places it on my lap. She backs away to the door and locks it.

'Let's make sure we eat it all, shall we?' she says, as if I'm a toddler. 'You're looking healthier.' She is constantly appraising me. I bring the toast to my mouth, take a bite.

'I'm glad we could do this for you.' She goes to the end of the mattress and tugs on the sheet, straightening it, then enters the ensuite and fusses about in there for a while; I eye the locked door. I'm finished with the food by the time she returns.

'Very good.' Patricia picks up the empty tray.

I watch her leave.

———

I eat steamed chicken and vegetables and a buttered bread roll, and Patricia is pleased with the resumption of my appetite. She is more relaxed, explaining that James had to return to work; he is simply too busy to take any more time off. I wonder if this means I've been here for a week.

'We're right though, just us girls, aren't we?' She continues to natter. Apparently, Woolworths prices are ridiculous; she spent ninety dollars for only two bags of groceries. Years ago, it was twenty dollars a bag. Patricia doesn't know how anyone can afford it. I nod along, devise possible ways I could disable her. The tray is only plastic, so that won't work. The mug is slightly heavier, but still unable to knock her out. She hasn't set foot in the ensuite again, but, if she does, I could close the door and push the mattress and side table against it. It would be pointless though, because she still locks the attic door behind her; she has the key. The best plan is to knock her out cold.

'Patricia,' I say. She looks at me. 'Thank you for everything you're doing.'

She smiles. 'You're welcome, dear.'

347

—

James comes in the evenings. He brings me soup for dinner, and we sit together for a while, just talking. He has new clients, including one with multiple neurological diagnoses, and he sighs. 'The psychiatrist won't even *consider* psychology sessions as a support, he only wants to sedate him,' he says with disdain, and I murmur my agreement, yes, drugs are terrible.

—

I don't know how many days I've been here. I'm not vomiting anymore, I no longer have diarrhoea. I'm sweating less and am not feverish. My skin is still sensitive, but the pain is receding. The headaches are milder. I stare a lot. I sleep a lot.

This morning I lie on the bed, spotting shapes in the wallpaper. I'm more mentally awake than I've felt in the last six months. Being off the medications has helped me focus. And I have nothing but time up here. Time to sift through information; to find the truth.

James told me that Renee left the farm and went back to her parents' home; then a few days later, her father turned up looking for her. But his story nags at me. James said Renee wasn't talking to her parents. So, if Renee *had* left the farm, wouldn't she have left for a friend's place? Rather than admit her parents were right? I know that's what I would've done.

Then, the ABC News article. Renee's mother, Sheryl, said clearly that Renee was only ever at the farm. If she had returned home, her parents would have said so. There would have been clear agreement on where Renee was last seen from the beginning.

And, something else: if Bob and Sheryl were the last people to see Renee, why didn't they report her missing to the police? The ABC journalist wrote that it was James who reported Renee's disappearance.

James.

I don't believe Renee ever left the farm: I believe her mother. I think James lied to me about Bob showing up to look for her. James sent Renee texts, made calls to her phone. He reported her missing, pretending to be worried. In truth, he did it all for one reason: because he already knew Renee was gone and that she was never coming back. James washed his hands clean of her, not even appearing in the press conferences to appeal for her return. Without a baby, she was of no use to the Crawleys.

And the police, allowed on the land of a founding family by John's grace, didn't bother to find or unseal that old, unused well.

—

Patricia brings me breakfast each morning and stands by the door while I eat. She comments at various intervals, usually to say my colour is good, or my face is filling out. I bristle but hide it by chewing and swallowing. Soon, I expect her to tell me I'm putting on weight, but don't worry, it's a compliment. I smile at her and thank her for every tray of food and tell her I didn't realise how much I needed this intervention.

Sometimes I pat her hand. The first day I did it, she winced, but now she's comfortable. Sometimes she'll squeeze my shoulder. We are building a relationship all our own, one in which I do nothing but make her feel important. One in which I've ceded control to her. *Professional, paid people-pleasing.*

'Finished?' Patricia leans forwards and I hand her the tray.

'What happened to Renee?' I ask. If Patricia truly wants me to be part of this family, to give her the grandchild she envisions, I'm guessing she might tell me what James won't.

She pauses by the door.

'James told you.'

'But you'll tell me the truth,' I say, and she wavers a little.

'I'm sure he already did,' she says.

'Patricia,' I say. I gesture to the room, the wallpaper. 'It's just us. There are some things women can only tell each other.'

She nods and grips the tray. 'It was an awful time for James. And there was nothing to be done.'

'I'm sure none of it was his fault.'

'It wasn't! And the parents went on a crusade against him.' Her fingers turn white as she squeezes the tray harder. 'Renee's aunt still, *still* leaves flowers at our front gate, harassing us.'

I feel a wave of respect for Amelia, marking where Renee died. Where she still is. 'That must be stressful for you.'

'James was in pieces when it all happened.' There's silence. She puts the tray on the side table, crosses her arms. 'Are you committed to my son?'

'Look at me,' I say. 'I love him. I'm getting clean for him, so we can have a family.'

She nods, leaning against the door. Takes a big breath in. 'Renee was here when she went into labour. She wanted a traditional home birth.'

I don't move or speak; I am still, attuned only to the buzz and vibration of Patricia's voice. The soft, drooping skin around her cheeks flushes as she recounts her memories.

'It was a terrible situation. The baby didn't survive the birth. It happens sometimes, feet first. Umbilical cord around his neck.' Patricia's words are clipped, clinical.

'And Renee?' I ask.

'Just a terrible situation,' Patricia repeats. 'James had no choice but to do what he did.'

For one long, woozy moment I consider pushing Patricia over and trying to run. But reality returns quickly: and what then? Where could I go? If they caught me, would they hurt me? What did James do?

And what might he do to me?

Patricia looks bereaved; I wait for more information, but she stares at the floor, struck by whatever memory she's been hoarding all these years.

'You buried Renee in the well afterwards.' I say it gently. 'And sealed it up.'

'We blessed her first,' Patricia says. She touches a small spiral pendant at her throat, the same as their cattle brand.

'I understand.'

'You don't.' Patricia pushes off the door, her posture rigid. 'It's been hard for this family to conceive, always. Our history isn't an easy one. One relative pushed out his first wife. Or maybe she wanted to leave, I don't know – she said terrible things about him around town. Not everyone can accept our beliefs. He married again, but it took a long time to repair the family reputation. And then, only one generation later – well, it was shameful. James's great-grandfather got the maid in trouble. I suppose he found it easier than dealing with his wife. But it got around of course, his wife found her in the marital bed. Francis had to do something about it, it couldn't go on.'

'The housekeeper? The one who died? Francis killed her?'

Patricia blinks. 'What's important is that there was a healthy baby boy.'

I grapple with this information. 'James isn't a full Crawley, then?'

'Of course he is. The male line continues unbroken. But it's a sore point in our family's history. I certainly didn't want you writing about it. That young girl made all sorts of claims before she died. Said awful things about Francis. About our beliefs. More gossip, more rumours! We simply couldn't allow it again.' Patricia is bright red now.

'I'm so sorry,' I say. 'You didn't deserve that.'

'No, indeed. We keep to ourselves now, and we protect the family. We do not involve outsiders; we prefer to use our traditional remedies to continue the line.'

'Remedies?'

She fusses with her rings before finally saying: 'Rituals. Each generation, we've had to complete them. And then we pass them down.'

I think of the fertility symbols crowding the house, the blood on the trees in the clearing. Was there a sacrifice? Of course: Matt's cows. The realisation hits every nerve; it's like being plunged into icy water. There can't be pregnancy without sacrifice, without giving something up. Isn't that what motherhood is all about?

'Matt's cows dying, was that part of this?' I ask, but she doesn't answer. Matt's face, crumpled and grief-stricken, comes to me and I push it away. 'I hope it works,' I say.

Patricia walks back over and I stiffen. She bends down and kisses me on the forehead. 'It will.' She pats the mattress. 'Lie down, dear.'

I do as instructed. She fusses over me with a blanket. 'Rest, and James will see you after work.' She heads to the door, then turns, fiddles with her wedding ring again, looks at a spot on the wall somewhere over my head.

'You know, we were all very disappointed about Renee.' Her face is pinched with displeasure, like a schoolmarm corralling unruly children. The sadness earlier was only for her son. 'But she wasn't truly committed. She wanted to give birth and go back to normal life. Like it wouldn't cost her anything.'

I feel intense sadness for that young woman, alone, isolated, and reliant on Patricia for help. No mother or father who she could turn to for help. In terrible pain, in utter vulnerability. But I say:

'How selfish of her.'

Patricia smiles and nods and settles her gaze on me; she has shared too much and is trying to determine if I'm lying to her. I maintain a sympathetic expression and do not look away, though I'm terrified. But I've been terrified before. I've looked into an empty face before. There's not a skerrick of empathy in her eyes. That, too, is familiar. A blankness would come over my mother's face before the verbal spars, before the physical attacks. Patricia shapeshifts and it shows on her face. She turns from captor to religious fanatic to loving mother-in-law within a single conversation. I don't know who she truly is, and in this moment I realise that's why I've never felt on solid ground with her. I wonder if the only true thing about her is her willingness to propagate the Crawley line. This is the role she has subsumed herself into, and it is not one she wants to fail at. Not again.

'I know you won't make the same mistake.' She reaches for the doorknob. 'It was a tragedy to lose that baby boy.' She leaves, the lock clicking as she turns the key on the other side.

I shiver, gathering the blanket around my shoulders, careful not to change my facial expression in case Patricia returns. But I think. I think of Tilly's injured face and neck. Think of the murdered female cows. Think of all the lies James told me about Renee, when this entire time, she lay dead in the well. *This is a haunted place.* Women become trapped here. Tilly, Renee, me: we are interchangeable. We each tried to leave. For our failings, our transgressions, we are punished, here in this house, where we cannot get away. All that's left of us is running footsteps, screams, the echoes of women desperate to escape.

My body tremors intensify; I rock back and forth. I don't know if I will ever get out of here.

—

James stays with me until late in the evening. He brings me a small television, pulls the side table in front of the mattress and sets the box on top. 'It's only the free-to-air channels,' he says apologetically, and I wave my hand and assure him I'm grateful. I say nothing of my conversation with Patricia. He lies close to me, and I make very sure not to recoil, and we watch reality programs. I'm too frightened to move, to sleep; I watch him out of the corner of one eye. His profile is relaxed, and he reaches over after a while to hold my hand. Finally, after eleven, he yawns, kisses me and leaves. I stay awake for as long as I can, in case it's a trick, in case Patricia and he have a plan, but nothing happens; and I eventually fall into a thin, fretful sleep.

—

Patricia brings a fruit plate and toast, juice and coffee. She's been squeezing the orange juice by hand, and this morning she's added a little ginger and lemon juice.

'Wonderful for lowering inflammation,' she tells me. I take a sip and tell her how much better it is than plain orange juice and that I wish my mother had known so much about health. After yesterday, I need her to feel that she has complete control. There cannot be the awkwardness of oversharing. She must know, without a doubt, that I'm on her side. I ask her for other dietary tips and tricks to help me conceive, and give the impressed response she craves with each one.

Managing her emotions, giving her what she wants, is the most effective tool I have. I have absolutely nothing else.

———

The next evening, James enters the room well after dinner. He holds a grocery bag. When he sits on the mattress with me, I scoot over to make room and he empties it out. Treats tumble onto the bed, all manner of sugars and chocolates and confections.

'You deserve a reward,' he says. I watch him scatter out the different options, a macabre repeat of our second date, and try to hide my disbelief with gratitude. I'm not an animal, being trained like Pavlov's dog. Is that how he sees me? Or is this meant to be a genuine kindness, something to mark my drug-free existence and good behaviour? I select a Lindt ball, the creamy chocolate forming a filmy coat over my tongue.

To think I used to live in a city, able to move about as I pleased, buying chocolate whenever I fucking wanted to.

James picks up the television remote, but I grab his hand.

'I want to talk,' I say. I spent the day weighing options. It's better if I show interest, if I extend empathy. If I wait too long, he might decide I'm keeping something from him.

He murmurs an assent, tracing a finger along my collarbone and holding my chin. He leans in to kiss me, and I hold a rictus position. *Do not shy away.* I ask James to tell me about his religion. Who they worship, what their belief system is, the different rites they follow. How am I involved; how will I learn?

'Soon,' he says.

—

James has left. I'm starting to doze. A heavy, drowsy feeling overtakes me; my limbs feel immobile. There might be a lapse in time, I am never quite sure up here. The moon isn't visible through the high window; it's always dark as pitch at night. There have been times when I was sure I'd slept for just a few hours, only to be surprised by Patricia coming in with a breakfast tray, and light struggling through the small glass pane. Then there were nights that dragged on and on as I tossed and turned, stuck in a state of myalgia, with even the light touch of the sheet setting off pain and discomfort.

It is different tonight. I try to break out of the unnatural drowsiness; try to lift a leg, to bend a knee. Nothing. My shoulders feel like they are being pushed down against the mattress. I am flat on my back. There is a creak, a slow, irritating utterance from the attic door. I can't see, but I hear murmuring, whispering. I try to call out, but my tongue is thick and slack. Shapes are approaching, but they, too, are dark. I cannot make out faces.

My feet are gripped, then pulled. I want to scream, but I can't. One leg is yanked to one side of the mattress: the other leg to the other side. The shapes move closer to my head. A fear envelops me that is more than terror; this might be the end for me. I'm paralysed; I'm *paralysed*, and I'm disgusted and furious at what is being done to me, but I am also absolutely fucking petrified. Nothing in my body suggests the fear I feel; no trembling, heat or sweat is evoked. I am sluggish and compliant, entirely at their disposal. Each arm is lifted and stretched out to the side; I am spread-eagled on the bed, vulnerable. I cannot move, cannot speak.

The whispering continues, mutterings in a language I don't recognise. Constant whispering. It snakes through my ears into my brain. My shirt is rolled up. The band of my tracksuit pants is pushed down. I want to react, to resist, but I can do nothing. I smell something sharp and dead and feel liquid dribble onto my stomach. Then soft bristles, moving round and round, and the murmuring stops suddenly, like a sound sucked through a vacuum. My shirt is rolled down, my pants hiked up. Steps retreat. Then the attic door jolts closed.

—

When I wake, I think, *That was a dream.* A sleep paralysis. I pull myself into a seated position and stare, confused. Soon, Patricia brings breakfast, smiles at me, says nothing of consequence. I smile and make gentle jokes, try to eat. I say nothing of the memory. She watches me. Finally, I push the food away. She leaves with the tray; I sit for a while.

Suddenly, a crash of trembling hits me. The memory of a ticklish feeling on my stomach. I pull up my shirt, slowly, torturously, because I do not want to know this. But it is there: a swirl, a spiral, painted on my abdomen, in brown, rotten blood. I cry. I cry uncontrollably.

I run to the bathroom to try and wash it off, but the remnants sit on my skin, flaky and sticky. I moan and sob, gripped by horror. I think of all the incursions on my body, great and small:

the wand, the miscarriage, the surgery, the hormone pills, the herbs, the isolation of the farm, this imprisonment; and still they have found another way to intrude on me, to force me into helplessness, manipulate me into being what they want. I have been a bystander to my own mistreatment for as long as I can remember, from the time I was born. I can only retreat into my mind for so long, because they will find a way to take that too, I know they will.

It's my decision, I insisted to James after visiting the doctor in Sydney. *My body.*

Then why did I let it be used? I stare in the mirror.

'It's my body,' I say.

—

Night.

I ask James why. Why he chose me.

He smiles at me. 'I wanted a woman who wanted a family. And I fell in love with you.'

'But why did you fall in love with *me*?'

James frowns. 'There's plenty of theories on the psychological experience of falling in love. We were similar ages, we had similar goals, similar levels of intelligence. Attraction.' He leans over and kisses my forehead. 'And then that intangible part of it. I felt close to you, quickly.'

'How could you be confident that I'd be open to all of this?'

He cups my face in his hands, looks deeply into my eyes. 'Love is a leap of faith. I felt you would commit to me. Properly commit. I knew that you wouldn't just leave.'

'That's not—' I stop. *That's not possible,* I want to say. Nobody knows if someone will leave or not.

'You had this look about you,' he says. 'Like that rabbit with its foot caught in a trap. One foot out, one foot in. Seeking rescue. At work, those are always my most interesting, complex clients. Clients who have been hurt. The hurt never leaves them. It's always there. Dragging on their ankle.

'I wanted to save you from the hurt. And protect you from it. Don't you think I've been good at that?' He runs his hand softly over my belly.

He has, of course he has, I assure him. And then, because I must know, there cannot be any ambiguity, I say: 'Did you protect Renee?'

He continues to swirl his hand over my abdomen. 'Mum said something?'

'She said it wasn't your fault.'

He looks up at me, his palm flat on my chest now. 'It was, it was my fault, but it was an accident. You believe me?'

'Of course,' I lie.

'She was trying to leave me, even before her due date. We couldn't have that, so we put her up here, made it comfortable for birth. We gave her everything she needed, but she didn't appreciate any of it. After the birth, she was screaming *nonstop.* She blamed Mum and me for losing the baby. Said I trapped her, abused her! That she'd call the police. Honestly, all I wanted was for her to – to—' He stops.

'You wanted her to shut up,' I say, hiding my disgust – disgust that he could be capable of something so repugnant, disgust that he then blamed Renee for it – because doing so is crucial if I want to stay alive.

'I just snapped,' he says, eyes glazed, staring at the wall behind me.

We sit in silence. He reaches over and takes my hand and squeezes it. I squeeze back. I close my eyes, unlock my jaw, un-grit my teeth. Then I say:

'I'm sorry Renee pushed you to it.'

He looks at me, relieved and absolved; he says softly, 'You know I'd never hurt you, right? You're different. You've rescued me, too.'

My stomach turns.

Then he leans in, kisses my cheek. 'Do you think you'll know when you're pregnant again?'

With a great effort, I reach down with my other hand and lay it over the top of our woven fingers. 'I'm sure I'll get a feeling.'

He squeezes my hand. 'I can't wait.' His hand is a fleshy straitjacket. 'And nothing will go wrong this time. We've made sure of it.'

James is hunting today. This takes the impediments to freedom from two down to one. An older, frailer, one. Patricia has been slacking lately. So busy talking, she forgets to close the door the whole way. This is how I've done it: be grateful, make no move towards escape. Let her really think I'm part of this, that I'm with them. Even if she doesn't quite believe that yet, she's warned me; she knows I won't risk it. It's been easier than expected. No; that's not true. I've been imprisoned in this room for at least two weeks, I think. Maybe longer. If I didn't have this plan, if I didn't tell myself it was easier to bear than it is, I wouldn't be able to bear it at all.

I think about what life will be like when James is no longer part of it. Going back to my apartment in Coogee, walking by the beach, buying takeaway coffee. Returning to work. Standing on a crowded bus, phone in hand, scrolling through emails. No *Good morning!* texts from a lover, no evening calls. No entwining of limbs, sweaty and flushed. Instead, quiet nights alone. Takeaway or ready meals again, because cooking for one is gloomy. The potential for a future, a family, a belonging, will be gone. Will I try again? Will I sit through dates and ask polite questions, disappointed by men who talk only about themselves, men with bleached teeth and waxed chests, men who excuse themselves mid-date to take a hit of coke in the bathroom, men who are disappointed when they find out I have a professional role and even more disappointed when they learn I come from nothing, that I didn't go to a Sydney private school and there's no inheritance forthcoming.

It seems untenable. As untenable as this.

I get plenty of notice when Patricia approaches; the attic stairs are steep and creaky, and she mutters as she balances a tray while she ascends. When I hear the movements, I jump up from the mattress and go to the ensuite, turn on the light and the tap and close the door, letting the water run. I position myself beside the attic door; when Patricia opens it, I'll be hidden behind it. Waiting, my entire body hot and thrumming, the air seems thicker and mustier than ever. I listen to her feet tread on each step.

She opens the door, which swings towards me. I hear her say, 'Oh, she's cleaning up.' I listen to the clink as she places the breakfast tray on the side table. I can't see her yet. Then I watch through the door crack as she approaches the ensuite and opens the door. She pokes her head in and says, 'Leila?'

and I *run*. I burst through the open door and drop to my bum and slide down the stairs, tumbling halfway thanks to the momentum. Patricia is screeching from the landing, but I ignore her. They detoxed me; I'm healthier now, and faster than her. I run to the front door, grabbing a set of car keys as I pass the sideboards. I'm out the door while she's still navigating the steep attic steps. I pull on the first pair of shoes I find on the verandah then fly down to Patricia's car and press the key button. I fling the driver's side door open, jump in and start the car. The shoes must be hers; they're small and tight but I don't care. The car revs and Patricia is running across the verandah, waving her hands, yelling my name. I back up as she stomps down the front steps, then turn the car, leaving a burn mark on the grass. I let out a triumphant shout: a long, guttural battle cry.

Then, in my rear-view, I see Patricia stumble. She is lying in the grass, dragging herself away from the steps. She starts to scream desperately, a scream of absolute horror and distress, and I brake.

I watch her in the rear-view, the car engine rumbling. She is shaking, shrieking, *Help! Help!* I see her tear-streaked face turning wildly. She grabs at her leg, pulling it along with her as she tries to move.

Fuck. *Fuck.* She is small and flattened. Did she break an ankle? Staring at her, I see my own mother, defenceless and weak. I am shocked into stillness, my hand gripping the park brake. I can't leave Patricia wailing on the ground. I cannot do this again, not *again*, leaving a mother to writhe in agony.

I reverse slowly. I'm not staying long. I get out of the car and approach her, keeping my distance.

'A tiger!' she cries. 'He bit me!'

I look around; at first I don't see it and think, *This is a trap*, but then I hear it, a hissing, and there it is: the angled, blunt head peering through the stairs, dripping from the mouth. I freeze for a moment, then run back to the car and look for something to bind her leg. There's nothing. I yell back to Patricia.

'Do you have a first-aid kit in here?'

She gulps a sob. 'I don't know.'

'Don't move,' I say. I pull off my pyjama top, leaving only my singlet. I'm losing breath, losing steam. When I get back to her, she wavers like she wants to lie flat, and I grab her by the shoulders.

'Sit up, sit up. Did you bloody step on it or something?'

She props herself up weakly. 'I didn't see it.'

'You've got an hour, Patricia, if you don't move.' I look back at the stairs, but the snake has retreated.

She shows me where the bite is, on the back of her ankle, just below the calf. It's deep and it's bleeding. I have to bind it, but don't know which way to do it: wrap it downwards first, or upwards? *Fuck, it doesn't matter*; I start downwards. She moans and cries, and I tell her to calm down and shut up or the poison will circulate faster. She whimpers, and I wrap the leg as tightly as possible and tell her to hold it firmly.

'Where's my phone?'

Patricia doesn't respond. Her eyes are glassy. 'Patricia. Where is James keeping my phone?'

She shakes her head. 'I – I don't know.'

I could search the house, but it would just waste time. The mobile reception is patchy anyway, and the landline is gone. If James returns, I'll never get away. I can't fight them both.

I need to leave.

'Patricia,' I say. She peers up at me. 'I'm going to go and get help.' She wails. 'Shut up. Shut up. I don't have a choice. I can't move you. I'll be back with help. Sit up and don't move, okay?'

She nods and wipes a hand across her face. I run back to the car and start it, skid down the dip in the driveway. The sedan's wheels lose grip, and the steering wheel loosens before I regain control. I distract myself with numbers. It's a seven-kilometre driveway. Seven. If I drive at seventy per hour, how long will it take me to get to the gate? Six minutes. But this is a dirt and gravel driveway. I'll probably only be able to do sixty. Seven and a half minutes? I hear a crack echo and shudder. James. He must be close. The gate. The gate. Will it be locked? Please, please be unlocked.

Dust rises behind the car. I lock on the curves of the drive, praying the wheels will hold, that the rocks spitting at the underside of the car don't cause any damage that will stop me. I hear another crack and jump; it's closer. At last, I see a glimpse of the bitumen road ahead, outside the farm, and then the drive dips again and it's gone. The sun is high in the sky and my chest tightens when I catch a glimpse in my periphery of a white truck hurtling through the paddocks towards me, rising and falling with the terrain. I speed up, but the truck is in front of me; it's faster, and built for this. The smell of burning rubber floods me and I watch in shock as the truck ploughs straight through the wire paddock fence and cuts me off. I brake, skidding off the drive into grass, and James jumps out of the car, carrying a rifle.

'Where are you going?'

I get out of the car, trembling. 'Your mum,' I say. 'The tiger snake from under the stairs. She needs help.'

He doesn't stop to ask me how it happened. 'Get in,' he says over his shoulder. I follow him to the truck, I have no choice. The rifle rests across his lap. He takes off with such force I'm thrown against the back of my seat. I scrabble for a seatbelt but can't get hold of it and just grip the car handle instead. We tear up the drive and I breathe in a metallic, rotting smell. I turn and see a bunch of bloodied fur in the tray. Kangaroos. I face forwards again and close my eyes, the jerking of the truck sending acid up my throat.

We reach the final rise and I open my eyes as we plough onto the front lawn. Patricia is lying down, unmoving, the leg binding loose on the ground.

'I told her to sit up,' I say, but James lets out a feral cry. He brakes hard, pulls the handbrake on and throws the car door open, leaving the ute running, the rifle on the front seat. He runs to her, dropping to his knees and cradling her, tapping her on the face. She rouses and grips him by the arms. I get out of the car and walk around to the driver's seat, lean in and pick up the rifle. Then I stand for a moment. James calls for me, but I don't answer. He calls again.

'Leila! My phone's in the car, grab it!'

I walk a few steps towards them. His arm is around Patricia's back and he's telling her to sit up, that if she lies down the poison will travel to her heart. He turns to me again.

'Get over here and hold her up! I need my phone!'

I stand still. I'm holding the rifle. He seems to work me out and holds out a hand, an attempt to placate; for the first time, I see fear on his face. I turn and climb back into the truck, laying the rifle across my knees. He tries to stand, to come and get me, but Patricia moans and lolls towards him. She is a boulder, rolling down a hill; she will pin him; he cannot leave her. He stops and holds her, staring at me. I release the park brake. Reverse the ute. He shouts my name, and I ignore it. Turn the truck around. Patricia grips him, eyes wild; he cannot move.

Maybe Patricia will live. I rev the accelerator. The truck speeds down the rise.

Maybe she won't. I hunch over the wheel, the rifle lurching in my lap.

Maybe the world doesn't need her anymore, now that her child is grown.

I reach the padlocked wooden gate and, without slowing, drive the truck straight through it.

In Coogee, my life revolves around therapy and court and lawyers and police. James is awaiting a hearing date. Patricia died. Renee's body and that of her baby – only bones – were recovered from the well. I don't keep across the news reports, though I caught a trailer for *60 Minutes* while channel surfing: Charlotte sitting next to Amelia, giving an interview, stating that she, too, always believed Renee was at the farm.

John maintains his innocence in all these affairs, saying he had no idea his son and wife were engaged in some kind of folie à deux. I don't know if the police believe him. I don't know if I do.

Matt returned Rusty to me. He lives in my apartment, sleeps in my bed, and we walk together for hours. The ocean frightened him at first, but now he loves running into the waves, then plonking himself down in the shore break, cooling his belly.

Once a week I go to a psychologist who thinks James love-bombed me, that he has narcissistic personality traits, developed by his parents' manipulation through a religion indoctrinated in the family over many generations. She thinks I was primed for this relationship by my mother. I don't know. James did care for me, I tell her. Because he looked after me when I lost the baby. He was there for me when I had a breakdown. He told me as much, and yes, I think I do believe him.

I don't tell the psychologist about the multiple women who sent me direct messages on Instagram, wanting to share their experiences of dating James: his fixation on younger women, his swiftness at suggesting they start a family. One of the messages said, *You're older, right? No other family members? I guess he finally picked someone who'd give it their all.* After that, I turned my account to private.

The psychologist says we have a lot of work to do.

———

I've been throwing up. My period is five days late.

I take a pregnancy test. It's positive.

———

What will my child's life look like?

I won't deny her a father like I was denied mine. I will right my mother's mistakes. There will be visits to a penitentiary; supervised visits.

I will be fair to her father. I won't hold this against him forever. I won't stay stuck in these moments forever.

He lost his mother, after all.

Our child will ask me if I loved him. Why we're not together. Whether we could still get married. I won't go into details – it would be unfair for a child to know the intricacies of pain so young. Instead, I'll tell her that once upon a time – not in a magical way, this story doesn't have a happy ending – once upon a time, I loved her father. When she asks about him, I'll say he helped so many people. Things will be different for my child; I'll be a different kind of mother. I won't burden her with the truth.

—

Only, it isn't really a lie. I did love him once, I did.

Sometimes, I think I still do.

LUTEAL PHASE

(lu·te·al) *noun*

if pregnancy does not occur, the corpus luteum
withers and dies. The drop in progesterone
levels causes the lining of the uterus to fall
away. This is known as menstruation.

The cycle then repeats.

ACKNOWLEDGEMENTS

Thank you for reading *The Farm*. I had the great fortune to be selected by Stella Prize-winning author Carrie Tiffany to work on the novel at the Faber Academy, and the amount I learned from her was tremendous. Thank you, Carrie. And thank you to the writers who studied alongside me; I look forward to every one of your novels being published – soon!

Thank you to my early beta readers: Hilary Longhurst, Catherine Gordon and my beloved Deb Bardon. They are three of the best colleagues I've ever had and I'm proud that we've become friends. Thank you to the talented Keryn Donnelly for our writing catch-ups, your sense of humour, and your support of the novel.

Thank you to my dearest friends, who are truly family: Brooke Hawley, Luke Gilpin and Anthea Wright. Your support means everything.

Thank you to my brilliant literary agent, Marina De Pass. Marina took the time to read this novel based on just a 2000-word excerpt – and then became the person who championed it endlessly. Whenever I had a crisis of confidence (often!) Marina was on the other end of the phone, assuring me that *The Farm* was a book that deserved to – and would definitely – be read.

Thank you to Rebecca Saunders at Hachette Australia for taking this story on and putting the full weight of Hachette behind it. Your commitment to the novel's message means so much to me. Thank you to Rebecca Allen for being the most thorough, comprehensive and supportive editor; and for laughing with me when we needed it! Thank you to Vanessa Lanaway for her thoughtful and detailed copyedit. Thank you to Rebecca Hamilton for her eagle-eyed proofread! Thank you to Ali Lavau and Alex Ross for your contributions to *The Farm*. Thank you to the Hachette Australia sales, marketing and publicity teams, including Holly Jeffery and Kirstin Corcoran, for their tireless support in promoting the novel.

A thank you to journalist Jessica Hill for her deep work on Australian domestic violence.

Thank you to Marylou and Peter. Mum, you fostered my love of reading from an early age, and sharing books with you is still one of my favourite hobbies, even after forty years. Thank you for reading everything I've ever written. And Peter was the father who believed I could do absolutely anything; he knew this would one day come.

The biggest love and thanks to my husband Charlie and our beloved dog, Buddy. Beloved doesn't really sum up the shared adoration and delight our trio enjoys. Fate, perhaps. Charlie: you not only read everything I write, you do so multiple times, and discuss with me the meaning and purpose of everything I do. You are one in a million, not only as a husband, but as a friend, family member and person in the world. It is no surprise that when you adopted Buddy, you found a dog that mirrors your soul exactly. All my love, always.

I finished the very first draft of *The Farm* on the same day it was announced that the United States Supreme Court had overturned *Roe v Wade*. As I went through querying, editing and releasing the novel, I watched the United States government introduce a federal bill to ban abortion and, at home, I watched Australia's domestic violence and coercive control rates continue to rise, with the number of women being murdered by their partners increasing to what is now called a 'national crisis'. It is truly disgraceful and deeply frightening.

We are living in a time when it is necessary to repeat, to defend, to shout: women's bodies are their own. We will never give them up.

Jessica Mansour-Nahra

hachette
AUSTRALIA

If you would like to find out more about Hachette Australia, our authors, upcoming events and new releases, you can visit our website or our social media channels:

hachette.com.au

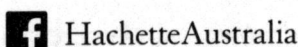 HachetteAustralia

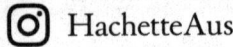 HachetteAus